Damned

By Genevieve Cogman

The Invisible Library series
The Invisible Library
The Masked City
The Burning Page
The Lost Plot
The Mortal Word
The Secret Chapter
The Dark Archive
The Untold Story

The Scarlet Revolution trilogy
Scarlet
Elusive
Damned

DAMNED

The Scarlet Revolution

BOOK THREE

GENEVIEVE COGMAN

TOR

First published 2025 by Tor
an imprint of Pan Macmillan
The Smithson, 6 Briset Street, London EC1M 5NR
EU representative: Macmillan Publishers Ireland Ltd, 1st Floor,
The Liffey Trust Centre, 117–126 Sheriff Street Upper,
Dublin 1, D01 YC43
Associated companies throughout the world
www.panmacmillan.com

ISBN 978-1-5290-8382-8 HB
ISBN 978-1-5290-8383-5 TPB

1 3 5 7 9 8 6 4 2

A CIP catalogue record for this book is available from the British Library.

Typeset in Palatino by Palimpsest Book Production Limited, Falkirk, Stirlingshire
Printed and bound by CPI Group (UK) Ltd, Croydon, CR0 4YY

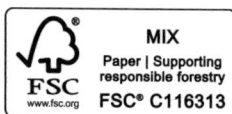

MIX
Paper | Supporting
responsible forestry
FSC
www.fsc.org
FSC® C116313

Visit **www.panmacmillan.com** to read more about all our books
and to buy them. You will also find features, author interviews and
news of any author events, and you can sign up for e-newsletters
so that you're always first to hear about our new releases.

This book is dedicated to Emma Magdalena Rozália Mária Jozefa Borbála Orczy de Orci, also known as Baroness Orczy

With thanks for the characters and stories which she created, and apologies for what I've done to them, including adding vampires, since without her, they would not have existed.

(Except for the French Revolution, which most emphatically did exist.)

THE FRENCH REVOLUTION
AND THE ENGLISH TERROR

'Frenchmen, you are already free,' declared the London Corresponding Society in 1792, 'but the Britons are preparing to be so.' At first there were many in England who saw the French Revolution as a glorious step forward, and one which would nurture new seeds of liberty and civil rights across Europe, as well as at home in England. However, this opinion was rendered unfashionable – unpatriotic, even – by the execution of the French king, and by the war with France. Where previously the English government had been willing to look approvingly on the changes abroad (and to try to annex some of the French colonies during the confusion), the situation now demanded overt disapproval – and action.

Besides philosophy and the spirit of revolution, however, there was genuine reason for unrest in England, and a desire for reform: riots in the countryside, soaring inflation, a lack of civil rights, the growing scope of industrialization, the war with France, and more. Popular opinion (encouraged by the government) promptly linked all of these together with the revolution in France. Reformers – or anyone expressing a contrary opinion – were labelled as radicals and associates of the French.

Patriotic support for 'Church and King' was shown in

public demonstrations against foreign enemies and domestic 'traitors'. The prime minister at the time, Pitt the Younger, issued a proclamation against 'seditious writing' in May 1792, which compelled Paine (author of *Rights of Man*, *Common Sense*, and other works) to flee to France, where he was quickly elected to the National Convention. In 1793 he was arrested and sent to prison in Paris, where he continued to write. Both sides of the Channel were concerned about where the new spirit for questioning might lead. (And, of course, other countries had similar issues, but for the moment the focus of these notes remains on England and France.)

Pitt set up spy networks (admittedly, hardly a new thing in English politics – see also Walsingham and other spymasters). In April 1794 the Habeas Corpus Act was suspended, so that political prisoners could be held indefinitely without trial, and in May a prosecution for high treason was launched against leading London radicals. This did not prevent dissent: writers, theologians, politicians, scientists and Society wits argued politics and philosophy openly in newspapers, pamphlets, journals, novels and lectures. It might be unpatriotic to publicly approve of any of the Revolution's ideals or ideas, but that failed to prevent talk of reform and change. The government knew – or feared – that a new revolt was still possible, this time in England.

The screws were tightening in France as well. The Law of 22 Prairial, also known as the *loi de la Grande Terreur* (the law of the Great Terror), was enacted on 10 June 1794 (22 Prairial of the Year II under the French Revolutionary Calendar). This law placed an active obligation on all citizens to denounce suspects and bring them to justice. ('For a citizen to become suspect it is sufficient that rumour accuses him.') It broadened the scope of charges, so that any criticism of the government could become a criminal offence; it limited trials to three days, forbade witnesses and defence counsels, and mandated a verdict of acquittal or death. The Committee of Public Safety saw enemies everywhere – including each other. Such severity had its consequences . . .

As in the previous books in this trilogy, these notes are a drastic oversimplification of historical events and attitudes. Yet it is true that anyone in England who moved in Enlightenment circles, or among those who proposed social change, would have been aware of the government's attitude, and the accompanying risks. Of course, this would have been less threatening for the rich and powerful, but for the poor and lower class? England was, after all, at war. And when a government feels threatened by the possibility of rebellions and uprising, civil rights such as *habeas corpus* – or other laws – may easily be put aside.

In any situation where change is proposed, those with vested interests will always be very aware of how much they have to lose. France was a bloody example of what *could* happen, and the English government and aristocracy (and surely vampires) needed only to look across the Channel to see it. And in these cases, enacting reforms is seldom as popular an option as cracking down on those who dare to argue for change or speak dissent . . .

DRAMATIS PERSONAE

The Blakeney household:

Sir Percy Blakeney and Lady Marguerite
 Blakeney, aristocrats
Mr Sturn, butler
Alice, personal maid to Lady Marguerite

The League of the Scarlet Pimpernel:

Sir Andrew Ffoulkes, aristocrat
Lord Anthony Dewhurst, aristocrat
Lord Charles Bathurst, aristocrat and scholar
Other gentlemen of noble birth and leisure
Eleanor Dalton, maid

Inhabitants of England:

Bow Street Runners, an inconvenience

KITTY MATTIS and SARAH MILT, passengers on the stagecoach

THE EARL OF BATHURST, aristocrat and father of Charles Bathurst

PROFESSOR JOHNSON, scholar in Oxford

Visitors from France:

ARMAND CHAUVELIN, agent of the Committee of Public Safety

FLEURETTE CHAUVELIN, daughter of Armand Chauvelin

Vampires:

LADY SOPHIE, Baroness of Basing

DE COURCIS, French gentleman vampire

CASTLETON, English gentleman vampire

PROLOGUE

The two elderly gentlemen rose as the woman entered the room. She might be a French spy, but there was no need for *rudeness*. Such a thing would stamp them as no better than the Republicans who had seized power in France. They waited only the bare minimum of time for her to take a seat, however, before resuming their own places behind a heavy and intimidating desk, in a whisper of coats and wigs which made the piles of paper rustle. Her escort stepped back to stand beside the door, his hands folded behind his back. He gave the slight nod which had been agreed on as a signal between them – she *had* attempted to pass a message to someone on their journey here.

The little clerk in the corner of the room, apparently beneath the notice of everyone present, scribbled down ceaseless notes on every word and action in the room.

'Lady Blakeney.' It was the first man who spoke, the older of the two. 'I trust we find you well today.'

'Mr Addington, Mr Ford.' She inclined her head politely. Her redingote and hat had the unmistakable touch of a top-of-the-line modiste, and her exquisite diamond earrings demonstrated her husband's wealth. A few red-gold curls fell becomingly to frame her face. 'I am indeed well, and I thank you for your courtesy in allowing me to remain at my husband's town residence until I am found innocent of these appalling charges.'

'That, madam, depends largely upon yourself.' It was Ford's turn to speak. The higher of the two stacks of paper on the desk rested before him, and he tapped it meaningfully. 'Permit me to say that if we choose to interpret matters more rigidly, then we would have every right and reason to lodge you in Newgate. Yes, you may well shudder!'

His mouth pursed in annoyance as he took in that she had not, in fact, shuddered. She looked placid and pretty enough to have been painted by the artist Reynolds. Though he, of course, had been a proper patriot and would never have agreed to paint a woman who'd once been associated with the Revolution, however rich her husband might be. It was truly a pity that instructions had come from above at the Home Office to handle this matter with a gentle touch. A few days in Newgate would crack that composure of hers – he was certain of it.

'I am still unclear on what evidence I have been charged,' the woman brazened it out. 'While I am most grateful to your good selves for the compassion and understanding with which I have been treated, nobody will tell me anything certain except for the constant cries of "spying" and "treason". What exactly am I supposed to have done?'

'You are accused of selling secrets to the enemies of His Majesty the King,' Addington intoned, with all the weight he would give a pronouncement from the Bench in court. 'By stealth you have persuaded men, who should know better, to speak freely in front of you, and then passed on this information to the spies of France.'

Lady Blakeney paled in shock, her gloved fingers going to her mouth and pressing against her rouged lips. 'But why would I do such a thing? The National Convention of France are hardly my friends. I've married an Englishman. I'm loyal to England!'

'Yes.' Ford and Addington exchanged meaningful glances. 'Indeed,' Ford continued, 'we find the matter of your marriage most . . . interesting. You were acclaimed as one of the wittiest women of France, with many friends who were prominent in the early days of the Revolution. And yet . . . you married Sir Percy Blakeney. A man best known for his sense of fashion and scarcely anything else – but equally, a man close to the Prince of Wales.'

'And an extremely wealthy man,' Addington added.

Lady Blakeney's eyes flashed as she straightened in her chair. 'I married my husband because I love him, gentlemen!'

'Indeed,' Addington said, and his tone dripped with disbelief.

She sniffed in a manner that would have done credit to the haughtiest English dowager, and folded her hands in her lap. 'Perhaps you gentlemen have spent too long as magistrates of Bow Street, but I can only tell you . . .'

Was that hesitation a crack in her facade? 'Madame, if you do not tell us *everything*, there may be no hope for you,' Ford prompted.

She met his gaze, and her own eyes widened. They were a lovely blue, brighter than the common grey so often described as that colour. 'Mr Ford,' she said softly, her pretty French accent somehow making her words all the more appealing. 'Many men courted me, yes, but when Percy offered me his heart, that was the truest treasure I could ever be given. I had no interest in his money. I gave up my career and my country to be with him. I left behind everything I had ever known . . . to be with the man I *loved*.' A tear began to form at the corner of her eye. 'And now I sit here, accused of treason, with my husband away in Antwerp. Dear heavens, I know he would speak for me, he would defend me, if only he were *here*! Many times I've wished he needn't go away on business so often, but I've kept silent because it is the duty of a wife to accept her husband's obligations. But now – now . . .' She flicked a dainty cambric handkerchief from her sleeve and pressed it against her eyes. 'Oh, if only my Percy could be at my side now, to contest these foul accusations . . .'

'Yet sadly he is not here,' Addington said. 'And in the meantime, in the absence of your husband, madame, you must answer for your own crimes.'

'I have committed no crimes!' she protested again. 'Gentlemen, is this England's justice? Where is the evidence against me? Who accuses me? This is the sort of thing I would expect from the courts of *France*!'

Addington's jowls twitched as he bit back a growl. 'You are being granted unusual leniency in staying at your husband's home, madame. Don't attempt to trick us into disclosing more information than is your due. These demands are futile.'

'I have contacted Percy's man of law,' Lady Blakeney said. 'I am sure he will be able to press these demands on my behalf.'

Ford and Addington barely troubled to exchange glances. This had already been planned for. 'We stand ready to receive his questions,' Ford said. 'As a man of law, he may be able to give you a more complete understanding of your position, madame. You are, after all, a foreigner to this country, as well as being of the gentler sex. Even if France may have acclaimed you as a wit, it is unlikely you realize how precarious your position is here. Were you to stand before a judge tomorrow, I have not the slightest doubt that you would be found guilty.'

Again the tears stood in her eyes. Ford was forced to remind himself that she had been an actress in Paris, and this show of weakness might be no more than a feigned display.

'But I thought . . . is there no justice in England, gentlemen? I thought now I had left France, I would be safe from malignant, baseless accusations! You are both magistrates at Bow Street. Surely you can look at me and perceive that I'm innocent of these charges?'

'Ah, would that it were so simple,' Addison said, briefly lapsing into jocularity. 'If it were, our days would be far shorter and less strenuous.'

'At least tell me who has accused me?' she asked, suddenly pathetic. She seemed to shrink in her chair, a rose cut down and wilting. 'Who has been so cruel as to say these things about me?'

'Immaterial,' Addison declared. 'The judge will be advised of it when your case comes to trial. Though of course . . .'

Lady Blakeney looked up again. 'Oh?'

'If you could be of any *assistance* to us . . .' He let the words trail off invitingly, waiting for a moment before he continued. 'We are aware that you move in the so-called "Enlightenment" circles, and that some of your acquaintances have spoken rashly in the past about the current government, and indeed about the King himself. If you wish to prove you are not some sort of French spy, then surely your course of action is obvious.'

At this she dissolved into full-blown tears, having recourse to her handkerchief and even her smelling salts. The odd phrase filtered through her sobbing, such as 'How could you?' and 'My poor friends who've already had to flee France' and 'What sort of woman do you think I am?'

We already know that, Ford thought resentfully. *You're a slut of an actress who married into luxury by way of the most stupid man in England, and we have every reason to suspect you're the most effective French spy in this country.* But if she was an actress, then he was a man of law, and he could manage his face as well as she did hers. He rang for tea, and watched as she calmed herself.

'It seems we are not going to progress any further today,' Addison eventually said, after several more sallies on their part and two more outbursts of tears on hers. 'We will have you returned to your husband's house. Pray remember that you are not to leave it under *any* circumstances.'

'I only hope my Percy will return soon!' she declared. 'He will lay all these false doubts of yours to rest.'

'I hope so too indeed, madame,' Addison agreed. They both stood as she left the room, before resuming their seats again.

'A tough character,' Ford said gloomily. 'I'm not saying she wouldn't crack if we put her in Newgate, mind, but it might take a while.'

'Indeed.' Addison poured himself more tea, even though the pot had grown cold. 'The stage is a hardening influence, and she's a practised liar. No doubt she could have wept her eyes out a dozen more times before we'd finished with her. I take it there's some reason why your ... connections ... want her kept in her home and not in Newgate for the moment?' He tactfully refrained from mentioning the Home Office.

'She must still have a way of passing information to her contacts, and on to France,' Ford explained. 'We hope to lay our hands on some of these other spies too, or to follow her if she attempts to flee.'

Addison shrugged. 'That'd be a confession of guilt in itself. Has her husband been informed yet?'

'Word's been sent to Antwerp.' Ford didn't mention that it had deliberately been sent as slowly as possible. The longer they had to work on Lady Blakeney without her husband – or more precisely, the influence which her husband, a fool but a well-connected fool, could bring to bear – the more they might be able to achieve. 'Of course, we could be agreeably surprised if he seeks a divorce, which would be most convenient. Last year they weren't on the best of terms.'

'Daily questioning for the moment, then, and keep her waiting a little longer each time she's brought here.' Addison made a note. 'And if any evidence should be found among her possessions . . .'

'Unlikely, unless we put it there ourselves.'

'Let us reserve that option for later. And do thank your *connections* for the tip-off. I feel we may have uncovered the root of an entire league of spies here.'

'I believe they have done England a great service,' Ford agreed.

CHAPTER ONE

It was not, Eleanor reflected, as though they were *unpractised* at this type of assignment. The League of the Scarlet Pimpernel might indeed be the most skilled group of men (and a couple of women) in England, or even Europe, when it came to snatching the unfairly persecuted and unjustly accused out of the jaws of law enforcement. It was their favourite sport, their preferred pastime, the game for which they'd ignore all other duties.

But this time it wasn't a game. They were at home, in England, and they were rescuing one of their own, from an enemy whom none of them had known about a month ago.

Eleanor couldn't see the sky above through the roof of the carriage, but she could feel the pressure of heavy clouds weighing down upon her in the heat of the July night – as heavy as a dozen wet sheets on laundry day, as oppressive as the eyes of a mob. She was grateful she had nothing more to do at the moment than huddle in the back of the carriage and let the men concentrate on driving and maintaining their disguises.

Sir Percy wasn't with them. While he was the person they could most have used – and who most *wanted* to be on this mission, to rescue his wife Marguerite – he was also the person who most required an alibi. Any suspicions of his collusion would almost certainly result in his arrest. At this moment, he was across town at a fashionable affair, losing money at piquet and becoming visibly intoxicated. (That, as he put it, was one way of making absolutely certain people remembered your presence.) He had planned the rescue in meticulous detail, however, and Eleanor was comforted by the knowledge he'd organized the whole affair.

She just hoped she'd be able to carry out her part of it successfully.

Charles – Lord Charles Bathurst – shared the back of the carriage with her, his shoulder comfortingly pressed against hers. His eye-glasses had been tucked in an inner pocket and he was squinting in the semi-darkness. On the outside of the coach, Tony – Sir Anthony Dewsbury – was guiding the horses, with Andrew – Sir Andrew Ffoulkes – next to him. Both of them were in the heavy coats and not-quite-gentlemanly clothing commonly seen on Bow Street Runners. Charles wore the same, but they didn't fit him as well, hanging loosely on his thinner frame.

Others of the League – Jeremiah, George, and a few young men whom Eleanor had never been introduced to – were currently roistering across London in its more select gaming hells and clubs, behaving like (or at least causing the damage of) twice their number of titled spawn of the wealthy. This would provide an alibi for Charles and the others tomorrow morning, should they need it. They could simply claim to have been part of that crew, drinking too much, throwing money to waiters and flirting with women who were no better than they should be.

'Almost there,' Andrew called from above, his tone deliberately gruff. 'Just a couple of streets away.'

Eleanor nervously reached up to touch some of the warts sculpted on her face, checking to ensure they hadn't fallen off. She'd powdered and painted her face as a disguise before, but had never worn quite this quantity of the stuff. If it were to rain, she'd look as though she were melting alive. Her clothing was also vastly inappropriate for her young frame, being that of an elderly woman in her sixties rather than her natural twenties, and as for the contraption in her mouth . . .

Well, she *had* said she wanted to be useful.

The plan was straightforward enough. Arrive at the Blakeney townhouse in London halfway through the night, while Sir Percy was out at a party and many of the servants would already have gone to their beds, and claim to be Bow Street Runners sent to take Lady Marguerite into custody. Leave with milady before anyone could object *too* strongly, while at the same time behaving in a suspicious enough manner that it would be remembered later. Smuggle milady to a safe location, well away from the conspiracy which threatened her and the League, leaving behind a false trail.

Of course, one of the weaknesses in the plan was that Andrew, Tony and Charles were all frequent visitors to the house under their normal identities, and Eleanor herself had spent months working there as a maid. Hopefully nobody would look closely enough to see beyond their disguises . . .

The carriage jolted to a stop, and Andrew jumped down as Tony soothed the horses. Charles gave Eleanor's hand one last squeeze for luck, then left the carriage to join Andrew. They stomped their way up to the front door of the house together, bulky and menacing in the dim light from the street lamp. Andrew thumped on the knocker with a vigour born of sweat from the oppressive heat.

The footman who answered the door was visibly taken aback by the identity of his callers. No doubt he'd been expecting Sir Percy. 'How may I assist you gentlemen?' he enquired, in a tone which laid significant doubt on the final word.

'We're here for Lady Blakeney,' Andrew growled, his hat down low over his brows. He seized an official-looking document from Charles and thrust it at the footman. 'Orders are that she's to come to Bow Street without delay. It's an emergency.'

'But it's the middle of the night!' the footman objected.

'You think we'd be here at this time if it wasn't urgent?' Andrew said. 'Now get this straight, lad. I'm Rupert Dallen of the Runners. The Bow Street Runners, before you get smart with me and ask me which ones. My friend here is John Card. And this bit of paper here, what you are currently looking at . . .' He jabbed a finger at the warrant. 'That's signed by Mr Ford himself, the magistrate. It says he wants to see Lady Blakeney right now, no ifs and no buts. So you'd better tell Lady Blakeney to come right on down straight away, without bothering to pack up her frills and whatnots, and hop in the carriage, see? It's not as if she hasn't been coming in for questions several times this week already.'

'I have to ask for orders. I'll only be a moment,' the footman said, sliding backwards with the deftness of practice. He nearly managed to close the door on Andrew and Charles, but Andrew got his boot in the way before he could fully shut it.

Eleanor resisted the urge to chew on her fingernails as she sat in the carriage and counted the seconds. Of course the footman wouldn't go straight to milady; he'd do what any sensible servant would, and go to the butler for orders . . .

'What is the meaning of this?' Mr Sturn arrived at the front door, silhouetted by the hallway light beyond. Eleanor felt a sudden pang of nostalgia twist her heart at his familiar heavy outline, his strict voice demanding to know what was going on. For the first time she truly accepted that she couldn't ever go back to being a maid in the Blakeney household again. Not now she'd been revealed to be a mage. Not now the vampires were hunting her and the League after what they did in Paris.

She would have complained *It isn't fair!* to the inside of her own head, just to hear the voice of the ancient mage who'd been haunting her – Anima would undoubtedly have scolded her for assuming such a thing as fairness existed. But . . . she was gone, too. Anima had passed on to her final reward, whatever that might be, and Eleanor was left bereft of her advice and complaints. To be honest, they'd more frequently been complaints but, like Mr Sturn's scoldings, Eleanor missed them now.

'What is going on here?' Quite against the usual canons of propriety, which dictated she should really be leaving her butler to deal with all this, Lady Marguerite had arrived at the door too. She was still dressed for dinner, though in a dark purple silk which Eleanor knew was among her least favourite gowns, and the light turned her bare neck and shoulders to creamy marble. 'What's Bow Street doing here at this hour? I'm not some sort of servant, to come running whenever you ring a bell!' Her theatre-trained voice rose beautifully, carrying down the street. If the nearby houses hadn't been paying morbid attention earlier, they would be now. 'I demand to see your authorization.'

'Here.' Andrew shoved the warrant into Mr Sturn's hands, ignoring Lady Marguerite. 'That's what gives us here the right to take Lady Blakeney off for a little trip to Bow Street, and she should think herself lucky it's not Newgate.' He was deliberately forcing a rougher accent than his usual languid tones: if Mr Sturn recognized him as one of Sir Percy's frequent visitors, well . . . Mr Sturn might play along. Or he might not.

13

'At least let me call my maid!' Lady Marguerite said. A brief gust of wind stirred the heavy air and toyed with her hair and the silk of her dress. 'I can hardly go alone—'

'There's a woman in the carriage to travel with you,' Charles grunted. 'One of the wardresses from Newgate.'

Eleanor took her cue. She swung the carriage door open and leaned out to wave a gloved hand. She smiled, drawing her lips back enough to reveal the carved bone fangs which were currently making her mouth a misery. It would be very useful if the witnesses could remember having seen a vampire in the carriage.

'That slattern's no fit company for her ladyship!' Mr Sturn protested.

'Enough of this!' Andrew caught Lady Blakeney's wrist with one hand, dragging her out onto the steps. He shoved her towards Charles, then forced his remaining papers into Mr Sturn's grip. 'Show this to his lordship when he returns. He'll know what to do with them.'

'I'll be damned if I let you drag her ladyship away like this.' Mr Sturn raised his fists, setting his jaw in lines of firm determination which showed even through his elderly jowls. 'John, Ben, Adam! Out here now! We're not allowing this sort of behaviour!'

Lady Marguerite gave a shriek, more for appearances than any attempt to seriously rouse the neighbourhood, as Charles manhandled her down the steps and into the carriage. Behind them, Andrew delivered a scientific punch to Mr Sturn's chin, dropping him like a sack of flour. He turned to face the attendant footman, who'd been standing back and gawping at the show, and grabbed him by his neckcloth, tossing him back through the open door. Brushing dust from his hands, he strode to the carriage, swinging himself up next to the waiting Tony.

He wasn't a moment too soon. The Blakeney servants

came boiling out of the house like wasps as the carriage rattled into motion, waving fists and shrieking fit to raise the dead. One enterprising young man – Eleanor recognized him as Timothy, from months of facing him at the kitchen breakfast table – tried to leap onto the running-board of the carriage. Fortunately he missed his step and went down with a crash and a groan.

'Dear me,' Lady Marguerite said as the carriage hastened down the street. At this hour it was quiet and empty in this fashionable part of London, conveniently for their escapade. 'I must raise everyone's wages. They're extremely loyal.'

'Time enough for that when we're safe, milady,' Charles said. 'Eleanor, can you . . .'

Eleanor nodded. With great relief she spat out the pieces of carved bone that had given the impression of fangs. 'Please forgive me, milady,' she said. 'This won't take a moment.'

'What do you mean . . .' Lady Marguerite began.

Eleanor concentrated, feeling the oncoming storm above them like the leashed weight of a superior's disapproval and the thick air like weariness. Behind it all was a flame – the movement of life, the spark which burned in the sun, which whipped the winds until they galloped across the land, and which moved each drop of blood through her veins.

This was so much easier when Anima was here.

But Anima was gone, and she'd left the weight of her responsibility on Eleanor's shoulders. Which meant the first and most important thing for her to do right now was to ensure that the vampires hadn't managed to control Lady Marguerite, in the same way that they'd controlled her brother Armand in France, and half the Committee of Public Safety. 'Look at this, milady,' Eleanor said, as a pale flame blossomed around her hand.

It lacked strength. It lacked definition. It flickered like a candle flame in a draught, as though it was about to vanish at any moment – it was simply *not good enough*. Eleanor forced herself to ignore the jolting of the carriage, the pressure of milady against her on one side and Charles on the other, and tried to pull herself into that part of her mind where magic was not only possible, but was more real than anything else around her. This wasn't just magic, she reminded herself. It was life – the flame of her own life, which she chose to burn. It was something the vampires did not have, and they could not endure its presence.

Lady Marguerite gasped in awe and delight as the sudden flare of white light lit the dark carriage interior as brightly as day. She reached out towards it, then snatched her fingers back again from the heat. 'Eleanor, what is this? What are you doing?'

'You don't feel . . . strange? At all?' A headache was blossoming behind Eleanor's temples, throbbing in time with the beat of the horses' hooves, but her great sense of relief lifted her spirits almost past the point of feeling it. This was why the League – even Sir Percy – had agreed they couldn't share any details of their plan with Lady Marguerite, not until they were safely away with her. If she *had* been controlled by the vampires, as Eleanor had just proven she wasn't, then she'd have betrayed the League to them without a second thought, confident that the vampires knew best.

'No. But *how* are you doing that?' Lady Marguerite wriggled around in the carriage to try to peer at the other side of Eleanor's hand. 'Is there a tube of some sort up your sleeve? Or have you coated your glove in some flammable substance?'

'I think she's safe,' Charles said, breathing a sigh of the same relief which had flooded through Eleanor. 'Armand reacted almost immediately.'

'So did the affected members of the Committee.' Eleanor

remembered how Marguerite's brother had instantly started convulsing at her light, a thin strand of dark liquid dribbling from his mouth as the vampires' influence was expelled from him. She let the flame vanish, leaving them in darkness again. The headache almost went with it, except for a few remaining twinges. It was getting easier, and she wasn't sure whether to be pleased or afraid of that. 'Please forgive us, milady, it's just that—'

Outside, on top of the carriage, Andrew swore, and the horses neighed on a note that was nearly a scream. A crack sounded as someone fired a shot.

'What's going on?' Lady Marguerite demanded.

'Tony, let me take the horses, we need to spring them!' There was a rattle of men changing places on the driver's box above, and then the horses jolted into faster motion. The carriage swayed from side to side as it speeded up.

Eleanor, Charles and Lady Marguerite squeezed side by side to peer out of the small rear window. Another carriage was close in pursuit, near enough now that the sound of their horses and wheels mingled with the League's own. One lightweight man was perched next to the driver, but others were leaning out of the windows on both sides.

'Halt or we'll shoot again!' the ratlike man on the driver's box commanded. He waved his pistol, still smoking from his earlier shot, as though it was the baton for some invisible orchestra. 'We're Bow Street! Bow Street, dammit!'

Lady Marguerite took a deep breath, almost visibly settling herself. 'I have two reasons to thank you, it seems,' she said, somehow maintaining her serenity even as she clung to a strap to counter the jolting of the carriage. 'If you *hadn't* turned up to take me away tonight, I'll wager those fellows would have done so.'

'Indeed,' Charles said gallantly, 'it seems we weren't the only people wanting to spirit you away by dead of night.

Now Sir Percy's back in the country, they surely realized they wouldn't have much time to secure your imprisonment before he intervened. It's only a pity we were forced into these drastic actions. The Chief's influential contacts proved not to be as . . . influential as usual.'

'Percy said very little when we spoke – I thought he suspected eavesdroppers, but it seems there's more to it than that. You have somewhere arranged to hide me?' The carriage took a sweeping turn to the right and they were flung together, catching hold of each other as the timbers of the vehicle creaked and groaned. Eleanor was astonished the two of them could talk so calmly while the carriage was going at this horrendously dangerous, bone-rattling speed.

'We have, but . . .' Charles didn't need to finish the sentence. If the Runners stayed close on their tail, they wouldn't be able to stop to leave milady there. And the longer they were chased through London, the more likely it would become that they'd be held up by some accident of traffic, or others might join the chase.

'Where are our horses from?' Lady Marguerite asked. A natural question from someone who was married to Sir Percy, who maintained a large stable and could handle any horse in it.

'Hired,' Charles confessed. 'We couldn't risk using any from our own stables – why, Andrew's bays would be recognized across town . . .'

'I could . . .' Lady Marguerite shook her head. 'No, it wouldn't work – I'm not fool enough to jump out at this speed, and in any case it'd leave you all in the lurch. Eleanor, why are you frowning like that?'

'I'm trying to concentrate, milady.' Eleanor had done this once before, with Anima guiding her. She should be able to manage it again. She surely *must* be able to. The sky was yearning to burst and flood the streets below; she would act as a mere go-between. 'Charles, tell me, would it better or worsen matters if the rain came down hard?'

'Can you do that?' Charles demanded in shock.

Eleanor was going to say, *I think I can*, but she seemed to feel Sir Percy's shadow behind her, and hear his voice. *Uncertainty's all fine and well in its place, but it's deuced unhelpful when a fellow's trying to make plans.* So she just said, 'Yes, but it may take a few minutes.'

Charles didn't question her further. Instead he rapped on the roof. 'Andrew! Eleanor says she can bring on the rain, but it'll take her a few minutes. Can you stay ahead of these fellows for that long?'

'Tell her the fewer minutes the better!' Andrew called down. 'And warn us first!'

Now she'd *committed* herself. Eleanor tried to ignore the look of curiosity and disbelief from Lady Marguerite, and instead focused on the fact that Charles – and Andrew, and Tony – all trusted her. Anima had called her *apprentice*. The old mage had admitted – eventually – that Eleanor possessed the ability to be a mage like her. The previous Queen of France, Marie Antoinette, had allowed Eleanor to sit in her presence, and addressed her as someone worthy of her attention. If they all thought Eleanor could do it, who was she to disagree?

She closed her eyes. The clouds were tangled masses of uncarded wool, prickling with the thorns of incipient lightning, tied together by a hundred separate cords of wind that alternately drew tight and then relaxed again. It was like a piece of sewing which had a loose loop of thread, where she had to follow it through dozens of other stitches until she could finally pull it closed, then tweak it into the order it *wanted* to be in, and . . .

A pulse of pain ripped through her head as though the lightning itself had lit it up. She pressed her hands against her temples, trying somehow to force the pain away, will it down, but it still throbbed blindingly harsh inside her skull. Yet at the same time the wind picked up, rushing down the street together with their carriage. She could *smell* the change in the air.

So could Charles. 'She's done it!' he called up to Andrew and Tony, his arm tight around her as he steadied her against the jerking of the carriage.

Lightning unseamed the sky. Thunder came a moment later, less than a second behind the blinding whiteness which threw the street and carriages into sharp relief, their shadows racing behind them. Andrew didn't respond in words but directed the carriage to turn sharply to the right, the horses obedient to his guiding hands on the reins and slowing their pace.

Rain began to rattle down, the first few drops crisp outbursts of noise as they slapped the pavement, the next ones more of a thudding beat as they hit already wet cobbles and newly formed puddles. Eleanor could feel the tension released from the heavens, the sheer relief of pressure unwinding and water falling, and it was a small balm against the pain in her head. It hadn't been that bad when Anima called a storm before. How much practice would it take before she could do such a thing as easily herself?

Of course, that depended on her *surviving* long enough to practise . . .

The carriage turned left, then right again. From the flashes of lightning which painted the sky, Eleanor could see the buildings around them were closer together now, leaning towards each other across the narrower streets. Andrew had driven them into an older part of London, away from the wide avenues and streets where he could let the horses out to their full speed, and into more contorted quarters. This meant he had to drive more slowly, and even at their reduced speed it was taking all his skill to guide the horses safely, to prevent a crash. However, the Runners in their carriage were just as handicapped by their surroundings, and by the oncoming rain. Nor did they know where Andrew was going: they could only follow him.

'You're bleeding from the nose,' Charles said, his arm tightening around her. 'Here.' He pressed a handkerchief into her hands.

Eleanor muttered garbled thanks and held the fresh cotton against her nose, unfortunately smearing it with face paint as well as blood. She caught a closer look at it in another flash of lightning. 'Charles, you didn't bring along one of your own monogrammed handkerchiefs on this mission, when we're meant to be in disguise?'

She felt his shrug. 'M'dear, if we're caught then we're already lost, and if we're not caught then I don't expect them to be checking my clothing for any embroidered initials. Faith, the worst I could have done would be to flutter it out of the window as we departed in token of farewell . . . Besides, I wasn't at the house to exhibit my personal linen, merely to hold the forged documents while Andrew played Bow Street Runner and terrified the groundlings.'

Lady Marguerite was looking at the two of them with an expression Eleanor could only describe as *satisfied*. Yet there was a certain wistfulness to her glance as well, as though she were imagining her husband next to her. 'And an excellent job you both did,' she praised them. 'Percy himself could scarcely have done better.'

Eleanor doubted that. Sir Percy would probably have intimidated his own butler by sheer force of will, without even the slightest risk of being recognized, and then escaped before the Runners caught sight of his carriage. But then, he *was* the Scarlet Pimpernel.

'Be ready!' Tony called over the rain. 'We're going to slow

down enough for you to jump out in a moment, directly after we turn left. Then run for the house on your right. The door will be open.'

'Understood!' Charles called back. Without turning a hair, Lady Marguerite gathered the luxurious folds of her skirts in her hands, ready to move at a second's notice.

The carriage spun sharply to the left, wheels skidding and screeching on the paving, and the horses neighed in protest. Another flash of lightning lit the street outside: narrow buildings stooped over the road like leering crones, and even the hammering rain couldn't wash away the stink of crowded gutters and piled garbage.

Charles kicked the carriage door open and jumped. He nearly fell, barely managing to land on his feet in a staggering, ungainly run. Lady Marguerite was a moment behind him, jumping out as daintily as if she were about to step into a ballet performance, but her slippered feet skidded on the wet filthy cobbles. Charles caught her before she lost her balance.

Eleanor was the last one out, throwing herself through the doorway in a blur of panic and terror. The rain and wind washed around her as she stumbled, arms waving frantically as she tried to catch herself. It almost worked. Instead of going face-first onto the wet cobbles, she fell to her hands and knees. For a moment she simply knelt there, breath coming in great heaving gasps as she felt the cold stone steady and unmoving beneath her, aware only of the important fact that she hadn't died.

Their carriage speeded up again, rattling away down the street, the loose open door banging against the side. Then the other carriage, the one full of Runners, turned the corner.

There was no time for finding the right house to hide in. Charles pulled Lady Marguerite against the wall and stood in front of her, his back to the street, an anonymous coated and booted figure in the rain. Eleanor took the obvious solution and simply curled up in a heap to the side, on the pavement, pulling her shawl over her face, a ragtag bundle that might have been a woman – living or dead – or simply a pile of garbage.

Another shot rang out from the Runners' carriage as they drove past. Eleanor wasn't a trained horseman like most of the League, but even she could tell their horses weren't holding up as well as the League's ones. If Andrew and Tony could just outlast them long enough to give themselves time to leave their carriage behind and slip away . . .

'Eleanor!' Once the Runners had disappeared, Charles abandoned Lady Marguerite and came rushing over to her side, offering a hand to help her up. 'Are you safe? You're not hurt, surely?'

'Nothing worse than bruises,' Eleanor said, grateful for the assistance. Yes, her face paint and powder *were* running down her face in the rain, but if she had to look like an idiot, at least she wasn't going to be a fainting maiden. 'Are you—'

'Of course,' he said, taking her other hand in his. She let the handkerchief fall, unimportant now, as she gazed into his rain-streaked face. She'd known him less than a year, but every time they put themselves at risk, the thought of him coming to harm worried her far more than any danger to herself.

It was easy to say, *He wouldn't be the man I love if he wasn't willing to face those dangers.* It was much, much harder to live with it.

'Over here,' Lady Marguerite said, laughter a golden thread running through her voice. She'd found the correct door, tried it and pushed it open. 'You two have a great deal to tell me, but we'd all better come in out of the rain first.'

CHAPTER TWO

'Well,' Lady Marguerite said, putting down her mug of tea and sitting back in her rickety chair. 'This is all . . . rather disconcerting, my dear Eleanor. What a good thing we are now at leisure to make our plans.'

She smiled. If Citizen Chauvelin, agent of the Committee for Public Safety in France, smiled like a cat watching its prey tremble in fear, then Lady Marguerite smiled like a fox that knew the prey hadn't yet seen it coming.

She, Eleanor and Charles had only paused long enough in the rackety dosshouse, where Tony had previously rented an upstairs room, to change their clothing. Then they'd decamped to another agreed rendezvous, before the Runners could come back to investigate anything they might have driven past and missed. They were now ensconced in a slightly more expensive house which, Eleanor understood, specialized in putting up groups of men and women for the night, and asking absolutely no questions about why a young man might go upstairs with a woman on either arm. (She'd mentally run through the League's members, trying to decide who might be well enough acquainted with this place to book rooms here, but had decided, in the end, it was none of her business. She wasn't sure she wanted to know in any case.)

Outside the rain still lashed at the windows. The storm which Eleanor had called wasn't ready to disperse; she felt in her bones that it would be raining at least till dawn, and probably well into the morning. 'You're taking this very well, milady,' she said.

'Admittedly it is a lot to take in,' Lady Marguerite acknowledged. 'Vampires, a normal part of society for centuries, are apparently conspiring against us all, and intend to rule from the shadows – if they do not already do so! And Lady Sophie is even more deeply involved in this than we ever suspected! Magi still walk among us, and you are one of them, and were until recently haunted by the ancient ghost of another one! And Chauvelin's daughter is a kind, sweet girl with genuine sympathies for justice! I must say I find that the least likely of all. Then again, when I knew him, years ago, I had no idea he had a child, or even once a wife. How little we really know about the people around us.'

Eleanor could feel an edge in the other woman's voice. 'Milady, I understand you might wish I'd told you some of this earlier . . .' she started, but wasn't quite sure how to continue. Anima, the ancient mage who'd possessed her, had sworn her to secrecy. But shouldn't her own obligations to her employers and friends count for more than that? She thought back uncomfortably to when Lady Marguerite had questioned her previously, suspicious of what was going on with her, yet Eleanor had kept her lips sealed on her secret.

It was easier for men. They could simply draw themselves up nobly and say, *It was a matter of honour,* and have everyone nod sympathetically. Maidservants would get a rather cooler reception if they were to try that approach.

'Eleanor had given her word of honour to her tutor,' Charles cut in protectively. He might not have his arm around her any more, but they were sitting side by side on the battered couch, facing Lady Marguerite in her own chair.

'I understand from her story that she didn't even meet this . . . this ghost, until we ourselves took her to France.'

'There comes a time to all of us when we're caught between conflicting obligations, and *I gave my word* simply doesn't stay the course, my dear Charles,' Lady Marguerite said, rather reflecting Eleanor's own point of view. 'If Eleanor knew something which could have helped the League, but kept silent about it, then . . . Well, I see her point, but I cannot entirely be in sympathy with her.'

'You'd have called me mad, milady,' Eleanor said, finally giving words to the fear which had troubled her for months now. 'This isn't the sort of thing anyone would *believe* if it wasn't waved right in front of their nose! And even if I had managed to raise a storm, would you have decided I was telling the truth, or just thought I was lucky and had picked the right moment to say it was about to start raining?'

'There was your demonstration in the coach,' Lady Marguerite said. 'I admit that conjuring a pretty light's not a great achievement, but it was something I'm quite sure you didn't fake. And – apparently – it confirms that I'm not under the control of these sinister vampires and their conspiracy.'

'It's true,' Eleanor insisted. 'We've seen it happen. Your own brother, milady—'

'You were supposed to keep him safe!' Lady Marguerite snapped, her eyes burning. She'd suddenly become the centre of the room, without the aid of any magic or mystical powers, simply by the force of her presence. 'And now you tell me he's safely back from Paris, but even so he hasn't come to see me, hasn't even sent me a letter. Percy said that he was in hiding, but wouldn't say where or in what condition he might be. All I know is that my brother, a victim of all this, was brutally coerced into betraying my husband and all the rest of the League, and now I can't even speak to him and comfort him!' For a moment her voice cracked with pain.

And we weren't victims? Eleanor thought, but had the sense – or the training not to disagree with her superiors – to keep it behind her teeth. Admittedly it was still a struggle, though.

Charles reached out to take her hand. 'It's all true, milady,' he said calmly. 'The Chief . . .' The League's name for Sir Percy. 'He couldn't tell you anything while we still feared you might be under the control of the vampires too. You could have been subverted just as Armand was. If we'd simply brought Armand to Blakeney House, we'd have been risking his neck all over again.'

Lady Marguerite snorted, a delicate yet imperious flare of the nostrils. 'Be that as it may, I am not happy to be the last with the news – especially when it's such important news.'

'You don't seem as surprised about the idea of a conspiracy of vampires, milady,' Eleanor ventured, thinking that a change of subject might smooth matters over. Besides, she *liked* Lady Marguerite. It hurt to have the other woman looking at her so suspiciously now.

'Oh, conspiracies, secret plots, behind-the-scenes manipulators, cunning *eminences grises* – they're ten a penny in theatre, and even more so in literature. The idea in itself doesn't astonish me. I'm more surprised that I never suspected it before – though I suppose that's the point, isn't it?'

'Milady?' Charles asked, looking confused.

'My dear Charles, one thing I learned as an actress in Paris was that one should be very careful what one takes on faith. When the producer promises you'll all be paid after the production's run for a couple of weeks, it's common sense to check the account-books yourself, and find out whether he's booked himself a ticket on the fast coach out of Paris. And one of the benefits to being a wit and having my own salon was that I also heard gossip from reliable sources, who were one step closer to the original information, rather than depending on the newspapers and broadsheets. People *will* nearly always tell you lies when it's in their interest to do so. How else does the League survive and operate, if not by being extremely good at lying?'

'I can see what you're driving at, milady, but there's good in a great many people too. Or why else would the League put itself in danger?' Eleanor said firmly.

Lady Marguerite threw up her hands in mock defeat. 'Point taken! Very well, there is good in all of us. I will strive not to be too cynical in front of you two sweethearts.' She ignored the flush on Eleanor's cheeks and Charles's sudden outbreak of coughing. 'However, I can very easily believe that there are enough vampires out there whose morality is sadly absent, and who are more interested in maintaining chains of influence than in the wellbeing of those around them. If humans can be like that, why not vampires?'

Eleanor felt uncomfortable to hear it put that way, but it made sense. 'And . . . the rest of it? The fact that some of them can sway men's minds and control their actions?'

'That leads to a train of thought I like very little – which is to say, not at all.' She leaned forward, and Eleanor and Charles did the same in unconscious reflex, making them look as though they were in a conspiring huddle. 'Charles, you're the trained logician, I think? Consider this proposition. That firstly, there is at least one group of vampires who know of this secret of controlling minds.'

'Only the one group?' Eleanor said.

'I'm hypothesizing here,' Lady Marguerite said. 'Let us assume not every vampire is aware of this ability. I personally know some vampires who are sad gossips and who couldn't keep a secret even if you promised them the entire Bank of England for their silence. If *they* knew about such things, then other people surely would too. We therefore must assume that not all vampires have the ability to . . . well, wave their hands and flash their eyes, or whatever it is they do. May I go on?'

Eleanor nodded mutely, blushing.

'Actually, it's done by feeding their victims their own blood,' Charles said meticulously. He fell silent as Lady Marguerite fixed him with a glare.

'Very well,' Lady Marguerite said, once the room was quiet again. 'Assume this group of vampires are all mutually bound to the highest level of secrecy, for three reasons. Firstly, if suspicion of this got out, then men and women such as the League would investigate. Secondly, the vampires would never be permitted near men of rank or wealth, for fear of how they might influence them. And thirdly – well, the people are easily roused, and very easily made afraid.' A shadow darkened her face, and Eleanor knew she must be thinking of France, and the mob which would cheer victims on their way to the guillotine.

'All of this seems eminently logical,' Charles said cautiously.

'Very good. Now, tell me, under what circumstances would these vampires ever allow anyone who knew their secret to live?'

'Do you think we haven't thought of all this?' Charles flared, in a sudden and uncharacteristic burst of temper. In the candlelight he looked older than his years, his thin bony face weighed down with the burden of his knowledge. 'The Chief's done his best to put a good face on it, to argue that there must be some way we can resolve the issue, but even if we're prepared to risk our own lives, what about our families? My father? Tony's wife, Andrew's wife . . . ? The charges laid against you show that they're willing to forsake all sense of morality in order to bring us down. They're no better than that damned Chauvelin!'

Lady Marguerite sighed. 'Chauvelin has more morals than they do, I suspect. Oh, he'd kill, he'd blackmail, he'd send us all to the guillotine, but he believes he's doing it for the sake of the Revolution, rather than his own personal power or the preservation of his life.'

'I'm surprised you have the slightest kind word for him,' Charles muttered.

Eleanor reached out to touch his hand, just as he had hers. 'Milady, you've scared us sufficiently. We agree that they intend to bind us to their whims or kill us. Myself especially.' Her throat was dry as she spoke. After all, she was something else as well as a member of the League of the Scarlet Pimpernel. She was a mage, and now the vampires knew it. And she wasn't just afraid for herself but for all the rest of the League, and even if she wouldn't admit it to him, Charles most of all. He was a scholar, and he'd already lied once to these vampires to save her. They'd assume he knew more than he did – more than *any* of them did, at the moment. They'd want to squeeze him for information, or turn him into a smiling lickspittle, just as they had with Armand Saint-Just in Paris. She *couldn't* let that happen. Even though she knew there was no way they could be together, that openly acknowledging their love was an impossibility, with marriage even more so . . . every drop of blood in her body yearned to keep him safe.

And what about her own family? Even if she wasn't close to them, what would she do if Lady Sophie sent her a letter saying *Come to me, or your family will pay the price . . .* ?

'And since Lady Sophie is a part of their conspiracy—' she began. The Baroness of Basing, Eleanor's previous mistress, hand in glove with the conspiracy of vampires who wanted to use the League as a catspaw and rule both France and England from behind the scenes . . .

'That is one aspect of it all I still can't believe – that Sophie's even more deeply involved in this than we thought,' Lady Marguerite cut in. 'She's always seemed the most reasonable, sensible, fashion-conscious woman, properly concerned with the management of her estate and her clothing. No more than any typical flower of society . . .' Her voice trailed away, then she laughed, though there was a note of bitterness to it. 'I can hardly be surprised if she should be just as good an actress as I am, I suppose. Or as skilful at identifying weak points – I am such a *perfect* target for accusations of spying.'

'How much did she know about the League?' Eleanor asked. She remembered listening to a conversation between her previous mistress and the Blakeneys, back when she'd been no more than a maid with dreams of working in a modiste's shop. There had been hints dropped which Eleanor had been too naive or ignorant to recognize at the time.

'Too much,' Lady Marguerite said sadly. 'No, she didn't know my Percy was the Pimpernel himself – even though she does now, from what you say – but she certainly suspected we were involved. She could probably have made some accurate guesses about other members of the League too. And if Armand has told her all he knows, then she knows *far* too much.'

Eleanor was silent. The words *What are we going to do?* boiled on her tongue, but she was afraid to speak them. She knew what Anima would have said: find the secret which the vampires are so desperate to hide. Use it. Destroy the vampires. They had a few clues from Bernard, the mage they'd uncovered in Mont-Saint-Michel – and though he was dead and couldn't help them any further, it was a place to start.

31

But the vampires *weren't* all murderers, conspirators and power-hungry tyrants. Some of them – probably most of them – were just people who happened to be vampires, and kept on surviving at the cost of a few cups of blood every night . . . At least they paid for it, didn't they, in coin of the realm and a decent wage? That made them, if not good people, at least no worse than any living man or woman?

But does that make it right? the memory of Anima's voice whispered in Eleanor's mind.

Eleanor was afraid what Lady Marguerite might say if she asked her what she thought they should do.

Someone hammered on the room's door, and they all jumped away from each other, as though they were servants caught whispering in corners. In a slightly shaky voice, Charles called, 'Who is it?'

'It's your friend!' Tony's voice was loud and clear – entirely recognizable, even if he was choosing not to name names. 'We need some help. Deuce take it, old fellow, hold together a bit longer and try not to bleed so much . . .'

Eleanor scrambled for the door, unlocking and opening it. Tony stood there, one shoulder under Andrew's as he supported the other man. Andrew looked to be barely on his feet, his face white in the lamplight. His right arm was bundled under his coat in a makeshift sling that was frighteningly stained with blood.

Charles and Lady Marguerite sprang to their feet and, with the help of all four of them, Andrew was settled on the couch, weakly apologizing for being an inconvenience. Before she shut the door, Eleanor peered down the corridor.

There was a trail of blood. Small drops, barely obvious on the panelled floor, but visibly there.

Eleanor then turned to see what the others were doing. Lady Marguerite had produced a knife from somewhere and was ripping Andrew's shirt open, contrary to his protests, exposing his right arm and chest. Tony and Charles were crowding around, both with the air of men who knew what to do and how to do it. Whereas she . . . she . . .

'I'll fetch some hot water from the kitchen,' she offered quickly. 'Charles, would you come with me to bring it back?'

Tony's notorious good nature showed signs of cracking. 'Are the both of you really needed to carry a jug of water?' he demanded. 'Normally I wouldn't have the slightest objection to you taking a quiet stroll together, but under these circumstances—'

'There's a trail of blood, Tony,' Eleanor cut in. 'Leading right to this door. Trust me, it'll be easiest to clean it up if I see to it now, while Charles brings you the water to clean Andrew's wound.' She tried to smile, but it was difficult when she looked at Andrew – always so strong, so much in control, a tall golden giant of a man – biting back a murmur of pain. 'I *am* the League's expert on scrubbing floors, aren't I?'

It didn't take Eleanor long to clean up the trail to their door. She wanted to be inside with the others, to find out what had *happened*, but if someone was hot on their tracks, Runners or otherwise, then she wasn't going to make life any easier for them. Half-remembered stories of magic tinderboxes, and dogs with eyes as big as millwheels, danced through her head as she worked briskly down the corridor, coming to a stop at the bottom of the stairwell. She didn't want to risk cleaning further downstairs, where one of the establishment's servants might see her and ask questions. The blood spots seemed to fade at that point anyway, trodden into the dirty floor down there.

There was even a certain comfort – and distraction – in doing something she *knew* how to do, rather than summoning thunderstorms or jumping out of moving carriages. *I'd wager none of the men could clean a floor this well.* It numbed the panicky thought of *What would I have done if Charles had been wounded and I'd been the only one here to help?*

Charles opened the door when she scratched on it. 'He's all right,' he murmured, answering her most pressing question. 'It was just a bullet to his arm. Though I fear the crash didn't help.'

'The crash?' Eleanor quavered, forcing herself to stay calm and not let her voice rise. She'd imagined bad, but this was worse.

'Merely a bagatelle,' Tony said. He pressed a glass of brandy into Andrew's good hand. 'I mean, Andrew was the one holding the reins when he took the bullet, and he did his best to spare the horses, but otherwise it was a hell of a smash. They shouldn't put lamp posts in such inconvenient places. Fortunately the Runners' driver had enough sense and skill to pull up their horses before they ran into us. In all the confusion, I dragged Andrew out of the mess and we staggered for it together. Took us a while to lose those Runners, though. Good thing you got out when you did – it'd have been deuced inconvenient if we'd been shepherding you as well.'

'You should sit down and have some brandy yourself,' Eleanor said firmly. The idea of being in the coach when it crashed, when it had been going at such a terrifying speed, made her shiver. Then she realized their current, most serious, problem. 'How are we going to explain Andrew's arm, if the Runners know they shot someone?'

'With difficulty.' Lady Marguerite had been rinsing her hands in the basin of hot water, washing off Andrew's blood. 'Can your magic heal him, Eleanor?'

'No,' Eleanor confessed reluctantly. 'I think the mage at Mont-Saint-Michel could have, but he had a different sort of magic . . . and he was much more experienced than I am.'

Lady Marguerite nodded. 'Then there will have to be

some foolish horseplay amongst you gentlemen, during which Andrew takes a pistol ball in his arm.'

'Can't do that,' Tony objected. 'We'd never duel. Anyone who knows us would know that.'

'It wouldn't need to be a duel,' Lady Marguerite argued. 'Just . . . someone being careless with a pistol.'

Tony folded his arms. 'I'm telling you, milady, none of us would do such a thing! We may be carousers, drunkards, fops and fribbles, but we don't play fast and loose with loaded pistols.'

'That's true,' Charles said. 'It wouldn't wash once they started asking serious questions.'

Eleanor looked between them – Lady Marguerite frowning in thought, and Tony's usually agreeable face stiffened into firm denial. Neither of them was going to budge. 'What if it was someone who doesn't know anything about pistols?' she asked.

'Some commoner off the street? They wouldn't *fire* a pistol, they'd take it and sell it,' Charles said.

'No, that wasn't what I meant.' It would be difficult to persuade *any* of the men to accept it, but it would be near-unanswerable if it passed. 'What if . . . Sir Andrew was returning late to his home, and his wife Suzanne woke from sleep and was confused, and accidentally fired a pistol at him?'

'Outrageous!' Andrew declared, sitting bolt upright and then going stark white as the pain from his arm dug in its claws. 'My Suzanne would never be so foolish!'

Lady Marguerite took the suggestion more seriously. 'We both know she wouldn't, Andrew . . . but there are people who'd believe it, and who'd consider it far more likely than the idea you and your friends would engage in horseplay with loaded pistols. They'd claim that nobody could expect any better from a Frenchwoman. Or indeed, from any woman.' The twist to her lips suggested she might be familiar with such accusations.

'I couldn't ask it of her,' Andrew said firmly. 'She knows nothing of our work—'

'Do you think she's stupid?' Eleanor couldn't help the words: they burst out of her, hot with bitterness for another woman who was ignored, patronized, and left to do the noble equivalent of scrubbing the floor. 'You rescued her from France. You married her. She's been helping milady here for these last few days while we've been away and milady was charged with treason. For pity's sake, Andrew, she constantly tells everyone that she has *no idea* who the Pimpernel and the League are, even though they saved her. How on earth could she say that so sincerely and honestly if she *didn't* know exactly what she was saying and why, and who she was protecting?'

Silence hung in the room. Then Tony coughed. 'It hasn't precisely escaped my knowledge that my own Yvonne's a sight too clever to be as ignorant as she claims to be. Of course, one couldn't ask her to jump out of a moving carriage or anything, but when it comes to her or Suzanne telling a tiny little falsehood to help us . . .'

'I couldn't ask her to bear such ignominy,' Andrew said, but his tone of stubborn refusal had weakened.

'Ah, bah!' Lady Marguerite interjected. 'So all the times she's told me that she only wished she could do something to help you, rather than sit around and assist the new émigrés in finding their feet here in London, she was merely exaggerating?' She wiped her hands dry. 'I don't think so. Andrew, you wouldn't be insulting her. You'd be giving her the greatest gift within your power – your trust. You'd be asking her to stand by you in danger as well as in safety – in sickness and in health, isn't that what the marriage service says?'

'I'd trust Eleanor with it,' Charles said, and the gaze which he fixed on her made her heart tremble. She so wished there was a way *they* could be together, in some world where he wasn't Sir Charles Bathurst and she wasn't just a common serving-maid. But even in France, where they'd had a Revolution for Liberty, Fraternity and Equality, the Rights of Men and a hundred other lofty-minded principles, such things were the province of romantic stories and fairy tales, not reality.

Andrew frowned. 'Even if I were to accept this – and mark that I'm not saying I do – we'd still have another problem.'

Charles struck his forehead. 'Deuce take it! Oxford.'

'What about Oxford?' Lady Marguerite asked. 'You mentioned there was some sort of important clue there, Eleanor . . .'

Eleanor nodded, but her face fell as she realized the scale of the problem. 'I did, milady, and part of the Chief's plan was that early tomorrow Charles would go there to investigate it further, and Andrew would go with him in case of trouble.' After all, the vampires knew who Charles was, and if they should be following him and catch him alone . . . 'But if Andrew's wounded and can't travel – perhaps Tony?'

Tony shook his head. 'The Chief's set me a few other pressing errands to run, and I'll be honest with you, my dear, I also came out of that crash with more than a few bruises. The Oxford trip will have to be put off for a few days.'

'Do we *have* a few days?' Charles asked, frowning. 'I could go alone—'

The chorus of simultaneous denial drowned him out.

'You can't travel with Eleanor either,' Tony said, cutting off that line of thought before Eleanor could even suggest it. 'On your own together, you'd need to pretend to be married or related, and they know you in Oxford, Charles. Your old chums and professors would have far too many questions.'

Eleanor pouted, but reluctantly had to agree his point. They'd attract far too much attention together on a public stagecoach without a good reason for being in company – and people travelling on the coaches had nothing to do but talk.

'There is another alternative,' Lady Marguerite said. She had that glint in her eye again, a fox on the prowl. 'Tony, you'll escort Andrew home to make sure he arrives safely. Then you can stage your little drama, with Suzanne "accidentally" shooting him. Don't worry, Andrew, she won't be scorned: half the women in London may laugh at her, but the other half will wish they had the nerve to do something like that themselves. Meanwhile, Eleanor will be travelling with *me*. You don't mind playing a maid again, do you, my dear?'

Eleanor's eyes widened as she took in what Lady Marguerite was suggesting. A woman travelling with her maid was entirely reasonable. 'But if you're recognized . . . then again, I suppose I shouldn't be counselling *you* on painting *your* face, milady.' If one of France's premier actresses couldn't utterly disguise herself, then Eleanor would eat her best bonnet.

Lady Marguerite nodded, but half her attention was on the men as she assessed their response. 'Quite. I'll be . . . oh, Bess Hardcastle or something similar. A widow in my fifties and travelling to Oxford to visit a nephew who's down with influenza, or a sprained ankle, or some other grave disorder, intending to soothe his fevered brow and threaten to cut him out of my will for his reckless behaviour. You'll be my maid . . . Annie. We may not be able to travel on the same coach as Charles, but we can make contact again once we reach Oxford, and assess the situation.' She tossed her hair. 'And before anyone else can say it, I know it's not what my Percy had planned. But he couldn't have foreseen things would go this way.'

'I trust you'll forgive me for voicing my concern, milady,' Andrew said, his tone subdued but firm, 'yet is this the wisest course of action? Should we not perhaps wait until we can contact the Chief and ask for new orders?'

'There's no *time*.' Lady Marguerite leaned forward, the lamplight turning her hair into a torrent of red-gold, bringing out the fine bones of her face, the intensity of her gaze. 'Charles was to take the coach tomorrow morning for Oxford, I believe? Which is *this* morning, now. It's too risky to get a message through to Percy tonight – he'll be swarmed by Bow Street for questioning after my disappearance, not to mention vampire spies keeping watch on him and everyone he speaks to. From what you and Percy have told me, they had me accused of treason bare days after you brought down their plot in Paris. And *they know who we are*. If they'll strike at me so swiftly to hinder Percy, then how long before they make targets of your own families? We need a weapon against them, and we cannot risk the slightest delay in finding out where to uncover it. Are we in agreement?' She looked around the room, her presence a call to battle.

Sir Percy might be the leader of the League of the Scarlet Pimpernel, but here and now, there was no further hesitation about obeying Lady Marguerite.

CHAPTER THREE

The night's rain had washed the sky clear: the dawn was unsullied by clouds, and the light seemed to fill every nook of the coachyard, etching the high roofs black against the pale sky. Outside the inn's coachyard Fleet Street was already bubbling with activity, full of the life and spirit of London at its best. Occasional shouts and screams suggested it was also full of the life and spirit of London at its worst.

The coachyard of the Bolt and Tun similarly buzzed with activity. As in the beehives Eleanor had seen when she was younger, everyone somehow dodged around everyone else with perfect smoothness and timing, as though it were a quadrille they'd rehearsed beforehand. Porters swung their piled barrows around travellers with barely a word of rebuke (well, perhaps a few words), grooms led horses to and fro between coaches, and customers in search of a morning drink cut through the whole melee with sublime disregard for anyone else's safety. As this inn was the main starting point for coaches from London to Oxford and beyond, it was particularly crowded and busy, so hopefully nobody would remember one more middle-aged woman and her humble maid if the Bow Street Runners came asking questions.

Eleanor felt as though the inside of her head had been

scoured out and left to dry. She hadn't had any sleep. None of them had. All their time had been taken up with preparing for the journey and changes to their appearances. Eleanor looked like her normal self again, with her pale hair pinned up neatly and a decent dress and shawl. It said something about the past few months that she'd needed to glance twice at her reflection in a pane of glass, because she seemed to be looking at a stranger.

Charles had been on the earlier coach, which left half an hour ago, at six o'clock, and with any luck he'd be able to close his eyes for an hour or two on the journey. Common sense might have said it was a good thing they weren't travelling on the same coach, since their false identities weren't supposed to know each other, but Eleanor couldn't help wishing in her heart of hearts that they *had* been. She could have sat next to him, squeezed in as they would have been, leaning her head on his shoulder . . .

'I demand to speak with your superior!' Lady Marguerite's voice shrilled through the air, twitching Eleanor to straight-backed attention, as though the woman was next to her rather than inside the booking office. Lady Marguerite's voice was normally so sweet and modulated, drawing attention without being at all demanding or sharp. Eleanor had to remind herself, again, that milady had been an actress before her marriage to Lord Percy. But that was really the mark of a good actress – or actor – wasn't it? When one forgot they *were* an actress.

One of the porters came to a pause next to Eleanor and put down the handles of the trolley of luggage he'd been pushing. 'Your mistress, is she?' he asked, with a nod towards the office.

'She is,' Eleanor agreed. 'Mrs Hardcastle. We had word that her nephew's ill in Oxford, and she wanted to catch the next coach there . . .'

'Well, I'm sorry to tell you this, my pretty, but there's no room on the seven o'clock, and then there won't be any more till tomorrow morning. Packed full it is, so tight you couldn't slide a card between the customers.'

'Oh dear.' Eleanor frowned. That meant Charles would be alone for a whole day without anyone to watch his back. 'She will be disappointed.'

'Don't you worry about it, sweet. Allen in there will butter her up and get her sorted with a ticket for tomorrow.' His expert eye took in the pile of luggage which Eleanor was guarding – two portmanteaux, one large and one small, and a couple of hatboxes. 'We'll have room for you and your bags then. And since you're such a pretty girl, if your mistress doesn't want you at her side all evening tonight, then perhaps you'd consider stepping round the corner with me for supper . . .'

'Annie!' Lady Marguerite came sweeping out of the office, the heavy silk of her old-fashioned dress rustling with every step. She was unrecognizable, powdered and painted like a woman twice her age, with a heavy grey wig concealing her natural hair, and her steps brisk and aggressive rather than their usual floating elegance. She walked like a woman who did not expect to be stopped, and would make anyone's life extremely unpleasant if they tried. 'I have managed – finally – to obtain a seat. Where is my fan? And my parasol? Fetch me some tea at once. We have half an hour to wait. This shoddy service is insupportable! I shall complain at the very highest levels. And find someone to take care of our luggage.'

'Yes, madam,' Eleanor said, and bobbed a curtsey. 'Ah, when you say *a* seat . . .'

'Silly girl!' Lady Marguerite rapped Eleanor on the knuckles with the fan. 'Inside the carriage for me, of course. You will be on the roof. Mind your manners and don't talk to any strangers.'

'Sounds like you work for your wages,' the porter muttered sympathetically as Eleanor trotted off to find some tea.

'Oh, you have no idea,' she murmured in response.

Eleanor was sharing the roof of the carriage with two other maidservants, a couple of staggeringly hung-over students content to lean on each other and doze, and an elderly gentleman wrapped in a coat far heavier than suited the weather. He constantly sucked pastilles and sniffled, reading and rereading a copy of *The Times* as though he intended to memorize the paper. By common consent, the three young women had crowded together on the rear seat, even though it was cramped, and left the front seating to the students and elderly man. They might not know each other, but they all knew the dangers of being a woman travelling among men.

Eleanor was wedged in on the far right. The woman in the middle was a few years older than Eleanor, and was in a *very* cheap dark blue muslin dress that didn't suit her – she seemed amiable enough. On the far left was a perky young miss in a much nicer dress and shawl, with brassy curls that foamed out from under her bonnet. She kept on shooting bitter glances in Eleanor's direction, the reason for which Eleanor could only puzzle over.

'Well now!' the woman in the middle said, ignoring the ebb and flow of London traffic below them (they were at least eight feet up, and Eleanor was trying not to think too hard about it). 'I don't know how far you ladies are travel-ling – I'm only going as far as Reading, which is where the Reverend Bottson gets off – he's in the carriage below us, you know – escorting me to take up my new position as under-matron to St Thomas's Home for Orphans – extremely proud of it, can't say otherwise, looking forward to taking care of all those dear little moppets whose parents are no longer with us, gone to a better place – name's Sarah Milt, and who would you be?'

It took Eleanor a moment to realize that Sarah Milt had reached the end of her sentence. 'I'm Annie Johns,' she said, doing her best to project shyness. 'Maid to Mrs Hardcastle – she's in the carriage, like your Reverend. Her nephew in Oxford has gone and sprained his ankle, or broken something, the letter wasn't very clear, and she feels it's her duty to go and minister to him, and tell him as how he should be more careful in future.'

'Does your mistress's nephew know she's coming?' the other woman asked, taking an interest.

Eleanor rolled her eyes. 'Well, she sent a message to say she was coming, but she took her time about how best to word it, and we can only hope it'll arrive there ahead of us. Not that that bothers *her*. She's one of those people who thinks everyone should be so pleased to see her that they don't need any warning she's on her way. She had me running around with notes to all the tradesmen to tell them not to make the usual deliveries, and sending letters to her lawyer to keep her will locked up tight, and the family diamonds in the safe, but write in time to make certain to tell her nephew to expect her? No, he's going to be lying in his bed, probably with a pint of porter in his hand to make him feel better about his poor ankle, and then the door's going to go flying open and she'll march in and—'

Sarah Milt giggled.

The third woman finally broke her sullen silence. 'I can't say as I was feeling particularly friendly towards you,' she said, 'but if you've got to put up with *that*, then least said soonest mended. My name's Kitty – Kitty Mattis.'

'I didn't offend you, did I?' Eleanor asked.

'Not you so much, but when your mistress forced them

to give her a seat on this carriage, it meant there wasn't room inside for me any more, like *my* mistress had paid for. So now I'm up here with you and let's hope it's not going to rain today. Probably will, though.' Kitty toyed with a metallic ringlet. Eleanor, experienced by now in the use of dyes to change one's hair colour, couldn't help thinking the wash she'd used was far too harsh. 'Miss Bethany – that's my mistress – likes someone to play a hand of cards with while she's travelling, or to read to her from the Bible.'

'Miss Bethany doesn't travel by public stagecoach often, does she?' Sarah asked, giving voice to Eleanor's own thoughts.

'Not likely! Her brother's got his own coach and if she needs to go anywhere outside London, he sees to it, and she never has to sport no blunt for it.' Eleanor recognized some of the racing cant which members of the League dropped from time to time. 'Her brother pays for most things for her, but he said he weren't going to drive to Oxford, not even for his dear sweet sister. Didn't want nothing to do with all them books or people reading them. He likes the horses and the Fancy – that's the boxing clubs – better.'

'Someone should tell him you can't catch an education like a disease,' Eleanor said, and all three of them laughed.

'So why is she going to Oxford?' Sarah asked. 'Is it for a holiday? The Reverend often says the architecture's a feast for the eyes – such pretty ways he has of talking. He's even better when he's in the pulpit, but it sounds like there's too many stairs for my liking.'

'Cousin of hers wanted her to visit,' Kitty said. She lowered her voice, and the three of them leaned their bonnets together. 'Fact of the matter is, I can't say I'm too upset to be getting out of London for the moment.'

'But why?' Eleanor asked. 'I mean . . . London.' She didn't have to elaborate further. All of them understood what she meant. The shops, the markets, the clothes, the entertainment, the company . . .

'Either of you walk out much in the evening lately?' Kitty asked.

A shadow came over Sarah's face. 'Not myself – I haven't got a young man to go out walking with, and I'm not the sort to go out otherwise – though naturally I wouldn't say a word against anyone else – and the evenings are later at the moment in any case, it stays light so much longer after sunset, such beautiful weather – and of course the dear little children take such a deal of taking care of – but – one hears talk . . .'

Eleanor shook her head. 'Madam's been having evenings with her friends to raise money for missionaries,' she excused herself, 'and it's kept all the household busy. What's the talk?'

Kitty stared at the road behind them as the carriage clattered through the streets of London, not meeting the eyes of the other women. 'You know about the blood trade?' she asked.

Eleanor thought back to what she'd seen in Covent Garden a month or so ago, with sellers on every corner touting blood – fresh human blood, supposedly from healthy young men and women. And there'd been the Victims' Ball she attended as a servant, where she'd been nothing but a source of blood for the vampire guests. Oh, not harmed, because one didn't smash the good chinaware. (Unless perhaps one was very drunk or careless.) But . . . it hadn't even been a matter of class, with the nobility disregarding servants as they usually did. It had been something else – as though the vampires were the human beings, and everyone else wasn't *real* in the same way, just a piece of furniture. Even the upper servants had been looking down on the lower ones who provided the blood.

Had this all been *spreading*?

'It's not from my mistress I heard it,' Kitty said, her voice pitched so it would carry over the noise of travel but still low enough not to reach their fellow passengers on the coach roof. 'It's from her brother, the one as pays for her – hired me and everything. He was the one who said that a pretty girl like me should be careful about where she steps out these days. There's talk, up there in them political circles. Worrying talk.'

Which Sir Percy wouldn't necessarily have heard, Eleanor thought, *as he's so busy taking pains to portray himself as a fool and unreliable lackwit, whose only interest is in tying his cravat.* 'Is your mistress's brother highly placed?' she asked. 'After what you mentioned he said about Oxford . . .'

'He's got friends as is in the military,' Kitty explained. 'They talk to him, and he talks to me, and they say as it's *women* who gossip!'

'It's not gossip if it's important,' Sarah said. 'That's a fact – if I tell you there's a lunatic with an axe running down the street, then that's not gossip, is it? That's a warning, same as I might give anyone who needed it, who was in danger – and if we're in danger, then it's not gossip to share what we know – it's the sort of thing that's in the Bible, with all the disciples writing each other letters about how the world was with them and if there was danger, and if they can do it, I don't see as we can't – because Lord knows there's few enough who'll look out for us.' She paused. 'Or those poor orphan children I'm going to.'

'But you said blood *trade*?' Eleanor asked.

'Well, you know how as normally vampires . . .' For a moment Kitty hesitated, her voice lowering on the word. 'As how *them* aren't in Parliament, and can't be ministers, or command regiments, or all that sort of thing?'

Both Eleanor and Sarah nodded. 'Been that way for

hundreds of years,' Sarah said, 'and can't say but that it isn't a good thing – otherwise how would they ever stop doing those jobs? You'd have all the government full of them with none ever leaving – and I don't have a word to necessarily say against any of them, but I can't help but feel that wouldn't be proper.'

London was falling behind them now. The air became cleaner, with the smells of the road and countryside wafting over rather than the stink of gutters and dung and crowded people. The sky was perfectly clear and beautiful, with the sun shining down, as though they were in one of the pictures Eleanor had seen in Blakeney House – all green fields, blue skies, and dancing shepherds and shepherdesses. It felt *wrong* to be talking of conspiracies and blood on such a day.

'Well, my mistress's brother told me – or I might have heard him talking to other people about it while I was fetching and carrying – that there was talk about some of that changing, what with the war and the King being . . . sick.' She chose the mild term, as if it was just a matter of a common cold, though Eleanor had certainly heard the darker rumours: babbling, foaming at the mouth, outright madness. 'They're saying as perhaps some of *them*, who have hundreds of years of experience in such things, should be stepping forward to serve their country, and the law should be changed so as they can. They're even saying maybe more of our young men as serve the King as soldiers – well, maybe if they weren't just human then we'd win more battles in France, so maybe . . .'

Eleanor's hand went to her mouth in shock. 'They'd *never*,' she said. The worst slang she'd heard from the League was insufficient reaction to this proposal. 'Surely not.'

'They say we're at war and we've got to do everything to win it,' Kitty answered.

'Well, and it wouldn't work in any case.' Sarah came in

as the voice of common sense, and Eleanor felt her stomach
settle itself again as the older woman spoke. 'Don't *they*
always say as it's a very difficult thing to turn people into
something like themselves? And even if perhaps it's not as
hard as they say it is, then what on earth would all them
soldiers eat on the ships over to France, and when they get
there? Or when they're in camps over here in England? It
stands to reason you can't have more of *them* without having
more of what they need to drink – like with foxes and rabbits,
my pa was a gamekeeper and he knew about that sort of
thing – and it just wouldn't work. People would object,' she
finished comfortably.

Eleanor thought about France and people 'objecting', and
how it had ended up with the vampires being dragged to
the guillotines – except for the ones who'd managed to hide
in the shadow of the leading revolutionaries. Yet Kitty had
spoken of a 'blood trade' as though it was an established
thing. 'Perhaps people wouldn't object that much if it wasn't
them in person opening their veins,' she said quietly. 'People
who aren't protected, though . . .'

Kitty shivered in spite of the heat, drawing her shawl
closer round her shoulders. 'There's girls I know who may
be on the street, but they don't deserve what happens to
them, not having someone to look out for them. You know,
don't you, Annie? You understand how it is.'

'I don't see as why Annie has anything to know about
it,' Sarah protested. 'With a nice steady upright mistress,
even if she sounds as if she could be a little difficult on bad
mornings . . .'

'Annie knows what I'm talking about,' Kitty said, and
drew one finger meaningfully in lines along the inside of
her forearm.

With a jolt, Eleanor realized that Kitty must have seen
her faded scars, from when she'd given blood to Lady

Sophie, her mistress, for . . . well, the whole of her life up until a year ago. She'd hoped they weren't too obvious, but the July heat was merciless, bringing every old scar from wounds to smallpox into view. Kitty was clearly aware of what they meant.

Likewise, Eleanor could make a few guesses of her own about Kitty. The other woman had friends who were on the street, had been employed by her mistress's *brother*, and was able to listen to his private conversations. She was clearly the most worldly-wise of the three of them. Which really wasn't any of Eleanor's business – after all, how could it compare in terms of scandal to being a member of the League of the Scarlet Pimpernel?

Eleanor hesitated, trying to find some way of phrasing things which wouldn't betray too much. 'The world's a hard place,' she said, 'and if someone in authority tells you to do something, then how much choice does a woman have, if she doesn't want to be turned off without a character and left on the street?'

Kitty nodded firmly. 'True enough,' she said. 'A woman does what she has to.'

'I'm worried, though,' Eleanor confessed. 'Perhaps none of this is going to happen, but the fact you've even heard talk about how it *could* happen isn't a cheering thing. There are already enough people in power saying as how anyone who speaks out against the government, or says anything they don't like, should be arrested—'

'Where did you hear about that?' Sarah asked. Kitty didn't look surprised, however.

'A friend of Mrs Hardcastle had been to some sort of social affair with philosophers, charitable types and blue-stockings, and people who talk about change and call it Enlightenment,' Eleanor explained, drastically paraphrasing a party she herself had attended a month ago, clinging to

Lady Marguerite's hem. 'She said the Bow Street Runners turned up and started arresting people – just walked in right through the front door!' This drew a gasp of shock from the other women, both of whom would know the proper entrance for tradesmen and Runners was round the back. 'And when some of the guests tried to walk out, well, the Runners knocked them over the head and took them off to Newgate.'

'There's a lot of people in Newgate these days,' Sarah said darkly. 'And the prison hulks – them ships they've got moored in the Thames – and they say Portsmouth and Plymouth too, on account of how there's not enough room in the jails. And the Reverend says there are more people in Bedlam every day, and places like it, with some still sensible enough, but packed off to there by their families, and dosed up with laudanum, because they weren't behaving proper in public – and . . .' She trailed off. 'It's not right,' she finished, but very quietly.

'Someone'll do something about it,' Kitty consoled her. 'It's not as if this is *France*.'

'What was that you were saying about France?' one of the young men demanded.

The women looked at each other. 'Nothing, sir,' Eleanor said virtuously. 'Just saying it's not as if it was France here.'

'Perhaps it should be.' He shook back lank hair and adjusted his neckcloth. 'For too long this country has avoided the questions which have plagued all countries since time immemorial. Albion must arise, as Blake writes in his glorious poetry! Our isle must shake itself from its slumbers and—'

'Oh do shut up, Segson,' his companion yawned. 'It's too early in the morning for this.'

'I will not be silenced!'

'If you haven't got a headache, I have. And I'm sure these

women don't want to be bored by your revolutionary thoughts.' The second young man attempted a charming smirk, which mostly came across as just a leer.

'Revolutionary? Bah! Pah! Feh!' The old gentleman nearly choked on his pastille, flustered. He waved his copy of *The Times* at the young men menacingly. 'The two of you should be joining the army! Defending England! Not wasting your time on . . . *philosophy!*' He put the sort of venom into the word which Eleanor usually associated with housekeepers discussing dust and tarnish. 'Spending your fathers' good money at Oxford like wastrels, rather than devoting yourselves to sensible studies and honest work. If I had my way, boys like you would be whipped! What's England coming to? Mohocks abroad on the streets of London, women kidnapped from their homes, French spies on the loose . . .'

'We're very sorry, sir,' Segson's friend said, kicking Segson's ankle meaningfully. 'My friend was misunderstood, or possibly misunderstanding. Are you on your way to Oxford too?'

As Segson muttered clearly insincere apologies and his friend continued to smooth the waters, Eleanor wished she could get her hands on the old man's copy of *The Times*. There might be something in it about Lady Marguerite's disappearance. But more than that, she wanted to assess how much of what her fellow travellers had whispered to her could be true. It was what Sir Percy would have called 'deuced unlikely' that she'd happened to be travelling with anyone carrying particularly important or secret information. So was what Kitty and Sarah had been saying just *common gossip*, albeit gossip which painted a particularly unpleasant picture?

Had she and the League been blind to what was going on in England, with their focus always on France? Perhaps it was vanity on Eleanor's part to think of herself as an integral part of the League rather than a mere adjunct, but she had eyes. She should have been able to see what was happening around her. Saying that she should 'know her place' and never think of standing up to injustice was . . . well, outdated. The Revolution had proven that, whatever else it might have done.

Yet Kitty's belief (or at least hope) that 'someone'll do something about it' left open the question of who that someone would be. The King? Known to be ill, possibly mad, and even then, subject to Parliament. Parliament itself?

Remembering how a hidden group of vampires in France had exerted their influence over the Committee for Public Safety – and beyond that, the National Convention – Eleanor wondered, her mouth dry with fear, just whose interests Parliament governed in these days.

If anyone could do something about this, it might be the League. But where in Oxford should they even *start*?

CHAPTER FOUR

The sun had set by the time they reached Oxford, though the sky was still pale and clear with the last of the light. Kitty and Eleanor stood side by side in a corner of the coaching inn's courtyard, minding piles of luggage and waiting for their mistresses. Eleanor was restraining the urge to rub various body parts which were complaining after the day's journey. She realized regretfully that she had grown spoilt: past journeys *inside* a coach, on padded seats, hadn't prepared her for a day travelling *outside* on the roof, even if they'd been lucky with the weather.

Though . . . it hadn't been precisely luck. She'd actually felt the twisting threads of the winds above, the shifting bulges of pressure like a god's eye bearing down on her, or like the massed feathers in an eiderdown quilt which needed a good shaking to even out its stuffing. In between the conversation, when all words had run dry and they'd been staring at the passing fields, she'd tried to soothe it, to stroke away the thick denseness which usually preceded another storm. And it had worked. Or at least, they hadn't had any more bad weather. That was a good thing – wasn't it?

'Your mistress should have booked rooms *before* she came down here,' Kitty said, not for the first time.

'I'm not arguing,' Eleanor said. 'I hadn't thought it'd be so busy, though. Aren't all the students supposed to have gone home to see their parents? I thought their – term, is it? – finished in June.'

'Probably most of them'd rather be here and studying if they want to study – or here and raising hell if they don't want to study.' Kitty spoke with feeling. Their coach had been interrupted on its way to the inn by a carousing group of young men who clearly hadn't been waiting for nightfall to start their drinking.

'Well, her nephew and his friends are still here,' Eleanor said, 'and one of them *should* have arranged rooms for Mrs Hardcastle. I only hope we don't have to wait too long for them to show their faces. They'd better not be off drinking or at lectures – do they have lectures here at night? If the vampires are their professors and teachers? Any which way, Madam won't be happy.'

So far Eleanor had come to three conclusions about Oxford. The first was that it was stuffed full of young men, and all of them noisy. Whether they were talking about their work, throwing names at each other that she'd never heard of, and declaiming in half a dozen different languages, or out to enjoy themselves, they went sweeping by in their black gowns. This item of clothing seemed to be a commonplace here, worn as casually as if it were a perfectly normal coat.

Her second conclusion was that it was *old*. It wasn't like London, with its new buildings piled on top of the old ones, or with older sections hidden behind fresh marble-fronted, white-doorstepped elegance. It wasn't even like Paris either, with whole swathes of new construction in progress and glaringly wide avenues. If there was anything Eleanor could compare it to, it would be Mont-Saint-Michel – centuries old and proud of it, in stone so fixed and permanent that it couldn't and wouldn't be changed. Any more recent parts felt like patches of new cloth sewed onto an older dress which still had its own integrity and dignity: out of place, unwanted, temporary and soon to be gone, leaving the original behind with no trace of their passing.

And her final conclusion was that people here were afraid – and angry. There was an undertone to passing conversations which she recognized from Paris, a note of resentment and brewing fury. It wasn't at the level which might raise shouting mobs to fill the street – not yet, at least. But it was there. She hoped Lady Marguerite and herself would be out of town before it boiled over, when someone threw the first stone that would start the avalanche.

Yet another student stalked into the inn yard in long ungainly strides, his gown flapping behind him. He nearly got himself run over twice as he stood in the middle of the yard, peering around short-sightedly at the darker corners. Eleanor's heart skipped a beat, then relaxed, and she forced herself to suppress a happy smile. Charles had found them.

In a gesture towards anonymity, he wasn't wearing his eye-glasses, which made it far less likely he'd be recognized by anyone who might know him locally. On the other hand, it made it far harder for him to see Eleanor in her corner by the luggage. She restrained an urge to wave at him. She wasn't supposed to know him, after all.

Finally he identified her from the other groups of waiting passengers and piles of luggage, and strolled in her direction. He looked between her and Kitty, appearing undecided. 'Excuse me, young women – are either of you in the employ of a Mrs Hardcastle?'

'I am, sir,' Eleanor said, and bobbed a little curtsey. 'Madam's in the office over there just now, speaking with the people in charge, but she'll only be a moment.'

'Ah, good, good. Trust you had a pleasant run up from

London? I always feel the countryside's so pretty this time of year. Extremely kind of Mrs Hardcastle to come so promptly. Her nephew – Philip, you know – was almost dragging himself out of his bed, saying she didn't need to, and threatening to throw himself out of the window if she showed up. Delirious, poor fellow.'

'I just bet he was,' Kitty whispered with a smirk, elbowing Eleanor in the ribs.

'Here comes Madam now!' Eleanor said, grateful not to have to extend the story any further than necessary. She was always afraid she'd start forgetting what lies she'd told if it became too complicated. She pointed in the direction of the office: Lady Marguerite was sweeping in their direction with a grand self-importance. No one came close to colliding with her, everyone removing themselves from her path and indeed her vicinity. It seemed even an agent of the Committee of Public Safety in France was not as terrifying as a dowager on a rampage.

She came to a halt a few paces away, looking Charles up and down, from every inch of his untidy hair and shabby coat to his muddy boots. 'And who is this?'

Charles swept a bow. 'Mrs Hardcastle?'

'Yes,' she admitted, in tones which suggested the word could be retracted if he proved insufficient.

'I'm James Phillimore, a friend of your nephew Philip. I've taken rooms for you at the King's Arms, and if you'll permit me to escort you there, I'll be glad to explain things further.'

Lady Marguerite visibly thawed and began pestering Charles for information about her fictional nephew's accident, which he was quick to supply. Really, Eleanor thought, the two of them took far too much enjoyment in the whole play-acting part of their scheme. Almost invisible in Lady Marguerite's presence, a thin woman in a limp grey dress and limp grey hat scurried up with a porter and took possession of Kitty, who left with a final wave to Eleanor, and murmured hopes they'd meet again.

A stamping and neighing at the inn gate announced the arrival of a new coach – heavy and anonymous, with no name or symbols painted on the sides. Eleanor, distracted from Charles and Lady Marguerite's prattle, wondered who it might be. A cold sensation ran up her spine as she saw the men who came stamping out of it. They were sturdy and well built, in heavy buff coats despite the hot weather, and moving with purpose.

She caught the words *Bow Street*.

'Madam . . .' she said softly, catching Lady Marguerite's attention, then flicking a glance towards the couple of men heading for the inn's coaching office. 'Should we be on our way?'

'Perhaps we should,' Charles said, disquiet showing in his eyes. 'We wouldn't want to attract any attention to ourselves.'

'On the contrary.' Lady Marguerite puffed herself up like a pouter pigeon. 'Attention is exactly what we want to attract. James, watch our luggage! Annie, follow me!' Swinging her parasol in one hand like a self-indulgent highwayman with a loaded pistol, she started back towards the office again.

What is she doing? But Eleanor couldn't disobey – that would be an obvious breach of proper behaviour. With an agonized glance back at Charles, she scurried in her mistress's wake.

The men – Bow Street Runners, Eleanor was sure of it – were in the process of questioning an already broken-looking man behind a battered desk. At the sight of Lady Marguerite, he choked back a groan, turning away from the Runner who was thrusting a piece of paper in front of him. 'I'm terribly sorry, madam, but these gentlemen have urgent business which I simply must attend to—'

'That we do,' the one with the sheet of paper grunted. 'Afraid you'll have to wait, missis.'

'The name is *Hardcastle.*' Lady Marguerite drenched the word in venom and then froze it for additional impact. 'And if you *people* are here to investigate the dubious goings-on behind this coach line, and their abominable failure to keep track of bookings – please note that I am *not* using the words *illegality* or *embezzlement* or even *outright theft*, even though I am entirely familiar with all of them, having a close acquaintance with our family solicitor – then I can only approve your actions.' She paused. 'Are you?'

The man paused. He chewed on a cud of tobacco in his cheek. 'No.'

'A shame. In any case, I desire a mere few words with this person.' She gestured with her parasol, indicating the clerk cowering behind his desk.

'But you've already complained!' the clerk snivelled.

'I have some further details I wish to add to my complaint,' Lady Marguerite informed him. 'Are you aware that in two of the inns where our coach stopped, the food I had ordered and paid for was not ready on our arrival? Indeed, I have positive proof that the food was in fact the remnants of a meal prepared for the previous coach, reheated for my consumption. And the other travellers,' she added as an afterthought.

Eleanor, meanwhile, was thinking how she might get a closer look at the paper which the lead Runner had slapped down on the desk. She couldn't step forward to look at it, of course; her place as a maid was behind her mistress. But if she were to just crook her fingers in the way Anima had taught her, hiding the gesture in the folds of her skirt, and call up a breeze . . .

Air rushed in through the open door, a breath of coolness on this hot day, carrying the scents of the inn yard with it. It slid through the papers on the desk and sent them wafting in all directions, a shifting mass of bills, orders, menus, schedules, and – most importantly – the Runner's document.

'Someone shut that door!' the clerk yelped. 'And pick up those papers, for the love of God!'

Eleanor joined the junior Runner in picking up the papers which now littered the floor, while the lead Runner and Lady Marguerite eyed each other dispassionately. With a murmured apology, Eleanor slid her well-mixed load onto the desk. She hadn't been able to read the Runner's document in full, in amongst all the timetables and passenger lists, but the glimpse she'd managed had been enough. *Lady Blakeney, by birth Marguerite Saint-Just, being of the following description, is sought by the Law as a victim of kidnapping. It is believed she and her captors may have travelled to the following locations from London . . .*

''Fraid this gentleman hasn't got the time for you right now, madam,' the lead Runner said. He shifted his wad of tobacco from one cheek to the other. Despite the hot day, he wore his heavy coat without a trace of discomfort and his eyes were cold and calculating. 'He's got some work to do for us, and that may take quite some time. Ain't that so?'

The clerk's eyes swivelled between the Runner and Lady Marguerite, and he visibly chose the unknown peril of the Runners rather than the known agony of her complaints. 'I'm afraid that's so, madam. If you want to come back later . . .'

Lady Marguerite drew herself up coldly. 'Your superiors will hear of this,' she informed the clerk, and swept out again, leaving Eleanor to follow with a sheepish, apologetic curtsey.

Behind her, she heard the Runner asking, 'Does she know your name to report you?'

'No, thank God,' the clerk replied, 'and I'll trust you not to tell her. Now about this woman you're after . . .'

*

'Audacity is a very useful tool,' Lady Marguerite explained later, as the three of them sat in the rooms Charles had booked at the King's Arms. She had removed her face paint and wig, and was now wearing a far more normal gown in pale green muslin. 'If you try to hide, and they notice it, then they become doubly interested in you. But if you make yourself so aggressively unpleasant they can't even bear to listen to you – heavens, I wouldn't have wanted to spend a single moment in conversation with myself! – then they will ignore you twice as much as they would under regular circumstances. A mirror of this, of course, is when my Percy disguises himself as a particularly unpleasant beggar. Have you ever noticed how far people will go to ignore beggars, or pretend that they don't exist?'

She sighed for a moment, her gaze distant, and Eleanor could guess she was thinking of Sir Percy, and wishing he were here. It was a simple enough deduction, given how delighted Eleanor herself was to have Charles beside her once more. But Lady Marguerite didn't have Sir Percy with her, and would be worrying about what accusations he might currently be facing in London, what suspicion he might be under, how the vampires might react now that Lady Marguerite herself was removed from view . . .

The antechamber of the suite of rooms was . . . well, it was neat and tidy enough, but Eleanor's fingers itched to give it a good scrub and dust, and make it that little bit neater and tidier. The furniture had been carefully arranged to hide the threadbare parts of the carpet, and a previous inhabitant had left behind a faint but persistent smell of pipe tobacco.

Still, she was here safely, as was Charles, and Lady Marguerite too – and for the moment the vampires couldn't be sure of their location. If only she could rid herself of this annoying nervous twitch every time she heard the creak of the floorboards outside, as someone walked by in the corridor, everything would be perfect. Or as good as could be hoped for.

'In any case!' Lady Marguerite clapped her hands together. 'I believe we'll have a day of safety before trouble may come to roost upon our shoulders. How should we – what is that phrase you men of learning use, Charles – prioritize our researches?'

Charles frowned. 'Only a day? Are you sure, milady?'

'Assume the worst,' Lady Marguerite advised him. 'If those Runners take a full list of everyone who was on the morning coaches from London, and send back to check all the names, then someone might discover that Mrs Hardcastle is not, in fact, taking a vacation in Oxford. And word would be promptly sent back here to detain the woman calling herself Hardcastle. Even given the best horses and the fastest coaches, I think it unlikely they'd be on our trail before tomorrow night. Of course, we may be fortunate, and Percy and the others will be doing everything they can to confuse the issue, but at the moment I am not sure we can depend on fortune.'

'But we can't be the only people travelling by coach who gave false names, can we?' Eleanor asked.

'Heavens, no. And if they're checking all the main coach routes from London, with any luck there will be a great many other criminals to confuse the issue. Still . . .'

'I take the point, milady. Action!' Charles sat upright in his chair, setting down his teacup. 'We must . . . You know, Eleanor, this would be a great deal easier if your friend Bernard had left us with more specific information, rather than a few elusive parting words,' he said plaintively.

Eleanor nodded ruefully. Bernard, the mage who had somehow preserved himself in a deep sleep for centuries, and then died less than an hour after Anima woke him, had known of something very important. The sleep of years had caught up with him, and over the last half hour of his life he had aged visibly with every passing minute. He had seemed a pleasant man although, admittedly, the grand total of mages whom Eleanor had met consisted only of him and Anima, whose spirit had now passed on too. So what *did* they know?

In the struggle between the mages and vampires, about five hundred years ago, the vampires had won, defeating, imprisoning or slaying all the mages. But apparently they had only *barely* managed to do so. The mages had intended some sort of last-ditch attack at a secret weakness the vampires possessed – something hidden beneath London.

'He told us his friend Matthew had known more,' Eleanor said. 'This Matthew – he said that he was a friend of the Dominican Order, who'd meant to build a priory here in Oxford?'

'Well, that at least is straightforward enough,' Charles said firmly. 'Blackfriars.'

Lady Marguerite raised an enquiring eyebrow.

'Blackfriars Priory was founded here in Oxford by the monks of the Dominican Order somewhere in the thirteenth century,' Charles said. 'Unfortunately, they were suppressed during the Dissolution of the Monasteries under Henry the Eighth—'

'The King closed down a great many monasteries and took their money when he became Protestant rather than Catholic,' Lady Marguerite explained to Eleanor. 'Religion is seldom so profitable.'

'So it no longer exists?' Eleanor asked, feeling as though – to borrow the terminology of the League gentlemen – her horse had fallen at the very first fence. 'But that means we have no chance at all.'

'If that had been the case, I'd have told you so long ago.'

Charles's tone was acerbic, but his eyes were warm. Away from the general crowd and the possibility of recognition, he'd donned his eye-glasses once more, and the lines of discomfort had eased out of his face. 'Blackfriars – the library, school and cloister – was all sold off. Deconsecrated, the stone used for other purposes, the land eventually ploughed over or built on—'

'But where does that leave *us*?' Eleanor demanded.

'I was thinking that I could try to trace any notes Matthew might have left,' Charles said modestly. 'I'll lay odds this Matthew was a scholar, and where better than to hide papers he wanted kept secret from vampires than with an order of monks? For all that vampires claim a place in society, they have an abhorrence to walking on holy ground. If this Matthew left his books or papers with the Dominicans, they're probably still in Oxford.'

Probably. The word sounded hollow to Eleanor. Yet what other hope did they have? She thought of Matthew, whatever sort of person he might have been, dying alone in Oxford without the support of any other mages. He must have felt as despairing as she did now . . .

Yet he hadn't been the only one, she reminded herself. Anima and Bernard had both been alone at the end, but they'd chosen to find some way to survive – to fling a light forward into the future and start a fire that might in time burn down the vampires they hated. If Matthew had done such a thing too, what form might this have taken?

She tried to explain this possibility to Lady Marguerite and Charles, but she knew she was stumbling. Anima would have had the words, the knowledge, for this – if only she were still here.

'So you think he might have left some sort of spell behind?' Lady Marguerite finally said.

'A spell can't survive the death of the mage who cast it,'

Eleanor said firmly. Anima had been quite clear on this point. 'That was why Bernard was still alive when we found him – if he'd been dead, his sleeping spell would have stopped working.'

'So he was only nearly dead. That makes it quite clear.' Lady Marguerite's smile took the sting out of her words. 'Yet your Anima – she was dead?'

'She said that she'd bound herself as a ghost when she died,' Eleanor tried to explain, hindered by the fact she understood very little of it. 'Though Bernard said this practice was forbidden, because those mages who tried it all became . . . mad ghosts who had to be exorcized.'

Lady Marguerite reached across the table and gently tapped her knuckles against Eleanor's forehead. 'Thank goodness you're solid English oak, my dear – we need have no fear of your stability. What is it, Charles? Why do you frown so?'

'There are stories of a ghost where the Priory of the Holy Spirit used to be,' Charles said slowly. 'Of course, Oxford is full of ghost stories, but . . .'

'But perhaps nobody has ever been there before who was a mage, mm?' Lady Marguerite twined one of her curls around her fingers. 'It's something to investigate, certainly, though I suppose we will have to try it tomorrow night rather than any sooner. One cannot expect ghosts to appear conveniently by day.' Her tone cast doubt on the idea, though, and Eleanor had to agree with her. Walking around Oxford hoping to meet a ghost was . . . well, even more lunatic than some of the League's riskier rescues.

'What else do you have in mind, Charles?' Eleanor asked. He had a look of concealed eagerness which all but shouted that he had some new scheme in his head. He'd been that way when he was writing up the false kidnap note for Lady Marguerite, or planning out their assault on Mont-Saint-

Michel a month ago. It warmed her, deep inside, to see this *enthusiasm* in his face. It would be heartbreaking to see him beaten.

'Why, only this, m'dear – your friend Bernard also dropped a few hints about matters which are normally considered settled history, but upon which he might be said to have a far closer viewpoint.' Charles leaned forward, and the candlelight gleamed on his eye-glasses. 'Do you recall him mentioning that vampires first became known of during the reign of Nero in Rome, at the same time as the rebellion in Britain?'

'Well, vaguely,' Eleanor admitted, 'which is to say, not particularly. We rebelled against the Romans? Did we win?'

'We lost,' Charles said, 'though technically, one could say we're all the descendants of the Romans by now, which I suppose means we also won. Time's a strange thing, and history more so. Admittedly all the records we have are Roman ones rather than British – Cassius Dio, Suetonius, Tacitus. My preference for Tacitus is because I found him far easier to translate when my tutor was rapping my knuckles . . .' He caught the *look* which Lady Marguerite was giving him and smiled ruefully. 'I may be wandering slightly from the subject: I cry your pardon, ladies. My ultimate point, I think, is that Bernard's hints differ from the common knowledge that vampires predated Julius Caesar. And there are certain historians in Oxford who have also, from time to time, raised disagreements with what one might term accepted history. Perhaps I should consult them, and see if they can give us any further clues to follow through this labyrinth?'

'Multiple sources for a story are all well and good when one is writing a play,' Lady Marguerite said, 'but they are singularly useless when it comes to discovering the truth. What other evidence do we have that this Bernard may have been correct?'

'Well, as Charles said, he *was* several hundred years closer to events than we are, milady,' Eleanor said, wanting to defend Charles's theories, even if she wasn't entirely sure she understood them. She was rewarded by a fond squeeze of her hand.

'But – correct me if I am wrong, my dear Charles – I understand that Oxford is positively teeming with elderly vampires, who could claim to be far closer to the Roman Empire than your Bernard. Surely . . .' Lady Marguerite's voice trailed off, and Eleanor could see her quick wits working. 'Ah. We should not only assume that certain vampires are lying in particular, but also that a great many vampires are lying in general about how long they have been haunting our shores.'

'Very few of them are *that* old,' Charles said. 'In fact, I'm not sure whether any currently here in Oxford would claim to be more than a century or two older than the founding of the university. The truly old ones have little patience for students buzzing around them, however flattering we may be. They weary of our questions – and of everything, I think. I've heard that in some colleges there are bricked-up cellars, where certain tutors and professors have laid themselves down to sleep for a century or two because they are simply tired of this modern world we inhabit. Indeed, there are also scandals about such retirements being by force, due to injuries to students – but I fear I'm wandering from the subject again. The fact remains, much of our history rests upon the word of vampires who have declared themselves the *fons et origo*, the original source of information, and . . . well, we have reason to believe that some of them may have lied. It might take me most of the day to arrange an interview, but—'

He was cut off by a sudden burst of shouting from outside – a chorus of yells which subsided to the slow mutter of a rising crowd. Eleanor flinched before she could catch herself: she'd known what it was to be caught in a mob before, in France. Magic couldn't help. Strong friends couldn't help. All one could do was run with the flow of people, shout whatever they were shouting, and hope to escape the tidal swell of the angry and violent all around you. People who might realize you were a traitor and a spy . . .

She could hear their words more distinctly now. *Whig!* and *Tory!* and *Revolution!* and *Bread!* and *Justice!* were fired across the street like pistol balls. If she'd been brave enough, she would have closed the shutters on the window, but she could see that Charles and Lady Marguerite were listening. Charles had drawn his brows together in concern, and where his hand still rested on hers she could feel his tension.

Perhaps there are people he knows out there in the street . . .

'Disperse in the King's name! Return to your colleges!' someone shouted, clear and arrogant over the mutter of the other voices.

A pause, then a mocking yell from multiple voices in response, and the sound of something splattering. It might have been a rotten cabbage. Eleanor hoped it was a rotten cabbage.

The sounds degenerated into baying yells, thuds and running feet. With an expression of disgust, Lady Marguerite finally rose to close the window. 'I don't believe we'll hear any more to our advantage,' she excused herself.

'It wasn't like that before,' Charles said softly, almost to himself. He looked at Eleanor, as though he was apologizing. 'Certainly we students might become merry and say more than we should, but outright riot on the streets?'

'It's been two years since you were here,' Lady Marguerite said gently. 'And perhaps this is an isolated incident, hm? There are disturbances across England.'

Charles shook his head. 'No. I met a couple of friends earlier, before I came to collect you, and they said there is unrest most nights of late. Sometimes it's merely a matter of a dispute in a tavern, but at other times it's worse. Like this, or more violent still. Innocent students out for an evening meal or attending night classes at their colleges have been caught up in it, and arrested for no more than being abroad at night. Men have even been killed. Oxford is not as it should be.' He tried to smile. 'Then again, as you say, England is not as it should be. We'll have to be careful not to go abroad at night, I fear.'

But Eleanor met Lady Marguerite's eyes, and she needed no magic to guess the other woman's thoughts.

They might not have that choice.

CHAPTER FIVE

There was no beautiful dawn the next day, no clear sky filling with light as the sun rose; only cloud, more cloud and additional cloud, making the heavens a dark morass of gloom. As Lady Marguerite's – or Mrs Hardcastle's – maid, Eleanor had risen early to lay out her mistress's clothes, and to fetch hot water, breakfast and all the other necessities a lady of quality required to prepare her for the day. This also gave Eleanor the chance to gossip with the servants in the kitchen. She reported her findings to Lady Marguerite as they shared breakfast, with Eleanor sitting on the end of the bed – most improper, but nobody else was there to see. Charles had already left to pursue his own investigations.

'This is one of the inns which takes longer-staying customers who need somewhere that's proper but inexpensive,' she explained. 'Ladies and gentlemen with more money go somewhere better, and people who don't care about having a good address go somewhere cheaper. Downstairs they think you must be either a skinflint or short in the pocket to have booked rooms here, milady. Though Mrs Dawkins – that's the cook – says she can recognize quality when she sees it, and was declaring she has no doubt you'll be moving to a better set of rooms if you plan to stay here in Oxford.'

'But she hasn't even seen me,' Lady Marguerite reflected, sipping her hot chocolate.

'I'm sure that never yet stopped her having an opinion about anyone,' Eleanor said drily.

'And what do they think of all that's going on in Oxford?'

That had been harder to tease out of the other servants, but being willing to lend a hand around the kitchen had helped. 'They're worried, milady,' Eleanor said. 'People are saying there's French agitators and spies in town, and that's why the students are all stirred up every night. They say as there are traitors—'

'They say *that* there are traitors, Eleanor,' Lady Marguerite corrected her. 'I taught you better than that.'

Eleanor sighed, thinking back to a year ago, when the Blakeneys had been training her to impersonate Marie Antoinette and talk like a lady of quality. Life had been easier then, even if she'd been ignorant of so much about the world – about the Revolution in France, and about everything outside Lady Sophie's estate. Perhaps that was why it had been easier. 'They say that there are traitors prowling the streets,' she continued, 'and that some of the students are planning to start a revolution, and all the young men should join the army and go to serve in the war with France, and . . .' She spread her hands helplessly. 'There's nothing *definite*, milady. But people aren't comfortable. Mrs Dawkins said the authorities had been hiring extra constables to walk the streets by night and put down improper behaviour.'

'Which authorities?'

Eleanor frowned. 'She just said, *Them in power* – her words, not mine! And Helen – she's the head maid, who's walking out with a young man from one of the colleges – said there had been a number of vampires visiting from London, and they were putting up at the colleges rather than staying at any of the inns.'

Lady Marguerite arched a thoughtful eyebrow. 'Any college in particular?'

'Merton,' Eleanor replied.

'One of the oldest Oxford colleges and a notorious haven for vampires among its senior Fellows, if I recall correctly. Charles would know better than I. There was something – I heard it at a party which Sophie was throwing, though I can't remember it clearly . . .'

'Milady,' Eleanor said hesitantly, 'I've spent most of my life with Lady Sophie as a mistress. You and Sir Percy knew her as a friend. How can it be that she's involved in all *this*?'

Lady Marguerite finished her chocolate and put down the dainty cup, but Eleanor had the impression she was doing it to buy herself time for thought. 'I suppose it comes down to how well any of us can know each other, Eleanor. Faith, how can I complain? Percy and I keep our own secrets – perhaps I shouldn't be surprised that someone else has done the same. Still, it wounds my pride.'

'That's all you have to say?' Eleanor exclaimed, infuriated that the other woman could treat it so lightly. 'It *wounds your pride*?'

Lady Marguerite shrugged. 'Maybe I have spent too many years with my beloved Percy to take matters entirely seriously. What do you want me to say, Eleanor? Would you prefer me to tell you just how *wounded* I am that someone whom I considered a friend is apparently a viper in my bosom?' She hesitated. 'No, that is too . . . theatrical. And I've been betrayed before by people I trusted. It would hardly be the first time. Still, I liked her. She *was* a friend. To you, she was a mistress. Does one like a mistress?'

'One can be fond of a mistress . . . milady,' Eleanor

answered. Although she'd never exactly felt fondness for Lady Sophie.

Lady Marguerite raised her hand in a fencer's salute. 'A fair point. Tell me then, do you trust a mistress? Enough to tell her your private concerns, your worries, your loneliness, your private dreams?' Her blue eyes narrowed. 'Do you go to your mistress to ask how best to manage your affections for someone inappropriate?'

'You know I wouldn't, milady,' Eleanor muttered, thinking of Charles. Why did Lady Marguerite have to press so strongly on *that* nerve? What was the point of yearning for a love which could never be?

'No, indeed! Yet . . . in the past, I've spoken freely to Sophie as a friend – now, it would seem, too freely. Your once-mistress the Baroness of Basing makes herself everyone's friend and nobody's enemy, Eleanor. She observes fashion while not being a slave to it. She manages to be on good terms with both the King and the Prince of Wales – and believe me, that's a difficult path to navigate. She has managed her estate for centuries, though I couldn't tell you when she took up its reins, and I fancy the dates might be somewhat obscure. Indeed, I wonder just *how* obscure . . . I pride myself on being a leader of society, my Eleanor – or at least, I did so before my arrest for treason – but Lady Sophie has been involved in Society for far longer than I have.'

'I didn't realize she was so well connected,' Eleanor said.

'No. I suspect that is the point. Equally, nobody realizes my Percy is so brave, and noble, and strong. Or that you are a mage and a member of the League, and a saviour to many who would have died in France.' She gave Eleanor a smile that was genuinely warm and affectionate. 'And nobody realizes just how many strings Lady Sophie has at her disposal, or what she might be beneath her pretty face –

or what she might currently be planning. If she were a character in a play, I'd vie for her part. But as matters stand, we must find a way to neutralize her – and whoever is in league with her.'

She clapped her hands together. 'Now! While Charles is pursuing his own leads, I suggest we investigate the Blackfriars site, or at least what remains of it. We shall be merely a couple of ladies strolling around town, quite unimportant and unworthy of attention.' Her critical gaze took in Eleanor's current dress. 'Hm. I will lend you one of my shawls. With that and a pair of gloves, I believe today you can be my companion rather than my maid – a poor relation, perhaps, or a distant cousin. It comes to much the same thing in Society, in that you'd be running my errands, but it will at least allow us to speak more freely to each other in public.'

'How will we find the old Blackfriars buildings, or where they used to be?' Eleanor asked.

'This is Oxford,' Lady Marguerite said serenely. 'It has a great many visitors who wish to see the sights. If the nearest bookshop can't sell us a book or pamphlet listing the sites of interest for the moral and aesthetic improvement of visitors, I will be extremely surprised. Let us enjoy the city together, and revel in the lack of guillotines. We are in England, after all.'

The benefits of being an assumed companion or younger relation, albeit a dependent one clinging to an employer or aunt for money, included Eleanor being able to walk next to Lady Marguerite rather than trailing behind her. This enabled them to make quiet conversation as they went, rather than Eleanor observing a dutiful silence as a maid should do. Yet to Eleanor's surprise, she found that in being disguised as someone a few steps up from the lower class, but still lacking in wealth, she wasn't even given the notice she would have received as a maid. Maids at least got a cheerful smile from shopkeepers, or an appreciative wink, or a commiserative nod at the mistress's high-handedness. A companion or poor relation was instead given the minimum of politeness and nothing else. It was a new standard in invisibility.

'I always thought Oxford would be prettier,' she said softly to Lady Marguerite as the two of them strolled along a crowded street. 'The vicar – that is, the one who was at St Thomas's when I was a child, on Lady Sophie's lands – said there were green lawns everywhere here.'

'Behind those walls,' Lady Marguerite said, jerking her parasol briefly at one of the high walls they were passing. 'A few are open for public viewing and admiration, but I fear most of the colleges prefer to keep their luxuries to themselves.'

Three students were approaching, heads together as they discussed something, and Eleanor caught a few words. 'Rational enlightenment . . . Regency . . .' They parted around the oncoming Lady Marguerite to resume their conversation on the other side of her, barely seeming to notice her.

'Politics,' Eleanor said, mildly disapproving. It was clearly very much on all the students' minds at the moment.

'Oh, you can't expect young university men to discuss Latin and Greek *all* the time. I fear not all of them are like Charles, my dear.'

Eleanor had been annoyed more than once by Charles's studious urges and constant wanderings from the subject – any subject – under discussion, in order to provide additional information from his excessive breadth of knowledge. Yet now she realized she would miss those traits if he were somehow to abandon them. They had become what she expected in an educated man. 'I've always wondered why he joined the League,' she said, a little wistfully.

Lady Marguerite glanced at her sidelong. 'I'll tell you at some point, if you're curious, but first let us reach the Thames. I believe it's not much further to Folly Bridge – and have you noted the name of the street we're currently on?'

Eleanor blushed, not having done so.

'St Aldate's. I will have to check my guidebook, once we're sat down for tea. A clue, perhaps!' Her eyes sparkled.

Eleanor wished she herself could be as enthusiastic. They had a whole *city* to search, and only a day or two to do it in – assuming there was anything to find here at all. Meanwhile, the rest of the League, back in London, would be facing the scrutiny of the law. Andrew had been shot – please God that the wound hadn't become infected – and Tony left the worse for wear too. And Sir Percy was undoubtedly suffering under questioning and threats – would his influential friends actually be any help? Lady Marguerite herself was being pursued as a criminal, or victim of kidnap, or both. And this was *England*. They were supposed to be *safe* here. 'Helen at the inn said this used to be called Fish Street,' she muttered.

'I think *someone* is in need of a cup of tea to restore her mood,' Lady Marguerite said brightly. 'Perhaps a cake, too! My dear, have some sympathy with me. After being under house arrest for the past week, even these clouded skies and busy streets are pure freedom and paradise to me.'

Eleanor murmured an apology, then was silent until they came in sight of the Thames. At this she couldn't help but pause and gasp. It wasn't like the Thames where it flowed through London – a great seething brown mass which swept along humans and garbage alike in its tides. It wasn't even like the Seine in Paris – as unstoppable as the Paris mob, seemingly calm and gracious but cold and grasping beneath the surface, as hungry as a vampire for anyone caught in its waters. No, the Thames here in Oxford seemed . . . tame, even pretty. It ran along between green banks on either side, where willows bowed to touch the water and any grasses caught in the flow pointed in the direction of the current. The bridge ahead, captured in a brief moment of sunlight, crossed the river in low pale arcs of stone. It might have been a painting, like the pretty ones hanging in Blakeney Manor, all landscapes and green fields, which Sir Percy claimed were the latest fashion.

'To the right, I think,' Lady Marguerite said softly. 'That is where we find streets with names such as Blackfriars Road and Preachers Lane. Let us be frivolous and look for a teashop there, then plot what to do next.'

When they were finally sitting down, and the waitress was hurrying off to fetch tea and cakes, Lady Marguerite leaned back in her chair. 'Well, my dear? I can tell you have been deliberating. What do *you* have in mind?'

Eleanor swallowed. She wasn't sure what Lady Marguerite would think of the plan she had been formulating – but she wanted to live up to what milady and the others expected of her. She was determined to try. 'Well, madam . . .'

There was a brief pause while the refreshments arrived. One simply could not discuss ancient mages, vampires and conspiracies with a waitress shuffling round the table arranging tea and cake dishes. Once the risk of listening ears had receded, Eleanor tapped a finger on the heavy *Guidebook to Oxford: Its Antiquities, Its Bowers And Its Many Charming Sights* which lay on the table between them. 'While we don't really know more from this about the Dominicans – the Blackfriars – than Charles could tell us last night, we do know that the site of their abbey was close to where we're taking tea at the moment.'

'Indeed,' Lady Marguerite agreed. 'Somewhere beneath the current assortment of fields, houses and streets. Yet I fear we will have little luck if we attempt to assault the place with spades.'

Eleanor nodded ruefully. 'This is a gamble, milady – well, multiple gambles, to be honest. I'm hoping that if I can, well . . .' The words were strange in her mouth, seeming ridiculous, but she forced them out. 'If I can use my power in this area and there is some trace left of Matthew – if he bound himself to the place somehow, just as Anima preserved her spirit – then I'll be able to sense it.'

To her profound relief, Lady Marguerite didn't instantly poke holes in the proposal or suggest that Eleanor was Bedlam-mad. Instead she frowned thoughtfully, her powdered brows drawing together as she considered. 'It's a reasonable scheme,' she finally said, 'and you know far more about this magic than any of us.'

'I know hardly anything,' Eleanor said quickly. 'I'm sorry. If only Anima had shown me—'

'My dear, pray cease this pre-emptive apologizing! Absolutely nobody blames you for any of this. Consider how much greater our danger would have been without your help. My brother Armand might still be a slave of those monarchist vampires in France.' The pinpoint flare of fury in her eyes was briefly as vicious as any sanguinocrat's bloodlust, but she kept her voice low. 'All that you've done, all that you've *achieved,* is far above anything we had any right to ask of you. Don't be ashamed because you don't know the secrets which were lost seven centuries ago. From what you've said, Anima shirked her duty as your teacher. If she were here, I'd give her a piece of my mind.'

Eleanor couldn't prevent the smile which crept to her lips as gratitude rose in her. 'Thank you, milady. You're very . . . comforting.'

'Perhaps, but at this moment I intend to be inspiring! Now how do you plan to use your power? A thunderstorm?'

'Oh, that won't happen till about five or six o'clock this afternoon,' Eleanor said without thinking. She could feel the sluggish weight of the clouds strengthening from the east. She knew when they would reach the point of no return – unless she were to prod them earlier, of course. 'No, I think I can do it if I persuade a breeze to blow. My concern is that I may react . . . oddly.'

'Oddly in the sense of a seizure, like a madwoman on the stage?' Lady Marguerite asked clinically. 'Or more in the sense of moaning and collapse?'

'I seem generally to huddle up in a corner with the air of someone having a violent headache,' Eleanor confessed. 'Or so Charles tells me.' She looked around the teashop. Rather to her surprise, instead of somewhere that was out of the way and off the main street, with convenient shadowy corners and nooks they could have hidden in, Lady Marguerite had chosen a popular one. Most tables were full of students discussing various matters – studies, politics and entertainment – at the top of their voices. The few remaining tables were occupied by groups of middle-aged women, who appeared to be mostly discussing the students. Lady Marguerite's sole nod to secrecy had been to choose a corner table which gave them a good view of the room and allowed them to sit with their backs to the wall. 'Perhaps we should go somewhere else . . .'

'This will do nicely, my dear Eleanor,' Lady Marguerite contradicted her. 'Everyone here is far too occupied with their own business to look at us. Had we been lurking in some otherwise deserted teashop, people who saw us would wonder why we were patronizing an outmoded, unfashionable place. Here we are merely a couple of customers – and quiet ones at that. The safest place is in the middle of the crowd.'

'Or directly beneath the hunter's nose,' Eleanor replied, remembering a previous ruse of Sir Percy's. 'Very well, milady. I'll try.'

'I have every faith you'll succeed,' Lady Marguerite said firmly. 'You have done so with everything else we've asked of you so far.'

'There was Mont-Saint-Michel . . .'

'A success plucked from the brink of failure is still a success. Now, on with it! Work your magic.'

Eleanor blushed, then lowered her head, her eyes half closing, and tried to feel for the threads which Anima had always plucked so easily in the past.

She could smell the breeze as it came creeping through the room, answering the summons of her crooked fingers. It carried scents from beyond the teashop's confines – river mud, rotting weed, drying grass that hungered for rain, sweat from straining muscles, animal dung, the stones of the road aching in the July heat. For a moment these overpowered the teashop's own odours of tea, coffee and hot chocolate, cakes and toast, perfume and hair-powder and newspaper ink. It felt as though Oxford was breathing around her and that the whole city was a living beast, which ate, excreted, sweated and bled, and the people moving through its streets were no more than drops of blood in its veins, necessary as a whole but singularly expendable.

She breathed out, and the city breathed with her. The little gusts kicked along the streets, around the teashop and south and west, to where the remains of the Dominican abbey ought to be – no, *must* be. Picking up dust and fragments of paper, they stirred the heaps of garbage and combed through the fur of panting dogs and cats that lay spreadeagled in the afternoon heat; they twitched at skirts and shawls and elegant lace cuffs; they pulled at curls and wigs; they ruffled the parched grass and swept across the surface of the Thames, brushing the other bank before returning. A hundred walls turned these gusts aside or made them divert their path; a hundred closed doors and windows barred their way.

All of it swept through Eleanor's mind in a flow of something that wasn't quite imagery but felt more as if she was exploring a thousand things at once with her fingers yet was unable to hold a single one in her mind. It drowned her as the Seine nearly had done once, carrying her along in a visionless blur of motion, a swirl of odours. And nothing – none of it – actually *meant* anything to her. She had no sense of specific geography or location, and could not recognize a single face. There was no prickle of awareness, no stab of a presence, nothing: merely sensation in dozens of different forms.

She stretched her senses outwards for as long as she could, searching for something, anything, to justify the effort, but still nothing came back that conveyed any meaning to her, only the flow of motion and constant interaction – as constant as the wind and as futile. Her head throbbed with effort.

Reluctantly, finally, Eleanor breathed in again, calling her own breath back to her, letting all the other twists and gusts of wind separate and fall away through the streets of Oxford. She had no room in her mind for anything except the thought of her failure. She'd tried so hard last night to think what to do, to remember Anima and what *she'd* been able to do. So much for her own powers, and for Lady Marguerite's faith in her . . .

Then something *caught* her wind. It was like a pin catching in the woven fabric of a skirt and leaving a long rip behind it as it dragged at the cloth. Her eyes flew open and she sat bolt upright, but she wasn't looking at the teashop around her. She had no exact comparisons for the sensation, but it was like burning ice, or slamming her elbow unexpectedly into a brick wall, or biting into an unripe apple while suffering from a toothache. She'd seen Anima's magic through her own eyes. She'd sensed Bernard's magic on Mont-Saint-Michel, though that had been a softer, more fluid thing. This felt as though not only had she perceived someone, but they had perceived her – and they were angry.

Most importantly, she knew where it *was*. Back the way they'd come, off St Aldate's, to the east. She couldn't have named the street, or even described the location by sight, but she was certain she'd recognize the place if she walked through it and felt the touch of wind against buildings.

The pin withdrew itself, and she could breathe again, but she knew this presence was still aware of her, just as she was aware of it.

'Annie!' Lady Marguerite exclaimed, shocked. 'Your nose!'

Eleanor lifted her fingers to it, blinking as her eyes adjusted to normal vision again, and found her hand covered in blood. 'Oh,' she said, swaying forward and nearly landing face-first on the table.

Lady Marguerite fussed over her, ordering the waitresses to fetch cold compresses and peppermint tea, passing the whole thing off as a nosebleed brought on by heatstroke. But Eleanor could see the sharp appraisal in her eyes – more than that, the hope that Eleanor had found something. A few of the establishment's other patrons glanced in their direction, but most of them were far more concerned with their own discussions.

It was then that the teashop door smacked open with far more than usual force, rattling against the wall. All eyes, even Eleanor's and Lady Marguerite's, turned to the doorway, where two bulky men were silhouetted. They were wide and muscular enough that they'd probably have become stuck if they'd tried to enter at the same time.

They looked around. One of them pointed out a table to the far right, occupied by several students. The other nodded. Then they stepped aside as a new figure strode in.

While vampires didn't *enjoy* going out by day, and especially not if the sun was shining, they were still quite capable of doing so. A day like today, heavily overcast and enshrouded by cloud, was the sort they liked best. The man who'd just entered the teashop had the typical pallor of a vampire, and as he saw the students at the far-right table, his lips peeled back in an arrogant snarl that showed a brief hint of fangs. His wig and shirt were stark white, but the rest of his clothing was dead black, and the heels of his shoes rapped on the floor as he walked through the now silent teashop.

Eleanor could see the students exchanging glances behind his back as he passed. Everyone apparently knew who he was – and nobody cared to attract his attention.

He finally came to a halt in front of the chosen table. Three of the students there had shuffled back in their chairs, as though wishing to disclaim all responsibility and never to have been there in the first place. But the other two rose to their feet – politely in one case, but with a noisy scraping of chair legs by the other.

'Mr Pells,' the vampire said. 'You are required to accompany me at once, to give an explanation for certain treasonous opinions you have voiced publicly.'

'I've done nothing wrong!' It was the student who'd pushed his chair back noisily. The colour stood in his cheeks as though he'd been drinking wine rather than coffee, and he balled his fists, ready for a fight, ignoring his quieter friend who was plucking at his sleeve. 'I was just talking with my friends about philosophy! We're here at university to learn, aren't we?'

'You've been spreading propaganda which is contrary to good public order, and which may cause harm to the morals of young people.' The vampire practically yawned. 'Don't make this difficult, Mr Pells. Come with me at once.'

'I don't think so!' Mr Pells shook off his friend's hand

and leapt onto the table. Standing among teacups and well-crumbed plates, he took a deep breath. 'Friends of Oxford! Fellow students! How long are we to labour under the oppression of a rotten Parliament – rotten to the core, stuffed with profiteers who make their money from the war with France and the traffic of slaves, and refuse to hear of any peace or abolition, whose sole concern is the preservation of their own power . . .'

'By the authority vested in me as proctor of Magdalen College . . .' The vampire shrugged, and beckoned to his two burly followers. 'Fetch him.'

'. . . and an insane King—'

The vampire – no, the proctor – snarled again. 'Fetch him *now* before he spouts more treason!'

No other students moved to help Mr Pells. Even the friend who'd tried to dissuade him edged back, eyes wide and face taut with fear. The two burly men dragged him down from the table. One of them slapped him across the face, then punched him hard in the belly when he wouldn't be silenced. They dragged him out of the teashop by his shoulders, his starched cuffs and calfskin boots trailing in the dust.

The proctor flipped a coin to the nearest waitress. 'Terribly sorry for the disturbance,' he said. 'Send any bills to Magdalen College.'

His gaze swept the room, moving across the students, none of whom met his eyes. He paused for a moment at Lady Marguerite's table, and his nostrils flared, but then he turned away, his face a cold mask, as though he hadn't been lured for even a moment by the smell of Eleanor's fresh blood.

Five seconds after he'd left the teashop, chatter broke out again, but it was different from earlier. Even though the volume was lower, the tone was more intense – the mice whispering at their tables so the cat wouldn't hear them.

There was real venom in their tones as well as genuine anger in their words. *Tonight*, Eleanor heard them mutter at more than one table. *Tonight.*

'Not a new occurrence, I'm afraid,' Lady Marguerite said softly, her voice a quiet twin to all the other ones murmuring angry complaints.

'Milady?'

'This isn't the first time someone's been vigorously suppressed for public speech here. That fellow will be lucky if he's only sent down – sent home from Oxford, I mean. I was listening to their conversation while you spent the past ten minutes in a trance, my dear Eleanor, and it seems that Oxford's seething with new ideas and philosophies – which, as we know, invariably leads to revolution. Students are being encouraged to think, but they are expressing their novel views too loudly for those in power to be pleased.'

There was something about the way Lady Marguerite said this – imbued with a world-weariness, and the aching pity of someone who'd seen it all before. Eleanor remembered she'd been in France before the revolution even started, and that she'd had friends among the people who first called for revolt, liberty and brotherhood. 'Is this what happened in France?' she asked, barely audible.

'It was part of how it began in France,' Lady Marguerite answered, 'and the next step was repression. You know by now how those in power respond when they are afraid. And after the repression, revolt . . .' She took a deep breath. 'But we have our own problems, don't we? Pray tell me, my dear Eleanor, that your nosebleed was not wasted, and you have some vital discovery to share with me.'

'I found something,' Eleanor said cautiously, but she thrilled with excitement at her success. 'It was in the wrong place, though. East of St Aldate's, somewhere between the Town Hall and . . . I think you said it was Christ Church

College when we passed it? I can't name it, but I could find it if we went there.'

Lady Marguerite frowned – an expression which went well with the paint covering her face and the fierceness of her hat and wig. She pulled the guidebook over to herself and leafed through it thoughtfully. 'Tell me, Eleanor, exactly *when* did your mage friends say all this took place?'

'Anima said she died in twelve hundred and ten Anno Domini, milady, in the reign of King John.' Eleanor wasn't sure exactly where this was going, but Lady Marguerite had clearly found a trail of some sort.

'Indeed. And the Dominicans didn't formally establish themselves in Oxford till ten years later, or build their main establishment here for another fifteen years after that.' Lady Marguerite closed the book with a snap. 'We were looking in the wrong place, Eleanor, and thank God you found the right one in spite of it. We need their *first* stronghold in Oxford, not their *last*, and given that this book says it was "near the grounds of what is now Christ Church College", I do believe you've found it.'

Eleanor sagged in her chair with relief. 'What do we do now, milady?' she asked, grateful to hand over the making of decisions to someone else until her headache ebbed.

'For the moment, we take a coach back to our rooms at the inn.' Lady Marguerite held up a hand in remonstrance as Eleanor tried to object. 'My dear, you look like death warmed over, and you clearly aren't feeling much better. Further discussions should be in private. We also need to see if Charles has had any success, or if he's left word for us. We did agree to stay in touch with each other, after all, given the current state of peril, so let's hope he's remembered that. And finally, if we are going to make an attempt on this site, I think it will need to be after dark, when prying eyes won't see us . . .'

CHAPTER SIX

Lady Marguerite had abandoned her chair, and was now pacing the room angrily, pausing from time to time to glare at the door. 'Where *is* the man?' she muttered. 'How does my Percy endure this casual slackness? Any actor so lax in attending rehearsals would deserve to lose his part.'

Eleanor was equally concerned, but didn't want to admit to it: it felt as if both of them saying it out loud might make the feared danger become true. 'It isn't his fault,' she tried.

'Oh, I'm sure it's not,' Lady Marguerite said, 'but who else am I to blame? Well, besides the whole of Oxford, and its professors in particular, as no doubt it's their dilatory habits which are keeping Charles waiting, and us more so. But still, a woman has a right to expect punctuality! We each have a duty to report in as and when agreed. And you and I cannot go traipsing around the city this evening without informing him of our plan first. I'm certainly not leaving a written summary of the day's work for him. The tales I could tell you about what happens when people do that sort of thing . . .'

She glanced out of the window again. The rain had come and gone, but the clouds still filled the sky. Eleanor could guess the hidden reason for Lady Marguerite's flighty behaviour: a coach could have reached London and be well on its way back by now, and it was possible that unwelcome visitors might be showing up at their door very soon. 'You are certain you're feeling better now, my dear?'

'Quite certain, milady,' Eleanor answered, not for the first time. She had been rather staggered by how drained and exhausted she'd felt after exercising her powers earlier. She'd encouraged storms to break before and been left with only a headache – well, to be fair, they had been extremely painful headaches, but that wasn't the point. Yet calling up that breeze from nowhere had left her fit for nothing more than bed for the next few hours.

Once more she wished desperately that Anima was still with her. She might have been able to explain it all, give *reasons* for her weakness, and help Eleanor find ways to be stronger. Though . . . if Anima had been willing to acknowledge her as her apprentice earlier, and been *willing* to teach her, then . . .

With an effort she forced away the mingled grief and resentment. It was something to which she'd never have an answer now, and brooding on it was little use when there were so many other desperately urgent problems to concern herself with.

'Perhaps we should consider at least a short trip to scout out the location you identified,' Lady Marguerite mused aloud. 'We could always leave a very brief and uninformative note in case Charles returns—'

She was interrupted by a knock at the door.

Eleanor answered it, opening it a crack and peering out. A boy stood there, barely ten years old by the look of him. His clothing was cheap – trousers rather than breeches, reminding Eleanor of France – and his hair poorly brushed. In one hand he carried a letter, and with a finger of the other he was excavating his nose. At the sight of Eleanor he straightened, removing finger from nostril, and said, 'You Mrs Hardcastle?'

'I am her maid,' Eleanor replied, adopting the tones of the haughtiest personal maid she'd ever had the misfortune to hear. 'Is there a message for her?'

'Letter for her. Said as she'd pay me a shilling for it.'

Eleanor knew this was an extortionately high rate for a boy to carry a message like this, and she fixed him with a cold eye.

He shuffled. 'Sixpence?'

'You'll get tuppence and be grateful for it,' Eleanor snapped. She held out her hand, and the boy dropped the letter into it. With a spasm of relief, she recognized Charles's handwriting. She fished out a couple of pennies from her purse. 'When and where were you given this for my mistress?' she asked, holding the coins in his view.

'Quarter of an hour ago, on Queen Street,' the boy said. He snatched the pennies from Eleanor's hand and was off down the corridor at a run.

Lady Marguerite in turn snatched the letter from Eleanor's hand as the door closed. 'Let's see what Charles has to say. He writes rather too much, given the chance that his message could have been intercepted, but I'm grateful to know that he's safe and well. Hmm – it seems that he has spent all day in search of information, much of it futile, but he believes he has found a scholar who can assist us. Apparently the fellow is known for being a skinflint and an iconoclast, as well as for general disagreement with – well, with everything. But he also makes claims about vampires which align with the information that Bernard hinted to you about, my dear. Charles has obtained an appointment with this Professor Johnson, at his house, and he suggests we meet him in the hostelry nearby afterwards – the Black Boar – where he has secured a table for us to dine. And we should be careful on our way, as apparently Oxford is feeling particularly rebellious tonight due to the arrest of various notable student firebrands. Something I could have predicted, but let us not be petty. Excellent! Where are my shawl, my hat, my gloves, my boots?'

'So he's safe, at least?' Eleanor said, a little wistfully.

Lady Marguerite paused in her preparations and turned to Eleanor. 'I'm sure if this letter had been addressed to you rather than to me, he would also have added some personal expressions of affection,' she said, more quietly.

It grew no easier to say it: it still felt like biting into a lemon and brought a pricking to her eyes. 'Milady, you shouldn't encourage him. Or me.'

'Why not, my dear?'

'Because nothing can come of it.'

'A nobleman can marry an actress,' Lady Marguerite said, referring to herself and Sir Percy, 'and did.'

'You were already a person of quality,' Eleanor said, trying to be resigned and practical about it, as she went down on her knees to lace up Lady Marguerite's boots. 'How could he ever take me to meet his father?'

'You assume he'd want *anyone* to meet his father.' Lady Marguerite tapped her on the shoulder with her fan. 'You give up too easily, Eleanor. I can see this will need my guiding hand. Have no fear! I am an expert in these matters.'

Eleanor swallowed nervously.

'But before that, I believe I am going to make some alterations to Charles's plans . . .'

Queen Street, like most of its neighbourhood, was overshadowed by the nearby Oxford Castle, which loomed in the distance like an ancient relation – the sort who was decrepit and gouty, but still held the purse-strings and must therefore be taken into account in all family calculations. Lady

Marguerite had said it had been turned into a prison fifty years ago, and it was difficult for Eleanor to think about the place without imagining herself in its cells.

How did a good girl like me become involved in so many improper and illegal enterprises?

It was only somewhere between seven and eight o'clock on this summer's evening, but the street lamps were already burning, and already necessary. The cloud-filled sky had brought on an oppressive darkness, earlier than usual for July. Still, there didn't seem to be too many students in this particular section of Oxford, and the streets weren't busy. Perhaps they were all attending late lectures given by vampires – or maybe they were simply drinking and talking philosophy.

Eleanor, having left Lady Marguerite sitting in state in the Black Boar, had slipped out of there by the back door – after a few words with one of the servers, who'd been happy to confirm Professor Johnson's address in Queen Street and provide directions. However, when she caught sight of the house, her steps stuttered and she had to prevent herself from staring.

The owner really *was* a skinflint. Even in the flaring, unhappy light from the street lamps, the deficiencies of the place displayed themselves like patches on a length of silk. The paint on the shutters was flaking; the brickwork was raddled and half covered with ivy, which was itself dying from lack of water; the glass of the windows was thick with dirt and dust; and the doorstep was most emphatically unwashed. Her lip curled in disdain.

She ducked around to the servants' entrance at the side. Lady Marguerite had suggested she come here to keep a close eye on the house. To be certain Charles *was* here, first of all, and also that he left safely, ensuring his note hadn't been intercepted and that the whole thing wasn't some devious trap. Personally, Eleanor thought it was all overly complex to be a trap – after all, if their enemies had been able to intercept Charles's note, then they'd have known where to find the women, and could simply have kidnapped them directly from their inn.

Eleanor rather suspected that milady just wanted to give her and Charles a few moments together without her presence – which was kind and generous of her, even if their future was impossible. Perhaps especially because their future was impossible. Though it was always a possibility that Charles really *was* in danger, and if that was the case, then . . .

She tried the latch on the side door, and to her surprise it swung open, unlocked. The kitchen beyond was not only empty and unlit, but had a feeling of staleness and disuse to it as she stepped cautiously in. Faint light penetrated through the murky windows, just enough for Eleanor to see. Dirty pots and plates stood waiting in the sink, and on the table a cloth covered something . . . ah, a cold collation, bread and ham and cheese, laid out for someone's later consumption. The dishes in the sink were freshly dirty rather than caked with days-old food; presumably the cook or maid had left her master's supper ready and stepped out for some reason, or left for the night.

All the better for Eleanor.

She tiptoed to the far end of the kitchen and opened the door that gave onto the rest of the house. Certainly Lady Marguerite had told her to watch from a distance, discreetly, but now she was actually here . . . well, any of the League would have seized the opportunity to investigate further, so why not her?

The draught that whispered through brought her the smell of old paper and expensive beeswax candles, but most of all the smell of dust. Bookcases and cupboards lined the hall, rising so high that there was no space on the walls for pictures. In fact, there was a total lack of any kind of ornament – no statuettes or urns or mirrors, only the stacks of paper, encrusted with dust and cobwebs. A single candle burned in a wall sconce, providing just enough light to avoid falling over the books or running into the wall.

Very faintly, somewhere above her, she could hear the sound of voices.

Eleanor followed those sounds through the house, along the hall and to the stairwell, testing each step carefully so as not to step on any creaky floorboard – in a house like this, what could the floorboards be but creaky? An impulse to be certain that Charles was safe drove her forward. She was already preparing a story if she should be intercepted by the house's owner – she was Mrs Hardcastle's maid, here to fetch Charles for his appointment. Candles burned at irregular intervals in the wall sconces, and she couldn't help but contrast the quality beeswax with the general air of disarray and dilapidation. The owner of this house – Professor Johnson, presumably – clearly paid good money for what he thought was important and skimped on everything else. Not unlike her previous employer, Lady Sophie.

At the foot of the stairs Eleanor hesitated. She could perhaps draw the words of the distant conversation to her on a breeze, but that would bring so much dust with it she feared her choking would betray her presence. Instead she edged her way up the stairs, moving with careful slowness, her eyes on the lit rectangle of a door halfway along the corridor at the top.

'. . . and as I've pointed out in my work *numerous* times, Celsus utterly fails to mention vampires in his *De Medicina*, which is justly regarded as a foundational text on health and related fields. So, given his death towards the end of

Claudius's reign, we can regard that as a *terminus* point, if you like, a convenient "before which none is known".' She didn't recognize the speaker. His deep voice wasn't unpleasant, but his sentences were cast in the same form she'd overheard multiple times today in Oxford, from both passing dons and students – as though he was delivering a lecture to anyone unfortunate enough to be nearby.

'Though of course we *do* only have part of the *De Medicina*, sadly,' Charles put in. His tone was quiet and unassuming, but it invited a contradiction. It practically stood up and waved a banner saying, *Tell me how foolish I am, and please provide all relevant details so I will recognize my own stupidity.*

Eleanor pressed her knuckles against her lips, muffling a sigh of relief. He was here; he was safe; he was well. And he clearly had things in hand. She'd never heard him discuss matters of learning with anyone else before (the other members of the League were not sympathetic to such topics and were prone to yawning). But even the few words he'd spoken demonstrated that he understood the issue in depth. Like forging warrants and other legal niceties, this was something only he, and nobody else in the League, could do.

She felt a flush of pride for him. Even if she barely understood a word they were saying.

'Yet it's supported by other evidence! In his *Symposium*, Asconius mentions the "new arrival of these strangers who by the drinking of blood", et cetera, et cetera, and that was written in the latter years of Vespasian's reign. My own analysis places his reference as being during the Year of Four Emperors, after the death of Nero. You see how we slowly but surely draw a net around the vampires' precise historical origin? But the crucial point in this is Seneca.' There was a riffling of papers. 'Here! In his letter to Cassius Dio – this was before the Pisonian conspiracy, of course . . .'

Eleanor pinched herself, trying to keep her focus. It was

difficult to follow the conversation with any sort of understanding when she didn't know a single one of the names being mentioned. Perhaps the best course of action, now she'd confirmed Charles was here and safe, would be to slip back out of the house and wait for him to finish. Then they could make their way back to Lady Marguerite together – and perhaps Eleanor wouldn't mention how she'd flouted her instructions, either. Although it seemed nothing short of an attack by cannons and muskets would disturb the flow of this scholar's enthusiasm.

'Tacitus discounts the matter, but then Tacitus is notorious for his lack of credence in anything resembling the supernatural. Though he does suggest that the downfall of Seneca was to some extent due to the loans forced on the British population which caused Boadicea's rebellion, and that there were, as he puts it, *those certain ones who held a grudge . . .*'

She began to edge backwards, being careful to keep her exit as silent as her arrival, but then froze mid-step as she heard a noise from downstairs. Someone had entered the house through the kitchen, just as she had done, but not as quietly. Ignoring the professor's droning, she strained every sinew to hear what was going on down there.

A rustle of skirts. Lady Marguerite? Could she have come here herself to join them? No, there were other footsteps following too – heavier ones. At least two people, possibly three. And Eleanor was caught in the middle.

She scuttled over to the nearest open doorway and ducked into it, narrowly avoiding toppling a pile of books which stood waiting to ambush any unwary arrivals. Dust sifted to the floor around her as she edged behind the door, out of any convenient line of sight from the corridor. The door itself was ill-hung enough that she could peer through the crack between door and wall and see who was approaching.

It was the full skirts of an elegant silk dress that came

into view first, the embroidery on them glittering in the candlelight. Eleanor knew those skirts, she knew that embroidery – her fingers ached with the memory of each careful stitch. Her heart sank as she realized who this was.

Lady Sophie walked past the doorway where Eleanor was hiding, her steps as calm and measured as if she was walking down the corridor of her own house. Behind her came the two vampires Eleanor had seen following her orders before – the dark French de Courcis and the pale English Castleton, with only the faint creaks and groans of the old floorboards betraying their passing. On better flooring they would have been as inaudible as ghosts.

Panic made Eleanor's pulse hammer so loudly in her ears that she feared it might somehow be heard by the vampires in the corridor beyond, only a few yards away from her. Oh, she could protect *herself* – she had the ability to call a light which would repel them long enough for her to flee – but now they were between her and Charles.

For a moment she allowed herself to entertain the hope that Professor Johnson might send them away. A man who spent his time investigating the history of vampires was unlikely to be popular among those same vampires. If Charles had a chance to hide . . .

Professor Johnson's lecturing voice broke off suddenly, leaving abrupt silence in its wake. Then he spoke again. 'My lady Baroness. You took your time, madam. I was afraid the bird would fly the coop before you arrived.'

The words made sense, *far too much* sense, but Eleanor couldn't allow herself to think about their full implications now, or to despair over the fact they were trapped like rats. Just as Lady Marguerite had feared! She had to get Charles and herself out of here before it was too late. But what else did she have to threaten them with? No guns. No League to back her up. Every move to drive them away from her would simply turn them loose on Charles. The weight of books and paper around her seemed to mock her, ignorant maidservant that she was, unworthy of the spires of Oxford.

Books and paper . . .

CHAPTER SEVEN

'What an unexpected surprise.' Charles's voice came clear and distinct down the corridor to Eleanor's ears. 'Madam, I don't know what you're doing here, but—'

'I do not have time to waste,' Lady Sophie said cuttingly, 'and you will oblige me, sir, by not doing so either. If you will answer my questions clearly and honestly, then this will be a great deal simpler and swifter.'

There was a brief pause. Eleanor could imagine Charles removing his eye-glasses to clean them, as he so often did when he was thinking. 'Well, madam, that depends entirely on what you wish to ask me.'

'How many of the League are here?'

'I have not the first idea what you mean.'

Lady Sophie sighed. 'I was afraid this would happen. Now we need to go through all the tiresome process of having you drugged and taken back to Merton for questioning – nobody will look twice at a drunken student being dragged back to his college, after all. And wasting precious time will not put me in the best of tempers, which will bring on one of my headaches. Have you no pity for a woman's headaches, Charles?'

'As a general rule, yes,' Charles said, 'but in your case,

madam, I delight in causing them. Surely you do not *expect* me to speak freely about such things?'

'Not as a general rule, no. I have endured for over fifteen hundred years, and I have yet to meet a man who acts *sensibly* once he has the bit of honour between his teeth. It grows wearisome.'

Eleanor inched her way around from behind the door as they spoke, every movement performed with twice the caution she'd used earlier. She could see the backs of the two men – large, muscular backs, not boding well for any attempt at physical heroics – blocking the corridor, where they stood behind Lady Sophie. Matters would be a great deal easier if they were to go forward and actually enter the room where the others were. Could Eleanor wait for them to do so? If they were going to manhandle Charles, they'd need to be closer to him. She didn't think Lady Sophie would soil her gloves by pouring a drug down his throat in person, vampiric strength or not.

'The young man has friends in town,' Professor Johnson said. 'He mentioned that he would be meeting them later.'

'Ah,' Lady Sophie said. 'Excellent. If they are the people whom I believe them to be, then we may almost have this matter under control.'

'Professor Johnson,' Charles said, and this time Eleanor could hear the note of betrayal in his voice. 'Why?'

'Be more precise, young man.'

'I can understand Castleton's choice, even if I disagree with it.' Eleanor saw the white-haired vampire's shoulders twitch, as though receiving a well-aimed shot. 'Though if I myself were afflicted by consumption, who knows? It's easy for a man to say he'd never be tempted until he is. Yet what about yourself, Professor? How could you tell this woman I was here? For pity's sake, you've spent most of your life declaring that there's more to vampires than we know!'

'Of course he has,' Lady Sophie said, cutting off Professor Johnson before he could answer. 'And the professor is entirely correct. There's still so much for him to learn. We tolerate him, nay, *patronize* him, because it means that foolish young men like yourself will come to him for help, and in return he will inform us of their enquiries. A mutually beneficial arrangement.'

'And one with an agreed payment, which I trust I will be granted soon,' Professor Johnson said. 'Imagine it, my boy. *Eternity* to seek the truths hidden behind the veils of history – not just vampires, but all the other facts which have been lost to time. Oh, I may have to publicly recant a few of my theories when I become a vampire myself, but I've never been a vain man. And after that . . . centuries! Centuries in which I will be able to dig through all the records in Oxford, in London, in Paris—'

'I can hardly see you being welcome in Paris if you're of the vampiric persuasion at that point,' Charles cut in. Eleanor could hear the stress in his voice, and wished she was at his side to reassure him that not everyone was so willing to sell their birthright – or their freedom, or their integrity – for a mess of pottage. She also hoped vindictively that Professor Johnson would be disappointed in his bargain.

'Have no fear,' Lady Sophie said gently, cutting across the spluttering noises Professor Johnson was making. He must not be used to contradiction – or at least, not from students. 'As a scholar of history, Professor, you of all people know how transitory revolutions are. Soon enough France will have returned to a more normal state, and you will be able to visit the Sorbonne and any other repositories of knowledge at your leisure.'

'Or the Revolution may reach the shores of England,' Charles suggested, 'and the two of you will face the guillotine and stake together.'

Lady Sophie sighed. 'I fear, Charles, that you have inherited a few of your mentor's less helpful traits, such as a tendency to impudent badinage.' She glanced behind her at the waiting Castleton and de Courcis. 'Gentlemen, if you would be so kind . . .'

Castleton and de Courcis charged into the room. There was a crack as something metallic hit the floor – Charles must have been carrying a pistol – and then a thud. Eleanor peered out from her shelter enough to see Castleton removing a small bottle from a pocket of his coat, while de Courcis restrained Charles, twisting both his arms behind him.

She had to act now. If they did manage to drug Charles, she wouldn't have the strength to carry him out of here. There was no time left for excuses or waiting for a better opportunity. With fear tying her belly into knots, she stepped out into the corridor and raised a hand, calling on the power which was hers. Light glowed around her fingers. 'No further, gentlemen,' she said, moving into their line of sight.

The light burned white, more brilliant than candles, hotter than lamps, and all three vampires flinched back from its radiance. The elderly man whom she could now see through the doorway, who must be Professor Johnson, stared at her in a mixture of shock and disbelief.

Charles bit his lip. 'You should have run,' he said simply.

'I for one am glad she did not.' Lady Sophie was forced to shield her face with her hand, and had backed away from the lambent flame until her shoulders were touching the bookshelves, but her voice dripped with sweet understanding and sympathy. 'Nellie has more sense than you do, Charles. She's prepared to make a deal. I can respect that in another woman.'

'How is she doing that?' Professor Johnson demanded. 'You told me the stories of mages were exaggerated!'

'Something can be exaggerated and yet still true.' Lady

Sophie edged sideways, trying to back out of the direct radiance of Eleanor's light.

Eleanor took a step forward into the doorway, ensuring there was no way the vampires could shelter. There were no other doors out of the room to allow their escape, and the windows were already shuttered for the night. 'The deal I am offering, madam, is that you release Charles to me and we leave together.'

'You used to call me milady, Nellie,' Lady Sophie said reproachfully. 'Why this sudden change of behaviour?'

'That was before you had me and the rest of the League locked up in cells below Paris, while you plotted to blow up the National Convention!' Eleanor snapped. *Calm*, she told herself. *Don't let her unsettle you.*

'Ah. So it's like that, is it? Very well.' Lady Sophie edged sideways again, one hand clamping on Castleton's shoulder. She dragged him in front of her, her hand white-knuckled with the force of her grip as she used him to shield herself from Eleanor's light. He grimaced but kept a tight-lipped silence, flinching from the light himself as far as she allowed. 'What have you to offer in return?'

'Your own safety, madam.' Eleanor's head throbbed with the effort of keeping the light burning steadily.

Lady Sophie laughed – a pretty, tinkling noise. 'My dear, we both know that your show of power, while effective, is temporary. You cannot destroy us with that alone, however painful it may be to us, or *force* us to release Charles. Eventually you will have to retreat in order to save your own skin. Surely an intelligent girl like yourself is capable of a better offer? I would gladly trade this young man for knowledge of the whereabouts of Lady Blakeney.'

'Don't do it, Eleanor!' Charles ordered. The white flame turned his eye-glasses into mirrors, concealing his eyes.

Eleanor restrained herself from saying that not only would

she not consider it, but even if she had been desperate enough to contemplate betraying Lady Marguerite, she had no faith in the promises of vampires anyway, however much they claimed to be noble and honourable. 'I have no idea where she currently is,' she lied.

'I imagine she's with one of the League,' Lady Sophie continued, 'and all the rest of them are currently in London. Charles here was the only one to leave London, bolting for Oxford, and naturally I took an interest in his movements. I don't know why *you've* come here with him, though. You're too sensible a girl to throw everything away for a night's passing fancy.'

'You followed *me*?' Charles exclaimed in shock, pausing his attempts to wrestle himself free from de Courcis for a moment.

'Since we are apparently laying our cards on the table – why yes, I did indeed follow you. My dear Charles, by now I know the identities of all the League! Why did you think I *wouldn't* have you followed?'

For a moment, Eleanor was struck by despair. The League had realized Lady Sophie was most likely aware of all their identities by now. The vampires had forced Armand Saint-Just into servitude, and naturally she would have interrogated him for any useful information he might possess. And, of course, she had later seen Charles, Sir Percy, herself and the others imprisoned below Paris. If she could have them all traced and followed, at any time and any place . . .

Then cold reason filtered through Eleanor's panic, strengthening her resolve. Yes, Lady Sophie might be able to trace them, but only when she knew where to start looking. She hadn't known they were going to rescue Lady Marguerite just a couple of nights ago, after all. She'd probably gambled on following Charles because he was doing an unusual thing in leaving London, while the rest of the League stayed there in public sight – and she'd been *lucky*. But that didn't make her omnipotent.

And Armand might have known a great deal, but not everything. Sir Percy was the one who knew it all. If Lady Sophie and her vampire friends ever managed to break *him* to their will – well, better not to think of that. Far more important to deal with the matter at hand, such as escaping together with Charles from a nest of vampires.

'Now, Professor!' Lady Sophie added, her voice like a whip, and Professor Johnson came barrelling towards Eleanor, one hand raised to shield his eyes.

Eleanor recoiled, taken aback, and for a moment her concentration wavered, causing the flame around her hand to ebb.

'Eleanor!' Charles cried out in turn, and his desperation drew a new fury from her. Her fire leaped up again, and with her free hand she pulled one of the books from the bookcase nearest her, tossing it directly at the professor.

His reaction was automatic: he stopped trying to grab her, instead lunging to save the leather-bound volume before it could hit him. 'Ignorant wench!' he snarled at her.

She didn't bother replying, addressing herself instead to Lady Sophie. 'Let me make myself clear, madam. You *will* order your men to release Charles, and he and I will leave together.'

'Or?' Lady Sophie asked. 'Will you strike us with lightning – here, inside a house? Will you call the winds to plague us, with all the windows shut? You've boxed yourself in, Nellie, and cut off the greatest part of your advantages.'

Eleanor suppressed a surge of bitterness – at Lady Sophie for clearly knowing her powers so well, and at Anima for falsely claiming Eleanor didn't have those powers and barely teaching her anything of use throughout the year she'd possessed her. 'Not quite,' she said, her voice almost as smooth as Lady Sophie's own, though it took some effort. She had to convince them all she was really willing to do this. 'You forget, madam. Fire burns.'

She moved her flaming hand towards the nearest shelf of books and saw, with satisfaction, the professor's look of horror. 'Which is your most precious volume, Professor?'

'You wouldn't dare!' de Courcis called from where he still held Charles trapped. 'The whole house could go up!'

'I'd probably get out alive, monsieur,' Eleanor answered. The obvious fear in his voice gave her strength. She might just be able to persuade them that she was sincere. Specks of dust crackled in the flame as they spiralled in the draughts. She let her hand hover a mere half inch away from the stacks of books and sheaves of notes. So much paper. So much very dry paper. 'I'm far closer to the door than you.'

'And what of him?' De Courcis yanked on Charles's arms, forcing a grunt of pain from him. 'Will you risk seeing him die along with us, after you've come here to save him?'

'It would be worth the price,' Charles said, before she could reply. He might have been ascending the steps of the guillotine, his head unbowed. Eleanor was grateful he could play along so well – it lent conviction to her bluff. 'To know that my friends would go free and no longer have to deal with your persecution and lies . . .'

Lady Sophie looked between Charles and Eleanor. 'Little Nellie isn't a murderer,' she finally said.

Wasn't she? Eleanor had shot a man in France who'd been about to hand her over as a prisoner and alert the guard to the approaching League. She'd also thwarted the prison guards at Mont-Saint-Michel in such a way that they'd likely faced punishment from their paranoid masters in the Committee for Public Safety, and could well have been condemned to the guillotine by now.

Yet if she set fire to these books here and now, and it

resulted in the burning rafters coming down on everyone's heads, would she truly be guilty of murder? Lady Sophie and her followers were vampires. But the professor was human and alive. And Charles . . .

She wouldn't do it, of course. She *couldn't*. But she had to convince them she would start torching the books, one by one, if they gave her no other choice. Books meant nothing to her – but to the professor, a man who stuffed his house with them till it was bursting at the seams, who'd sell his soul for knowledge? How far was *he* prepared to risk what he loved?

'Perhaps I'm ready to risk killing you all,' she replied to Lady Sophie, attempting to imitate Sir Percy at his most flippant. 'Perhaps not. The question is whether you want me to find out here and now, or if you'd rather postpone the answer to a later date.'

'This is ridiculous.' Professor Johnson put down the volume he'd been cradling like a baby. Panic gleamed in his eyes and drew threads of sweat down his face, trickling from under his threadbare wig and over his jowls. 'The idea that this ignorant slut would torch a priceless repository of knowledge – it's unthinkable. Do something, Baroness!'

'Stop her yourself,' Lady Sophie said, 'and I promise you will receive what I know you want most. Here and now.'

The professor looked between Eleanor and Lady Sophie. And then he moved, but not in the direction Lady Sophie had clearly been expecting. Instead of jumping for Eleanor, he threw himself at Charles and de Courcis, knocking both of them off balance. The three of them went crashing down. 'Let the boy go!' he shouted as they struggled together on the dusty floor.

Apparently he values his books more than his hope of immortality . . .

Eleanor seized the moment. She stepped into the room

and focused on the light – her own flame, her knowledge of the force of life which drove the blood through her veins and which the sun woke from the sleeping earth. The very thing vampires lacked and feared. Her pulse hammered in her ears like the rattle of carriage wheels, and the world seemed to sway around her like a painted sign in the rain, unreal and dribbling at the edges.

With a gasp Charles broke free. He struggled to his feet, booting the quailing de Courcis in the stomach on the way, and staggered over to Eleanor. 'Let's be out of here!'

'You'll need to lead me backwards,' Eleanor said through gritted teeth. 'If I let go too early . . .'

Thank heaven, he understood. He set a hand on her shoulder and towed her backwards, down the corridor and to the head of the stairs. 'When I say now,' he murmured in her ear, 'you can stop doing that and we'll run for it together.'

The sounds of struggling from the room had stopped. 'Charles?' Lady Sophie called, her voice sweet and persuasive. 'Nellie? You're wasting your time running, children. We've found you once. We'll find you again. Come back and make terms with us while you can. We don't want to hurt you – you're far too valuable for that. Stay and talk with us . . .'

Eleanor jerked a nod to Charles, ignoring Lady Sophie's words. Everything around her was growing hazy. The light was the only real thing in it. She was burning herself up in it, and it was beautiful.

'Now!'

She blinked, and the light was gone. Together they ran down the stairs in a world suddenly dark, lit only by the flickering candles, and stumbled out through the front door into the noisy street.

There were people everywhere. No, more precisely, there

were *students* everywhere. It wasn't like the mobs in Paris, where everyone came together side by side, men and women, a hundred different types of citizens mingling, with the only constant being the red, white and blue of flags, cockades and sashes. This street – and perhaps every street in Oxford – was full of young men in their scholarly gowns, shouting and declaiming, their faces lit with anger.

Eleanor was still too muddled to do more than gawp at the people around her. Fortunately Charles had more sense and dragged her down the house's steps and into the crowd, pulling her shawl up to cover her head and dropping his own eye-glasses into a pocket of his coat. As they stumbled away, Eleanor glimpsed Castleton and de Courcis in the doorway, looking around for any trace of the fugitives.

She was still trying to come to terms in her own head with what she'd almost done. It had been an enormous bluff, and she'd only been *pretending*, but at least Professor Johnson had believed her. He'd really thought she was prepared to set fire to the books, and risk killing them all. But playing with fire that way, in all aspects, could have gone terribly wrong. She'd been willing to risk Charles's life in order to save him.

What has happened to me?

It would have been easier if there was someone she could blame for the way her entire world had been rewritten a year ago, when she'd been no more than just another maid with a talent for embroidery. The fault of the League, or Anima, or her own magic, or the vampires in general, and Lady Sophie in particular. Someone else, anyone else, other than that of Eleanor herself. But the truth was, it was no one's fault, or it was everyone's, including hers . . .

'*Respice ad haec; adsum dirarum ab sede sororum, bella manu letumque gero,*' Charles murmured in her ear as they retreated together into an alley to allow a group of students to pass.

108

They were nearly at the Black Boar, where Lady Marguerite would be waiting for them – it backed onto this alley, and it was close enough that they could smell the odours from the kitchen.

'What?' Eleanor asked.

'Oh, a little Virgil. When one of the Furies appears in the *Aeneid* to give Turnus his marching orders, she stands before him with a blazing torch – just like you, my dear. And she says, "Look at me! I come from the home of the Dread Sisters and in my hand I carry war and death." You were the most incredible thing I've ever seen, Eleanor. You faced them down without a moment's hesitation. I was so proud of you.'

Now it was all over, now there was no *point* in crying, tears came leaking from her eyes. 'I was afraid they wouldn't believe me,' she confessed. 'I thought they'd realize I must be bluffing, that I couldn't have done it. I was so relieved when you played along.'

'Played along?' He blinked at her, shocked. 'But . . . Eleanor, I was sincere! It was the least I could do, when you'd dared so much for my – for *our* sake. I thought . . .'

'How could you believe I'd ever do that to you? Risk you burning?' The words she'd been trying to avoid for both their sakes came spilling from her mouth. 'I *love* you, Charles!'

'You love me?' His arm tightened around her. 'Eleanor, I've wanted nothing but to hear you say that to me for these past months . . .'

She clung to him, desperate, forgetting all sense and rationality and practicality, and for the first time their lips met. The mob of students continued to shoulder past them, lost in their own dreams of revolution and enlightenment, but for that moment it felt as though Eleanor and Charles were entirely alone. She could have stayed there in the circle of his arms for ever.

Charles was the first one to remember where they were. Reluctantly he released his hold on her. 'We have to find Lady Marguerite,' he said, looking to the Black Boar's back door.

'No need.' Lady Marguerite's voice was somewhat acid. 'I believe I could have stood here coughing until any passer-by thought I had consumption, and the pair of you would not have noticed me. While I sympathize, we are in a state of crisis. Have you heard what they're shouting?'

'No,' Eleanor confessed with a blush.

'A great deal about Pitt, and his government, and the war with France, but very little that's practical. In a way that may be worse than definite proposals. A group of excited young men might do anything at all. Charles, I'm assuming your mission didn't go entirely to plan?'

Charles gave a quick report on events. 'But it wasn't time entirely wasted,' he finished. 'No doubt the professor only wished to keep me there while he waited for Lady Sophie to arrive, but he did give me some useful facts which I'll share later. But what do we do now?'

'We need to check the spot which I identified earlier,' Eleanor said quickly. 'But there are so many students in the streets, I'm not sure we'll be able to do so unobserved. And Lady Sophie's men will surely be scouring the city, looking for us.'

'There may be a way to kill two birds with one stone,' Lady Marguerite said thoughtfully. She unclasped her cloak, offering it to Eleanor, and removed her hat, tearing false pieces from her hair, while brushing off powder with the skill of an actress accustomed to quick changes. 'Eleanor, give me your shawl – yes, that'll do. A little rouge . . . there. Am I recognizable?'

She no longer looked like the elderly dowager she'd been impersonating, but equally she didn't resemble her normal self either. The light from the street lamp caught on her eyes and the red slash of her mouth, giving her a dangerous air.

'I'd need to look twice to know you, milady,' Eleanor confessed.

'And I'd need my eye-glasses,' Charles said. 'What have you in mind?'

'Give me ten minutes. I'm going to go a little way north, and address the mob. I've heard enough speeches in France to know how it's done.' Her smile shifted from dangerous to positively vicious. 'While I'm drawing the crowd away, Eleanor can lead you to that spot she found – east of St Aldate's, I think you said? Do whatever needs doing as swiftly as you may, then we'll meet up at our rooms in the inn afterwards. Are we agreed?'

Eleanor knew what Sir Percy would have said about this. From his frown, she suspected Charles did too. But Sir Percy wasn't *here*, and Lady Marguerite was, with a plan, and she clearly had the bit very thoroughly between her teeth. Objections would not be entertained: they would merely result in Eleanor and Charles being overridden.

Eleanor had no idea exactly what she was going to do when they found the spot, but if Lady Marguerite trusted her to do it, then she'd give her utmost. 'We are, milady,' she said.

It took Charles a moment longer, but he nodded. 'I feel almost sorry I won't be able to hear you,' he admitted. 'I'm certain you're a far finer orator than most of the popinjays in tricolours I've overheard in France. But please, milady, I urge you to take all precautions not to be arrested.'

'Ah,' Lady Marguerite said, 'but I was a revolutionary myself, once. And like every true actress, I know when to make a carefully timed exit from the stage.'

CHAPTER EIGHT

'She's just started on the Girondins,' Eleanor reported, as they hurried through the emptied streets. She wasn't sure whether her hearing was simply better than Charles's, or that the breezes carried the words to her ears without her conscious desire. Frightening if so – another piece of magic dropped into her life which she had no way to refuse. 'About how they were the true exemplars of liberty, and other factions in the Revolution dragged them down.' She frowned, trying to catch the drift of the speech. 'Now she's quoting Madame Roland: "O Liberty, what crimes are committed in your name!"'

Charles pursed his lips in a whistle. 'I'm astonished they're listening to her so attentively. Not that I don't have the utmost faith in milady, of course,' he added hastily. 'But I wouldn't have thought they'd just settle down to hear her speak, rather than marching across to Merton to throw cobbles.'

'Well, they *are* students of Oxford,' Eleanor said.

As they approached the spot she'd identified earlier, just to the east of St Aldate's, she focused her attention. The air itself felt different from the normal winds and breezes, like a larder where a single piece of fruit has begun to turn rotten, tinting the air with a barely perceptible odour that would alert any good housewife.

No, that wasn't quite right. It wasn't *foul*. It didn't stink. It was just . . . wrong. Something here was out of place, and she could sense it.

'Are you suggesting we're liable to seat ourselves and listen to any passing speaker, whatever our mood?' Charles teased her.

'Better than not to listen to anyone at all,' Eleanor answered, distracted. 'She will be all right, won't she?'

'I have absolutely no doubt that she can handle herself a great deal better than we can,' Charles said. 'She may not have been so frequent a visitor to France recently, but the others have told me that she's undertaken jaunts there with the Chief before now.'

With the Chief – so she'd had him and others of the League by her side to help in any escape. But Lady Marguerite was alone right now, trapped in front of an audience of hundreds of students, and who knew where Lady Sophie and her followers might be . . .

Eleanor bit her lip, trying to distract herself from the fear creeping over her. The sooner she and Charles managed – well, whatever they were going to manage – then the sooner they'd be able to assist milady. The best thing she could do was to focus on the matter at hand.

When they turned a corner into a side street which ran along the high stone wall of one of the colleges, she *knew* this was the place she'd sensed earlier. There was nothing here that she recognized with her eyes, but it still felt as though she'd stepped into some familiar spot from childhood.

She looked around. On one side of the street, houses were shuttered and quiet – perhaps due to the late hour, or perhaps because of the riotous students. On the other side was a stone wall which could have been hundreds of years old, its large yellowish stones washed to pallor by the thin moonlight. There were no convenient street lights in this narrow road: the shadows overhung the pair of them in a way which felt almost like safety.

'Do you think someone buried something here?' Charles suggested. 'It might be distinctly awkward if we're required to dig up half the street.'

'I hope not!' Eleanor said fervently. 'But I think . . . Charles, my knowledge around this is very scanty. Anima didn't tell me even a tenth of what she knew, and I suspect *she* didn't even know a tenth of what *could* be known. She said magic is a thing of life, and that a mage's spells can't survive their death. And that the dead aren't able to cast or abide magic, which is why vampires detest it.' She trailed her fingers along the wall, walking along beside it, hoping for some sign that her thoughts might have drawn the high card, as Sir Percy would put it. 'Yet she believed she was a ghost, and isn't that being dead? Bernard had seemed to understand it better; he'd said that the last piece of her magic was holding her onto the edge of life. Which I suppose makes her not exactly a ghost, but merely a . . . living soul? I fear I haven't the words to explain something like this. One would need a student of theology.'

'Whereas I'm merely a historian and scholar who never planned to take Holy Orders,' Charles said. 'But where does this argument lead us?'

'Well, I felt *something* here earlier today.' Was that a prickle against her fingers, like the brush of an unexpected nettle in a pile of weeds? *Yes.* She was sure of it. It was at this section of the college wall, like an invisible stain in the stone, and just as she could sense it, she knew it could somehow sense her. Like some large and dangerous animal – a bull, or a boar – which had been asleep on a hot day, yet now its eyes were flickering open.

'Have you found something?' Charles asked, his brows drawn together in a frown.

She carefully pulled her hand back, unwilling to risk fully awakening the presence. 'I think so. I believe it may be the same sort of thing that Anima left behind.'

'A spell, then?'

'I don't know,' she confessed. If only Anima were still here to answer her questions! 'But if it is magic, a spell, and it feels as if it is, then the mage must still be alive. Perhaps it – he – is alive in the same way that Anima was – by binding his soul to some item or place in the hopes of future aid. Which is why I want you to stay well back, Charles.' She turned to look him squarely in the face. 'I will *not* run the risk that this Matthew may attempt to possess you as Anima did me.'

'Interesting choice of words,' Charles said cheerfully. 'Some people would have said "as Anima did I", but I agree with you that grammatical consistency is better left to pedants. Which bit am I to take care not to touch?'

'Here,' Eleanor said, keeping her hand a careful six inches away from the part of the wall in question.

Without a moment's hesitation, Charles slapped his palm against the stone.

'Charles!' Eleanor nearly shrieked.

'Curious thing,' Charles said. 'I can't say I feel anything in particular except stone, and some rather unfortunate liquids. I can only hope they're not the result of some poor fellow coming to grief here after drinking too much. I'm dreadfully sorry if I startled you, m'dear, but at the moment I'm the least important person here . . . *Quis es, puella?*'

His eyes had focused on her in a way that was entirely out of place with the rest of his features. He was now looking at Eleanor in the same keen way he might scrutinize a manuscript, or a book, or a document which he was forging.

It felt wrong to see that degree of dispassionate fascination in the face of someone whom she knew and loved so well.

'Matthew?' Eleanor said, praying she was right. Her eyes strayed to the wall, and she bit back a gasp of horror: Charles's hand had sunk into the stone as though it were mud or thick starch.

'*Ita vero.*'

'My name is Eleanor. Please speak English, sir. I only know a few words of Latin.' She prayed silently and desperately that Charles was still *there*, and that Matthew hadn't simply replaced him somehow.

Charles cleared his throat as though it was rusty. 'You are one of us?'

'Yes, of course,' Eleanor said, 'or why else would I be here and have woken you? I'm the student of a mage who called herself Anima. She commanded the winds and storms.'

Charles rubbed his chin thoughtfully with his free hand, the gesture of a man used to a beard. 'I know none of that name.' He looked down at his body, then around at the surrounding street and walls. 'What strange clothing is this, and what buildings are these? How long have I slept?'

'Anima woke Bernard, who was asleep in Mont-Saint-Michel.' Eleanor continued her planned speech, one ear cocked for the sound of any approaching students, vampires, or other inconveniences. She purposely skimmed over how long Matthew and Bernard had slept – if she had to answer all his questions about the current state of the world, they'd be here till dawn. 'Bernard sent me to find you. He said you'd uncovered some vital information which could help us against the vampires.'

Charles nodded slowly. He looked around at the surrounding buildings, then more closely at Eleanor herself again. 'And how do I know that you speak the truth, and

116

aren't merely some agent of the vampires, sent to cajole me into giving up the last of my secrets?'

'I fully appreciate your caution, sir,' Eleanor said through gritted teeth, 'but there is currently a mob abroad in the streets here in Oxford, and there are vampires hunting me and the man whom you are possessing. I fear we have little time to discuss the matter. Isn't the fact that we woke you proof enough?'

'You could still be a paid agent of theirs,' he argued stubbornly. 'I've often feared some of our kind might become their minions.'

Something inside Eleanor snapped. They'd come all this way, faced all these dangers, and *Charles* might be in peril of his very soul, and now this – this *nincompoop* – felt the need to be as petty as a Revolutionary official demanding to see her papers. 'Very well!' she exclaimed, putting her hands on her hips. 'Have it as you will. The man who's currently risking his life and soul to give you speech and perception is nothing but a cunning forger and schemer. I'm an ignorant slut who's defiling the streets of Oxford with her presence and should go back to my needle and thread. We're corrupt minions of the vampires who secretly control England. Why should I contradict you? I will merely point out that the vampires are currently *on the retreat* in France, where the population's taken to publicly executing them, and the League I work with have finally seen for themselves how vampires can control the minds of their victims.' A memory of one of Sir Percy's favourite sayings came to her. '*Fortune is flying past us with a single hair on her bald head, and this is our chance to catch it.* But for that, I need your help. Will you take this opportunity to stop them at last?'

'You need my help.' He stroked his chin again. 'Well, I'm sure for a price it can be arranged.'

Eleanor now perceived the depth of the hole she'd just

stepped into. 'A price?' she demanded hotly, trying to disguise her sudden panic. 'Would you charge your sister in magic a price for your cooperation?'

What might he ask for, she wondered fearfully? What other than a new body – that of Charles?

'You talk of sisters and brothers.' He rounded on her like an offended cockerel. 'Where were you when I needed you? I spent my days among the Dominicans, like any other common brother. I grew old on a diet of bread and water and prayer, and *none of you came!*'

There was an odd light in his eyes, a flicker of deep fire. Eleanor found herself uncomfortably reminded of what Bernard had said about other mages who'd tried to preserve themselves in this way. *The few successes were all mad ghosts who had to be exorcised . . .*

This wasn't about her pride, or her self-respect. This was about convincing Matthew to give them what they needed, whatever it might require.

'I'm sorry,' she said, bowing her head. She went down on her knees in the muddy lane. Lady Marguerite's rich velvet cloak draped around her in misplaced elegance, and she suppressed a wince at having to draggle the fine fabric in the mud. 'Bernard at Mont-Saint-Michel would have come, but he was unable to leave. He said you might be the only person who could help us. I beg you . . .' What was the most appropriate way to address him – one that would combine respect with a reminder that she, too, was a mage? 'Elder brother, I and my friend have woken you because you may be able to save us all.'

'Your friend?' Charles raised his hand to his eyes, inspecting it. 'This man is no mage. And his body cannot support my presence for much longer. Why did you not bring another mage with you?'

'Because there is nobody else,' Eleanor said quietly. 'The

vampires won. For centuries mages were forgotten. I only discovered my powers through chance.'

Charles snorted. 'You should have let me sleep on.' His fingers stirred inside the stone as though it was a bowl of dough.

'No!' Eleanor was growing desperate. *His body cannot support my presence for much longer.* Did this mean Matthew would simply cease his possession of Charles, or would he ride him to exhaustion and death, like a fool overworking a good horse? 'Elder brother, we've been hunted here all the way to Oxford by the vampires chasing us! Are you merely going to stand by and watch us die? Is this what you waited all these centuries for?'

Charles hesitated, gnawing his lip. 'If Bernard did send you, then . . . what did he already know? How much did he tell you?'

'He said that you – the mages – had discovered there was something very important below London, something which could not be moved,' Eleanor recounted hastily. 'He said the vampires were guarding it, but didn't dare go near it for fear of discovery.'

Charles nodded. 'Yes, that is so. I managed to take certain castings before I left London to seek refuge here – the rhythms of the earth, the patterns of the stone. The same things you can do with the air and winds. Oh, I recognize a storm-caller and air mage when I see one! You can't hide yourself from another mage, girl. Every footstep of yours on these cobbles speaks to me of your strength. Yet Oxford . . . Oxford itself is strangely quiet.'

Eleanor could still hear the sounds of the distant mob, but she suspected that wasn't what he meant. Would she be like this when she was older, conscious of every movement of air around her? Of course, that did assume she'd live to be old . . .

'What is it that frets you so?' he demanded. 'Any mage should have more self-control than you do. You sweat and panic like a serf afraid of displeasing her master.'

'Because we have so little time. The vampires are just behind us,' Eleanor said, giving him half her reason. She wasn't going to admit how worried she was about Charles. Matthew seemed the sort of person who'd turn it against her as an accusation of weakness. 'They're pursuing us still, searching the city. Their leader, the Baroness of Basing, Lady Sophie—'

'Who?' Charles knotted his brows in thought, and his face grew dark with fury. 'Sophie, Sophia . . . Is this woman you speak of Sophia of Port-en-Bassin? Is she behind all this?'

The names were similar. Even the place names – Port-en-Bassin, Basing – were within spitting distance of each other. Could Eleanor's previous mistress, undoubtedly ancient – heavens only knew how ancient – be the same woman he was thinking of? 'She's a vampire, elder brother, but I've only ever heard her called Lady Sophie.'

'Does she have a sweet tongue,' Charles snarled, 'and eyes the colour of black violets? A woman who veils herself and prompts men to act for her, but beneath it she has a heart of pure ice, and a tongue which could teach the Devil himself new sins?'

Eleanor blinked. 'Elder brother, it does *sound* like her, though to be honest I'm sure there are a hundred other ladies of society who could fit that description.'

He was no longer listening to Eleanor, too consumed by his own anger and suddenly convinced of the connection, seizing on it as though it was his hope of salvation. 'You should have told me she was involved at the beginning of our converse. How was I supposed to know how serious this was? I've long suspected she had her fingers in the London matter. Now you bring me proof of it. If . . .'

He paused, staggering; his fingers sank deeper into the stone which he leaned against. 'Why did you let me grow so distracted, young Eleanor? I have so little time in this body.'

Eleanor was used to dealing with unjust accusations from superiors, such as *Why did you let me drink that brandy?* or *How could you be so careless as to spill a single drop while overloaded with the dishes and crockery that I ordered you to carry?* One ignored the injustice and apologized humbly, while getting on with one's tasks. 'I'm sorry, elder brother,' she apologized. 'Please tell me about the London matter.' That single repeated word – London – had renewed her hope. There definitely *was* something to be learned here.

'I have not enough time in this body to tell you all that needs to be said.'

'Then take mine instead!' Eleanor cried, forcing out the words before she could stop herself. She'd survived Anima's possession, after all. She could do it again if she had to, though the thought made her skin crawl; Anima had been like an elderly aunt, annoying but tolerable, while this man was a stranger and she disliked the little she knew of him. But if it was necessary, and if it persuaded him to release Charles . . .

Charles shook his head, biting back a snicker. 'What, a woman's body? What manner of man do you take me for? I would not . . .' He staggered again, his face pale in the dim moonlight.

Eleanor rose to her feet, moving to support him. She could feel Charles's pulse as he leaned against her; it was far too fast for her comfort, galloping like a runaway horse. 'Please,' she begged. 'Help us. Don't let Sophia win this war.'

Where appeals for help had failed and calls to brotherhood had proved useless, spite finally succeeded. 'That spawn of the Devil – no, you're right, she cannot be allowed to come out victor, with the blood of so many of us on her hands and mouth. But I no longer have the strength, and this body has no innate power . . .'

This, Eleanor thought she *could* do something about. She'd let Anima use her power when the old ghost had possessed her. She'd even managed to share her power with the mage Bernard in Mont-Saint-Michel. So she reached into that part of herself which could feel the movement of the winds and see the tangled net of forces which pulled the clouds into a storm, then tried to force it through her hands and into Charles.

Sparks crackled around the pair of them as though she'd dropped water into a pan of hot oil. Charles recoiled, stiffening in her grasp, and glared at her. 'You clumsy fool! Have you no training at all? Must you try to force it down my throat?'

'I was trying to help you!' Eleanor retorted, her fingers tingling unpleasantly. 'Show me how to do it then, so I don't harm the man you're possessing!'

Charles's eyes met hers, but the spirit behind them was still that of a man she didn't know and wasn't sure she wanted to. He seemed the sort of tutor who'd have been rapping her knuckles for the slightest mistake. 'I've no time to lesson you properly,' he snapped. 'Return to the basics. Surely you were taught those? *I* extend to you, and *you* then accept my touch and will your strength to me. Do you feel it, dolt?'

Eleanor supposed she could hardly complain at his lack of courtesy – she was actually learning something useful, after all. Now she *could* feel something reaching out from him – his power, the last of his strength. But it extended blindly, as though he could scarcely see or feel her own presence. It was like feeling the shaking of Paris streets under the feet of the rioting mob, hundreds or even thousands strong, or looking down from a height at the rolling spread of summer fields and sensing the whole earth's pulse below it. She caught at this sensation, then linked her own anger and desperation with it, as she might have interlaced fingers with another woman, letting him breathe it back in.

'Yes,' he said hoarsely. 'Yes, that will do. Hold me upright a little longer.'

As Eleanor supported him, Charles reached *further* into the stone in which his hand was immersed, as though it were a nook or hidey-hole. When he drew his hand out again, he was clasping a tubular leather case. 'My findings are within,' he said, his voice shaking. 'I took the readings of London with reference to the mighty buildings such as the Tower. I wrote it down before I was forced to flee to Oxford for safety. For all their claims of righteousness, I knew the blood-drinkers would not cross the Dominican Order. I later concealed this within the stones that made up the foundation of the priory.' He grabbed her, his hands tightening with a clasp like living bone. 'You must put an end to this! Ever since Nero's days they have walked these lands, and the worst of it is, I believe they came from this kingdom! We are the source of this plague which was loosed upon the world! You must put an end to it, girl – I have not the strength, but it lies in your hands now. Take this to your master, whoever he may be, and bid him cleanse the world . . .'

It was a dreadful thing to see the light go out of his eyes as the last thread of Matthew's life and magic snapped, and made even worse by the fact it was Charles's eyes she was looking into. His breathing slowed, fluttered, and for a moment Eleanor knew sheer panic and despair as she feared Charles was about to die in her arms too. But then it resumed in a more natural rhythm, and she took a deep breath herself, one of relief. The last sensation of Matthew's power was gone. He had exhausted himself, and departed to meet whatever judgement might lie in store for mages.

Stonework near her creaked as pieces of the wall crumbled to dust. She could hear what sounded like buildings collapsing in the distance – or was that just the riot? Had the very earth here contained some part of Matthew's power, or been reinforced with his spells in the past? And now he was gone, and all his spells broken with him . . .

Eleanor eased Charles down to the ground, wishing she had a better place to put him than the muddy paving stones. She turned the leather case over in her hands as she waited – and prayed – for him to wake. From things Anima had shown her of the old mage's memories, Eleanor guessed this was a scroll case, holding a roll of paper or vellum. Could this pinpoint exactly where the vampires' great secret was in London? Could it be as simple as that? And would this somehow persuade the vampires to leave them be?

She was well aware of the principles of blackmail: one found another person with a secret, and extorted goods, services, or assistance in freeing prisoners in return for not making that secret widely known. Aristocrats did it. Servants did it. Every social class, as far as she could tell, practised the art. Sir Percy had managed a few escapes from prison this way – it was astonishing how some of the apparently purest and most devoted Revolutionaries had private lives which they preferred to conceal from the public eye. But – and this had proved inconvenient on one occasion – sometimes the person being blackmailed was so desperate to retain their privacy, they would go to any lengths to kill the blackmailers who knew too much. If this secret was too dangerous, then Eleanor and the League might just have jumped from the frying pan into the fire.

Eleanor sighed. All this *mess*, merely because certain

vampires wished to keep their hold on power and privilege, whatever the cost might be to everyone else around them. She remembered something Anima had said about vampires before she passed on: *No vampire can* remain *virtuous. They may begin with the best of intentions, but nothing lasts. In the end, survival is all that matters. And the longer they survive, the more that becomes the cornerstone of their heart. It isn't the sinners I should have been blaming, it's the sin.*

She put aside her thoughts before they could veer too far into theology or self-pity. The important thing was that they'd *succeeded* in their mission here, against all hope or expectation. Now they had a chance, so long as they could stay out of the clutches of Lady Sophie and her faction while Sir Percy determined how best to use this information. It wasn't as though all vampires were determined to dispose of them, after all. Many of them presumably just wanted a quiet life and a peaceful home, and might have no idea at all that others of their kind went around feeding their blood to humans in order to influence the strings of power. To call them all evil, corrupt sanguinocrats would be . . . well, as bad as saying that every single Frenchman was a regicidal revolutionary.

She tenderly brushed a loose lock of hair from Charles's face, then snatched her hand back as he opened his eyes.

'Dear me,' he said. 'I fancy I've done something which I ought not to have done. Your expression doesn't bode well, m'dear.'

'You did exactly what I told you not to,' Eleanor answered, torn between exasperation and a niggling suspicion that if he *hadn't* done so, they'd still have been standing here trying to decide what best to do. 'Thank heaven you're unharmed!' She paused. 'You are unharmed, aren't you? You don't feel any pain? Your soul is still your own?'

'Merely a certain lassitude, no worse than after a hard

day's riding,' Charles reassured her. He sat up despite her attempts to stop him and rubbed his head. 'I fear I have no memory of what just passed, but I see you're holding an item of interest. Where did it come from?'

'It was *inside* the stone,' Eleanor tried to explain. 'He seems to have been a mage who worked with earth and stone, so he was able to somehow reach into this stone to hide his notes there. He said it was part of the priory's foundation, though . . .'

'They used some of the stones from the priory to build Christ Church College,' Charles explained, a covetous hand reaching across to stroke the ancient leather. 'Thank heavens they kept this stone intact rather than breaking it up for rubble, what?'

Eleanor shuddered at how close they might have come to disaster. 'Can you walk?' she asked. 'I think the mob's gone further north. We should return to our rooms, or go looking for milady if she's still not back when we get there.'

'If she's not, you can wait in the rooms while I track her down,' Charles said immediately.

They were still discussing it as they headed north together, one ear cocked for rioters and the other for vampires. Charles was now carrying the scroll case tucked under his coat; it had cost Eleanor a pang to hand it over, but it was safer than her walking around with it displayed in her bare hands. The signs of the mob's passage became more obvious as they advanced: windows smashed, crates broken, pieces of clothing hanging from signposts or lamp posts, the occasional young man pleading with the inhabitants of a building to be allowed in.

Eleanor was bone-weary. The day felt as if it had lasted for far longer than it had any right to. Charles also walked with a heavy tread, and she wondered if he was still aching from the earlier betrayal by a fellow Oxford scholar. She would have to ask him about that and try to cheer his mood, later.

The buzz of voices ahead became audible, and Charles turned to Eleanor with a sudden seriousness. 'Please wait here by this archway while I scout ahead, Eleanor. I give you my word I won't leap into any folly, but I'd feel safer assessing things first, with you well out of it. A young woman's liable to draw eyes in a situation like this.'

'True,' Eleanor said, somewhat sarcastically. 'We're not in France, after all, where both men and women riot together.'

'You can complain about that to milady soon enough.' He pressed her hand, though the look in his eye suggested he wished he could do more, and then strode down the street away from her.

Eleanor drew her borrowed cloak close around her, enjoying its weight and the rich softness of the velvet. She knew she'd never be able to afford anything like this for herself. And she didn't resent that – well, at least, not very much. She did wish, though, that when all this was over, and she could finally work in a modiste's shop (or maybe even *own* a modiste's shop, if she allowed herself to dream), she'd be able to design and sew for the women whose beauty would truly suit such clothing. People like Lady Marguerite, or her own friend Fleurette. It was folly, of course; a modiste probably made a great deal more money from people who depended on their clothing rather than their looks to attract admiring eyes. Her best customers might well be elderly ladies in their sixties, demanding a thousand nips and tucks and embroideries to make them look ten years younger. But still . . .

Strong arms suddenly closed around her from behind, shocking her out of her daydream, and a hand flipped the hood of her cloak over her face. She screamed as best she could, struggling against the iron-hard arms that held her imprisoned and seemed ready to crush the breath out of her. She couldn't see who was doing this. She couldn't hear anything.

Then something struck her on the head and she knew no more.

CHAPTER NINE

They had cut her hair. That meant she would be going to the guillotine in the morning.

Eleanor curled up in a ball on her pallet, trying to warm herself, but every passing breeze brushed against the back of her neck, reminding her that her hair had been shorn, and the morning light would mean her last day on earth. She'd seen it happen to other women, to prisoners whom the League hadn't managed to save. The guards always sheared their hair off, at the nape of the neck, to make room for the guillotine blade that would come down on the neck itself and slice through it.

She couldn't stop shivering. Air came in through the open window – open, but barred – carrying the sounds of Paris beyond, the throb and bustle of a huge city. She was a single fragment caught in the millwheels of law and justice: soon she would be utterly crushed.

Though why were all the voices she heard speaking English?

They'd taken away her own clothing, both Lady Marguerite's cloak and her dress, even her stays, and left her in a dirty old grey gown and her shift. Her arms were wrapped in bandages, some of which were newly stained with blood, and her mouth tasted of vomit.

But if she was in the hands of the Guard, subject to the justice of the Revolution, then why had she been freshly bled? The Revolution didn't bleed people. Vampires did that.

Questions circled in her head, and she was unable to find answers, unable to construct any sort of explanation which made sense. She was only conscious of her own misery and utter inability to focus her mind and emotions, to apply her will and rouse anything in herself resembling power. She felt as sick as the time when she'd caught pneumonia in Paris, when Anima had told her the truth about mages and vampires, when she'd been lying in a bed with the League caring for her . . .

Where was the League? What had happened to Lady Marguerite? What had happened to Charles?

Someone was screaming – not far away, elsewhere in the block of cells – and someone else was crying. She was so cold, and she couldn't sleep. She opened her eyes and stared at the floor of her cell without anything resembling deliberate thought. The only thing that filled her mind was how dirty it was.

She should get up and find a bucket of water and a cloth and scrub it clean – because she was a maidservant who knew her duty and did a good job. No, she was a servant of Lady Sophie, and provided blood for her mistress like a good girl, which was why her arms were marked with fresh slashes. Surely that was all there was, all there had ever been, and everything about the League of the Scarlet Pimpernel, magical powers and riding in balloons, summoning storms and impersonating the Queen of France, was just a dream, a story someone must have told her . . .

Now Sir Percy was sitting on the floor next to her, in the plain shirt and trousers that he'd worn as a disguise in France as a common workman, his legs outstretched in perfect comfort. 'It's a pity, m'dear,' he said. 'I thought we'd get further than this.'

'Further?' she mumbled, her mouth dry. She looked around for water, but there was none.

'With anything.' He shrugged. 'So many things not done, so many innocents not rescued. Who will do it if we won't, mm? That's what they forgot in France. A gentleman has to do his duty.'

Eleanor tried to turn her head away. She hadn't *asked* for this. She hadn't *wanted* this. She was going to be executed along with him – for why else would he be here with her? – and it wasn't *fair*. She was just a maidservant. None of this was her fault. She should be cleaning and sewing and doing everything that she was told. 'I'm not a gentleman,' she whispered. 'I don't want to die.'

'You could always tell them everything,' Sir Percy suggested gently. 'A mere slip of a girl like you, led into bad ways by your superiors – it's the sort of thing that happens all the time, m'dear. Shed a few tears and make a clean breast of it, what? Nobody could possibly blame you.'

Eleanor blinked, and imagined Charles in the room with her – Charles, Andrew and Tony, and Lady Marguerite, as well as all the others – people who'd trusted her with their lives and secrets. This wasn't Sir Percy. He'd never expect her to betray the others. It was some sort of bad dream.

What would Anima have said? 'Get thou behind me, Satan,' she whispered.

'For that you'd need to know which way you were facing,' Sir Percy said unhelpfully. 'Besides, I've always thought it the worst of ideas to tell the Devil to place himself where you're most vulnerable. Dreadful strategy. No doubt the error's in the translation. I'm sure the original text was a great deal wittier. But perhaps we shouldn't look too closely at such things, hey? We run the risk of seeing something that we'd rather not know.'

'Is milady a prisoner too?' Eleanor whispered. 'Or Charles? I can't remember . . .'

'What do you remember?' His voice was casual, but his blue eyes were suddenly very intent.

'I think someone hit me over the head.'

'Oh, that.' He shrugged again. 'It happens to us all the time. Well, not to me very often, because as I said, I don't like anyone getting behind me, but to Andrew, to Tony, to Charles, to all of the League. Let's call it a baptism of skulduggery hm?' His laugh was as braying and asinine as it always was when he was affecting his Society persona of rich nobleman and utter idiot. 'You want to be up and about as soon as possible afterwards. I strongly recommend fresh air and healthy exercise. Bleeding and purging – well, the doctors may be in favour of it, but I myself have never really seen the use of such things. I'd far rather retain my own blood and food, what?'

'Do you blame me?' The idea seized her and wouldn't let her go. With unsteady fingers she tugged at the bandages on her arms. 'Do you and all the others think that selling my blood as I did was no better than selling my body? Do you all look down on me like some sort of . . . whore?'

'No, Eleanor,' Sir Percy said gently. 'We don't.'

'They do. He's lying.' Anima was seated at her writing table opposite Eleanor – though since when had there been a writing table in the cell? – and toying with a quill pen which gleamed palely in the darkness. Just as when Eleanor had seen her in her memories before, Anima wore a furred mantle against the cold, and a wimple of white cloth was wrapped round her head. Her eyes were a pale, faded blue, and she looked at Eleanor without compassion or mercy. 'They considered you a useful tool. So did I. But now you've failed both of us, you know what happens. Out on the street without a character.'

'But I didn't fail you.' She knew Anima was dead. Long past dead. Her ghost had left Eleanor, deserting her in the middle of Paris and neck deep in danger. Now she was just sitting there, writing with an angel's feather as her quill, looking down her nose at Eleanor as she grovelled on the floor. 'I've been trying—'

'Trying isn't good enough,' Anima said crisply. 'In your current situation, it's either success or death. It's like the law in France – you're either innocent or you're dead. Do you have any witnesses to speak in your favour?'

Sir Percy raised a hand. 'If I might say a word?'

'You talk constantly and say nothing.' Anima dipped her pen in ink and wrote something down. 'The Recording Angel will not be deceived or mocked. Why do you encourage this child to waste her time on petty rescues when she should be doing something *important*? This work outweighs her life. She has no time to rest.'

'I wouldn't say the people whom we saved thought they were *petty* rescues,' Sir Percy objected. 'And do you expect her to die for your cause? You're no better than one of those revolutionaries, madam. She has a right to the things every woman wants – a happy life, a husband, children . . .'

'Tell that to your Marguerite next time you put yourself at risk,' Anima snapped. 'Do you ask for her permission before you go gallivanting off to play your *game*, to enjoy your *sport*?'

'I can't say I noticed you asking Eleanor's permission before anything you did,' Sir Percy countered. 'Since when did she agree to enrol in your crusade against the vampires? 'Pon my word, I believe you'd rather have thrown in your lot with the National Convention if you had a free hand in the matter. At least they'd have let you pursue your vendetta without consequences.'

'You're arguing without me,' Eleanor said weakly. 'Aren't I here? Wasn't it my own blood? Doesn't that matter?'

'Ah, the very person I wanted,' Anima said. 'Eleanor, tell this *English gentleman* that your life is unimportant when it comes to a higher purpose. You are to write your name on history in blood. Hurry now, I have no time for the lazy and incompetent.'

'Nonsense,' Sir Percy said. 'Eleanor's on my side entirely, aren't you, m'dear? Why, I can offer you money and comfort and happiness, and all you need to do is sit back and take my orders like a good girl. What more can you ask for?'

But she wasn't listening any more. She curled up, tears trickling from her eyes, hot and unstoppable, as she thought of every time she'd cut into her own flesh to provide blood for her mistress. *Her owner.* Fragmented echoes of revolutionary speeches from France danced in her ears, phrases glorifying the equality of the people, that no man was born superior to any other, that nobody had the right to anyone else's blood or body or toil. And even though she knew from practical experience that those words were idealistic dreams, which only someone like her friend Fleurette could believe, and that daily life in France simply wasn't that sort of paradise, still she *wanted* them to be true.

Was it really so bad to want such a life?

Dawn light started filtering in through the window. Someone was weeping in the next-door cell. Keys jangled at the door of her own cell. She tried to blot away the tears from her face, but her hands still trembled. At least if she was going to die, she could try to be brave . . .

The door swung open. Two men stood there, heavyset fellows wearing stained linen smocks over their normal clothing. They weren't wearing tricolour rosettes, though. That was strange. Everyone else in Paris wore the tricolour by day and night, if only because they were too afraid not to. She looked sideways at Sir Percy and Anima to gauge their reactions, but they were gone.

'Now you don't give us no trouble, lass, and this'll be easier on you,' the first one said.

'You're speaking English,' Eleanor said, confused.

The two men exchanged glances. The second one muttered something in the other's ear, and he nodded understandingly. 'That we are. This is London, after all.'

Eleanor reached up to touch her hair, confused. Why had her hair been shorn if she wasn't going to the guillotine? Where was she? 'I don't understand,' she whispered.

'At least she ain't making no fuss,' the second man said. Unshaven patches dotted his cheeks, and the smell of his pomade turned Eleanor's stomach, even from where he stood in the doorway. 'Now you stay sitting down there and I'll bring you your dose and the bowl, and then the medicine. James, you keep the door and mind she don't run for it.'

Eleanor would have liked to feel strong enough to run, but her legs were weak beneath her and she knew she'd simply end up measuring her own length on the floor, in front of these two strangers. 'I won't make a fuss,' she lied. 'I just . . . please, sirs, tell me where I am?'

'Don't you know?' the first one said.

The second elbowed him. 'Course she don't. The Physician said as how she thought she was in France half the time, didn't he? Poor lass,' he added, in an afternote that was clearly meant more for form than out of any genuine sympathy. 'No, you're in London, and you should be glad of it. Who'd want to be in France?'

Eleanor thought she could see light through her confusion. She must have been knocked out by Lady Sophie's agents, and they'd brought her here – wherever *here* was – as a prisoner. Her mood rose, and she felt the imagined cold breath of steel against her neck recede. 'I see. Thank you, sir. But then where am I?'

'You're in Bedlam, lass.' He stepped forward, and she fell

back in response, but the cell was small and she had nowhere to run. 'Now open your mouth and take your dose like a good girl.'

She'd fought back, struggling weakly in their grasp, but they'd treated her like a dog being dosed, forcing a cupful of bitter liquid down her throat and then holding her head over a bowl while she vomited. Once that was done, she'd been made to drink from another flask that the second man was carrying, and finally left to lie on her pallet while her head spun and her stomach ached.

'Now don't you fret, lass,' the first man consoled her, with the jolly heartiness of a man who hadn't just been purged and drugged. 'This is good for what ails you. It's clear you want to be of sound mind and body, and they say that's what gets a man or woman back on their feet fastest of all.'

'I want to go home,' Eleanor whispered. She'd meant to say it more loudly. The fragility of her voice terrified her. She couldn't speak. She couldn't concentrate. She couldn't do anything.

A fragment of memory came back to her. Anima telling her of how the vampires had managed to capture her and keep her subdued with drugs, then left her to die. Eleanor's eyes wandered to the flask hanging on the second man's belt – a leather bottle of much better quality than the one holding the medicine which had made her vomit.

More pieces fitted themselves together in her mind. Lady Sophie . . . she was old. She'd been there back then, during the war between mages and vampires. She'd know about such drugs. If she was behind Eleanor's imprisonment, and had given these men the means to keep her subdued – though no doubt she'd have lied about *why* they should administer it to Eleanor – then Eleanor could whistle for any hope of being able to command the winds, or even the faintest breeze. She had only her mortal abilities, and here and now, she couldn't even stand upright.

'The sooner you're of sound mind, the sooner you'll be out of here,' the first man reassured her. He patted her shoulder, his firm hand painful against some of the bruises he'd inflicted earlier while they held her down. 'Get some sleep. The visitors will be here soon.'

The door closed behind them, and the key turned in the lock.

Eleanor rested her head in her hands and tried to think. She knew about the visitors who came to Bedlam. Rich men and women paraded around, peering into the cells, and laughed at the madmen. She'd disapproved of it in a perfectly rational and charitable way before, and then not bothered thinking about it any further, because she'd never once imagined she'd be locked in here herself.

A brief, blinding hope came to her – that one of the visitors might actually be acquainted with a member of the League and could carry a message for her. This was just as quickly extinguished by painful common sense. Why would any person of rank and quality believe a dirty, half-dressed woman in a cell here? They'd simply assume she was . . . mad.

She was also dreadfully aware that while she hadn't been treated well by any stretch of the imagination, she could have been treated a great deal worse. Better not to risk offending the guards until she was absolutely certain what to do and how to do it.

Until? the back of her mind mocked her. *You're assuming that you'll find some chance to escape. What if no such opportunity ever comes? What if this cell is going to be your home for the rest of your life?*

No. She couldn't, *wouldn't* think that way. The League had rescued helpless victims from worse gaols than Bedlam.

In fact, she tried to convince herself with tentative optimism, Bedlam might be a great deal *easier* than many gaols, because nobody ever expected intruders to break *into* a madhouse. It was always the other way around.

Eleanor tried to remember anything she knew about Bedlam, or about madhouses in general. The few fragments she could recall were either utterly prosaic or obviously the stuff of fiction. On the practical side, she knew from the newspapers that such places were generally for the relatives of rich people who could afford the fees to lodge an insane family member there, but Bedlam was one of the few hospitals that would accept the poor and indigent. The more extravagant three-volume novels she'd read had informed her that such places were where a hapless innocent was locked up by a cruel relative who intended to steal her money, force her into marriage, or both.

She realized she was giggling uncontrollably. Now it was her turn to be shut up in a madhouse. But that only happened to beautiful waifs who wandered around in trailing white gowns and fainted at the slightest threat. Such lovely maidens were usually rescued by their heroic true love, who would snatch them out of peril, and then the story would end with a wedding.

Eleanor bit her tongue until she stopped snickering. She had to do something. Perhaps if there was a doctor who made some sort of rounds of the patients, she could convince him she wasn't mad? She had no way of knowing what story Lady Sophie might have told to ensure she was locked up here, but a real doctor – a man of education and experience – would surely recognize her sanity?

Noise echoed through the building. Other patients were awake now too. There were murmurs of conversation, cries, screams, whimpers – a background tapestry of sound, like the noise of a busy market, or the chorus of the opera Eleanor had been present at a month ago. With an effort of will, she tried to ignore it.

What would the Chief do? Everything she'd seen earlier must have been a hallucination. Sir Percy wasn't here with her, not in Bedlam, and Anima even less so. But she'd heard a great many stories – from the others, not from Sir Percy himself – of daring escapes from French gaols and how he'd gone about it.

Eleanor waited till her stomach was more settled, then pulled herself up against the wall and staggered over to the window. Again she noticed there were no panes of glass, no shutters, merely closely spaced bars – too close for her to attempt any escape by that means. It was set high enough in the wall that she had to go up on her tiptoes and hold on to the bars merely to peer outside.

She was astonished to see green space beyond, with lawns – looking ill-kept in the early morning light, and yellowing from a lack of water, but still lawns. Across from them ran a parallel wing of the building where she was imprisoned, studded with cell windows like her own on the ground and first floors. As far as she could see, the whole building was shaped like a U, and she was in one of the long wings which formed its verticals. She was at least on the ground floor – that was something. *Never turn down an advantage*, the Chief would say. But it was little comfort when there was no hope of squeezing out through this window. Even though the wall showed signs of age, with crumbling plaster and rusty bars, it was a thoroughly impassable barrier.

She heard the sound of approaching footsteps and voices, and quickly slumped back down on her pallet, finding very little difficulty in adopting an air of dejection. Some of the voices had the refined accents of the upper class, and her throat tightened with desperate hope.

But the voices retreated, laughter mingled with disgust in their tones, and she was left sitting on her pallet alone.

Imprisonment in Bedlam was many things, she decided eventually. It was miserable, it was cheap (that realization came after lunch, when she was given a slice of bread and a cup of gruel, and watched by the hard-bitten woman who doled out the gruel as though she expected Eleanor to go for her throat at any moment). It was noisy at the worst moments and quiet at the most terrifying, and the building itself was old enough that it needed a revolutionary commission to tear it down and build something more useful. But most of all, it was *boring*. She'd never sat so long alone with nothing to do and nobody to speak to. Her hands ached to be sewing or embroidering or tatting, or simply cleaning. It didn't help that she still felt sick and dizzy as well, yet she couldn't bring herself to try to sleep. Every second noise outside had her catching her breath in tense hope that it might be one of the League, or a servant they'd suborned, or . . . anyone.

It was late afternoon by the time one of the parties of visitors chose to peer in through the grille in her door. She could see the outlines of expensive hats and elegant coiffures of powdered hair, and hear every casual word.

'And what is it that troubles this poor child?' A man's voice. 'Faith, she seems quiet enough, sitting there by herself. Is she a melancholic?'

'That ain't it precisely, sir.' She'd heard this voice on and off throughout the day, explaining the maladies of other prisoners for the benefit of the visitors. He must be one of the regular staff here, like the two men who'd dosed her this morning. 'This poor girl here is a victim of what the doctors call haematological crisis.' He sounded out the long word, clearly unsure of its pronunciation, and probably even more uncertain of its spelling. Eleanor wondered what it meant. 'It's driven her to insanity, poor child.'

'Oh, really? Do tell us.' There was a clink of coins being exchanged. 'My dear Petronia here simply *loves* hearing about new diseases. Something to do with blood, I take it?'

'You're dead right, milord. There's some folk whose bodies make too much blood, the doctors say, and if it's not released from their bodies, it puts pressure on their brain and causes mania. Maybe even an aneurysm.' Another word which clearly required thought. 'This poor girl was in service and giving blood, and because of that nobody knew as how she was subject to the ravages of this here disease. But when she wasn't giving blood for long enough . . . well. It's a shame to say what happened, it truly is.'

Eleanor was reasonably certain there was no such disease. At least . . . she didn't think there was.

'Oh, how dreadful!' a woman's voice gasped. It had a tone to it which suggested she was constantly gasping in shock, awe, or horror at the state of the world. 'To think a helpless young woman like this might be condemned by the cruel touch of Fate in such a way!'

'Well, do go on,' the male aristocratic voice said. 'Can't leave us dangling in the winds of curiosity, what?'

'She was afflicted with delusions,' the Bedlam attendant said solemnly. 'And committed murder, milord, bloody murder! She'd go sneaking out of the house by night, and she took a knife to three young men of good family! It was a proper tragedy. Now you might ask why she's not chained up with the more violent types on the upper floor, milord . . .'

'I am rather curious about that,' the male visitor said. 'Strikes me that she's a sight more dangerous than you'd expect from the winsome little chit that she is.'

'It's because once she was got back on a proper course of bleeding, she didn't remember none of it, milord,' the attendant said. 'When she gets into her mania and into a bloody spasm, she's fair delusional and claims she's a revolutionary from France, come over here to gut all the aristocrats. But as long as she's bled regular and dosed, she's as meek and mild as milk. The Physician says it's right tragic, but she's too dangerous to be allowed outside these walls. Why, what if it happened again?'

'The poor young woman!' That was the female visitor. 'Oh, pitiful girl, to be so abused by Nature! I wish we could do something about it.'

Such as offer to take me out of here? Eleanor wondered cynically. Somehow she doubted it.

'Gervase, do give the fellow half a crown, will you? He can at least see that the girl has a clean gown. It seems too much for her to be sitting here in squalor of body as well as of mind.'

Eleanor wanted to scream. She wanted to lunge up against the door, wrench at the grille and tell these virtuous, high-minded, obnoxiously curious visitors that this was all a lie – she'd been imprisoned here against her will and they should tell Sir Percy Blakeney where she was. Also, that the attendant certainly wouldn't spend any of that money on getting her a clean gown. It'd only go to cover his tab at the nearest alehouse.

Instead she bit her lip and kept her head lowered. Being underestimated had always served her well so far. Let them think her meek. Let them think her broken. Let them assume she wasn't dangerous. She'd find some way to use that against them while she waited for the League to rescue her from the asylum.

But the fear at the back of her mind wouldn't go away: what if Lady Sophie decided she was too dangerous to be allowed to live? What if the wardens of Bedlam were used to lunatics pretending to be harmless?

And what if the League never came?

CHAPTER TEN

It was late that evening, after a second dose of the drug and a couple of slices of bread, when they took her out of the cell. She stumbled on the tiled floor, her bare feet recoiling from the cold surface, as the two warders marched her down the long gallery. Detritus from the day's visitors – orange-peel, paper cones which had held sweets, newspapers, fragments of sweet-smelling bouquets – had been swept into corners, leaving the main passage mostly empty and uncluttered. To right and to left the grilles set into cell doors seemed to watch her. She wondered how many other prisoners had crept up to the bars to see her go past, in search of a moment's distraction from the grinding misery of this place.

The two wardens were the same men who'd come to see her this morning, and while neither of them was harsh, they treated her warily, as though she was a rabbit who might bolt at any moment. *No, not a rabbit. A mad dog who could bite.*

'Can't see why he's come this late,' the second man grumbled to the first over Eleanor's head. 'And can't see why the Physician's sending a specialist for this girl, either. They already know what the problem is with her, don't they?'

'Ah,' the first man said, meaningfully, 'but he's one of *them*. Stands to reason *they'd* take an interest in this sort of case. Fact is . . .' He lowered his voice, but Eleanor could still hear every word, given that he was walking less than a foot from her. 'I've heard some doctors say this sort of thing is more common than they think. Look at France.'

The second man frowned, chewing on his tobacco. 'You mean . . .'

'I mean look at how these things go together. No vampires, and a bloody revolution. Stands to reason, see?'

The second man's frown deepened. 'But didn't they have their revolution first?'

'I'm just saying it makes sense,' the first man said, retreating, as Anima would once have put it, from the logical grounds of cause and effect to the more comfortable position of *sounds reasonable to me*. Oh, the stab of misery Eleanor felt at the thought that the old mage had truly left her.

The same man gave Eleanor a prod in the ribs. 'Now remember, girl, stand where you're put, don't sit down until you're told you can, and don't you touch nothing. Understand?'

'Yes, sir,' Eleanor whispered. She was desperately trying to raise her power – any power at all – and finding herself as empty as a dry rain-butt in July. Silently she cursed the drugs they'd given her.

The gate at the end of the gallery was opened – a serious piece of ironwork, Eleanor noted, and something which would stop a grown man, let alone a housemaid. It was closed behind them and locked again. Eleanor tried to observe events as she was sure other members of the League would have done, looking for any sign of carelessness or laxity. But all she could see were sensible habits carefully observed. While she wasn't exactly wishing they would be loose enough in their habits to allow the lunatics here to run free, she *did* wish they could be a little less reliable.

Her sense of the building's geography told her they were

now in the horizontal part of the U, between the two wings. This part of the building was *much* nicer – or at least, much cleaner. She could identify the direction of the kitchen and laundry just by sniffing the air and picking out the odours of bread, cabbage and bleach. However, she wasn't led to either location, which she regretted. She'd have known how to deal with those. There was an odd smell behind them, though, something sweet which she didn't recognize . . .

'Here she is, Doctor,' the first guard said, shepherding her into what was clearly the study of a gentleman of leisure. 'Will you be wanting us to stay in case she attacks you?'

The man – no, the vampire – who was seated at the mahogany roll-top desk looked up and set his pen down. 'No, I think not. Wait outside, and I'll call you when I need you.'

It was Castleton, looking just as he'd done in Oxford. His white hair – natural, not even needing the services of wig and powder – was caught back in a club, and his clothing was in restrained shades of black and grey. A flush on his cheeks suggested he had fed recently. Incongruously, there was a plate on the desk in front of him, with white bread and sliced ham, and a cup of water, though such things would be of no use to him.

For a long moment the two of them stared at each other, while the door closed behind Eleanor. Castleton finally said, almost gently, 'Well, you might as well sit down.'

There was only one place for a visitor to sit: a high-backed chair, set directly in front of the desk, heavy wood with no cushioning. Straps on the arms and legs suggested it could and would be used to restrain violent prisoners. Eleanor obediently took a seat, but she couldn't bring herself to rest her forearms on the sides of the chair, so close to those innocently dangling pieces of leather.

'Aren't you going to say anything?' he asked.

'You know I'm not insane,' Eleanor said flatly.

'Oh, absolutely,' he agreed. 'Unfortunately for you, Maggie Johnson – that would be you, of course – has been admitted here with all the necessary folderols and standard matters of form. There is no question at all of permitting her to leave. A case of murder – have you heard?'

'I heard one of the wardens talking about it,' Eleanor said sourly. 'Have you actually had three men killed, in case anyone asks questions?'

'My dear girl, what do you take us for? We would hardly go around killing people wastefully.' He smiled, and there was a flash of fang. 'Besides, nobody is going to ask any questions.'

Eleanor had to admit this was true. Her head ached, but she forced herself to sit up straight and ignore the churning of hunger and nausea in her belly. 'Why are *you* here?' she asked. 'Have you become a doctor in your leisure time?'

'Hardly. There are three gentlemen in authority here – the Apothecary, the Physician and the Surgeon – and the Apothecary's the only one of the three who lives on the premises. No, I am a visitor, come purely out of charity and helpfulness – sent by your mistress, who is paying your bills. I trust you are grateful?'

'I'd gladly spare her the trouble and take myself elsewhere,' Eleanor said drily. She rubbed her arms and shivered. Despite the July weather, it was cold in here. 'If she has no wish to waste her funds, I've no desire to make her spend them.'

'A noble attitude, but quite out of the question. For the moment, at least, you will not be leaving.'

That wasn't a surprise. 'Then what do you want, sir?'

'Ah. Straight to the point. You have no idea how much of a relief that is. So much of my days are spent dancing around the circumlocutions and hinted suggestions of my

elders. Then, when one fails a task due to a quite unreasonable lack of information, one is . . . well, let's not go into
details.' He smiled again. 'Lady Sophie is disinclined to visit.
She's taken a shocking aversion to you. The words *betrayal*
and *traitress* were used frequently. I believe she mentioned
that she took you from a broom – or is that the Duchess of
Marlborough and Abigail Masham I'm thinking of? Never
mind. The allusion is clear enough. Short of an extremely
sincere apology, she has no desire to see you.'

'She was going to kill Charles!' Eleanor snarled at him.
'Don't you have anything to say about that? I thought you
were Charles's *friend*.'

'He wouldn't have been killed,' Castleton said patiently.
'Quite the contrary, considering matters in the long term. He
would simply have needed to reconsider his loyalties. It would
be a pleasure to journey side by side with him into eternity.'

'Or you'd lock him up in Bedlam?'

'Oh, that only happens to the poor, the weak and the
defenceless.' That smile of his could be surprisingly
unpleasant. 'Charles is none of those things. You, on the
other hand . . .'

Eleanor's attempts to appear innocent and helpless finally
burned up like paper in her sheer fury at the way he was
looking at her. It was of a piece with all the others – vampires,
servants of vampires, people who wanted a few extra pence
and saw her as saleable goods – who simply considered her
a lesser being. Not even as a some*one*, but just a some*thing*
that could be sold, could be bled and could be killed. She
took a deep breath and adopted the manner of Marie
Antoinette, which Lady Marguerite had worked so hard to
train into her. 'My dear sir, would you kindly omit the
attempts to frighten me and come to the point? I am sure
you have a busy night ahead of you, and I would not wish
to detain you.'

'Very well.' He sat back in his chair. His eyes glinted green in the light from the candles. 'We are reasonable people. We are prepared to negotiate. I am certain you know what we want – or rather, *who* we want.'

'The League,' Eleanor said flatly. 'No.' Relief spread through her in a wave that for a moment almost quieted her stomach and soothed her headache. Castleton still didn't know where they were? She'd been trying not to think about whether the others had been captured too – and what had happened to them if they had. The vampires could hardly imprison them in Bedlam under false names, given the chance that aristocratic visitors might recognize them, but there were so many places in England that one could hide prisoners . . .

He blinked, long eyelashes giving him an air of boyish confusion. Had he been a living man, Eleanor had to confess she would have been attracted. 'Don't play the fool. I mean your superiors. Your teachers. The details of your initiation and lessons. Lady Sophie may not value your company, but she is highly interested in your answers to such questions. And what were you doing in Oxford with Charles? What were you looking for there?'

Eleanor's breath caught in her throat, and she lowered her gaze, seeking a moment of clarity to decide how best to answer. How best to *lie*. If they were asking this sort of question, then they *didn't* have Charles – or any of the others – and they didn't have the scroll case. They didn't have anything except her.

This had happened before, in the tunnels under Paris, when Marie Antoinette had assumed she was merely one member (and a very junior one) of a greater order of mages who had succeeded in remaining hidden until now. The whole business had given Eleanor some practice in bluffing on the subject, and did at least mean she wouldn't respond to Castleton with blank shock and obvious incomprehension.

Because, she suspected, the fact the vampires believed there were other mages had just saved her life. To them she was a useful tool, who could be used to hunt down those others. Had they known she was the only one – in England, at least, though who knew about foreign lands? – then they would simply have disposed of her, as one gets rid of a rotted apple before it can corrupt the barrel.

'You must think I'm very easily convinced to turn traitor,' she finally said. The raw emotion behind her words was entirely sincere.

'I think you're sensible, as are we.' His shoulders had relaxed a fraction. 'Tell me, is it worth it?'

'Is what worth it?'

'Being a prisoner here in Bedlam, Eleanor.' It was the first time he'd called her by her name. 'A diet of bread and broth and daily purges. Being bled every two days. Sleeping on straw and listening to the screams from the cells alongside. Knowing the rich and famous will come and peer in on you as a curiosity. The choice of whether or not you die here is entirely your own.'

'How much choice does a maidservant ever have?' Eleanor parried. She needed time. Dear God, she needed time. The longer they kept her alive, the more chance that the League might somehow find her and rescue her. But if they decided she was uncooperative and of no further use to them . . .

'Clearly some choice, or you wouldn't have reached this far.' He leaned his elbow on the desk, resting his chin on his hand. 'I must say I'm quite impressed. You have, after all, worked your way in among the League of the Scarlet Pimpernel: quite a feat for someone who isn't one of *them*.' He used the pronoun with a different inflection from the warders and their earlier talk of vampires; there was a subtle note of anger to his voice.

'One of them?' Eleanor asked. She wasn't sure why he was bitter, but she was prepared to pursue any clue to the personality of this man who held power over her.

Castleton twitched a shoulder in a shrug. 'The rich. The well born. Those who simply stroll into their positions and never even consider how close death and disaster come to them.'

'I don't understand,' Eleanor said. 'I thought you were one of Charles's friends . . .'

His green eyes had become distant. 'Yes, we were friends, at Oxford, and before that. Even though his father was an earl and mine was only a vicar. But when consumption invades the lungs, how much use is friendship then? When you must struggle for each breath, wealth will not save you, birth and lands are of no avail. Whatever he might have *said*, however many times he might have expressed his sympathy, he could *do* nothing. And so instead I went in search of those who could help me. Isn't that what any sensible, reasonable person would do? What sort of fool lets himself die when there are other options available?'

What would Charles have done, if he'd felt the slow death of consumption in his own lungs? Eleanor didn't know. She didn't *want* to know.

'So you approached them?' she asked tentatively.

'Oh, there are ways to make such arrangements, even if the channels are petty and frivolous. De Courcis . . .' He sniffed, making his opinion clear. 'The fellow's a wastrel and worse, a bore. But he was my path to life. If that means I have to pretend to be his friend and run the errands of Lady Sophie and others for a few decades, then it's a small price to pay.'

'That seems . . . almost a shame,' Eleanor said, feeling out the boundaries of this strange new intimacy carefully. 'When I saw you at the Victims' Ball last month, I thought you seemed good friends.'

'I suppose there's little actually wrong with him,' Castleton allowed grudgingly, 'but frankly I would rather spend my time more productively. There's work being done on which I would far rather spend my time, together with some like-minded companion who could challenge my thinking and restore my passion for knowledge.'

The word *Charles* formed in Eleanor's mouth, but she kept it firmly behind her lips. If he didn't realize he'd just given himself away, then she wasn't going to tell him.

'And now that I've told you something, I think it's your turn,' he said, without changing his tone. 'Tell me about your magic, Eleanor.'

She shrugged. 'What could I tell you that Lady Sophie doesn't already know?'

'A great deal, I imagine.'

Could it be that Lady Sophie wasn't inclined to share the information she held? 'I know so little,' she parried, 'and understand even less. But I'm told that vampires are unable to use magic.'

'That would be because it's unnatural,' Castleton said, 'and as vampires are a natural thing, what you call magic is repulsive to them.' He paused. 'Or so *I'm* told.'

'By Lady Sophie?'

'By Lady Sophie.' He pushed the plate on the desk forward slightly. She could see the sleek butter on the white bread, the rich pink of the ham. 'Would you like something to eat, Eleanor?'

Her stomach seized into knots at the very thought of being filled with such good food. Her face must have betrayed her, for he said encouragingly, 'There is no need for you to *harm* yourself by allowing yourself to be starved.

We are merely talking, making conversation. Why not strengthen yourself with something a little better than gruel and crusts?'

'Because it might be drugged,' Eleanor said quickly, wanting to convince herself this was so, before her treacherous thoughts could come up with a dozen reasons as to why it wouldn't do any harm for her to eat.

Castleton shook his head. 'If I wanted to drug you, I'd simply have the wardens do it. You must know that by now.'

Eleanor had no counter to that. She took a deep breath. 'Because you want me to,' she said.

'And now you're behaving like a child throwing a tantrum, declaring *I will not* merely to spite me, and spiting yourself by doing so.'

She looked him in the eyes. 'I'm not sure you're any older than me, sir. And I don't know about you, but I was always told bullying was a mean, vicious thing to do.'

That had been close. She'd nearly said *my mother always told me*. By the grace of God Lady Sophie hadn't yet seemed to think of threatening her mother, and she wasn't going to offer this new tormentor any helpful ideas.

'My dear Eleanor – I may call you that, mayn't I?'

'I prefer it to Maggie Johnson,' Eleanor said sweetly.

'Is it too much to ask you to be reasonable? You don't *have* to sit in squalor and live off crusts. It isn't *necessary* to drug you daily and bleed you every few days. You are the only one forcing us to do this. I'm not even asking you to hand the League over to us – they're an entirely different problem, and one that is being dealt with even as we speak.' He let the words hang in the air for a moment, just long enough to inspire the worst possible ideas as to what he might mean. 'We simply want to discuss magic, and who taught you, and other such things. There's room for all of us. England is a large place, and the world still larger. Our paths have come into conflict, it's true, but they don't have to stay that way. Why, in the long term, you might even find it more rewarding to join us.'

'Join you?' Eleanor said slowly.

'We recognize talent. Consider my progression. How often do you think a vicar's son rises to this level of power?'

Eleanor dragged herself back from trying to argue the point. She could recognize a carrot when it was being dangled in front of her. No doubt he'd be back to the stick again once the carrot failed to work. 'Are you going to promise me riches and land, and a patent of nobility as well, sir?' she asked politely.

'I'm promising you the most important thing of all,' Castleton said calmly, not rising to provocation. 'Life. From what Lady Sophie has told me, a mage dies within a man's normal span of years – or a woman's. If you want more than that, and if you want to accompany Charles into eternity, then you'll think about what I've just said.'

For a moment his words tempted Eleanor into imagining it. Herself as a vampire, immortal, unchanging, a young woman forever, never touched by age, never fearing death, with Charles beside her . . .

Then she remembered the Victims' Ball, and the vampires walking around her, along with the other servants who'd been providing blood, prowling like wolves around them all, breathless and cold and *famished*. Perhaps she could, in her worst nightmares, have seen herself as one of the vampires there – but not Charles. Never Charles.

He'd been ready to die in Oxford to allow her to escape. That was something a vampire could never do. Because, as Castleton had confirmed, and as Anima also had told her before, life was to them the most important thing of all. In the end, the *only* important thing.

Castleton must have read the rejection in her eyes, for he

shrugged. 'Perhaps you will change your mind later. We are in no hurry.' He moved the plate away from her again and smiled as she deliberately averted her eyes from the food.

'How much has Lady Sophie told you?' she asked, returning to the earlier point.

'Very little.' His eyes narrowed. 'You could make a good friend of me by telling me more, Eleanor.'

I could, couldn't I? Just for so long as I'm useful. Eleanor wondered how many other young vampires like him were as hungry for power as they were for blood. And she wondered how long Lady Sophie might survive if she were to turn her back on Castleton once too often.

She forced herself to sit up straight again. 'I'm not making any deals,' she said. 'And I'm not telling any secrets.'

Castleton shrugged once more. 'In that case, I will leave you to your sleep,' he said. 'We have no need to force you, when we can simply wait. I believe they will be letting your blood again tomorrow. It is a regular treatment for the afflicted here. As are the cold baths – though perhaps you will be grateful for a little cleanliness.'

Curiosity pricked at her. 'Is there truly such a thing as a haemo— no, haematological crisis?' She tried to remember what the warden had said. 'Some disease which demands that people must be bled, or they will go insane?'

'The doctors have begun to say so,' Castleton said softly, 'and who'd argue with his doctor? There may be a good many rich men and women who are relieved to discover the insubordination of their servants has such an easy explanation, and such a convenient remedy.'

Eleanor shivered, from fear and disgust rather than the unseasonable cold. 'Yes. Very convenient.'

'The more of us there are, the more blood we require. It is a simple enough equation.'

Fragments of conversation from the coach ride to Oxford

flocked at the back of her memory. What was it Kitty had said she'd overheard? '. . . *maybe more of your young men as serve the King as soldiers . . . if they weren't just human then we'd win more battles in France . . .'*

France had changed with the Revolution. How much might England change in response? And how much blood might England need to provide, to sustain her vampires?

'You're very quick to talk about *them* and *us*,' Eleanor finally said. 'How long has it been that you've been a vampire, sir? Less than a year?'

Castleton didn't answer this. Instead he rose to his feet. 'I'll call the warders to have them return you to your cell, *Maggie*. A deluded girl like you needs her sleep. In a day or two I'll return to speak with you again. Hopefully you won't have done anything by then which might cause you to be moved upstairs, to where they house the violent lunatics. It could be an unpleasant experience – but sadly necessary.'

Eleanor bit her lip and didn't answer.

'I suggest you not leave matters *too* long,' he added. 'After all, you are only a human – and humans are such fragile things.'

CHAPTER ELEVEN

'Please listen to me, madam!' Eleanor had begged, clinging to the grille in the door. Her patience had run dry after days of imprisonment, hunger and drugs; she had resolved to at least attempt an appeal to the onlookers. 'I promise you that I'm a sane woman. I've been shut up here due to the cruelty of my mistress – first she accused me of theft, then when my innocence of that was proven, she called me mad and had me locked up here instead.'

The two elderly ladies by her door had looked at each other and tutted, the fringe on their bonnets shivering with every shake of their heads. Their escort, an elderly clergyman, merely frowned. 'The mad will lie as easily as breathing,' he had pronounced sadly, 'and think themselves to be telling the truth. Poor child. I will pray for you.'

Eleanor had bitten her tongue so hard she could taste the blood. She couldn't afford to lose her temper and scream or beg; that would merely confirm to them that she was deluded, insane and untrustworthy. Tears stood in her eyes. 'Please, ladies, sir – if you will carry a message for me—'

That had been yesterday. Her fingers still ached where the warder had casually used his strap on them, knocking her back from the grille to flinch against the wall. 'It's a right shame,' he'd said to the visitors. 'If the poor young woman is claiming these things, then it stands to reason her haematological crisis is afflicting her again. I'll leave word that she's to be bled tomorrow.'

Eleanor found herself looking back to the house arrest she'd been caught under in France with a certain fondness. After all, while she hadn't been short of honest work to do there, they *had* fed her. Baths had not consisted of a bucket of cold water – or worse, several buckets of cold water. Fleurette's society had been a joy. Chauvelin himself might be a cold-blooded agent of the Committee of Public Safety, who'd happily send the entire League to the guillotine and consider it a job well done, but his daughter Fleurette had been a delight. She was open, friendly, cheerful, sweet-natured and everything Eleanor could have asked for in a friend. It was saddening to think that now Fleurette was safe with her father in Paris, Eleanor would probably never see her again.

Unless perhaps the war with France ended, and France's revolution failed – or changed somehow, so that it was no longer the terrible scourge which drove half of France's citizens to betray the other half for fear of going to the guillotine themselves. And oh, yes, Eleanor herself was somehow freed from here, and became able to save up the money to travel to France, with Fleurette actually *wanting* to see her or being allowed to do so by her father . . .

There was nothing to do here except daydream. That was the worst of it. The constant dizziness from the drugs and the gnawing pangs of hunger could be endured. The weariness from too-frequent bloodletting worried Eleanor, though. Like most servants who'd given blood, she knew how much she could give and stay healthy, and being bled every couple of days would soon have her unable to stir from her pallet. But her boredom and the utter lack of anything to do was even worse. She could only stare at the walls or out of the window, listening to the screams and crying from the other cells along the long gallery, or be bitterly amused by the comments of the warders as they pointed her out to rich visitors. So far her tally had been raised to killing a dozen men by slashing their throats. At this rate they'd soon be accusing her of building a guillotine for her private use.

She still hoped, of course. She could hardly prevent herself from doing so. With each visit by wealthy sightseers – the idle nobly born, the newly rich who had grown that way through trade, the visitors from the countryside wanting to see the sights of London, or would-be novelists and play-wrights looking for inspiration – she prayed to hear a voice she might recognize, however foolish its apparent words might be. But then she had to remind herself that Lady Sophie, and the vampires working with her, already knew who most of the League were, and would be watching all the visitors coming here . . .

The back of her neck was still cold where her hair had been shorn. The whole building was cold. It was as though some icy chill permeated the entire hospital, wafting up from the cellars (where, the woman in the next cell whispered, the bodies of murdered patients had been secretly buried). It defeated the July heat with an iciness like that of death itself. Even Castleton's visits – three, so far – were a welcome distraction.

Footsteps came tramping along the gallery outside and stopped outside her cell. She raised her head to stare at the grille out of curiosity. She'd already been given her daily doses, so it shouldn't be *that*, but it was too early for visitors.

The key turned in the lock. Castleton was there, strategically standing behind a pair of warders. Did he worry she might still have enough power to light a fire which would burn the flesh from his bones? If only she did.

'Not sure she's up to walking, sir,' one of the warders said.

'She can walk or be dragged,' Castleton said flatly. 'The choice is hers.'

Eleanor swayed to her feet, supporting herself against the wall. She'd been plunged in cold water yesterday, so she wasn't as dirty as she might have been, but her dress would mark her as a slattern from fifty paces distant. 'Where are we going?' she asked, her voice a whisper.

'To the men's side of this establishment,' Castleton said. 'I wish you to meet a man named James Tilly Matthews.'

The warders glanced at each other on hearing that name, but made no outright sounds of disapproval, and Eleanor's mood lightened slightly. The warders might be carelessly cruel, but the ones who'd dealt with her weren't outright vicious. She pulled her courage together and followed him, flanked by the two heavyset men.

The men's gallery was laid out exactly like the women's, and there was little difference between the two in practice, except for the pitch of complaining voices behind the locked doors. Castleton didn't bother to pause before any of the cells, though Eleanor caught the glitter of watching eyes as she was escorted past. At length he came to a stop before a cell near the far end, and he waved Eleanor up to the grille. 'Observe,' he said.

Eleanor peered inside. The man sitting in the pale early morning light showed no signs of violent madness. He had, it appeared, been allowed charcoal and paper, and was scribbling something down. Stains on his sleeves showed that he, too, had been a victim of this place's regimen of bleeding its patients. His hair was unkempt and he was unshaven, but he looked a mild-mannered fellow. 'What am I supposed to see?' she asked.

Castleton's mouth quirked in an almost pitying smile.

'Mr Matthews,' he said, addressing the man, who looked up at his voice. 'We have a young lady here who wishes to hear about the air loom.'

'Ah.' The man set his papers aside and rose to his feet. Like Eleanor, he supported himself against the wall. 'Have you also been afflicted, madam?'

'Afflicted?' Eleanor asked.

'By their malignant workings.' He staggered to the door, meeting her eyes through the grille. 'They have placed a magnet in my brain, you see, which allows them to work upon me with the air loom, even here. I should perhaps be flattered to be the subject of their conspiracies. Many of their other victims are powerful men, rich and noble – they have corrupted Pitt himself and others of his party, as well as the revolutionaries in France. That is why we are kept at war, you see. They force it on us.'

'But how?' Could this man somehow also be aware of the vampire conspiracies? Eleanor felt a sudden surge of hope. If other people believed . . .

'The air loom, madam, the air loom!' His hands tightened on the bars of the grille. 'It is a device they have which allows them to implant thoughts into our heads. They go about their business thought-making and apoplexy-working, and should any man know too much, they burst his brain asunder, with lobster-cracking or bomb-bursting. They would do so to me, but I am not considered important enough. The magnet in my brain permits them to attain my thoughts and whisper in the shadows. They constantly attempt to poison me by emitting stenches into my cell.'

Eleanor sagged against the door. If this man was aware of anything that was going on, it was by pure coincidence or happenstance. He was quite mad.

'The air loom is an ingenious contrivance,' he went on, 'and I have been drawing diagrams of it for Mr Haslam the

Apothecary. They keep it in an underground room near here. It generates gaseous charges, and is fed with effluvia of copper and sulphur, vitriol and aqua fortis, hellebore and nightshade. There are fumes from cesspools and plague burial pits, and other liquids which I should not mention to one of your gender, madam. But you may be assured that they stink. They all stink.' He shivered. 'It is vital the men in power be made aware of these facts!'

'Mr Haslam the Apothecary takes a great interest in Mr Matthews,' Castleton remarked. 'It is by his grace that Mr Matthews is permitted charcoal and paper. Of course, Mr Matthews has visited France as well, which is how he knows that Frenchmen are the victims of the air loom too.'

'It is true, madam,' Matthews said. 'I was arrested and detained as a prisoner in Paris. But this only gave me a greater understanding of the scope of this conspiracy. When I returned to England, I found my business – I am a tea dealer, madam, an excellent tea dealer – had been declared bankrupt and my property taken from me. You see how even then the men and women behind this were working against me? They knew, they *knew* I would rise to oppose them, and they thought I might be eliminated before I could cause them any trouble. Yet I am not altogether silenced. Mr Haslam may not trust me, but he listens to me, and I have confidence that soon enough other men will do so too. They will be stopped. Jack the Schoolmaster, the Glove Woman, Sir Archy – once we have rooted them out and exposed their work, we can hope for peace in Europe. Is that not a glorious thought, madam?'

'And . . . vampires?' Eleanor asked.

He blinked. 'Why, vampires have nothing to do with it. Besides, it is known they have little sense of smell. I have heard of experiments being conducted, in which it has been proved by men of science that—'

'Enough,' Castleton said. His hand fell on Eleanor's shoulder, cold even through his glove, and he pulled her back from the door, letting the warders catch her as she staggered. 'A most enlightening conversation. Thank you, Mr Matthews.'

'Will Mr Haslam be calling by today, sir?'

'I'll let the Apothecary know you asked,' Castleton said. The rest of the journey back to Eleanor's cell was silent.

Once she was locked in her cell again, Castleton waved the warders back and watched her through the grille. 'Have I made my point?' he asked.

Eleanor's heart was like lead. He'd just demonstrated exactly what *she* would sound like if she tried to speak the truth more widely. That vampires really could control minds if they fed their blood to their victims. That men of power in both England and France – and probably other countries as well – were influenced by those vampires, and they could affect the course of the war, as well as more besides. She'd be rated as nothing more than a madwoman, properly locked up in Bedlam for her own safety. Previously she'd only suspected people would think her mad, but now she'd had her face well and truly rubbed in that knowledge.

She wouldn't give him the satisfaction, though. 'Is it true that you can't smell?' she asked.

Castleton's eyes widened in anger, and for a moment his fangs flashed as he opened his mouth to snarl a reprimand at her. Then he took a deep breath, and smiled, albeit with a perceptible effort. 'So you still have some spirit. Good. I wouldn't like to think you broke so easily. Some matters are worth taking one's time over.'

'If you aren't in a hurry, then why did you take me up there?' Eleanor said. 'Is Lady Sophie unhappy with your progress?'

'Believe me,' Castleton said, and this time his voice had a vicious edge to it, 'if Lady Sophie expresses her unhappiness to me, I will endeavour to make you feel every ounce of her displeasure. Are you enjoying your current lodgings? Would you rather be lodged on the first floor, with the violently insane? It would expand your education to hear them scream and scrabble at the walls all day and night. You have been gently treated so far, but if you make any further attempts to spread your lies to visitors . . .'

He turned and walked away.

Eleanor sat down on her pallet and rested her forehead on her knees. If Castleton thought it worth threatening her to enforce her silence, well then, surely her efforts weren't futile. She might still find someone among the visitors who'd listen to her. And she'd thought, the past couple of mornings, that perhaps she had a crumb or two of power left, though she hadn't dared try to use it. Maybe Lady Sophie's drugs grew less effective with constant use. And . . .

All her hopes felt hollow. She could recognize her own attempts to keep her spirits up, to believe she might have a chance. She knew just how small that chance was, and diminishing by the day.

She remembered again what Anima had said about her own death – imprisoned, drugged, left to starve to death underground, and ultimately binding her soul to a book in the hope that some future mage might find it. But she didn't have Anima's knowledge to perform such a spell.

The question was, did she have Anima's strength of will to keep fighting?

Eleanor had to believe what Sir Percy had once told her – that the League never left anyone behind – because the alternative would be despair.

The day dragged by in more long hours of boredom. Outside the sun beat down on the withered lawn with pitiless fervour, heavy and oppressive, but distant clouds spoke of a storm – the sort which would come on without warning and with sudden hammering gusts of rain. The visitors were in the gallery again, and she could hear their laughter and questions as the warders pointed out the most interesting patients to them.

'. . . and this one here's a very sad case,' the warder said, reaching her cell. Over the past couple of days they'd been moving from dire warnings about how dangerous she was to calls for pity for her sad affliction. Perhaps they got more tips from visitors who felt sympathetic to the prisoners? Eleanor wondered drearily how she'd be described by the end of the month, if they continued on her current diet and bleeding. *Perhaps they'll be saying it was a merciful release, and the poor girl would have wanted it that way, if only she'd known how mad she was . . .*

'Really?' a man asked. 'Do tell us more.'

Wait. She knew that voice. She *knew* that voice. But it was someone who couldn't possibly be here. She must be dreaming again, as she had with Sir Percy and Anima earlier. There was no other explanation for it.

'The poor young woman's suffering from a haematological crisis,' the warder said. He'd grown much better at pronouncing the words with practice, no longer having to sound them out syllable by syllable. 'If she's not bled regular, she has delusions, sir, and she runs wild with a knife. It's a sore pity, that such a sweet young thing should be so lost to the afflictions of her body and mind.'

'How dreadful!' That was a woman's voice, young and sweet with a heavy French accent. Eleanor knew *her* too. 'What a tragedy!'

It might all be a dream . . . but she had to know.

With an effort she dragged herself to her feet, leaning against the wall as she stumbled towards the door. She had to look through the grille to see who was on the other side, because if it was who she thought it was, if she hadn't finally gone stark staring mad and become a worthy inhabitant of Bedlam, then . . .

The two people whom the warden was escorting finally came into view. A small thin man, in a plain wig and drab black clothing, his waist for once bare of its usual tricolour sash, but his yellow-green eyes as sharp and cold as ever. And beside him, a young woman with golden curls foaming from under her fashionable hat, brilliant blue eyes filled with tears at the misery around her, and a face which spoke her feelings more loudly than words ever could. She was carrying parcels, as though they had been shopping earlier and come here for a brief noon diversion.

What were Chauvelin and his daughter Fleurette doing here? How was this *possible*?

Chauvelin met her eyes. A thin smile curved his mouth. He drew out a pocket-watch and consulted it. 'Almost midday,' he said to the warder. 'We have a little longer, I believe?'

'That's true, sir, though we'll need to be giving them some food soon. All the other visitors are already gone . . .'

There was a clink of coins.

'Right you are, sir. Now I'm sure that a gentleman like yourself and your pretty niece here know all about the dreadful things going on in France, but they seem to have worked on this woman's brain to a dreadful extent. It was a sad night when they first discovered the truth of her goings-on—'

The expanding narrative was interrupted by a shuddering boom. The warder broke off mid-exaggeration, and Fleurette gave a little squeak of horror. After a moment's silence, cries of shock and confusion began to rise from the other cells. There was a smell of gunpowder on the air, drifting through the barred window which looked onto the lawn outside.

The warder bit back an oath, perhaps conscious of Fleurette's shocked blue eyes. 'Right, sir, no time for anything more. I'm afraid you and your niece will have to leave while we look into whatever's going on here.'

'Of course,' Chauvelin said smoothly. 'Lead the way, good fellow.'

Eleanor then had an excellent view of Chauvelin removing a small heavy club from his coat as the warder turned to lead the way out. The fellow went down without a murmur, the keys on his belt jangling as he hit the ground.

Fleurette dropped her parcels and pounced on the keys, running over to Eleanor's cell door to try them one after another until she found the right one, while Chauvelin watched the gallery door. 'Be quick,' he instructed her. 'We have no time to waste.'

'I know, Bibi, I know, you've told me!'

Finally the right key went in, and the lock opened. As the door swung free, Eleanor stumbled out into the gallery, taking deep disbelieving breaths of the smoky air. 'This is a rescue?' she asked tentatively, aware of how stupid the question was but unable to prevent herself.

'We have no time to explain,' Chauvelin said curtly, 'so for the moment do as you have always instructed your own targets to do, restrain your questions and follow orders. There are shoes and a cloak in those parcels: put them on. Fleurette, help me drag this man into the cell.'

Eleanor fumbled the parcels open. There was a plain brown woollen cloak, with a hood which could be drawn up to hide her shorn hair. There were shoes – regular black walking shoes, tight on her feet but welcome after days of going barefoot on Bedlam's floors. But most thrillingly of all, there was a small piece of paper – a square of white marked with a five-petalled red flower.

Tears blurred her eyes as she pulled on the shoes and

draped the cloak around herself, while Chauvelin and Fleurette dragged the warder into her cell and locked the door on him. Chauvelin took custody of the keys, eyeing the other cells thoughtfully.

Eleanor could guess his thoughts. A gaolbreak was always improved by additional confusion. 'I'm not sure it would help,' she said, feeling a sting of guilt that she was leaving the other women imprisoned here. Were any of them unwilling residents, like Eleanor herself? 'The violent ones are all upstairs on the first floor.'

'True,' Chauvelin admitted. He looked her up and down, assessing how well the cloak covered her. 'Not perfect, but it will do. Keep the hood raised. Follow me, and stay close.'

Fleurette put a strengthening arm around Eleanor as Chauvelin led the way down the gallery, keys in his hand. There was more shouting from elsewhere in the building now, and the stench of smoke was stronger. 'I'm so glad that you're alive,' she whispered.

'And I've never been so glad to see someone in my life,' Eleanor replied. *Even Citizen Chauvelin.* 'But what's going on?'

'We are rescuing you!' Fleurette said cheerily. 'Your Pimpernel and my Bibi have come to an agreement. Soon we will have you out of here and safe, and then Bibi has a task for you—'

Chauvelin turned the key, and the heavy gallery door swung open.

A warder stood on the other side.

CHAPTER TWELVE

Eleanor's hopes, so recently raised, came crashing down. She had no strength to use her magic, such as it was; Fleurette was certainly not a combatant, and the man looming ahead of them was big enough to make two of Chauvelin . . .

'You took your time,' Chauvelin remarked drily.

'Sorry, sir,' the man said. He stepped back and gestured for them to walk through, before closing and locking the door behind them. 'Fair amount of running here and there at the moment, so I had to be sure our passage was clear. This way, if you please.'

Eleanor could only mumble, 'How?' as she stumbled along behind Chauvelin, leaning on Fleurette.

Chauvelin heard her, and glanced back with a thin smile. 'The warders here are shockingly ill paid,' he said, 'and there are people who are willing to devote good money to your safety and freedom. Now, to the left here, am I correct?'

'That you are, sir. But you'll be bearing in mind that I ain't never been down there—'

'That was understood, yes.'

For the moment the corridors and rooms were empty, but Eleanor knew it couldn't last. 'What's the diversion?' she asked Fleurette.

'Smoke bombs on the first floor on the men's side,' Fleurette said. 'Oh, Eleanor, this is such a miserable place! I'm so angry with whoever had you sent here.'

'Here now, don't be unfair,' their guide complained. 'We do our best for the poor afflicted ladies and gentlemen, it's not our fault they're sent here. We never mistreated you, did we, miss?'

Eleanor realized he was talking to her. *Starved. Bled. Purged.* Was it her moral duty to speak up in the man's defence because it hadn't been *worse*? More importantly, should she risk aggravating the man currently being paid to lead them to safety? 'You didn't,' she agreed prudently. Fortunately he wasn't looking at her face. 'You had no way of knowing I was being held here against my will.'

'Course we didn't,' the man said cheerfully. He paused, gestured for them to remain where they were and checked the junction ahead. 'Right, they're all still upstairs . . .'

'And we are going down.' Chauvelin glanced at Eleanor again. 'To avoid any misapprehensions, or attempts to, shall we say, run in the wrong direction, we will be departing through the cellars. Your compatriots are due to breach them from the opposite direction, tunnelling from a nearby house. Can I trust you not to do anything unwise?'

Eleanor could see his point. If she'd been her normal self, she'd have done her utmost to find a way to escape that didn't involve him. Rueful memories of aristocrats in France complaining about their own rescues seemed to mock her. She needed his help, here and now; she had no choice but to hope the story of her waiting friends was true, and not another deceit to trap her. 'I won't be stupid,' she said, rather unwillingly.

'Good.' Chauvelin left it at that, and Eleanor could only pray she hadn't made the wrong decision.

The door which their guide led them to would have

caught Eleanor's attention whatever the circumstances. It was larger than any normal door down to a cellar, and its frame was new, suggesting that part of the wall had been knocked down to expand the entrance and accommodate it. The lock on the door was large, heavy and very clearly in earnest. Chauvelin removed a key from an inner pocket of his coat – shiny, presumably newly cast – and applied it to the lock. It took him an effort to turn the key, and while he struggled with it, Eleanor found herself looking back down the corridor behind them for fear her escape had been discovered. She knew that urging Chauvelin to hurry would be of no practical use, but her tongue still itched in her mouth with the need to encourage him to work faster.

Finally the wards clicked, and Chauvelin pulled the door open. Cold air came billowing up to meet them – bitterly, bone-chillingly cold, with the same sweet smell behind it that had permeated Castleton's office, only stronger and more pungent. All of them flinched.

'What's *down* there?' Fleurette gasped.

'Dunno,' their guide said, 'and most of us ain't never been allowed down there either. They take crates in and they take crates out. And all the patients' blood gets taken down there, too.' He shrugged. 'Well, you got to do something with it, right? Can't just pour it down the drain. It attracts rats, see. More rats.'

Chauvelin's mouth thinned in disapproval, but he chose not to deliver a diatribe on the subjects of vampires and blood. 'Hurry,' he advised, waving the guide and women past before he joined them, closing the cellar door behind him.

There was light: Eleanor didn't think she could have borne it without light. The very latest Argand lamps burned on the walls as they made their way down the stairs, with additional layers of glass shielding the wick and reservoir, as though to protect them from the chilly air. The light was clear enough for Eleanor to see previous footprints on the stairs, the marks in mud of thick hobnailed boots. Something heavy had been brought down here, and back up again, for the treads were scuffed in both directions. Could it be true what people had whispered, that dead bodies were buried down here?

'What is that smell?' Fleurette asked, giving words to Eleanor's own thoughts, her voice hushed in the silence.

'Ether,' Chauvelin said flatly. 'I do not know why, and I like the possibilities even less.'

For once Eleanor had to agree with him. Why should there be such dense quantities of ether down here, below Bedlam? Were they keeping an entire village-worth of people drugged? She added it to her list of questions for later, as they came to the bottom of the stairs. The door there, at least, was unlocked.

As it opened, Fleurette and Eleanor drew close to each other at the blast of still colder air. It might have been the middle of winter. Light from still more Argand lamps burned on what seemed at first to be large cubes of glass – no, wait, it was *ice*. The warehouse-like cellar beneath Bedlam, far larger than Eleanor would have expected, was stacked with chunks of ice. Gutters in the floor allowed a steady trickle of melt-off water to the drains in the corner. Between the pieces of ice, like flies in amber, stood heavy ceramic jugs, all of them sealed as though they were some housewife's prized jams and preserves.

'All this is plain unnatural,' their guide opined with a shiver. 'No wonder they don't let us down here. Can't say most of us would want to work here if they knew all this was below – whatever it is.'

Chauvelin's frown dug new lines in his forehead. 'This is somewhat more extensive than the official plans for the cellars suggested,' he said. 'Still, that should only make our departure easier. Here.' He passed a small pouch to their guide. 'The rest will be given to you this evening, at the inn, as we agreed.'

'Right you are,' the man said, the pouch swiftly vanishing into a pocket. 'I'll be upstairs making sure nobody looks twice at me. Best of luck with everything, miss.' He tapped his brow in Eleanor's general direction and backed away quickly.

The thud of the closing door behind him was worryingly loud.

'To the north of the cellar,' Chauvelin directed firmly. 'The north-east corner.' He consulted his watch, frowning once again.

Eleanor wondered what he was thinking. Should the League already have made themselves known, if they'd breached these cellars? Or were they scheduled to breach them at a specific time, and if so, were they late?

'What can they be freezing down here?' Fleurette wondered out loud, looking at the jugs amid the ice as they hurried past them. 'And why?'

'I suspect it's blood,' Eleanor said. While Fleurette was hardly dressed for this temperature, wearing a typically fashionable walking dress, Eleanor was even less so. It was hard to imagine it was July outside when it was so bitterly cold down here.

'But why?' Fleurette frowned far more prettily than her father. 'And how did they manage to get so much ice down here in the first place?'

'Maybe Castleton wasn't just here to persuade me to speak,' Eleanor said slowly, thinking it out. 'Perhaps this is part of some greater scheme in which he's involved. He knows about the developments of science, and many of the older vampires don't. And Bedlam is a convenient source for blood, with many of the patients bled daily. What if they're trying to find ways to preserve large quantities of blood once it's been drawn?'

'That would agree with certain recent developments,' Chauvelin said. 'But there will be time for more speculation when we are safely out of here.'

'At least this cellar is well lit,' Fleurette said. 'How repulsive it would be if we had to fumble through here in the dark!'

Eleanor's brain was crowded by a thousand other thoughts, such as the likelihood of their erstwhile guide betraying them and returning with other men in tow to take them all prisoner, and the weariness and nausea which still possessed her. But even so she could recognize Fleurette had a point, if not the one she thought she was making. Why *was* this cellar so well lit, with all the expensive lamps burning even when it was empty and locked?

'I quite agree, m'dear.' The voice of de Courcis came from directly behind them. 'I do abominate sitting around in the dark.'

Fleurette squeaked and spun around. Eleanor, still leaning on her, nearly went sprawling and had to grab at the nearest block of ice to stay upright. It was punishingly cold against her fingers. Chauvelin's hand was already going into the pocket of his coat.

'Now please let's not make this more awkward than is absolutely necessary.' De Courcis appeared not nearly as fashionable as he'd been on previous occasions when Eleanor had seen him. His neckcloth was in disarray, his dark hair unpowdered, and he leaned against a pillar with the attitude of a man suffering from a painful hangover. Although Eleanor had thought vampires couldn't get hangovers. 'Deuce take it, can't a man sleep in peace?'

'Did we disturb you?' Chauvelin enquired politely.

'I'll say you did, by Jove! I'll admit to a long night at the cards last night, which gave me reason to rest down here for a while. Imagine my surprise when I heard the door open.' He almost looked sympathetic. 'Tell you what, old fellow, you retrace your steps and go back up into the house above, and I won't lift a finger to stop you.'

'Where we'll encounter your friend Castleton,' Eleanor said sharply. 'I think not.'

De Courcis rolled his eyes. 'I've nothing against you, young woman, but the situation's placed us on opposite sides. I don't actually *enjoy* manhandling ladies, you know. I don't even have any great urge to thump men over the head – though I'll make an exception for anybody who tries to shoot me with a wooden bullet.' His eyes met Chauvelin's, momentarily serious. 'I don't know who you are, my good chap, but you're readying a gun, aren't you? And you expect it to inconvenience me, which means a wooden bullet, doesn't it? Think this through very carefully, because if you *don't* kill me on the spot, then what happens next won't be at all pleasant for you.'

'You talk like a man who would risk his life!' Fleurette said, somewhat appalled. 'Why would even a vampire be so careless of his safety?'

De Courcis shrugged. 'I grow bored when there is no work for me, and gambling is one of the ways I can distract myself from the endless wasteland of eternal life.'

Eleanor wondered, again, exactly what the relationship was between Castleton and de Courcis. Had they ever truly been friends? Or had Castleton simply seen de Courcis as a convenient pathway to the life he so desired?

Still, any issues that might lie between the two men were scarcely significant now. What Eleanor needed to find was a way out of this cellar, and since the League was apparently behind schedule – please God let it be no more than that – only Chauvelin's gun stood between them and utter failure. Chauvelin's gun, and Eleanor's magic – although for the moment, Eleanor still had no magic worthy of the name. When she tried to reach into those parts of herself which had previously been wellsprings of strength, there was scarcely more than dust and ashes. Had this been how the mages felt when the vampires had first defeated them?

What would Anima have done? She would have drawn on Eleanor's strength. But if Eleanor had no strength . . .

The mages of the past had been able to draw on the strength of those who trusted and supported them. Anima had said so, as had Bernard in Mont-Saint-Michel, and Matthew in Oxford. And perhaps, just perhaps, there was someone standing right next to Eleanor who trusted her enough to help her in this way.

'Stand back!' she hissed at Fleurette, pulling her away from the confrontation, the other woman's arm warm against her hand. The only warm thing, it seemed, in this whole cellar.

'Yes, be sensible,' de Courcis agreed. 'This really doesn't *have* to be unpleasant.'

Unpleasant for you, Eleanor thought bitterly. It would certainly be unpleasant for herself and Fleurette if they went along with the vampire's demands and retraced their steps. Yet perhaps, if he'd been born in a different time and place, and his life had left him as something other than a vampire, he'd have been one of the League and following Sir Percy's orders.

She didn't know. She couldn't know. She could only work with the tools she had in front of her.

'Stay back,' Chauvelin ordered, echoing her. His hand came out of his coat pocket, and there was indeed a small pistol in it. 'You have assured me that if I miss my shot, I will regret it. I assure you in turn that I am not accustomed to missing my shots.'

'I need you to help me,' Eleanor whispered in Fleurette's ear as Chauvelin and de Courcis faced one other, each apparently waiting for the other to move first. 'Remember Mont-Saint-Michel, where I helped Bernard? I need you to help me now, in the same way.'

Fleurette's blue eyes widened. The wetness of the cellar, full of melting ice and dripping water, combined with the light from the Argand lamps to create a damp haze throughout, turning her tumbled curls into living gold. 'Of course,' she murmured back. 'What do I do?'

'You have to *want* to help me,' Eleanor said, desperately hoping this would be enough. 'And trust me.'

'Always.' Fleurette squeezed her hand.

Eleanor shut her eyes, trying to find the fragmentary spark of power within herself. She chewed on her lower lip, her head aching with the effort. And for just a fraction of a second, a single heartbeat, she felt that lightning – like the first drop of rain from a sky that seemed clear, or the glimpse of brightness in a cloudy sky, which is gone when one turns to look for the sun. *It's there. I know it is. Just because I'm having trouble seeing it doesn't mean it isn't. It's part of me and I choose to use it.*

Whatever it costs.

The spark inside Eleanor flickered again, and she tasted her power, breathing it out in the palest shadow of a breeze. It brushed against Fleurette – trembling, nervous, yet determined – and came racing back to her, like a tennis ball which had been loosely tossed over a net and struck back twice as hard. Through that breath of her power, through the contact of their hands, she could feel Fleurette's will to aid and support her. Just as her spirit had once been with Anima, Fleurette's spirit was in sympathy with hers.

It all seemed to happen in a single moment. De Courcis moved, lunging forward to knock Chauvelin aside. Chauvelin fired his pistol. Eleanor raised her hand, and the light which burst from it dwarfed the brilliance of the Argand lamps.

De Courcis had taken the pistol ball in his shoulder and blood streamed down his coat to mingle with the run-off from the ice. He recoiled with a furious snarl, his mask of good-humoured amiability slipping to leave his face a rictus of skin, bones and fangs. The spatter of his blood on the floor hissed and steamed, darkening to black as he threw himself behind one of the stacks of ice.

Chauvelin didn't pause for arguments or demand explanations. He caught Fleurette's free hand, towing his staggering daughter through the pillars of ice cubes and support columns which turned the cellar into a maze. Eleanor followed, every step a weary struggle; she knew she had no choice but to keep the flame burning. To let it lapse now would unquestionably mean the worst for all three of them. She didn't want to keep drawing on Fleurette like this – she could feel the other woman's eagerness and determination flutter like a candle in a draught, with the knowledge that this was her own life she was burning. But Eleanor had to trust that the League would be waiting, that they *would* come, that this wasn't all in vain . . .

'How do you plan to get out of here?' de Courcis called from the shadows. 'There's no secret passageway, no priest's hole here. You're merely wasting time and effort!'

'Do you think I'd go back up there?' Eleanor demanded. Specks of darkness danced in front of her eyes as she struggled with exhaustion. 'What have I to gain from letting them bleed and kill me? You know what they've been doing to me!' Some memory of the League – Charles, Andrew and Tony – prompted her to add, 'And you call yourself a gentleman?'

'A gentleman who wants to live.' His voice came from a different area of the room this time. He must be dodging between stacks of ice, waiting for her flames to die away. 'It all comes down to that, m'dear. And if it's a question of you or me, then I'm terribly afraid it must be you. All due regrets, but I haven't lived centuries just to give it all up because of some idea of proper manners.'

'But then *why* have you lived?' Fleurette demanded, her voice carrying through the room. The reflections of Eleanor's fire danced in her blue eyes. 'What is the *point* of your life, if it is just an endless wasteland for you? Surely there is something you love, some hope, some kind of faith?'

'There is nothing left except the fear of dying.' His voice was now to their right – too close! Eleanor spun around, flailing her hand towards him, and he darted back again, a wolf returning to cover. 'You'll understand, pretty girl, when you become older.'

'God forbid I ever should,' Fleurette said with utter sincerity, utter conviction, and the flame around Eleanor's hand rose fiercely enough to burst into a dozen separate fires, lighting their surroundings with painful clarity. It caught reflections in the ice throughout the cellar, turning the room into a hundred glassy panes of light shining through some distant casement.

A sudden crashing thunder echoed through the cavernous space – not from the corner of the cellar they'd been making for, but a few yards further south down the wall. Dust came flooding in, spoiling the beauty of the light, and mingling with the dripping water to trickle down as mud.

'Not before time,' Chauvelin muttered, shaking his head as though to clear the noise from his ears. 'With such a lax attitude towards punctuality, I'm surprised you ever succeeded in France.' He tucked his pistol away, pulling Eleanor and Fleurette towards the ragged cavity which had appeared in the wall.

Tony leaned through it, peering through the dust and

light, a spotted handkerchief suitable for the most rakish of highwaymen covering most of his face, yet failing to render him unrecognizable. 'Is anyone there?' he demanded, looking from side to side. 'Deuce take it, is anyone there? I say, fellows, we may have blown a hole into the wrong place. This doesn't look like the cellars of Bedlam at all.'

'Here,' Chauvelin snarled, thrusting Eleanor and Fleurette in his direction. 'We have no time for delay. They already know we're here.'

'Organizing escapes really isn't your forte, old chap.' That was Sir Percy's voice, and the relief which surged through Eleanor almost brought her to her knees. It was all right now. Everything was under control. Her light ebbed and flickered away, no longer necessary. She released her grip on Fleurette's hand. 'It should be left to the professionals . . .'

'De Courcis is here, in the cellar,' Eleanor gasped. 'Chauvelin shot him, but it didn't kill him.'

'Is he indeed.' Sir Percy stepped through the gap, handing Fleurette in the opposite direction with grave courtesy, and frowned into the mists of the cellar. 'De Courcis, old chap! Would you care to make a deal?'

De Courcis coughed and spat – still out of sight, but audible. 'And what sort of deal did you have in mind, Blakeney?'

'I thought you might consider changing sides. I suspect dear Sophie won't be too pleased with you over today's events.'

De Courcis's laughter had an unpleasant gurgling note to it, and Eleanor wondered whether Chauvelin's wooden ball had taken him in the lung. 'I was just about to offer you the same bargain. You can't win, you know. Really you can't.' There was a dreadful weariness to his voice. 'Once enough of us realize the magnitude of the danger you pose – that *she* poses to us – then all England will be roused against you.'

'There's more to England than drinking blood and eternal life,' Sir Percy said calmly. 'Zounds, look at France! Do you really want to fan that sort of fury here?'

'You seem to think I have any level of choice in the matter.'

'Of course I do. Deuce take it! If men and women have free will and choice, how can vampires be otherwise?'

De Courcis paused. 'I can give you five minutes head start. Don't ask for more.'

'Most kind,' Sir Percy said, flipping a vague salute in the direction of the shadows. 'Till later.'

He turned, and at that moment de Courcis came rushing from the shadows, his hair loose and tangled around his face, blood fresh on his shirt. He seized Sir Percy by the throat, his nails digging into his victim's flesh, and spun, throwing the Pimpernel to one side as though he were a child's doll. The whole thing seemed to happen between blinks; one moment he was moving forward, the next Sir Percy had gone sprawling. De Courcis darted forward again, savage as a wolf, death in human shape, his face like a skull.

He knocked Chauvelin aside, his eyes on Eleanor. Fear held her as immobile as a corpse. Between heartbeats she sought for the place where her power was, but found it empty.

A pistol spoke. The ball took de Courcis from behind, in the heart, and he fell, all his momentum draining away into a long collapse. The light faded from his eyes. His flesh fell to dust, his clothes collapsing to the floor. Within the space of two breaths there was nothing left of him, and Eleanor could not have said which fragments of the dust and ash littering the place had been from the explosion, and which part of the vampire. She stood there, one hand at her throat, trying to slow her heartbeat, trying not to think of his face as he'd lunged for her.

'It seems you, too, have learned to use wooden bullets,' Chauvelin said, picking himself up and dusting himself off.

Sir Percy was back on his feet, scanning the cellar for further threats before turning back to them. 'It's a shame,' he said soberly. 'I thought better of the fellow than that.'

'You were a fool to expect the "English sense of honour" from him,' Chauvelin retorted.

'Ah, but I'm trusting your sense of honour, aren't I?'

Chauvelin made no reply.

A moment later Sir Percy had Eleanor by one elbow, and Chauvelin had her by the other, and the two of them practically lifted her through the hole in the wall. Another cellar lay beyond, and there was Charles, and Andrew, with other members of the League. It was Charles whom Eleanor's eyes clung to – dusty and smeared with gunpowder, his eyeglasses glinting in the light of the lantern someone else was holding. She saw his lips move in the shape of her name as he came forward to support her.

She was safe now. She could rest.

Eleanor closed her eyes and let herself fall into darkness.

CHAPTER THIRTEEN

The carriage was bumping on cobbles, the air was hot and breathless, and Eleanor's head was spinning with incoherent thoughts, yet it was *still* better than where she'd been imprisoned for the past week. Weeks.

'You should have shot him when first you saw him.' That was Chauvelin's voice. There was a good reason for Chauvelin to be here, but for the moment she was having difficulty remembering it.

'It hardly seemed a case of obscuring our identity, old fellow.' That was Sir Percy. His voice reassured Eleanor. She didn't need to open her eyes yet. 'Dear Sophie was going to know perfectly well who blew a hole in the cellar and plucked Eleanor out of her clutches. Why shoot de Courcis as well, if he'd been prepared to leave us be?'

'You would have been removing a future enemy,' Chauvelin said drily. 'Which you had to do in any case. Were you truly surprised that he was more afraid of the Baroness of Basing than of you?'

Sir Percy sighed. 'There, I fear, you may have a point . . . Are you worried about our escape, old fellow? I assure you that it's been planned out in the most exacting detail, and doesn't even rely on anyone being disguised as a member of the Revolutionary Guard.'

'I am worried about my daughter. You have still not explained the full details of what happened there. I have refrained from breaking our alliance, because it was clearly to our mutual benefit, but so far you have given me nothing but excuses, and the last time our carriages changed horses, she was still as fast asleep as your protégée.' Eleanor could hear the concern beneath the etched fury of Chauvelin's voice. Concern for Fleurette, that is. Not for her.

'I've already told you.' That was Charles's voice, coming from right next to her. He was the person against whom she was leaning. Eleanor smiled in her half-sleep. 'Eleanor said other people can support her while she's doing magic – what happened with Fleurette must have been an example of this process in action. I wish I could have seen it.'

'Magic.' Chauvelin's voice dripped with scorn.

'You still don't believe it after what you've seen, old fellow?' Sir Percy sounded quite serious.

'I know that I have seen . . . something. I do not believe in magic any more than I believe in God.'

It was a good thing Fleurette hadn't heard that, Eleanor decided dreamily. It would hurt her feelings so much to hear that her father was an atheist. How shocking.

'Magic is perhaps the wrong word,' Charles said thoughtfully. 'Consider all the new developments in science, everything man is now discovering! I use the term "magic" for want of anything better, but in truth I conceive of it as something like magnetism or electricity. Franklin's experiments with lightning, and more recently that Italian fellow Galvani's work with what he calls bioelectromagnetism . . . There's so much we don't know. Magic is simply what it was called when we knew no better.'

'And vampires would keep it that way. The news of the riots at Oxford – and Cambridge, now – is most instructive.'

'There are riots across England,' Charles said, his voice troubled. 'Or so the newspapers would have us believe. Letters in the journals, motions in Parliament demanding that action should be taken . . .'

'And now this discovery in the cellars of Bedlam.' Chauvelin sounded quite smug, as though he expected nothing less when exploring an English cellar.

Eleanor decided, reluctantly, that she should open her eyes. It was more difficult than she'd expected. Her whole body ached, as though she'd been running from pursuit across half of France, instead of merely – merely? – being locked in the same room for the past couple of weeks. Still, needs must, and the conversation had become increasingly intriguing.

She raised her head and blinked in the late afternoon sunlight that filtered in through the carriage windows. Charles sat beside her, his clothing now that of a proper gentleman rather than the less stylish garments suitable for blowing holes in cellars. Across from her, on the facing seat, were Sir Percy and Chauvelin, both choosing to sit edged into opposing corners rather than endure the other's presence, a clear space of seat visible between them. Sir Percy was in his full glory as man about town, with an immaculate cravat, overcoat with multiple shoulder-capes, velvet jacket and breeches, and boots which fitted like a glove as well as reflected like a mirror. Chauvelin was in aggressively simple black and white.

Outside the window she could see a hazy image of English countryside rolling past, green and gold under the hot summer sun. They were well outside London, then. Good.

'Eleanor?' Charles said sharply, voice torn between relief and concern. 'Are you awake?'

Eleanor nodded and regretted it. She couldn't quite bring herself to meet anyone's eyes, conscious of the danger they'd put themselves in just in order to rescue her. 'Thank you for getting me out of there,' she whispered. 'Thank you so much.'

'I only regret we couldn't do it sooner,' Sir Percy said. He was regarding her with his full attention, rather than affecting his usual attitude of foppish unconcern. The sunlight gilded his hair an even brighter gold, and while the carriage still rocked with speed, he lounged in his corner seat like a great cat. 'I fear it took us a little while to discover where Lady Sophie had placed you.'

'How did you find out?' Although Eleanor had tried to speak to some of the visitors, she hadn't thought any of them had actually listened to what she said. They'd been more interested in the warders' stories of insanity and murder. 'I wouldn't have thought to look in Bedlam . . .'

Charles chuckled. His arm went around her shoulder. 'We took a leaf from milady's own book, Eleanor. If she thinks she can trace the League by having all its members followed – well, the League can do as much to her *and* all her frequent visitors. And Bow Street's more than willing to assign Runners when they know their fees will be paid. She might have been keeping to her London house, but when Castleton began to spend all his time in Bedlam, that was the clue we needed.'

Eleanor smiled up at him in gratitude. 'I'd never have thought of that,' she confessed.

Sir Percy coughed. 'While I regret disturbing tender moments such as this—'

'I have no such regrets,' Chauvelin said flatly. 'Will my daughter wake soon?'

'I'm sure she will,' Eleanor said, fervently hoping she

was correct. Anima had said this was a common practice when she was alive, after all. It would hardly have been sensible if it had left the friends of the mages slumbering for days on end. 'If she hadn't helped me like that, I wouldn't have been able to drive back de Courcis. I'm truly grateful.'

'Hm.' Chauvelin eyed Eleanor speculatively. 'And can *anyone* assist you in that way? To drive back vampires?'

'Only somebody who trusts me,' Eleanor said quickly. She was still dizzy, but she could sense a wealth of loaded questions and dangerous topics behind his words. 'Besides, she was the first person who'd ever tried to help me do it . . . And why were *you* two there in the first place? What are you doing in England?'

'Later,' Sir Percy said. 'For the moment, Eleanor, you have my word that Citizen Chauvelin's not a threat to us – and his daughter even less so. We have a temporary alliance.'

Eleanor's mind leapt to the previous occasion when this had happened. 'Has someone attempted to murder the Committee for Public Safety again?' she asked.

'Not to my knowledge,' Chauvelin said. 'Though that does have something to do with my interest in you, Anne Dupont, or Eleanor Dalton, or whatever you are currently calling yourself.'

'You might as well call me Eleanor Dalton, citizen,' Eleanor said, resigned. At least it would make matters easier if she wasn't having to answer to multiple aliases. She coughed. Her throat was painfully dry. 'But if you could explain—'

Sir Percy passed her a flask which proved to contain water. 'First and foremost, Eleanor, we need to know if you've discovered anything over the past couple of weeks. Discussions of our future plans can wait until we've reached Bathurst Manor, several hours to the north of London, at which point – yes, m'dear, stop staring at Charles, it is indeed his family establishment towards which we're heading. And we will be engaging in some minor deceptions so as not to draw his father's wrath. My beloved Marguerite is with Fleurette in the carriage behind us. We will be casting ourselves on his father's mercy and asking for lodging for the night, or even a couple of nights, due to some excuse which I have yet to fully determine. During all this, you will be posing as one of the two daughters of the Marquis de Chauvelin sitting next to me . . .'

Eleanor wanted to gape open-mouthed at the scale of all this. Then she saw Chauvelin's face – as sour and pinched as if he'd bitten into a lemon – and had to suppress a giggle. 'Couldn't Monsieur Chauvelin just be a private citizen?' she suggested, her voice trembling.

'Not if we want to keep my father on side,' Charles said glumly. When Eleanor turned to look at him more fully, she saw how his whole face was set in lines of foreboding and resignation. 'My father has very little time for anyone below the rank of a baronet, m'dear. It'll make life simpler for all of you if we tell a few little lies. It's not as if he's in Society enough to recognize any names or faces, thank the heavens.'

'But, my current, ah, condition . . .' Eleanor waved her hand at herself, shamefully conscious of her stained garments, shorn hair and general improper state of dress.

'You were kidnapped,' Chauvelin said curtly, 'by a Revolutionary faction attempting to put pressure on me. They are still at large in London, which is why Sir Percy Blakeney has prevailed upon his friend to bring you to a safe place.'

'There, you see! I knew you were as capable as I am when it comes to conjuring up a good lie.' Sir Percy shifted as though to clap Chauvelin on the shoulder, but Chauvelin edged further into his corner. 'And now, before we go any further, Eleanor – your story . . .'

It was late at night by the time they arrived at the Bathurst estate, and they had already changed horses twice. The surrounding town crowded around the mansion on the south side, held back by a vast yew hedge which curved like the arc of a bow, and was tall enough that it surrounded and overtopped the gatehouse through which the carriages entered.

Eleanor had been drooping more and more throughout their journey. Fleurette had awoken at their last halt to change horses, to her father's poorly concealed relief, and now Eleanor was the one dozing. If she hadn't been in public – well, sharing the carriage with Sir Percy and Chauvelin – then she would have tried to press Charles for some information on his father and home. She was reminded how little she knew about him and his family. He never wanted to discuss those matters, and she was usually careful to avoid them. She was aware his mother was dead – had died when he was a boy, to be precise – and that his older brother John had died too, in some sort of accident which had forced Charles to cease his studies at Oxford and also made him the new heir. It was a difficult situation: she *wanted* to know more, if only to ensure that she wouldn't say the wrong thing in casual conversation and prick Charles's more painful memories. The number of times she'd managed to do so before had convinced her he must have a great many of them.

'Are there grottoes and ruins?' she asked, peering out of the window. 'I cannot see any on this side of the house.'

'They're all to the back, m'dear, further out in the grounds,' Charles said, tucking his eye-glasses away in a pocket. 'Take a deuce of a lot of maintaining, if they're to look properly quaint and elegant for picnics and strolls and all that manner of thing.'

Eleanor imagined shadowy grottoes and ruins lurking in the moonlight, filling the elegantly landscaped grounds, and each ready to hide a double handful of vampires lying in ambush. She hadn't forgotten how narrow their escape from Bedlam had been. How soon might Lady Sophie discover their whereabouts?

A butler, flanked by a bevy of footmen, waited at the mansion's great door. The building loomed above, pale as bone in the moonlight, dozens of windows peering down at them.

Charles sighed. 'Here we go.'

As the carriage rolled to a stop, one of the footmen came running up to it to open the door. Charles stepped out, then assisted Eleanor in leaving the carriage, before Sir Percy and Chauvelin followed. His hand was warm on Eleanor's, and he gave her a little squeeze of encouragement. Out of the corner of her eye Eleanor could see Lady Marguerite and Fleurette exiting the second carriage, and more footmen running up to help with the baggage strapped to the roof.

How can anything this large and obvious be a secret? Eleanor thought, despair creeping in. *Surely Lady Sophie will already have heard about our arrival . . .*

But then what? Lady Sophie couldn't exactly have a mob storm the estate. That might perhaps have worked in France, where Revolutionary mobs had been known to riot and attack the local aristocracy – though less so now, because the aristocracy were generally no longer there – but this was the middle of England. The local village would laugh her to scorn if she were to demand their obedience. Even if she had people like Castleton executing her will, and doing such illegal things as kidnappings and so on, Eleanor would be safe in the middle of the League, and inside a large and well-built manor house. And she certainly wasn't the sort of woman who went for long walks on her own in the estate grounds at midnight. She had *slightly* more sense than that, she assured herself.

Lady Marguerite came running up to her and swept her into an embrace. 'Eleanor, you darling, foolish, stupid, careless, reckless child! How could you have made us all so worried?'

'Pray do not suffocate my daughter,' Chauvelin remarked, taking a pinch of snuff as he surveyed activities with the air of a man reviewing a military position.

In between tearful embraces by Lady Marguerite and Fleurette, trying not to burst into tears herself in response, and general utter exhaustion, Eleanor was barely conscious of what else was going on around her. It was only when Fleurette tugged her towards the mansion that she realized the others were already entering the place, strolling in as though the shadows of League, Revolution and vampires didn't hang a few paces behind them.

'The master is in the green drawing room, sir,' the butler confided to Charles, 'and awaits you there.'

Even from a distance, Eleanor could see the jerk of Charles's Adam's apple, the forced straightening of his shoulders. 'Of course,' he said, leading the way through the entrance hall.

Eleanor would have liked to look around, but by now she was so tired it demanded all her concentration to place one foot after another and not to stumble. She was once more painfully conscious of her shorn hair – something she'd almost started to forget during the days in Bedlam – and the dirtiness of her dress. She couldn't even huddle under her cloak, here inside and about to be presented to Charles's father.

An unseasonable fire burned in the fireplace of the green

drawing room, adding to the summer heat. The man who stood beside the fireplace paid no apparent attention to it, setting down his glass as the group of visitors entered. He was in black and gold, colours which suited the room, and his powdered hair was held back by a black velvet bow at the nape of his neck. While he had a generous mouth which should have been suited to amiable smiles, there was something mask-like about his face, and his eyes were narrowed into slits as he looked them over.

'Well, Charles,' he said. 'It appears you have an excuse to call upon me at last.'

'Sir.' Charles bowed, his attitude so carefully and precisely formal that Eleanor could almost feel the edge of fear which lay behind it. 'I trust my visit with my friends is not an inconvenience to you.'

'Oh, think nothing of it. A day's warning is more than enough to have to deal with you and all your . . . associates.' He turned his attention to Sir Percy. 'Blakeney, it's been a while since I've seen you or your friends. You have my thanks for tolerating my worthless brat. Perhaps over time you can instil some proper behaviour into him.'

Sir Percy swept a bow. 'I assure you that Charles has been nothing but a credit to you, old chap.'

'Yes, I'm sure you'd say that. You always were too kind-hearted for your own good.' His eyes shifted to Lady Marguerite. 'And you seem to have your wife with you. Now, correct me if I'm wrong, but I could have sworn the journals were claiming she'd been accused of high treason and was then kidnapped by vampires. Would anyone care to enlighten me?'

'Before we go any further,' Sir Percy said, 'it'll make things the deuce of a lot easier if I can introduce your remaining guests, as this whole matter is connected to them.'

For the first time Eleanor felt the full force of the Earl's attention. He didn't look at her in the way that vampires – well, some vampires – did, as though she were nothing more than blood stock or furniture. And of course, when it came to normal English aristocrats looking at serving-maids, most of them didn't bother to notice them at all. Instead, he considered her as though he were out hunting and she was a small animal hidden in the grass; he hadn't yet decided whether she was prey or insignificant, and his final decision on whether or not to tolerate her would be entirely on his side, with nothing she could do to change matters.

He looked at her, she realized, in much the same way that Chauvelin had at their first meeting. It wasn't reassuring.

Charles swallowed. 'Indeed, sir – these three people are refugees from France, fleeing the cruelty of the Revolution and the guillotine, and now pursued even here where they should be safe. Permit me to introduce Armand, Marquis de Chauvelin, and his daughters Eleanor and Fleurette.'

The Earl's gaze moved between the three of them. Chauvelin gave a small bow, of much the same degree as Sir Percy's, though with less flourishing of the hands and cuffs. Eleanor and Fleurette both curtsied. 'Indeed,' he said.

'Evil walks the streets of London,' Charles declared with gravitas. 'A conspiracy of egalitarian vampires, devoted to the same folly as the Revolutionaries of France, is attempting to seize power, and has—'

'Get to the point, boy,' his father said. 'Also, where do egalitarian vampires come from? All the ones I've ever met have been sensibly proud of their families and their proper place in society.'

'We're still trying to find that out,' Charles admitted. 'But so far they've falsely accused Lady Marguerite of treason—'

'Treason is the act of betraying one's own country, whatever the journals may care to call it,' the Earl said. 'The worst of which *she* could be accused of is spying, I believe. And if I did consider it true, madam, I'd have you thrown out of my house this minute. I trust your husband will convince me otherwise.'

Charles swallowed. 'These vampires attempted to black-mail the Marquis de Chauvelin by kidnapping his eldest daughter,' he tried again. Eleanor could see the desperation in his eyes, the wish not only to convince his father of the League's lies but actually to *please* him, to impress him with his diligence and urgency. 'We only managed to rescue Eleanor today.'

'Your ability to present facts is abominable.' The Earl sounded merely . . . weary, as though this was something he had said dozens of times before, but felt the need to repeat, in the same way that a man might hope that grinding his puppy's nose into its own excrement would finally train it not to soil the floor. 'Why did I bother to send you to Oxford, to have you come back so poorly educated? I should send you to St Petersburg instead to look after the family interests there. Even an idiot could manage those – which might make it the best possible position for a son like you. If your brother was still with us—'

Eleanor considered the situation. She considered the fact that she – and the others – had been left standing, practically ignored by the Earl, with no offer of food or drink. She might only ever have been a servant in great houses, but she knew better than *that*. And most of all, she considered the way Charles was being treated by his father – in front of his *friends*. The vicious choice of words, obviously done so often that it had been reduced to mere habit. The condescension. The actual *cruelty*.

Society's standards might indicate that an unmarried young woman like herself should keep silent and refrain from interfering in a perfectly well-deserved scolding of son by father. Fortunately, there was one route which Society positively encouraged young women to take, and it was in perfect alignment with Eleanor's own inclinations. She was, after all, exhausted.

Eleanor let go of her attempts to remain upright, to hold herself like a proper young woman of the nobility, and deliberately allowed herself to swoon.

CHAPTER FOURTEEN

When Eleanor opened her eyes again, it was to dawn light filtering through the windows and birdsong outside. The house around her was quiet, free from the sobs and cries which had permeated Bedlam like maggots working their way through meat. Her mouth was dry, and her head was hot and heavy. But she was in a clean nightgown, in a bed with lawn sheets – lawn sheets! – and a room which spoke of a house wealthy enough to allot elegant bedchambers to even the most uninvited guests.

She looked around cautiously. Lady Marguerite's maid Alice dozed in a chair next to the bed, lines of care smoothed away from her face as she slept. Beside her stood a small table with a jug and glass.

Water? The very thought made Eleanor's mouth feel twice as dry. For a moment she thought she could taste the drug that they'd forced down her throat every day, but no, that was only the shadow of a nightmare – the warders weren't going to come stamping through the door to hold her down and make her drink it . . .

She realized she was sweating. A breeze tore through the room, rustling the papers which lay on a table by the window and rippling through the drawn curtains.

Alice blinked, then knuckled sleep from her eyes as she glanced at Eleanor. 'Looks as if all the titles and luxuries in the world, true or false, can't stop an honest woman waking up at dawn when she should be at her tasks,' she said quietly. 'How are you feeling?'

'Not very well,' Eleanor confessed. 'Alice, what are you doing here?'

'And how should milady travel without her maid with her?' Alice demanded. She poured out a glass of water from the jug and slipped an arm around Eleanor's shoulders, helping her to sit upright and sip from it. 'I hope you don't think she's the sort of woman who'd go on a visit to one of her husband's friends without having her maid, and his valet, following along. That'd not be the done thing at all, and milady knows when it's important to be seen to be proper.'

'Even when milady's been accused of things – *falsely* accused,' Eleanor added hastily, 'and everything else?'

'All the more so,' Alice said firmly. 'We wouldn't want our host the Earl noticing anything out of the ordinary, would we?'

Eleanor's throat was working properly now, but her head still ached with confusion. 'You once told me before that it wasn't your place to ask questions,' she said.

'No more it is,' Alice said firmly. 'But if you think I'm going to let milady get into trouble when I can be a help to her, then you and everyone else can think again! Milord tipped me the wink, and I told the household I was taking leave to see my sick aunt in Budleigh Salterton. Then I met up with milady and came down here. Not an ounce of trouble to it.'

Eleanor wanted to laugh. She lay back against the pillows. 'I hope milady's grateful,' she said.

'I should think she is! Nobody else can do her hair as

well as I can.' Alice pressed her hand against Eleanor's forehead. 'And you should be getting some more sleep. You're hot enough that you'll be taking a fever at this rate, and the weather isn't any sort of help.'

'It is July still?' In Bedlam, Eleanor had marked the days by making scratches on the wall of her cell, but the thought haunted her that more time might have passed while she was unconscious or drugged. She didn't *know*, and it frightened her.

Alice's expression softened. 'Poor girl. Now don't you worry. They can't get you here. Nobody knows we're all here, and milord and milady have something in mind. Just as usual,' she muttered, in a lower tone. 'And milady told me to tell you when you woke up, that if you behave yourself and don't make any fusses, then young Lord Charles will come and see you in the morning. He's got news for you about some sort of old book or something that he found in Oxford.'

Eleanor's heart jumped, and she tried to sit up again, but Alice stared at her so fiercely that she relapsed back into the pillows. Thank goodness they still had Matthew's scroll safe. Castleton's apparent ignorance of it had given her hope of this, but relief flooded through her at this confirmation. And of course Charles could read it. He knew how to read Latin, just as Anima had done, and just as Eleanor herself most emphatically could not. What might he have learned from the scroll? Would it be enough to save them all? The sort of secret which could cow Lady Sophie and her servants, and persuade them to restrain their ambitions?

But once again the fear stirred in her – what if the League might uncover something too dangerous for the vampires to allow such a blackmail? They had already shown how far they were prepared to go to protect whatever lay hidden beneath London. And if they could wipe out all mages as they had once done, then what hope did the League have?

'Now you listen to me,' Alice said firmly. 'I can see from your eyes that you're wide awake and thinking all manner of things about Lord Charles. If you don't shut your eyes right now like a good girl and go back to sleep, you'll be yawning your head off by the time he wakes up, which will be halfway through the morning. You know what young men are like, and young noblemen even worse. So hush now, and sleep.'

'But—' Eleanor protested.

'Are you arguing with me about any of this?'

'No, Alice,' Eleanor said. 'But just one thing – is Lord Charles in trouble with his father?'

'And how do you expect me to know that?' Alice asked.

Eleanor simply looked at her.

'Oh, very well. Not more than usual, by all accounts. His father is – well, it's not as if I've been here before, but heaven knows I've encountered men like that. From what I hear, perhaps the less Lord Charles came home, the happier a man he'd be. But maybe if he did send Charles off to Russia, as he keeps on threatening to do, and then had to do without him, he might realize how good a son he is. But I'm not one to tell tales. Now hush and close your eyes.'

Eleanor did as she'd been ordered. She'd spent the past two weeks wanting control over her own life, but perhaps she could let things be for just a few more hours.

But poor Charles . . .

And what could it be that he'd read in that scroll?

The afternoon sun leached colour from the dry grass, making it more sage-green than the ideal emerald, and glared off the distant lake. Eleanor was grateful for the small group of ash trees which shaded the bench where she was sitting, and for the breezes which made the leaves dance and tickled the bare back of her neck. Her shorn locks were doubly embarrassing now that she was back in the company of women with a decent length of hair. She wondered how long it would take until she was no longer ashamed to be seen this way in public. At least she was dressed properly – indeed, in far better than her normal clothing. Lady Blakeney had brought down suitable dresses (and other necessities) for a young woman of Eleanor's age in her own luggage.

At least, suitable dresses for the type of young woman as whom Eleanor was masquerading.

Still, this was hardly public. She had Fleurette on one side of her, and Charles on the other, and truly she couldn't ask for better company. The only *slight* problem was that she wished it was either one or the other, but not both at the same time. She had urgent questions for Charles, but she wasn't sure Fleurette should hear them; and she wanted to ask Fleurette dozens of things about why she was here, and what Chauvelin's schemes might be. But when she'd broached it before, Fleurette had dimpled and said her Bibi's affairs were private and no doubt he'd discuss them with Eleanor later.

Possibly, Eleanor had to admit, she was making the matter worse by not wanting to speak about her time in Bedlam. Both Charles and Fleurette had encouraged her to share the story, but Eleanor only wanted to forget it. The confining walls, the purging, the bleeding, the meetings with Castleton, the gay chatter of the visitors peering in at the poor lunatic inmates . . .

Were there other men and women there who'd been as unjustly imprisoned as Eleanor herself? The idea was sickening. Yet what could she actually do to help them?

''Pon my soul, we're all very dull today,' Charles said, not for the first time. 'I feel I should apologize for not making better conversation.'

'I think it's because of the weather,' Fleurette suggested. 'Is there a storm coming? Can you tell us, Eleanor?'

That was one undiluted blessing. Now that she wasn't being dosed with that medicine daily, her sense of the weather was returning. Eleanor nodded. 'I believe it will be on us tonight,' she said. She could feel the slow creep of pressure across the land, as though giant hands were forcing the flat blue sky down like a piecrust and squeezing out every last breath of fresh air. 'But there's nothing to stop us from enjoying the sun for now.'

'Perhaps we could go down by the lake, later?' Fleurette suggested. 'It would be a charming stroll. If Eleanor is feeling well enough, that is. You should have told us yesterday how ill you were. I was positively horrified when you collapsed like that! And Charles—'

'Even my father cannot complain when I try to help a woman who's just fainted in front of me,' Charles said quickly. There had been something askew in his face at the beginning of Fleurette's speech, when she'd mentioned the lake, but he had pulled himself together quickly enough, if only to avoid her saying any more about his response to Eleanor's swoon. 'Besides, I was hardly the only one. Citizen Chauvelin – er, the Marquis—'

Fleurette giggled.

'Yes, I know, I must be more careful about these things. In any case, he was bending over your unconscious body a moment later, and Lady Marguerite was only half a breath behind him, calling for spirit of hartshorn to revive you, and feathers to burn under your nose.'

Eleanor wrinkled her nose in disgust. 'What, at the same time?'

'It was just like a scene from the theatre,' Fleurette assured her earnestly.

Eleanor could believe that. Lady Marguerite would know

all the best dramatic touches. 'And did Sir Percy do anything?'

'Raised his quizzing-glass, shook his head, expressed astonishment and shock, and generally waited for the rest of us to pick you up and see you to your bedroom,' Charles said. 'Which was quite in keeping with what my father expected.'

Swooning to distract attention from Charles had seemed like an excellent idea at the time, but Eleanor now worried that if she'd provoked him to an obvious reaction in front of his father, she might only have made matters worse. 'Where is everyone now?' she asked. 'It was nearly lunchtime when I woke up, and Alice insisted I eat something, then come out here with you. I've barely seen anyone else all day.'

'Percy was looking over the stables when last I saw him,' Charles said, 'and milady and Chauvelin were taking tea in the parlour and fencing – purely figuratively, I assure you. My father spent the morning in his study. He hasn't requested my presence yet today, so I'm happy to be able to spend the time with you. He seems convinced, for now, that Lady Marguerite should not be turned in to the authorities.'

Eleanor squeezed his hand. 'I do hope your father won't be annoyed about all this,' she said. A moment's thought compelled her to add, 'And that we aren't bringing any sort of trouble down on him.'

'Oh, Father's never been particularly fond of vampires,' Charles said quickly. 'He blames them for the execution of Charles I during the Civil War. Do ask him about that – he's fond of explaining his views on the matter and will be glad to have a new listener. He's maintained a low opinion of them ever since he was old enough to learn the family history. You must see the paintings in the Long Gallery while you're here, by the by. I know you won't be overly interested in the past of our family, but their clothes are depicted very well, and may be of interest to you . . .'

He was evading the subject of what they were planning to do next, but Eleanor couldn't force the question while Fleurette was sitting next to them. 'I suppose it comes down to how long we will be here, then,' she said drily. 'Pray don't think me ungrateful, either of you: I cannot thank you enough for rescuing me from Bedlam. But I'll confess the whole experience has left me uneasy about any sort of safety, for the moment. And – forgive me, Fleurette – the longer we have to continue this masquerade, the more chance that one of us will slip up.'

'Oh, it's an easy thing to pretend to be an aristocrat,' Fleurette said gaily. 'Bibi said I need only tell everyone that I've lived all my life in the country and know nothing of cities, and to agree with everything a man says to me, but to be careful never to be alone with one. And nobody expects me to speak English like a native – the way you do, Eleanor – because Bibi has told everyone that he only recently escaped from France with me.'

'But how does that explain my speaking good English?' Eleanor asked, diverted.

'Oh, you are my older sister! Naturally you are more scholarly than I am, and you studied languages when I was too young and frivolous to take an interest.' Fleurette dimpled. 'Lady Marguerite thought that was an excellent story. She said I had a true talent for this sort of work.'

Eleanor felt a moment's pang of jealousy at the image of Fleurette and Lady Marguerite dealing together so very well. The intimacy – friendship, even – which she'd shared with milady during their trip to Oxford seemed reduced by comparison.

This is folly, she rebuked herself. *The League rescued me from Bedlam. What greater proof of friendship and trust do I require?*

Fleurette glanced between Eleanor and Charles. 'I believe I will go and play chaperone a few dozen paces away,' she said cheerfully, 'and allow the two of you to speak in private. You must have a great deal to say to each other. I will wander around and pick flowers, or gooseberries, or whatever the phrase is.'

Eleanor couldn't prevent herself from blushing. 'You're very kind, Fleurette. Thank you.'

'Oh, it's nothing.' Fleurette rose and shook out her skirts, smiled at Eleanor and Charles – who was also blushing – and strolled across to admire the nearest clump of bushes. The flowers that studded it were all dying in the heat, but it was the thought which counted.

'I'm not sure what I can say to you under these circumstances,' Charles mumbled. 'Even if we're being left in temporary privacy.'

'You can tell me about what happened to that document we recovered in Oxford!' Eleanor exclaimed in a hiss. Fleurette might be generously strolling at a distance, but she wasn't deaf. 'Please tell me it wasn't all for nothing.'

'Far from it!' Charles brightened, and his fingers twitched as though longing to adjust his eye-glasses meaningfully. 'You did far better than we could possibly have hoped for.'

'We,' Eleanor contradicted him. '*We* did far better. Weren't you just as much a part of it as I was? Didn't you risk yourself by letting yourself be possessed?'

'I promise not to disregard your advice on that point again,' he said, pressing her hand. 'But we did indeed find something vitally useful. Matthew's plans and diagrams gave us the location of this secret beneath London. We know where it is.'

That was more than Eleanor had dared hope for. 'But he

drew those up hundreds of years ago,' she said uncertainly. 'And there was the Great Fire of London, as well as everything else . . . Will it still be there?'

'Fortunately he chose some buildings as landmarks which are still holding their own,' Charles explained. 'Such as the White Tower – the oldest part of the Tower of London – and other places that have survived, or whose locations we were able to trace. The Chief's had me sitting over old maps for the past week, trying to correlate all the points and diagrams.' He rubbed the bridge of his nose. 'Faith, it's strange for me to say that I've had enough of books and papers for the moment, but this once I'll own to it. He told me it was the best thing I could do . . . for you . . . while he and the others were endeavouring to find where you were being held.'

Now it was Eleanor's turn to squeeze his hand. 'It was,' she reassured him. 'Truly, it was. If we can find this secret . . .' She didn't know exactly what they were going to *do* when they had it, but Sir Percy would probably have a better idea of how to apply pressure to Lady Sophie and her pets than Eleanor herself. There might even be some way that Eleanor could fulfil her promise to Anima, to break the power of the vampires – though for the moment, simply escaping their threats would be enough. 'Then perhaps they'll be forced to stop hunting us. And we could even put an end to this vampire conspiracy, and stop their interference in politics.' After all, it was only the specific vampires hunting her with whom she had a grievance. She wasn't some sort of crusader like Anima had been. There must be some sort of third path.

Charles sighed. 'Deuce take it, I loathe being a fugitive like this in my own country. I could live with being one in France, what with breaking the law and all that, but this is England!'

'At least we haven't got the law pursuing all of us yet, as well as Lady Marguerite,' Eleanor said, hoping that was true.

'No, they've held off from unleashing those hounds,' Charles agreed. 'I wonder why. Possibly they fear the consequences of escalating this game.'

Eleanor glanced across to Fleurette. The other woman was still a safe distance away, but she couldn't be expected to stare at dead flowers for ever, and there was still more that Eleanor wanted to ask Charles. 'On the matter of this great secret, did Matthew's notes say what this actually *was*?'

Charles rubbed between his brows again. 'I fear Matthew was more concerned with the elegance of his Latin and the salvation of his soul than in providing definite facts on that point,' he said ruefully. 'No, perhaps I do the man an injustice. Some of his ramblings were those of a man who seemed deathly afraid of what he suspected. Like Bernard, he used the phrase *fons et origo* – source and origin. Eleanor, do you think it could be that this dire secret, this hidden matter of importance, is . . . the first vampire ever created?'

'The vampires claim there is no single first vampire,' Eleanor said slowly, 'but then, that's what they *claim*, and we saw in Oxford how eager they are to conceal their true history. So your thoughts might well be correct. Though why would that have made Matthew worry about the salvation of his soul?'

'I do not know. Perhaps Bernard could have told us more. They were brothers in their craft, after all, and he seems to have had some inkling of this secret too, even if he would not share it with us.'

Eleanor realized that in the discussion, she'd lost sight of the most important point. 'And where *is* this secret hidden?'

Charles looked almost embarrassed. 'I believe it's beneath the Houses of Parliament.'

Eleanor was torn between shock and laughter. 'Of all the things for Parliament to be built upon! At least the National Convention only had gunpowder beneath it.'

'Parliament's managed as much in the past,' Charles noted. 'Remember Guy Fawkes and his plot – though pray don't mention that in my father's hearing, as he's been known to wish the fellow had succeeded.'

Fleurette turned from her flowers, glanced to their right, and began to hastily walk back towards Charles and Eleanor. She was affecting a casual manner, but her eyes betrayed concern.

'Hsst!' Charles commanded, following Fleurette's gaze. Eleanor naturally turned to look and stiffened as she saw the two figures approaching.

CHAPTER FIFTEEN

On one side was the heavy, trudging form of Charles's father, in black and gold again, and beside him strolled the smaller, leaner shape of Chauvelin, also in black but undiluted by any brighter shades or metallic accents. Once again, it seemed strange to see him without a tricolour sash or Revolutionary rosette. Charles and Eleanor rose to their feet to join Fleurette, and all bowed or curtsied as the older men came closer.

'Your daughters show good manners,' the Earl remarked to Chauvelin. 'For a couple who never attended Court, extremely good manners. I must commend you, sir.'

'I thank you for the compliment, sir,' Chauvelin returned. 'I will confess I had no great wish to take them to Court. A man who has devoted himself to his family does not wish to expose the softer blossoms to injury.'

'Very true.' The Earl's gaze flickered over Eleanor and rested on Fleurette. 'Charming, absolutely charming. Perhaps you and my son would care to walk with me to the lake, my girl?'

'I'd be honoured, milord,' Fleurette said. 'But poor Eleanor—'

'Tush, your father will remain with her. He told me that he wishes to speak with her in any case. Come now.' The

Earl offered Fleurette his arm, and Fleurette took it with a sweet modesty which Eleanor suspected disguised a lack of enthusiasm. 'Charles, come with us. What passes between a father and his daughter is not for the ears of any careless stripling.'

Charles flushed, then paled, then flushed again, and bowed. 'As you wish, sir.'

Eleanor watched the three of them stroll away with rather mingled feelings. True, she was losing Charles and Fleurette – and neither of them seemed willing to go – but if Chauvelin was willing to tell her a little about what was going on, then that would redress the balance somewhat. 'Do you want to seat yourself first, sir?' she said softly. 'I wouldn't wish to appear lacking in daughterly manners if the Earl should happen to glance back at us.'

'I may be excused a degree of laxness for the sake of fatherly concern.' Still, Chauvelin took a seat on the bench, disdaining the scattered cushions. 'Sit. You and I have urgent business, and I don't know how long we can remain at this house before we are discovered.'

Eleanor found herself strangely reassured by this statement that they were all in danger. However much she tried, she couldn't convince herself that they were truly safe. To have someone outright declare it was, in its way, a relief. She seated herself neatly, straightening her skirts. 'I am at your service, sir.'

'You say that very prettily, and I am sure you were well coached in proper manners, but we both know there's not a word of truth to it.'

'As you wish, Father. Or should I call you Bibi?'

Chauvelin winced. 'Restrain yourself to "Father", if you would.' He extracted an enamelled box from an inner pocket and took a pinch of snuff from it, then sneezed. 'So. I believe we can be . . . useful to each other.'

Eleanor blinked. 'I, useful to you?'

'Undoubtedly. You will recall your actions in front of the Committee a month ago?'

They were painfully clear in Eleanor's memory. She'd managed to purge the taint of vampire control from some of the Committee members and their subordinates. Anima had expended the last threads of her essence to help Eleanor achieve this and had passed on in the process, her ghost leaving Eleanor behind once and for all. It had been reckless and foolish, and Eleanor had been manipulated into doing it in the first place, but she couldn't entirely bring herself to regret it. Some things should be done, no matter how foolish or reckless they were. The question was, how much did Chauvelin *really* know about her abilities? 'I do,' she said cautiously.

'Excellent. We make progress already.'

'What do you know about that?'

'I have over a dozen eye-witness accounts,' Chauvelin said smoothly, 'most of which are indisputable – or at least come from people who cannot be contradicted. Some of them are, would you believe, truly grateful to you? They hardly *chose* to be the victims of vampires. You came from nowhere and saved them.'

Eleanor didn't want to admit it to Chauvelin, but this did make her feel better about the whole episode. 'Has the Committee set you to investigating the affair?' she asked.

'The Committee has set quite a number of people to investigating the affair.' He took another pinch of snuff, letting her sit and wait impatiently while he sneezed. 'Their particular interest in my views come from the fact that Saint-Just – that would be Louis-Antoine de Saint-Just, rather than our dear Marguerite or her brother – reported having seen you in *my home* a couple of days previously. Citizen Robespierre himself discussed the matter with me.'

Normally Eleanor would have been only too pleased to know that Chauvelin was in political trouble, but the current circumstances made things more awkward. She felt an unwilling blush creep across her cheeks. 'I'm sure you were able to explain matters easily,' she said hopefully.

'Within reason. I explained that you were an innocent, easily frightened young woman, whose society I was cultivating. One possessed of unusual gifts.'

He was watching her as they spoke, like a cat at a mousehole. Eleanor tried not to feel uneasy. After all, they were in the middle of England, and the League was all around her, ready to protect her. Why should she feel so exposed?

A stupid question. This was Citizen Chauvelin, one of the best agents of the Committee for Public Safety, a hunter who'd more than once given the Pimpernel a run for his money. It was only common sense to be afraid when dealing with such a man, however secure her own position might seem.

Yet now he was waiting as though he expected her to leap to some conclusion from his words. 'And . . . what do you think those gifts are?' she asked.

Chauvelin sighed wearily. 'The obvious. You are some form of natural response in humanity to vampires, it would seem. The world creates them, but it also creates human beings who can repel them. Nature may produce snakes, but she also gives us the mongoose.'

'That's an extremely interesting theory,' Eleanor said. She wasn't lying. The more she explored the questions of magic and vampires, and why magic repelled vampires, the more she wondered whether Anima had actually been *right* about a great many things. Charles had suggested that her powers were merely something as yet unknown to science, and worthy of investigation. It seemed that Citizen Chauvelin had similar opinions. 'You don't believe in magic, then, I take it?'

His expression was as bitter as lye. 'I do not believe in magic, nor have I ever had any inclination to do so. What *you* can do is real and tangible. Drugs render you incapable. Vampires who consider their own self-preservation the only cause worth believing in think you are a threat. They do not believe in magic, and neither do I.'

Oh, don't they? Eleanor thought, but she kept that to herself. 'Yet none of this explains why you went to such trouble to rescue me,' she said. 'Though please don't think I am ungrateful.'

'I hope you will not forget that gratitude.' He leaned forward, eyes glittering, his narrow face intent and hungry. 'Since you apparently intend to ignore more subtle suggestions, I will be forthright with you. Eleanor Dalton – Citizen Dalton – I wish to offer you employment.'

Eleanor sat back, astonished. 'What?' she demanded, her brains apparently having deserted her and left her without the capacity to express herself more fluently.

'I would have thought that a working woman was more aware of how the market for labour operated,' Chauvelin said. Her bemusement clearly amused him. 'You have a useful skill. I wish to hire it.'

Eleanor tried to reduce her whirling thoughts to some semblance of order. 'Or do you mean that the *Committee for Public Safety* wishes to hire me?' she asked, suspecting she wouldn't like the response.

'For the moment, the Committee doesn't know about you in person,' Chauvelin reassured her, smiling thinly. 'They only know that you are somebody whom I know. Certain highly placed people have expressed a wish that I obtain your services. I do not want to disappoint them.' He left unsaid how far he might go to avoid that disappointment, and what it might mean for Eleanor. 'However, I'm not a fool: I can see I must offer you something you want – that

211

you *need* – in return. The current situation makes it extremely obvious what that is.'

Given Chauvelin's previous actions, Eleanor wondered for a moment if he was going to offer her information that would allow her to blackmail Lady Sophie. She had never previously realized how tempting such a thing might be. Perhaps she had been unfair in the past to judge blackmailers so hastily. But he'd changed his phrasing from *want* to *need*. 'What do you think I need?' she asked cautiously.

'Safety.' Self-satisfaction at his argument was clear in every line of his body. 'You have made yourself a target for vampires. The safest place for you is one where they will be unable to reach you. In short, France.'

'You can say that when just a month ago they were controlling half the Committee and planning to blow up the National Convention?' Eleanor exclaimed. 'For shame, Citizen Chauvelin!' Her words were meant as mockery, but they felt hollow to her.

'They were, they did, they attempted, and they *failed*.' His mouth curled in what was not a smile. 'Do you think you're any safer here? Are the airs of Bedlam so congenial to your tastes?'

'I'm not safe anywhere,' Eleanor said slowly. The shining surface of the distant lake, the green rolling lawns, the pleasant countryside all seemed to mock her. She was here in disguise, and would be thrown out without a moment's hesitation if Charles's father were to discover the truth. She was reliant upon her friends to protect her, defend her and save her. She was a leaf on the surface of the water which could be plucked under by any stray current.

'I suppose one of your friends in the League would re-assure you at this point,' Chauvelin said flatly. 'He would pat your hand and urge you not to worry your little head about such things. Marguerite Saint-Just had more intelligence than that – and so do you, I think. If the world is not safe for you, then you must make it so. And you will find it easier if you are not in a country which allows those who abuse you to act as they wish, and with impunity.'

Eleanor tried to ignore the many parts of her mind which were in agreement with him. 'France is not a safe place,' she said, 'even if it may have fewer vampires than England. What about the law which was passed less than a month ago? Under that law, a single anonymous accusation could mean my death. Or yours, or anyone else's. How is that safety? What is to stop someone who's being controlled by a vampire from simply killing me one dark night? How is *anyone* there safe?'

'I'm glad to see you are considering the matter rationally,' Chauvelin said, still with that air of satisfaction. 'Precautions would be taken. For the moment, as the only person capable of doing what you can do, the Committee would take an interest in your safety. Perhaps you have forgotten that some of them *know*, from personal experience, what a vampire's control feels like. They have a strong motivation to ensure that it does not happen to them again. Trust their self-interest, if nothing else.'

'So I would be on uncertain ground, rather than no ground at all.'

'Would you prefer Bedlam?'

Eleanor couldn't control her flinch. And Chauvelin saw it, damn him. 'Don't think that your Pimpernel is unaware of this, by the by,' he added. 'Part of our . . . bargain . . . was his permission to make this offer to you. He knows that you may accept it.'

'Why does he think I'd want to?' Eleanor bit her lip, and forced self-control on herself. This was no time for hysterics, however well merited they might be. Sir Percy wouldn't want to just . . . get rid of her, like an old servant pensioned off. This must surely have been a mere concession to Chauvelin, in order to secure his assistance in a situation where any of the League would have been known and watched for. Surely.

'As I have said, safety. Perhaps he also wishes to separate you from Lord Charles Bathurst – and I admit I can see his point there. Marriage with you would be impossible for the young man. In France, you could find a husband more suited to your abilities and position, and he will be able to forget you in time.'

As Eleanor sat there mutely, attempting not to vent her feelings, he continued. 'Don't think me unreasonable. Impossible attachments are common among young men and women. But I suspect from your own behaviour towards the young man that you realize just *how* impossible it is, don't you? Such a marriage could not take place in England.'

'And in France?' Eleanor got out, nearly choking on her words.

'If he wishes to forsake his rank and family, and come to France to take an honest job, to begin a new life there, I will consider him as a possible suitor.'

'If you suggest such a thing to him,' Eleanor snapped, cold fury infusing itself into her voice, her fingers curled into claws, 'then not only will I never forgive you, but you may whistle for any chance of my even *considering* your suggestion!'

'Ah, I thought so.' Chauvelin smiled, thinly but genuinely. 'In that case, no, I will not mention the possibility to him, since we both know he loves you well enough to do it. And you love him well enough not to wish him to forsake his life and family. It is convenient to have these things clearly understood, isn't it?'

Eleanor fumed with anger, but at least it was better than curling up and dying on the spot from mortifying embarrassment. Of all the people she would least have wanted to understand her feelings and weaknesses, Chauvelin topped the list.

A growing breeze plucked at her skirts and ruffled her shorn hair. She forced her hands to unclench themselves, trying to calm her feelings. Chauvelin *didn't* know about the nature of her magic – or didn't believe in it – and that might yet be vital. 'So, Citizen Chauvelin,' she finally said. 'You've explained the advantages of your offer. No doubt there would also be a salary of some sort, a place to live, perhaps even a state pension for my old age . . .'

Chauvelin nodded warily. Clearly he didn't believe she had chosen to accept his bargain, but he was willing to allow his prey time to run. 'I will be frank with you. Your demonstration in the Bedlam cellars that you can work with other people to do . . . whatever it is that you do, will enhance your value. Naturally my Fleurette will not be taking part in such work, but we can find other people who will support you.'

'But I would have to support your Revolution.' She deliberately gave the word its full value, as though she could encompass everything in it – the trials, the mobs, the hunger for victims, and ultimately the guillotine. 'There is also the minor matter of England currently being at war with France.'

Chauvelin shrugged. 'You've shown little enough interest in that business prior to now, other than to dress as a soldier when you and your League wish to pass unnoticed. Perhaps if there were fewer vampires on both sides, hostilities might lessen. And what's more . . . though of course locked away in Bedlam, you would hardly know about it.'

'About what?' Eleanor demanded, conscious she was being baited and yet unable to stop herself.

'I understand certain proposals have been put before the English Parliament regarding the military – and vampires.

Proposals that some soldiers be "elevated" to that rank.' His tone dipped the word in acid and left it hanging in the air like a curse. 'They would, it has been suggested, do more damage to the French in their new condition. It has yet to be decided whether they should choose such candidates from particularly heroic officers, or from murderers in gaols awaiting hanging – though perhaps there is little difference between the two. And of course, there is the question of how to preserve and transport blood, since they would need to *feed* these new soldiers, who could hardly be turned loose on their own ranks . . .'

Eleanor stiffened, remembering the cellars under Bedlam, the blocks of ice and the frozen containers of – what else could it be? – blood. No doubt all provided from the daily bleedings of the patients. 'I believe they have already solved that problem,' she said, her voice shaking. Just how many games had Castleton been playing?

'Yes, very likely,' Chauvelin agreed. 'Even your Pimpernel sees the errors in these suggestions. However, he may have gone too far in portraying himself as a fool in public. There will be little he can do to change what they have in mind.'

Eleanor had no doubt this was the sort of thing which Anima would have wanted Eleanor to stop. But how could she affect anything at the highest level of politics? Was she supposed to single-handedly persuade Parliament to change their mind? She felt like a mouse surrounded by towering buildings – unnoticed, perhaps, and capable of running around in their cellars, but unable to actually *affect* the mightier powers which formed the foundations of her world.

Once more, it all came back to the vampires' secret. If the League could use it, could *stop* them, then all this talk of Chauvelin's became no more than conjecture. The League now had to save both England and France – and perhaps more beside. After all, if England began using vampires as soldiers, how many other countries might follow out of self-defence? And where would that end?

'I can't give you an answer now,' she said. 'I can't. I need time to think. And Charles will be back soon.'

'I doubt it,' Chauvelin said. 'I imagine his father will keep him by the lake for as long as possible.'

'Why?'

'You don't know?' Chauvelin actually sounded pitying, for once. 'His elder brother died there. A boating accident, I was told – one of those strokes of chance which can befall even the most athletic young men. A slip, a fall, a blow to the head, and the heir was drowned without even a chance to struggle. Charles saw it happen from the shore, and his father has never forgiven him for it. I believe he likes to remind him of it whenever he can.'

Eleanor shook her head in disbelief, her eyes suddenly burning with tears. That explained so much about Charles – his diffidence, his lack of self-worth, the cruelty with which his father treated him. It was hardly *his* fault; but from her year of acquaintance with him, she was quite certain he blamed himself and only himself, however little he deserved it.

Chauvelin rose to his feet. 'I will be charitable and wander down to join them. Perhaps I can distract the Earl. In the meantime, I suggest you return to the house. However safe this estate may appear, I think it unwise for any of us to wander around it alone.'

'You don't think that we've evaded notice, then?' Eleanor didn't like agreeing with Chauvelin, but on this point she was willing to make an exception.

'I think it is only a matter of time.' He offered her his hand for her to rise. 'And so, I believe, do you.'

CHAPTER SIXTEEN

It was cooler inside the house. The heavy timbers and old stone held off the weight of the sun. But equally it was stagnant, like living underwater. No breezes disturbed the scatter of papers and journals on the table, or played with the tassels that hung from the cords of the heavy velvet curtains. The servants had done their duty for the time being, and then disappeared, leaving the rooms clean yet empty. Eleanor wondered what it was like when Charles's father was alone here with no family nor guests, and how he endured the *weight* of the house's history.

She looked around, finding herself unexpectedly at a loose end. Were things normal, she would have been working like any maid; cleaning something, or helping in the kitchen, or sewing . . . Her fingers ached for needle and thread, for work that she enjoyed – productive, creative work which would culminate in her having added something useful and beautiful to the world.

Perhaps that was how she should be thinking of Chauvelin's offer. Would she be saving lives, if she took him at his word? Did it really matter what she wanted, if this was her duty? Was it what Anima would have wanted her to do?

218

No – she had instructed Eleanor to uncover the vampires' secret, and they were getting so close to that now. Nothing else mattered until she'd done all she could to aid in that mission.

There was one thing, at least, which she could do here and now, and that was to find out if Chauvelin had been speaking the truth about recent events. The newspapers – *The Times* and others – lay there in open invitation to guests. She was about to do battle with the most prominent-looking article when a cough startled her and she turned to see the household's butler.

Lifelong reflex impelled Eleanor to bob a curtsey, and she had to deliberately lock her knees to prevent herself from doing so. She felt far more like an impostor here, in her own country and facing another servant, than she had done in France when disguised as Marie Antoinette and confronting the warden of the Temple Prison.

'Madam,' he said, and proffered her a silver tray. On it lay a sealed note. The name on it read, *Eleanor*.

Lady Sophie's handwriting! Eleanor's hand shook as she reached out to take it. 'Thank you,' she said, her voice trembling – yet she wasn't certain whether anger or fear was the stronger emotion. 'Might I ask who delivered this?' Thankfully it was easy to fall back on the manners which the League had trained into her when she'd been intended to impersonate the Queen of France.

'Young master Castleton, the vicar's son,' the butler said. 'He informed me that the two of you have prior acquaintance, madam, and requested that I should mention he is staying at the King's Head in the village below.'

Eleanor's fingers tightened on the note. So much for the League's certainty that they wouldn't be traced here for a few days! So much for their thoughts of safety! Why hadn't Charles – or Sir Percy – thought of Castleton's connection to the area? She took a deep breath. 'Thank you,' she said. 'Would you kindly inform Lord Charles that I wish to see him, when his . . .' How should she put it? *When his father isn't demanding his presence to berate him for imagined faults?* 'When he is at leisure,' she finished.

The butler inclined his head in a dignified, imperturbable nod, and drifted out of the room in silence. Eleanor sank into the nearest chair, staring at the note in her hands. Hadn't Lady Sophie said quite enough already? Didn't actions – such as kidnapping Eleanor and committing her to Bedlam – speak louder than words?

With a little sob she tore the note open, breaking the wafer which sealed it, and began to read.

My dear Eleanor,

At least, Eleanor reflected, she was no longer calling her *Nellie.*

I consider it highly unlikely you will accept any apology which I might offer, so I will spare us both the trouble. As far as I am concerned, I did what was necessary. When you have lived as long as I have, and when you have as many people under your protection as I do, you may understand my actions. For now, I cannot expect you to appreciate my position.

And in any case, one didn't apologize to the servants, did one?

I am ready to negotiate. There must be a way in which we can both secure our future safety and independence. I am willing to extend this lenience to your friends in the League, and I depend upon you to make my case to them, as I believe you can view this situation from a more pragmatic point of view than they will. I was born long before the age of chivalry, or the age of honour, and certainly long before the age of English gentlemen. I have little time for sensibility, except when Society demands it. As the saying goes, I know when half a loaf is better than no bread.

Eleanor chewed on her lower lip. If she had been wholly concerned for her own safety – and for that of the others in the League – then this would have been everything she wanted to hear. Assuming, of course, that there was a word of truth to it.

We have both demonstrated that we can seriously inconvenience the other, which is the usual prelude to negotiations. Let us omit the war and go directly to the peace treaty. I am currently staying at the King's Head in the village below. Send me a message – either that you will visit me, or that I should come to you. Bring whatever company you desire. I only wish to make my case. My side of the matter has been prodigiously exaggerated, and I have acted throughout with no more than the simple motive of self-preservation. I dare say you will argue the same. Let us meet and talk the matter through like sensible women, and avoid further casualties.

Sophia Basing

Eleanor sat in the chair, turning the contents of the letter over in her mind, as though inspecting a dress which looked clean enough but had a suspicious smell to the seams. While every mention of *sensible women* and nod towards assumed equality was balm to her sensibilities, she realized Lady Sophie had no doubt chosen every word with the intent to flatter her, and persuade her to agree to this meeting. She was old and practised enough to be able to lie – and lie convincingly.

221

And just how old is she, in any case? Matthew's angry words came back to Eleanor suddenly – *Sophia of Port-en-Bassin, involved in the London matter . . .*

At least it wasn't a letter inviting her to come out alone at midnight to a lonely copse somewhere on the grounds of the estate. She supposed she should be grateful that Lady Sophie had *some* respect for her intelligence.

'Lost in thought, m'dear?'

Eleanor looked up to see Sir Percy and Lady Marguerite – he with his quizzing-glass raised, she with an affectionate hand on his arm. A great weight lifted itself from her shoulders. 'I was about to come searching for you,' she confessed. 'I've just been given this.' She handed him the note, with a brief explanation of its arrival, and watched as he and Lady Marguerite scanned it together.

'Well,' Sir Percy finally said. He waited for Lady Marguerite to seat herself, and then allowed himself to sprawl across one of the heavy chairs. 'I must say that dear Sophie's stolen a march on us. Demned if I can think how she managed to track us here *so* swiftly! There are a dozen places where the League might have holed up, so how did she seize on us here? It's not as if she has the resources to track every coach leaving London.'

'And there aren't even any optical telegraphs here,' Eleanor said, trying to lighten the tone. She'd seen – and helped burn down – one of the new devices in France which could send a message across the country in a matter of bare hours.

'True, true. One couldn't hide something that large behind the chicken-house.' Sir Percy held the note up to the light as though scrutinizing it for secret messages, inspecting it through his quizzing-glass. 'Now what is it that dear Sophie really wants, mm?'

'Possibly her first aim is to rattle our nerves,' Lady

Marguerite suggested. 'A display of power, to convince us she knows our every move and can predict our slightest decision. Faith, she'd probably claim she knew how many cups of chocolate I had with my breakfast if she imagined it'd make us believe there was a traitor on the premises.'

And what if there *was* a traitor among the people here? Not just the League, but Alice, or Sir Percy's valet, or one of the local servants, or even Charles's father? It wouldn't even need to be a deliberate act of betrayal. The person might be an innocent who'd been fed the blood of a vampire over a month or more and forced into becoming their faithful servant.

Sir Percy seemed to guess her thoughts. 'Have no fear, Eleanor,' he said. 'That's one of their greatest weapons, I fancy. Our friend Chauvelin's an example. He trusts nobody, and never will, lest they might be an agent of the sanguino-crats whom he so detests.'

Lady Marguerite laughed, and tapped her husband's wrist with her fan. 'He never trusted anyone in any case, my love. It's hardly a new development for the man.'

'Perhaps that's true,' Sir Percy allowed, 'yet my own point's sound. If we start by suspecting each other of betrayal, then where will we finish? I'd rather believe that dear Sophie had some trick up her elegant sleeve which we've yet to fully comprehend.'

And yet Armand Saint-Just had betrayed them in France, Eleanor thought unwillingly. She couldn't just reject the idea.

She chose to turn the conversation to a different path. 'Chief – why are we working with Chauvelin?'

'It came as a surprise to me as well,' Sir Percy confessed. 'But when he approached me, and offered his services to locate and rescue you, I realized that here was a man – with his own agents, I have no doubt – of whom dear Sophie knew absolutely nothing. Think of it as a fashionable marriage of convenience, Eleanor. We are currently being civil to each other over breakfast, but by lunchtime we'll be at odds, and come the evening we'll have separated to different quarters of the world.'

'He's made you an offer, hasn't he?' Lady Marguerite said. 'I recognized that prowl of his when we saw him from the upstairs window. Trust me, my dear, I know that man's self-satisfaction far too well.' Her mouth twisted with bitterness, and Sir Percy touched her hand – much as, Eleanor realized, Charles had squeezed her own hand for comfort earlier. 'Whatever he may have offered you, I assure you it is not worth it. That little weasel never makes a deal unless he's convinced he'll come out ahead. Whatever you may decide, we'll back you to the hilt, of course. But I do hope you'll tell him no.'

While Eleanor was somewhat reassured by this absolute declaration of support, she couldn't help but note a certain flaw in Lady Marguerite's logic regarding deals with Citizen Chauvelin. 'But the League's own current arrangement with him . . .' she said tentatively.

Lady Marguerite rolled her eyes. 'Fie! How shall I live with one of my own students outsmarting me?' But there was laughter in her voice. 'I'd have more qualms about this *arrangement* were it not for the fact that we're both allied against this particular group of vampires. My belief is that little Chauvelin thinks we'll exhaust ourselves against each other, and that he can walk away with you afterwards.'

'A presumption which we do not share,' Sir Percy said firmly. 'His daughter may be a charming innocent, but under no circumstances will we let you fall into her father's claws. Now, to business. I think dear Sophie may have handed us an opportunity.'

'You think the woman's serious?' Lady Marguerite asked.

'Oh, not a bit of it. I have not the slightest doubt she's

only making this offer in order to gain a temporary advantage. Much like certain other people on this estate who are currently listening behind that door.'

For a moment his words hung in the air – and then the door in question opened, and Chauvelin walked in. He showed not the slightest trace of embarrassment, or awkwardness, or even annoyance at a slight to his professional skills concerning listening at keyholes. 'Pray continue,' he said, taking a seat. 'I find this conversation most interesting.'

'And I would in fact have invited you to join it at some later point,' Sir Percy replied amiably, 'but who am I to argue with the benefits of eavesdropping? My thought is that Sophie has, for once, made a mistake.'

'Which is?' Chauvelin queried.

'We know precisely where she is. Assuming she actually *is* down in the King's Head. In fact, I think it best to make sure of that as swiftly as possible. Excuse me a moment.' He leapt to his feet and strode from the room.

Lady Marguerite picked up the note which he'd discarded and passed it to Chauvelin. 'The cause of our discussion,' she explained.

Chauvelin looked it over, then shifted his gaze to Eleanor. 'Do you believe a word of it?' he asked.

'I believe she wants it all over, and for us to stop frustrating her schemes,' Eleanor said. 'I don't believe she wants a truce on equal terms.'

'Well, you'd know her best of any of us, as her servant. Marguerite Blakeney here was her friend . . . but we all know that friends can be deceived.' There was a vicious edge underlying his voice.

'She was Percy's friend before she was mine,' Lady Marguerite said, not rising to the bait. 'I never thought unkindly of her until – well, until all this came to the light.

I suspect she herself would claim that she'd prefer still to be on good terms with us, were it not for minor considerations of power and self-preservation. And there's little difference on those points between a person who's a vampire and one who's not.'

'Perhaps,' Chauvelin allowed, 'but I've yet to meet a sanguinocrat who would not ultimately betray anyone and everything else to save their own life. You know the sentiments I hold towards your husband's League. These have not changed. I will, however, allow that foolish as they are, they have a certain . . . ability to sacrifice themselves.' His tone suggested he'd gladly see them all do so. 'I have yet to meet a sanguinocrat who'd do as much.'

'Faith, you damn us with faint praise,' Sir Percy said, striding back in. The door swung shut behind him as he flung himself back down into his chair. 'I've sent my man John down into the village to have a pint at the King's Head and determine whether Sophie and Castleton are there, and if so, how many friends they may have brought along to keep us company. Because if they are in fact haunting our local rafters, then our choice of action seems clear, I think?'

It does? Eleanor wanted to say, but she didn't want to show herself as *entirely* ignorant in this company. Especially as from their expressions, Chauvelin and Lady Marguerite both seemed to understand what Sir Percy had in mind.

Chauvelin steepled his fingers. 'How do you propose to divide your forces?' he asked.

'Myself, Charles and my beloved Marguerite to London. You, your daughter and Eleanor remain here.' He turned to Eleanor. 'I fear, Eleanor, that I must ask you to undertake what may be the most dangerous and difficult task I've yet demanded of you.'

'You know I'll do it if I can,' Eleanor said, her lips dry.

He nodded. 'I have no doubts of you. The task, you see, is to remain here and play bait.'

'What?' Eleanor was about to complain, to expostulate, to give a thousand reasons why she'd be needed with them, but then Sir Percy raised his hand. She shut her mouth and bit her tongue to keep herself patient until he could give an explanation.

'You've pointed us to the whereabouts of the prize we wish to retrieve from London,' he said, 'and one which we all believe could give us the advantage we need in this dispute with dear Sophie and her vampire friends.'

'An item which you refuse to describe to me,' Chauvelin said pleasantly, 'or tell me where it lies hidden. I cannot blame you, and I'd do entirely the same thing in your position, but I trust you will understand my extreme curiosity.'

Lady Marguerite snorted. The more amiable Chauvelin grew, the more irritated she seemed to become. 'Sophie will doubtless have taken precautions to keep it safe, although we've been told it cannot be moved. However, the situation has changed, because we now know precisely where *she* is. She's left London, if this letter is true, and is sitting just outside the Bathurst gates.'

'Precisely,' Sir Percy said, picking up the thread of her discourse as easily as if he'd caught a ball she threw to him. 'And so long as she delays here for a few hours more, if we leave at once and can reach London first, we have an opportunity which I hadn't dared expect.'

'But will this item not be guarded?' Chauvelin asked. 'If it is so important, surely as an intelligent woman she'll surround it with guards a dozen deep. She has both money and servants – and loyal sanguinocrats.'

'But she cannot do so *secretly*,' Sir Percy said. 'Much like the trouble you've had in the past, old chap, when attempting to transport some prisoner of high importance, but were stymied by the fact that the more guards you set around them, the more likely that someone would talk too much or take bribes. I fancy that Lady Sophie cannot even trust her fellow vampires on this point. Did you not say, Eleanor, that Castleton seemed in the dark about it? And we've seen that they have their own power struggles in France. I fancy it's no better in England. If word got out that she was concealing some item of prime importance, well – half London might be awash in blood. So we just need to hold her focus here to expose her weakness elsewhere, so that we can slip past her defences.'

Eleanor put the pieces of Sir Percy's plan together. 'And if she thinks she has a chance to convince or remove me . . .'

'Quite,' Sir Percy said. 'Which is why you need to convince her that you are within reach – while remaining safely inside the house and *out* of reach. I wish to make that absolutely clear.' He glanced sidelong at Chauvelin. 'Even if you might be tempted to stray elsewhere.'

'Why should I wish to place her in danger, after having gone to such lengths to remove her from Bedlam?' Chauvelin enquired.

Sir Percy gave him a lazy smile. 'You might be tempted to remove her before the rest of us return. Though I'm sure you'd tell me no such thought has crossed your mind.'

'You're quite correct. That is what I would tell you.'

Eleanor was finding it somewhat bruising to have to sit next to such naked dislike, however much it might be disguised by the politest of language. 'But how will you get out of here and to London without anyone realizing?' she asked. 'When we arrived here, the road up to the house came through the village outside.'

'Well noticed,' Sir Percy congratulated her. Now he'd resolved on a course of action, there was a keen sparkle to his blue eyes. This new challenge had worked on him like strong brandy. Eleanor wished painfully that she could be swept along with him, rather than remaining at Bathurst House. 'Once my man gets back with confirmation of dear Sophie's presence, we'll ask permission from Charles's father to take some horses from the stables for a ride, then cut across country to one of Charles's neighbours. There we'll beg the loan of a coach to reach London as swiftly as possible. With luck we'll be in the city before night falls.'

It was reckless, it was hair-raising and it was everything the Scarlet Pimpernel lived for – and in which he succeeded. 'You'll need to tell me what to write to Lady Sophie, milord,' Eleanor said, already knowing she'd agreed to it.

From two rooms away, Eleanor listened to Charles's father express his disapproval of his son – yet again – in measured, curt tones. The breeze carried the words to her ears, but couldn't convey the expression on the Earl's face. And that was probably a good thing, because it would have stoked Eleanor's anger still higher. Her mother might have scolded her from time to time, but never like *this*.

With Sir Percy, Chauvelin and Lady Marguerite hanging over her shoulders, she'd written – and rewritten, and rewritten again – a note to Lady Sophie. This should, if there was any justice, keep her waiting for Eleanor to pay a call at the King's Head that evening. One end of their ruse was in play; now it was merely a matter of the League reaching London as swiftly as possible.

'I had thought,' the Earl was saying, 'that when my son actually troubled himself to visit me, it was for proper reasons such as dealing with the estate, or even wishing to spend some time in conversation with his father. Instead I find you pressing your attentions on a young woman barely risen from her sickbed. And now, when I request your presence, you tell me that you . . . wish to go riding with friends. In the heat of the afternoon.'

He spoke as though he were addressing Parliament, Eleanor thought, seething on Charles's behalf. Everyone within earshot would be gaining the full benefit of the Earl's opinions. Which was to say, a fair number of the servants, and certainly all the guests. Eleanor was two rooms away, and even then she barely needed to call a breeze to assist her hearing. This sort of scolding might be appropriate from a butler or a housekeeper berating an inadequate servant in front of the whole household, but from a father to his son it simply felt cruel.

'Lud, sir!' Sir Percy exclaimed. 'Pray don't be so harsh upon poor Charles here. I hoped that he'd escort myself and my lovely wife on a ride and point out the local areas of interest. We'd no intention of causing you inconvenience, nor of bringing your wrath down upon his head.'

'Indeed not,' Lady Marguerite put in. Eleanor could imagine her charming smile, her attitude of sympathetic understanding. 'Can you not spare him to us for a single afternoon?'

'Blakeney,' the Earl said coldly, 'I permitted my son to spend his time with you because I thought you might be able to coax him into proper social graces. I'll admit you've managed to turn him into a proper figure of a man, rather than a snivelling Oxford scholar like the Castleton boy. However, you have no sons; I cannot expect you to sympathize with a father's feelings in this situation. I'll allow you to be the most fashionable man in England, but when it comes to the management of your estate, everyone knows you leave it entirely to your stewards. As to politics – well, I'd be astonished if you can even tell me the name of our prime minister.'

'Then I fear you'd lose any bet you might make,' Sir Percy

said cheerfully, 'because I can tell you that it's Pitt. Heard a poem about him when he took the position ten years ago. How did it go – *A kingdom trusted to a school-boy's care . . .* Not a patch on my own work. You might have heard it? *They seek him here, they seek him there . . .'*

'Spare me the doggerel,' the Earl sighed. 'I make allowances for you, Blakeney. I see no reason to make them for my son. God knows that had John lived, he would never have behaved in this manner—'

'Sir!' Charles exclaimed, the word seemingly dragged out of him.

'At least *there* you show some proper feeling. You don't want your responsibilities, and frankly you don't deserve them, but by God I'll make you live up to them if I must beat them into you. You could be spending your time in some useful manner, here or in our holdings in St Petersburg, but no, you are determined to disappoint me. Let me be plain. Since you have chosen to impose yourself upon this household, you will not go gallivanting off as you might do in London, ignoring your responsibilities. You will present yourself to me in my study on the hour, ready and willing to discuss the estate. Your guests will have to take their leisure without you. Feel free to use any horse from my stables that you wish, Blakeney – I know that *you* are competent to handle them.'

Eleanor clenched her hands into tight fists and silently thought curses upon the Earl's head. She wouldn't even give him the kindness of believing he meant well. He didn't. His every word was chosen with intent to wound. She wondered if things would have been different if John, the elder son, had lived. Or would their father simply have found new grievances with *both* his children?

'And do not think yourself secure in your position, Charles,' the Earl added. 'I can marry again. Perhaps another son, reared with more attention and discipline, would be better suited to the title and lands. Then you could go to Russia – or go to the devil. I suggest you do not give me cause to consider this more carefully, boy.'

A door closed with a click.

Footsteps approached the parlour where Eleanor was sitting alone. She rose, and Charles came in, walking as if each step required conscious thought, a curiously blind look to his face. Nothing to do with whether or not he was wearing his eye-glasses, but instead the fixity of one who did not want to see what was in front of him.

'Charles?' Eleanor said softly.

'Oh, I'll go.' His voice was numb. 'I can't abandon the Chief now – I'm needed, I know it. He'll forget what he's said, his temper will cool and later he'll ignore my behaviour . . .'

She took his hands, enfolding them in her own. They were cold. 'Charles, I'm sorry. I didn't know.'

'I'd rather you'd never known, m'dear.' He managed a smile, but his eyes were still distant. 'I cannot blame him. My older brother John was a far worthier heir to the title and lands than I. When he drowned that day, and I could not reach him, could not save him . . .'

'It wasn't your fault,' Eleanor said urgently, as though the sincerity of her words could pierce his pain.

'Maybe not, but I've forever felt as though I was running to catch up.' Charles sighed. 'I took his place with the League, as well – did any of the others ever tell you that he was one of them first? No? They do me that kindness, at least. I make what little contribution I can, but even so I fear I'll never fill his shoes, there or elsewhere. He was the man of action, and I a mere scholar.'

Eleanor tightened her grip till he made a noise of protest. 'Indeed? Then pray tell me who'd have forged all those papers for the League in France if it had been your brother with them rather than you. Who would have translated the documents from Oxford which you risked your life to obtain?' She dropped her hands and pulled him close. She couldn't, *couldn't*, let him leave in such a state of despair. 'Perhaps John was a good man, but I never knew him, and it's you, not John, who . . .'

She wanted to say *I love*, but she couldn't bring herself to do it in this moment – and especially not in this venerable house, so full of heavy silence and disapproval. She could only look him in the eyes and try to share her feelings without speaking the words aloud.

For a moment he stood there in her embrace, his own arms wrapped around her. Then he jerked away. His father might not be in the room, but his shadow – and the shadow of his heritage – lay between them.

'I must be on my way,' he said. 'The others will already be in the stables. Stay safe in the house, Eleanor – there are enough men here that even Lady Sophie won't be foolish enough to stage some manner of assault.' He hesitated for a moment. 'If – if anything should go wrong with our endeavour in London, then you'll find my notes in my bedroom. And Chauvelin will protect you. I have no doubt that will prove unnecessary, though. The Chief knows what he's doing.'

'I trust the Chief,' Eleanor said forlornly, as though it were a prayer for all their safety, and watched Charles go.

CHAPTER SEVENTEEN

The sky was aflame with sunset. The view from the window of Fleurette's first-floor room – next to Eleanor's, similar but decorated in blue – was the sort of thing which should have been painted by masters and hung up in galleries for future generations to admire. Yet all of it was flawed by the desperate worry gnawing at Eleanor's guts.

She clenched her hands on the window frame, wondering whether the others had reached London yet. Even with the best of luck, they were probably still on the road. And once they got to London, they'd need to contact the rest of the League, gather their resources, put the plan into motion . . .

'Eleanor, will you not play cards with me?' Fleurette asked. Her English was coming on in leaps and bounds, though her French accent was even stronger than Lady Marguerite's affectation. 'Otherwise either I must play chess with Bibi and lose, or I must read, and I do not read English as well as I speak it. Besides, all the newspapers speak of people and places with whom I have no acquaintance.'

'You may as well do something other than stare out of the window,' Chauvelin said, with rather less sympathy than his daughter. 'Even if all goes well, we're unlikely to have news before tomorrow morning at the very earliest. If you continue staring at the horizon and fretting, then I will need to send your excuses down to the Earl, and claim you are still recovering from your ordeal and unfit for supper.'

'That might be the easiest thing in any case,' Eleanor said coldly. She hadn't forgiven the Earl for his words to Charles earlier. Having to face him over the supper table and make polite conversation would almost be as bad as eating gruel in Bedlam.

'If I can sit at meals with the Scarlet Pimpernel and keep a civil tongue in my head, then you can manage the same with the Earl while posing as my daughter,' Chauvelin said. There was a note of steel to his voice. 'If you are to come to France, then you'll need to learn to do as much and more. I had thought that simple acting was within your capacities.'

'You are coming to France, Eleanor, aren't you?' Fleurette's voice was . . . wistful. Eleanor could imagine her face – trying so very hard not to lay her wishes on Eleanor as an additional burden, yet wanting to have her nearby as a friend.

Bitterly she wished that she could invite Fleurette to stay in England. *That'd* show Chauvelin. But what could Fleurette hope for here in England, without family or friends other than the League? Why would she actually *want* to remain in a foreign country at war with France? And was England actually safer for her than France, with Lady Sophie liable to take measures against anyone connected to the League?

'I don't know,' she finally said. 'I'm sorry, Fleurette, I don't know.'

'A better answer than *no, never, certainly not, it is impossible, why are you still here when I have already refused you,*' Chauvelin commented.

Eleanor was attempting to devise a suitably cutting reply when something happening below caught her eye. She leaned forward to look more closely. Two of the Earl's men, in clothing which suggested they were grooms or gamekeepers or similar, were dragging a third man between them towards the house.

Below her, the Earl stepped out onto the terrace. Eleanor could have dropped a penny out of the window and had it land on his powdered hair. He moved with heavy deliberation, the dying sun in the bloody sky picking glints from the gold embroidery on his black clothing. When he paused, the two servants quickened their pace, pulling their struggling prisoner along.

'A poacher?' the Earl finally said, his voice carrying in the still air.

There was a rustle behind Eleanor as Chauvelin, then Fleurette, came to join her at the window.

'We found him in the spinney to the south-east, milord,' one of the servants said, sparing a hand to touch his brow. 'Broke and ran for it as soon as he laid eyes on us, so we ran him down and brought him in. Says his name's Brewster, but he's not a local man.'

The prisoner stopped struggling. 'I never done nothing wrong!' he declared. 'You can't set your dogs on a man just because he's walking in your woods!'

'Actually, I can,' the Earl murmured. 'Did he have any game on him, Jenkins?'

Jenkins hesitated. He looked as though he dearly wished he could have said yes and provided evidence. Finally he muttered, 'No, milord. Just this.'

Without speaking, the second man held up some sort of contraption of wooden slats and rope. It looked barely large enough to hold a kitten.

The Earl walked close enough to inspect it. 'Hm. Did he have a ferret in there?'

'No, milord,' Jenkins answered. 'Just a pigeon. Fell on it when we brought him down, he did, and it flew away.'

At Eleanor's side, Chauvelin tensed. His lips drew back from his teeth in a silent snarl.

'Well, I suppose pigeons are hardly dangerous,' the Earl said. 'Have you anything to say for yourself?'

Brewster sucked on his lower lip, hesitating, then shrugged. 'Nothing that you'd care to hear. Milord.'

'No excuse for being on my land?'

'Didn't know it was yours, did I? I was going to meet a friend. He never showed.' Brewster shut his mouth with what should have been an audible click, from the vehemence of his chin.

'Have him beaten, then throw him off the grounds,' the Earl instructed Jenkins. 'By the by, have you seen my son and his guests?'

'Yes, milord,' Jenkins said. 'And no, milord. Though if they went west—'

Chauvelin closed the window softly, avoiding noise, then turned to Eleanor. 'I fear the situation is not as we thought,' he said crisply. 'I am as guilty as anyone of underestimating the vampires. Tell me, when Blakeney sent one of his men down to scout at the inn, had that man ever seen Lady Sophie before in person, or did he merely have a description of her to go by?'

'I don't know,' Eleanor said, her stomach beginning to curdle with dread. What had she missed? 'Why?'

Chauvelin shrugged. 'We must determine whether the vampire at the inn *was* Lady Sophie of Basing, or merely another female vampire dressed in her clothing and staying in her room, conveniently avoiding public attention. It would be an easy role to play.'

'What have pigeons to do with all this?' Fleurette asked.

'*Homing* pigeons,' Chauvelin said. He seemed to be calmer now. '*Carrier* pigeons. This would also explain how they knew so quickly where we were hiding.' He glanced at

Eleanor. 'Do you still not understand? Your enemies don't need to follow you and the League if they can plan ahead. They penetrate your network – you said Armand Saint-Just had been subverted, I believe? – and ensure that they know most, or all, of your members, then send servants with carrier pigeons to the villages nearest to their estates. Any arrival by the local aristocracy, especially with a coach full of guests, will be the immediate subject of gossip by the locals. At which point, within a few hours your Lady Sophie can expect a message with details of our arrival, our location and our numbers.'

'She's hardly *my* Lady Sophie,' Eleanor protested weakly. She was too busy reeling from the impact of Chauvelin's theory. 'But in that case . . . if she isn't actually here . . . then she expected Sir Percy to believe she *was*, and to seize the opportunity to take action?'

'Being able to lure one's adversary into over-extending is as useful in security as it is in intelligence,' Chauvelin said. He seated himself in front of the chessboard again. 'Poor Brewster downstairs was probably one of several men planted around the estate to watch for an unscheduled excursion by Blakeney and others, and send word of their direction via carrier pigeon. The operation would require a number of loyal servants, but money can buy a great many of those, and sanguinocrats have a great deal of money.'

'But surely this is bad news, Bibi!' Fleurette exclaimed. 'If our friends are walking into a trap . . .'

'If our *temporary allies* are walking into a trap, then it's no more than they've done a dozen times before,' Chauvelin replied. He toyed with a pawn in a contemplative manner. 'No doubt they will extricate themselves as easily. Indeed, nobody knows better than I how skilled they are at such . . . cleverness.'

'And if they can't?' Eleanor demanded.

He looked up at her, his greenish eyes as uncaring as a cat's. 'I suppose in that case the League of the Scarlet Pimpernel would no longer be able to cause me trouble in France.'

Eleanor turned away sharply, unable to look at him any longer. It was only guesswork on his part. It might be completely wrong. Surely something as simple as a carrier pigeon couldn't bring down Sir Percy Blakeney and the League?

She needed some way to prove or disprove what he was saying. The easiest thing to do would be to determine whether Lady Sophie really was at the King's Head in the village. If she was, then Chauvelin was probably incorrect. But if she wasn't, or if it was some other vampire there playing her part . . .

Yet going down to the inn *herself* would be the action of a fool. She would be exposed, running directly into danger. She needed somebody else who knew what Lady Sophie looked like, yet all those in the League who did had left her behind to go to London.

But perhaps there was someone else in the house who *could* help her.

'Excuse me a moment,' Eleanor said, not looking behind her at where Chauvelin was arguing with Fleurette. She left the room, glancing around for a servant. It took her a few moments to find one of the footmen. She had to remind herself that as a presumed lady of quality, she would not be asking for a favour; she would be giving an order. 'Please have Alice – Lady Blakeney's maid – sent to me in my room,' she said.

'Of course, ma'am,' he murmured, and retreated with a bow.

Eleanor fretted as she walked up and down, fiddling with the bandages which covered her arms. The cuts from her daily bloodletting would take a while to heal. She wanted to be *doing* something. Why had the Chief not thought of this possibility? How could he have made so dreadful a mistake?

We don't always win, he'd once told her, but at the time she'd written it off as an attempt to ease her tears at her own failures. *We've frequently been lucky, but that's not always the case.* Had their luck finally run out?

There was a scratch at the door, and then Alice entered without waiting for any invitation, carefully closing the door behind her. 'You wouldn't have called for me like this if there weren't a problem,' she said, getting directly to the point. 'Is milady in trouble?'

'There's a risk that milady and milord, and all of them, may be walking into trouble,' Eleanor said, grateful for the other woman's directness. 'Alice, do you know what Lady Sophie – the Baroness of Basing – looks like? My previous mistress?'

'I do indeed,' Alice said, and Eleanor suppressed a sigh of relief. 'A face like fresh cream and eyes like pretty stones. I've seen her more than once when milady was visiting her, or the other way round.'

'She's supposed to be staying at the King's Head inn down in the village below, but there's a chance it's actually another woman masquerading as her.'

Alice nodded. 'And you'd like me to take a walk down there and find out the truth of the matter. Well, I'll be honest with you, from all I've seen you do in the past, I'd expect you to run down and do it yourself. Now I'm not eager to stick my head into a nest of evildoers—'

'I wouldn't ask you to do that!' Eleanor said quickly. 'I don't want you to put yourself in danger.' She realized she'd been unfair to ask this of Alice rather than do it herself. 'Don't worry about it. I'm sorry. I'll need to borrow a maid's dress—'

'But they'll know your face, as without a doubt they're looking for you.' Alice sighed, folding her arms. 'If you've learned enough sense to ask someone else for help rather than risking yourself, then you've learned something more than milady has. You're right to think she'd never have looked twice at me, if it is her. And if it's not her, then so much easier. Thank goodness the heat of the day's passed. I wouldn't care to be walking there and back under the midday sun.'

'Then you'll do it?' Eleanor said, taken aback.

'That I will. I'll say I'm in need of spirits of hartshorn, or something of that nature, and have one of the young men here escort me down to the village. You can expect me back in an hour or so. Don't you go worrying yourself, now! You're only just out of the sickbed.'

'No, Alice,' Eleanor said meekly. 'And thank you.'

'I've sent someone down to the inn to see if Lady Sophie is actually there,' Eleanor reported, rejoining Chauvelin and Fleurette. Fleurette was peering in dismay at the chessboard, while her father sat back and watched. 'Somebody who's seen Lady Sophie before and knows what she looks like.'

'A logical step,' Chauvelin said. 'But what do you intend to do after that?'

This was the point on which all Eleanor's plans beached themselves, running ashore to founder on the rocks, with no lighthouse to guide or stars to show her the way. 'I'm not yet certain,' she said, and hated the weakness in her voice.

'You were, perhaps, considering hurrying to London to warn them?' Chauvelin suggested. 'Finding your way to their homes, or whatever meeting point they had arranged? All highly laudable.'

If it had been Sir Percy saying this, he might have been praising her. Since it was Chauvelin, she knew he wasn't – and that however mild and pleasant his tone might be, he was mocking her. 'You have a better suggestion, sir?' she enquired bitterly.

'A passable one, I think. I could find some excuse to persuade the Earl to lend us his carriage to return to London. That would provide the means of travel which you require.'

It would indeed. Eleanor had no money, no influence with the Earl and no way to fly from here to London, even if God had somehow ripped the heavens open and reached down to grant her a balloon. Yet she winced inwardly, because she knew Chauvelin's offered favour would come at a very high price. And she knew precisely what that would be.

'Yes, this would seem to resolve everything,' Fleurette said cheerfully.

'Almost everything.' Chauvelin slid a bishop forward on the board. 'After all, I have no actual *reason* to persuade the Earl. Why should I assist you in running headlong into danger? Wouldn't your own League order you to remain here, where you are safe?'

Eleanor closed her eyes for a moment. She could feel despair weighing her down – despair, and a future stretching in front of her away from almost everyone she knew and loved. 'It's still to your advantage if the League succeeds,' she pleaded, knowing it wouldn't work, yet hoping somehow it might. 'Lady Sophie was working with the sanguinocrats in France who tried to blow up the National Assembly. Surely that's a more immediate threat than the possibility of the League inconveniencing you in the future?'

'You argue very prettily,' Chauvelin said. 'But I would rather that we be frank with each other. After all, it is possible that time may be an issue here, so we should not waste too much of it. You know what I want.'

There was one hope left in the room, one way of possibly changing Chauvelin's mind. Eleanor looked to Fleurette, hoping for sympathy, and saw it – but she also saw the cheerful brightness in Fleurette's blue eyes of one who sees all her wishes come true. 'Fleurette . . .' she said, looking for words that might persuade the other woman to stand against her father.

'I think you're being unfair, Eleanor,' Fleurette said flatly. 'Unfair to Bibi, but also unfair to *yourself*. Why shouldn't you come to France, where you'll be respected and appreciated? You can stop the sanguinocrats from corrupting and destroying the Revolution. If you stay *here*, they'll still keep trying to kill you. They already locked you up in Bedlam. But now you're asking Bibi – and me – to come with you and help save your League. I've met the League and . . . well, they're good people, and I don't *want* them to be hurt, but at the same time they've done nothing but put you in danger and lead you into trouble. Bibi would never do such a thing to me.'

'No,' Eleanor murmured, thinking of how Sir Percy gambled the lives of all the League again and again, her and Charles and everyone else. But at the same time, he trusted them to survive and succeed. Chauvelin might never put his daughter in such peril, but would he ever ask her to aspire to something higher, to risk herself for a cause they both believed in? 'Perhaps he wouldn't.'

'He's always tried to keep me *safe*!' Fleurette jumped up and stamped her slippered foot on the floor. 'That's what fathers do!'

'And I'm sure a great many noblemen of France tried to do as much for their own daughters, before they were sent to the guillotine!' Eleanor flared back. 'How long before someone accuses me under the new law? And have you forgotten how they imprisoned you at Mont-Saint-Michel?

You yourself are still in hiding in this supposedly safe country!'

'That's because of corrupt people in power! They were probably being controlled by the sanguinocrats, like the ones you purged in the Committee! If you just came and helped us, if you used your powers that God has given you to help everyone, then maybe it could even stop the war!'

That was something Eleanor didn't want to think about, because what if it was true? What if God had really given her her powers in order to do something like that? How could she possibly take up such a burden – yet how, with a good conscience, could she refuse it? And again, what of her promise to Anima?

She resorted to brutal practicality. 'That won't stop a war. Nothing stops a war except one side killing enough people on the other side. Ask your father if you don't believe me.' That was one belief Anima had expressed quite strongly while she was still with Eleanor, and Eleanor had seen nothing in the meantime to contradict it. 'I'm no Joan of Arc. And in any case, she was burned at the stake, or had you forgotten that? I'm not a martyr.'

'No, you're a woman of France—' Fleurette broke off, apparently having temporarily forgotten that Eleanor *was* actually English. 'You're a woman of England,' she started again. 'And you have a responsibility to your motherland! You should be working to find common ground between our nations, to liberate your people as we've liberated ours.'

'But if I do go to France with you, I'll have to pose as French for as long as I'm there,' Eleanor pointed out. Her eyes burned with unshed tears at the thought of it. It would be as much a lie as it would have been if she'd pretended to be a French heiress to ensure the Earl agreed to Charles marrying her. And it would be as much a lie as her *current* situation, pretending to be Chauvelin's daughter and having

244

all the servants nod to her as though she were a lady of quality. It was *all* lies, whichever way she looked. She was going to have to live a lie, one way or another, and the only choice she had was which one.

Fleurette swallowed. 'But we'd be together. I'd look after you and help you, and you'd be doing something which nobody else can do. Eleanor . . . I thought you were my *friend.*'

'I am!' Eleanor protested.

'Then why can't you see this is the best solution? I know you and Bibi don't get along very well . . . but over time you'll come to appreciate each other's good points, I'm sure. I'll *make* sure of it.' Determination glittered in her eyes. 'I want to make a better world – one where we can all be safe. And you're not safe here.'

I just wanted to work in a modiste's shop, Eleanor thought. But that was no longer an option. Perhaps it hadn't been for some time now. 'England is my home,' she said. 'You're asking me to give up my home, my family, everything . . .'

'To make a new one.' Fleurette stepped forward, taking Eleanor's hands in hers and squeezing them warmly. 'Besides, you'll be able to return here, won't she, Bibi? It won't be for ever. Just long enough to deal with the worst of the sanguinocrats. And would it be so bad, to have a new home somewhere else, somewhere where you were valued?'

Eleanor couldn't face Fleurette. She looked aside and saw that Chauvelin was twiddling a pawn between his fingers, an expression of solicitous neutrality on his face. Of *course* he'd just sit back and let his daughter make his case for him. He'd know just how much Eleanor might reject any offer from him, purely on the grounds that he was the one making it.

She would have liked to call Fleurette a hypocrite, to ask if she'd do the same if she were in Eleanor's position, but one huge barrier loomed in the way of that line of argument:

the pure and simple fact that Fleurette *would*. If someone were to grant her the same power that Eleanor had, she'd devote herself to the job without – well, with *barely* a second's hesitation.

There really wasn't any choice, and the sooner Eleanor accepted it, the better.

'No,' she said to Fleurette, trying to push aside thoughts of Charles, thoughts of England, thoughts of pleasant hours embroidering, of being merry with the other maids, of Sir Percy and Lady Marguerite and Tony and Andrew and all the rest of the League. Anima would approve of what she was about to do. That had to help, surely? 'No, it wouldn't be so bad.'

As Fleurette's face brightened, Eleanor turned to Chauvelin. 'You understand, monsieur,' she said, 'that my agreement is conditional on our fears actually being true? If it turns out that Lady Sophie is sitting down at the King's Head and thoroughly deluded by the League's stratagems, then—'

Chauvelin shrugged. 'In that case, I will not hold you to our bargain. I understand your position. But if my theory is correct, then in return for your willingly joining me in France and cooperating with the Committee to root out vampire influence, I give you my word that I will help you reach London and rejoin your League as swiftly as possible.'

And he would keep his word. Even the League agreed on that. Eleanor swallowed, then nodded. 'Agreed.'

Fleurette squeaked in delight and flung her arms around Eleanor. 'My sister!'

Eleanor returned the embrace. Fleurette was warm, and at the moment Eleanor felt so very cold.

Yet now she'd made the decision, her thoughts seemed clearer. Despair had a way of doing that. 'And you won't stop me helping the League in London?' she asked Chauvelin.

'As you have pointed out to me, it is in my interests for them to inconvenience Lady Sophie, or even destroy her. And if this secret is so vital to all the vampires, then perhaps it could be used against those in France too. Your assistance can only add to the League's chances of success. However, I will expect you not to risk yourself unduly, and to leave for France with me immediately afterwards.'

For a moment Eleanor let herself toy with the idea of Sir Percy and Charles forcibly stopping her from leaving, saying that she'd had no choice but to make the deal, and . . . well, doing the dishonourable thing which Eleanor didn't want to have to do herself. But that would be cheating, wouldn't it? Even letting them do something like that would be cheating. Housemaids might not be gentlemen, but they had their own sense of honour. And if she wanted Chauvelin's willing cooperation, then she must surely volunteer her own.

'I understand,' she said. Part of her mind set that word *unduly* aside for possible later use. 'But while we are waiting for Alice to return, there is something we can do. Or rather, something Fleurette can help me do.'

'Excellent!' Fleurette said. 'I am at your service!'

Chauvelin waved them away, his eyes abstracted. No doubt he was planning whatever excuse he'd give the Earl to explain their departure.

Eleanor took Fleurette's hand and led her towards the door. 'We need to search Charles's bedroom,' she explained.

That caught Chauvelin's attention. 'I would be glad to assist,' he offered smoothly.

Eleanor was certain he knew all about searching people's private possessions, but the idea of his hands prying through Charles's belongings made her wince. 'No,' she said firmly. A thought that courtesy would ease future interactions made her add, somewhat untruthfully, 'Thank you. I think Fleurette and I will suffice.'

Fleurette waited till she and Eleanor were in the corridor before whispering, 'You don't want Bibi to see any love poems he's written you, do you?'

Eleanor sighed. 'I'm not even sure I want to see them myself.'

In view of what she'd agreed to not ten minutes ago, it would quite simply break her heart.

CHAPTER EIGHTEEN

It was night before they reached London. They had been chasing the sunset, with every passing minute of light by which they could drive a victory. As darkness fell, the driver had slowed the horses without waiting for any direction to do so, and Chauvelin had shaken his head at Eleanor's appealing glance. 'It will do none of us any good if we crash,' he said curtly.

Alice had returned from the King's Head as quickly as she could. She'd managed to inveigle her way upstairs, since 'the lady guest' was keeping to her room, and had caught a glimpse of her and her attendants when one of the maids had briefly opened the door. Her report to Eleanor had been quite definite: whoever the vampire guest at the inn might be, she wasn't Lady Sophie. Chauvelin had promptly made their excuses to the Earl, who was already stalking and fuming over the disappearance of his other guests and his son. They'd surreptitiously slipped away – hopefully without followers or homing pigeons to mark their passage.

Eleanor and Fleurette had spent the time talking quietly, and Fleurette had replaced the bandages on Eleanor's arms. Chauvelin had spent most of the journey leafing through the folder of documents which Eleanor and Fleurette had located beneath Charles's mattress. Eleanor had felt a certain amount of guilt about letting him examine the League's plans for an assault beneath the Houses of Parliament, but . . . well, it would be worth it if it saved their lives. Besides, she had difficulty imagining Chauvelin imitating Guy Fawkes.

She would absolutely refuse to admit it to Charles, Sir Percy, any of the League, and least of all Chauvelin himself, but it was a relief to have him on her side. He was *intelligent* – sufficiently so to have almost managed to kill the League when he was their enemy. But now he was, however briefly, their ally. She only hoped he would remain their ally for long enough.

Chauvelin held up some of the papers to inspect them more closely in the lamplight, and frowned at what he saw.

'Is something wrong?' Eleanor asked hesitantly.

'This . . . narrative,' Chauvelin said, 'which you and Bathurst retrieved from Oxford, and which he was kind enough to copy down and enclose in this portfolio. I am uncertain about some points of Bathurst's translation. Oh, do not bristle at me, I am not attempting to insult the man. In fact, I congratulate him on his excellent research and his convenient compilation of information.'

Eleanor forced herself to suppress her urge to bristle. She would have to learn to tolerate these jabs from Chauvelin with more fortitude, she knew, if she was to look forward to months, if not years, of his company. 'Isn't a translation just, well, a translation?' she asked.

For once, Chauvelin hesitated before answering. 'I may be reading more into this text than is appropriate. The author is clearly insane in any case, with his babbling about sorcery and secret wars and hidden brotherhoods . . .' For a moment his eyes flicked to Eleanor, as sharp as a needle, but she kept her face blank and eventually he looked back to the papers.

'Yet I believe the man who wrote this was in a state of turmoil. I am accustomed to listening to confessions – in fact, you might say I am an expert in such things. This statement . . .' He tapped the papers. 'It seems to me to be the last words of a man who is sorely afflicted by guilt.'

Eleanor's flesh crawled at his words. *I am accustomed to listening to confessions . . .* Yet Charles had said something about this too, hadn't he? 'Charles spoke to me about it, but only a little. He said the ramblings were those of a man who was afraid of what he suspected.'

'Afraid, but also . . . incriminated,' Chauvelin said thoughtfully. 'Not a personal guilt, but much as a man might sound who fears that one of his family has committed a crime and that it has come back to haunt him.'

'You read a great deal from that document,' Eleanor said rather sharply. If Charles – and Sir Percy, of course – hadn't discerned all this, she found it doubtful that Chauvelin could have done so much better than them.

Chauvelin shrugged. 'Perhaps I do. After all, I must have something to occupy myself during this interminable journey. Let us change the subject. What do you plan to do, once we arrive in London? We will be there within an hour or two.'

This was a point on which Eleanor had strongly been hoping for divine inspiration, which had not, alas, arrived. She resorted to common sense. 'We're already several hours behind the others. If we try to go to anyone's house, we'll probably find they've already been and gone – and no doubt there will be people watching them, if what you suspect is true. But equally, it will have taken time for Sir Percy to assemble the others. My best suggestion is that we go directly to where they're planning to enter the Houses of Parliament, and intercept them there.'

'How are they planning to enter?' Fleurette asked curiously.

251

'If Parliament is anything like our National Assembly, then it must be surrounded by guards, and only the most serious of men and the people's representatives are admitted!'

'Sadly, if it *is* anything like our own National Assembly, then it's quite simple to walk in through the kitchen disguised as a servant.' Chauvelin sounded drily amused rather than bitter – then again, it hadn't been *his* failure in security.

Fleurette was quite capable of putting two and two together. 'Did *you* do that?' she asked Eleanor admiringly.

'Yes,' Eleanor admitted. 'But I don't think it would work in this case, with three of us.'

'Perhaps Bibi could pose as a reporter for the journals?' Fleurette suggested. 'Or . . . or we could pretend to be the mistresses of important ministers of state, being let into the building through a concealed side entrance!'

Now Chauvelin looked less than amused. 'That will not be necessary,' he said icily. 'The League's planned its method of entry elsewhere. The sewers, where they discharge into the river.'

Eleanor had been trying to avoid thinking about that. The tunnels beneath Paris had been bad, the sewers even worse, and now necessity obliged her to plunge back into foul water, slime and corruption. Hopefully they'd be less noxious than the sewers of Paris had been. 'At least we have a map,' she said hopefully.

Chauvelin shook his head.

'At least we have an entrance?'

'That we do have,' Chauvelin said. 'And if we don't find them near the entrance, I imagine there will be traces of their passage – open doors, greased bolts, unconscious guards. All the detritus which the League usually leaves in its wake. Of course . . .'

'Yes?'

'I do have some men in London,' Chauvelin said idly.

'They might have more information on the League's current goings-on. However, contacting them would cost us time . . . But the choice, of course, is yours.'

'What might they know?'

'Perhaps where members of the League were last seen, and where they were going. I have men watching most of their town houses – the Blakeney house, the residences of Sir Andrew Ffoulkes and Sir Anthony Dewhurst, and so on. I paid them within the past week, so they should still be enthusiastic. Such vigour tends to wane as the money runs dry. If the League have been sending messages to each other and gathering for action, then they will know about it.'

A qualm of unease stirred Eleanor's heart. She looked aside, trying to decide on her response.

'You are no doubt wondering how I know so many of the League,' Chauvelin said, guessing her thoughts with unpleasant accuracy. 'They have not always been so careful as they are now. And once I had my finger on a few of them, well, it was easy enough to trace the threads which led to the others. To be a spy is a risky and dangerous thing, Eleanor Dalton. It is an occupation best pursued in solitude, without friends or family who can be used against you or lead your enemies to your doorstep. It is not a *game* with which the rich and idle may amuse themselves.'

'I'm neither rich nor idle,' Eleanor said quietly. 'Nor would I call myself a spy.'

'There is a world of difference between what a man – or a woman – calls themselves, and what they actually are,' Chauvelin hit back. 'I allow you a measure of forbearance because you were dragged into this, and because you have agreed to cooperate and work for me. Do not think I will extend that lenience to the aristocrats of the League.' There was real venom to his voice, and his pale eyes gleamed like a cat's in the light of the oil lamp.

'But, Bibi, we are allies for the moment,' Fleurette put in. 'And they are not all evil people – merely misguided. They did save me from Mont-Saint-Michel, after all.'

'Permit me to speak to you as a fellow citizen rather than as your father,' Chauvelin said. 'Yes, they are our allies because we have a greater enemy in common for the moment. But even good men can do great harm to others if they are misguided – especially if they are misguided. Do not expect me to *like* them.'

'And when this alliance is over?' Eleanor asked. *When I'm in France working for you, and the League are free to do as they wish? When Charles is no longer by my side . . .*

'Our countries are at war!' Chauvelin snapped. 'It is all very well for you women to wring your hands and exclaim, *Are we not all human beings and children of Reason?* That will not stop bullets or turn back soldiers. France presses forward as a republic, governed by the people, while England and other countries cling to their monarchs, their despots and their sanguinocrats. As a dog that returns to his vomit, so is a fool who returns to his folly. If the League avoid France once this matter is over, then all the better for them. If you care for them, Eleanor Dalton, you will convince them to do so. Because if they are caught in France again, the courts will have no mercy on them – and neither shall I.'

Yet there was a glint in his eye, a note to his voice, which suggested he hoped they *would* venture to France once again. Because how else could he have his vengeance upon them? How else could he send them to the guillotine? In England, the most he could do was spy on them. But in France, he had power – and the League would regret every prisoner they had rescued, every time they had thwarted him, each and every time they had humiliated him and the Republic with him.

It had been easy to forget all this while Chauvelin and

Sir Percy both spoke amiably of alliances of convenience, and Chauvelin courted her with promises of employment. But Eleanor knew now that she must never allow herself to forget the true and absolute hatred which rankled at the core of Chauvelin's heart.

She wrenched her attention back to Chauvelin's original question. 'I think we should go to the sewer entrance directly,' she said. 'Or would it be better to go to some place a short distance away and then walk from there? In case someone notices the coach?'

'A fair point,' Chauvelin agreed, all amiability once more. Though was he a little disappointed by her decision? Had he hoped she'd agree to contact his agents instead? She couldn't be sure. 'The sooner we find them, the better.'

The time crawled by during their sojourn in the coach. Outside, the London streets were crammed full, with the July heat lying like a suffocating blanket atop the busy crowds. It was late at night, but not so dark that the law-abiding citizens had retreated into their homes and locked the doors. Street vendors sold food – bread, sausages, pies, oranges and apples, spun sugar fancies, little cakes, pickled onions, roast pigeons and salted pork and jellied eels. The smells of London rose hot and strong around them – perfumes and animal dung, herbs and vegetables and sweat, flowers and rotting meat, and the stink of the river thick and close above them all. Chauvelin's expression was that of a dyspeptic thundercloud, clearly wishing he was back in Paris, where the people would have parted nervously before the carriage of an agent of the Committee for Public Safety. He looked as though he would like to hold a cloth in front of his face and ignore the whole of London's existence.

Fleurette was peering out through the window with avid curiosity, having twitched back the curtain enough to see the street beyond. Eleanor still wasn't sure what she should do. She might need Fleurette's strength, just as she had helped her in the cellars below Bedlam. Yet was it fair to drag Fleurette along in her wake, possibly into even deeper danger? She knew what Chauvelin would say. He wouldn't risk his daughter. But worse, she knew what Fleurette would say. She would cheerfully volunteer to help, heedless of peril. Did Eleanor have any right to . . .

'We're here,' Chauvelin announced, as the carriage drew to a stop. 'Follow me, and keep your hoods up and your faces hidden.'

They'd halted beside the Red Dragon tavern, a busy establishment with windows overlooking the river. A wafting smell of mussels and eels displayed its kitchen's specialities and made Eleanor's stomach clench with hunger. Chauvelin helped them out of the carriage, tossed a coin up to the driver and muttered some sort of explanation, then led the way into the busy tavern. Eleanor paused to look around, ignoring his hissed instructions to follow, and saw the bulk of the Houses of Parliament further up the river. It squatted there like a huge church or even a cathedral, its windows gleaming with light along its length. She should have been impressed by it, but the knowledge of what might lie below made it seem somehow unsavoury – like an animal that seemed to be asleep, but was already dead and infested with maggots.

Chauvelin's thin hand descended on her wrist, and he tugged her along viciously. 'A little attention to our current surroundings,' he muttered. Then he had to pause to take Fleurette in tow, who was also displaying great fascination with England, the English and a typical English tavern. Eleanor could almost have felt sorry for him.

A few minutes later they had slipped out through the back door of the tavern and were hastening along the street beside the river. Eleanor would not have cared to fall in. It seemed as wide as the Seine in Paris, and just as full of boat traffic – and sewage. There were people everywhere – buying, selling, flirting, arguing, drinking – and she wondered how precisely they would be able to sneak into the sewer entrance, which Chauvelin claimed the League's maps had placed here, without being observed.

Yet the answer came soon enough. A side alley led to stone steps, which in turn ran down to the water's edge, where a wide orifice spilled filth into the Thames. Even London's poor avoided this spot, driven back by the ferocious stench. The days of heat and the lack of rain must have marinated it to its utmost. Only one person had the will to remain here – an elderly woman curled up in a corner of the steps. She was a mass of shawls and white hair, without even the strength to lift her head and curse as they edged past.

'There,' Chauvelin said, pointing to the oozing mouth of the outlet tunnel, a trail of sludge dripping from it and down into the Thames. 'We should be grateful the weather is dry; it would be folly to attempt this approach if it were raining or the sewers were running high.'

'I never thought I would be glad to see you, my little Chauvelin.'

Eleanor spun, steadying herself against the wall. That had been Lady Marguerite's voice!

The bundled figure unfolded from her tangle of shawls and skirts, shaking back the tendrils of a wig which had concealed her face. It hardly seemed enough to transform her, but abruptly it was Lady Marguerite Blakeney standing there – in filthy rags and smeared with mud, stinking of gin, but recognizably herself rather than a denizen of the gutters. 'Who would have thought the day would come when I would thank God for your arrival?'

'Your theology is hardly my concern,' Chauvelin retorted. He was as acid as ever, but in the light from the lamps above Eleanor had seen his hand slip inside his coat, feeling for some concealed weapon. 'I take it we have come to the right place?'

'And barely in the right time. My husband and the others went in an hour ago. But I have seen men – vampires, I think – patrolling further down the river, and I fear that Sophie's agents suspect something. It is most fortunate that you are here to assist.' Her smile was all sweet charm and iron will. 'How *did* you know to come?'

'Your husband made a mistake,' Chauvelin informed her with satisfaction. 'The woman at the King's Head was not the Baroness of Basing. You have been tracked by servants using homing pigeons, and no doubt once she knew you were coming to London, she had all your houses watched. It is little comfort to think she must be bankrupting herself to pay for all this surveillance.'

'Why are you still out here?' Eleanor asked. Too late, she realized the many ways it might be understood. *Why have you not gone inside to inform them of the vampires? Have you let them walk into danger without warning?*

Lady Marguerite tossed her head in anger, and the lank curls of her wig twitched like a serpent's coils. 'You think I wanted to be here? I would rather have been with Percy, but he insisted that I stay out here, whatever happens, so if they – if they should not return . . .'

'Then he did understand they might be walking into a trap,' Chauvelin murmured. 'I thought as much.'

A dozen small pieces came together in Eleanor's mind. The way both Sir Percy and Lady Marguerite had insisted she stay at Bathurst Manor, where she at least would be safe. The manner in which Charles had left her, embracing her as though he might never see her again, and informing

her where to find his notes should something go wrong. Sir
Percy had realized this might be the League's most dangerous
mission yet, with every chance of failure – but that it could
also be their only chance of stopping the vampires.

'You should have been honest with me about the risks!'
she said to Lady Marguerite, woman to woman rather than
maid to mistress. 'I might have been able to help!'

'Eleanor . . .' Lady Marguerite held out a hand towards
her, then let it drop. 'I would have done, but you had already
suffered so much. My Percy said that we had no right to
demand more from you.'

'Not demand, no.' Eleanor set her jaw. Her hands tightened into fists. 'But you could have *asked*.'

'Then you will—'

'Wait!' Chauvelin said. 'You gave me your word that you
would not risk yourself unduly. If you go in there after them,
you will be putting yourself in mortal danger.'

'I'm quite aware that I'm of no further use to you if I'm
dead,' Eleanor answered. Her mood seemed one with the
heavy oppression of the air, the thick tension of the sky: a
thunderstorm, ready to burst. 'I will do my best to stay
alive.'

'And I, too!' Fleurette declared. 'But . . . is there not some
better way than this?'

'Of course there is!' Chauvelin said angrily. 'Retreat.
Gather information. Gather allies. Our enemies won't *kill*
the League, and it will take time for them to break their
wills and suborn them. But you, with your powers, they *will*
kill. Surely you are not such a fool as to rush to your death?'

'I'm not prepared to gamble on that,' Lady Marguerite
said softly, 'and neither, I think, is Eleanor. Come with me.'

'You gave me your word, Eleanor Dalton, and I've done
everything that I promised. Is this the honour of the League
of the Scarlet Pimpernel?' Chauvelin spat out the words as

though they were anathema, as though he – an atheist – was invoking God against his will. Even though Eleanor suspected he might say anything in order to sway her to his side, she could feel his words sink into her like barbs.

'I am not concerned with honour,' Lady Marguerite broke in. She had a pistol in her hand, and was pointing it at Chauvelin. 'I am concerned with my husband's life.'

'No!' Fleurette gasped. Without a moment's hesitation, she stepped between Lady Marguerite and Chauvelin, blocking the shot.

'Foolish child!' With the strength of desperation, Chauvelin pushed her out of the way, sending her cannoning into Eleanor, who barely managed to catch her before the two of them went into the Thames. 'Don't risk yourself like that!'

'Indeed, stay out of the way.' Lady Marguerite's pistol didn't waver. 'This is between the two of us.'

'And will you tell your husband that you pulled the trigger?' Chauvelin challenged her.

'Enough of this!'

The shout drew all eyes. Castleton stood halfway down the stairs above, flanked by a couple of large men. His white hair was disarrayed and his clothing thick with the dust of travel. 'I have not killed three horses to reach London in order to listen to your bickering. I *will* know what's going on here. Surrender or die!'

CHAPTER NINETEEN

Surely, Eleanor thought, *surely* this must attract some attention from passers-by? Was London not just as crowded as Paris with busy-bodies, gossips and scandalmongers? Was there nobody here who would come running to help on hearing threats to commit murder?

Apparently not. Or if they did hear anything, they were too sensible to come running into mortal danger.

'The poor horses!' Fleurette gasped, tender-hearted as ever.

'I asked a *question*,' Castleton snarled. 'I expect an *answer*. I see a great many people down there who could give me one. Who would like to be the first to volunteer? It will significantly reduce the odds of my shooting you.'

'Forgive me if I doubt the odds of you letting us live after we have provided you with the information you want,' Chauvelin replied.

'Playing for time? It will do you little good. And don't try anything foolish, Eleanor Dalton. That little trick of yours with sparks and a show of light might inconvenience me, but it will mean nothing to these gentlemen behind me. And it won't stop a pistol ball, will it? Which of your friends should I shoot first?'

Fleurette pressed her hands to her bosom, her hood falling back to bare her glorious gold hair. But the glint in her eye suggested to Eleanor that she was playing to the men behind Castleton rather than to the vampire himself. 'I do not understand,' she said, her pretty French accent almost as charming as Lady Marguerite's own. 'We are refugees from the Terror in France. Why are you threatening us like this?' A big tear welled in the corner of her eye.

Her words gave Eleanor time to think. Castleton was probably correct – using her light to drive him back would be useless here. It might deter him, but wouldn't necessarily repel his human servants. And if he did fire – well, a pistol ball might go anywhere, and she had no wish for anyone in her group to be killed. Even Chauvelin.

She looked up at Castleton. 'Given your apparent ignorance, I'm assuming Lady Sophie has told you little of what's really behind her actions? You want to know the truth of all this, sir? What truly happened over five hundred years ago, when John Lackland was on the throne?' It was almost as though Anima was still here, prompting her, wanting to throw her anger in the vampire's face.

Castleton shifted his aim, pointing the pistol at her rather than any of the others. 'You know I do.' There was something like madness in his eyes; they gleamed red like chipped garnets in the shadows. 'I won't be treated like a gaming piece any longer. She . . .' The identity of the *She* was clear enough, but he spoke with a venom which seemed hard to justify. What had Lady Sophie done to him? 'She thinks all of us are nothing but her pawns. Well, once I have the truth I'll be able to set my own terms. Speak, girl!'

'Five hundred years ago,' Eleanor said, gauging the distance between herself and Chauvelin, 'a man named Matthew fled to Oxford. He was pursued by the vampires of the time, and I think Lady Sophie was one of them. He left his last confession behind, and together with Charles, I found it. And . . .' She took Chauvelin by surprise, snatching the leather satchel holding Charles's notes from his hand and brandishing it. 'Here it is. Is this what you're after, Castleton?'

She saw his pistol swing wide as his gaze fixed on the satchel. A hunger even deeper than the thirst for blood disfigured his face, drawing his lips back to reveal his fangs, twisting his mouth into a snarl. 'Yes. Once I have the truth—'

With the full force of her body, Eleanor spun and tossed the satchel out into the Thames. 'Then go and *fetch* it!'

The satchel bobbed for a moment before beginning to sink.

'Grab them!' Castleton yelled at his men, and then threw his pistol aside, diving into the Thames after it.

'I would advise you to stay back.' Lady Marguerite raised her pistol once more, pointing it at the men. With her free hand, behind her back, she waved Eleanor and the others towards the sewer entrance.

While the men above were hesitating – clearly neither of them wished to be the first to charge – Eleanor and the others slipped into the outlet, followed a moment later by Lady Marguerite. They hastily began to edge their way along the tunnel, dodging the worst of the waste. For a few yards the light from the entrance sufficed to let them see their way along the narrow walkway, but soon they were in near darkness.

We don't have time to hesitate. They will surely follow us in here. With an inward sigh, Eleanor raised her hand and summoned light. It only cost her a brief moment of pain, and she wondered if she should be concerned at how easy it was becoming to do what Anima had called *burning your life*. But this was what the League chose to do in any case, wasn't it? Use themselves as candles to light the way for others in the darkness . . .

263

In the new brightness she saw Chauvelin's eyes narrow with speculation. No doubt he was already considering what this might mean for him. Enough time for that later; it would be easier to argue when the lives of the League weren't in the balance.

They turned a corner, the women holding their skirts tightly to their legs to avoid brushing against the filth everywhere, everyone breathing shallowly against the stench – and then halted.

There was a hole in the wall to their right. Someone had removed the old bricks with hammers and crowbars, leaving a space large enough to crawl through. Eleanor raised her hand to direct the light onto the other side, but nothing was visible there except barrels and crates.

'This would be it,' Lady Marguerite said, taking the lead. 'Citizen Chauvelin, you first.'

'Why my father?' Fleurette asked, bristling with sudden distrust.

Lady Marguerite gave her a brief, charming smile. 'Because only he and I have pistols, my dear, and without skirts he will find it easier to crawl through than we will. Then he can stand guard on the other side.'

'Quite true,' Chauvelin agreed.

He has a pistol? Eleanor mentally chastised herself as Chauvelin slipped through the hole. *Of course he has a pistol. What was I thinking?* She glanced back the way they'd come, but there were no signs of pursuit yet. Perhaps they would be lucky, and Castleton's men would have dispersed after their master threw himself into the river . . . She hadn't been sure that ruse would work with him, but he'd taken the bait hungrily, giving them those precious moments to escape. Just how desperate was he to learn the truth? How many of them – humans and vampires – were seeking it?

She was the last to crawl through. The cellar was old but

dry, stacked with heavy barrels and crates, and beneath the stink wafting from the sewer opening, Eleanor could trace the odour of old dried wine.

And . . . was there something else?

Casting around by the glow from Eleanor's hand, Lady Marguerite found a lantern and striker, which she used to provide another source of light. The hammers and crowbars which must have been used to break the wall were neatly piled up in a corner.

'How tidily organized,' Fleurette marvelled.

'Probably in order to facilitate a rapid escape,' Chauvelin said sourly. 'This whole project is more hasty and violent than I would expect from the Pimpernel and his League.'

'We had very little time to work,' Lady Marguerite excused herself. 'My Percy was planning an infiltration disguised as tradesmen bringing in the latest supplies of wine, port and brandy, but there was insufficient time to prepare for it. And in any case, few would have believed in such a delivery late in the evening.'

Chauvelin shrugged. 'They might have done. One hears stories about the thirst which Parliament inspires in its members. Now, which way from here? I would have consulted the map, but I fear we have . . . lost it.' His flick of the eyes at Eleanor suggested that *he* would have found a better solution than tossing everything into the Thames for Castleton to dive after.

'Follow me – and beware. The League may be here, but so are the minions of our enemy.'

The cellars of Parliament were rank. It wasn't just the smell of the sewers, which wafted from behind them with every draught, and which clung to skirts and shoes like a permanent defilement. There was something about this place which set every nerve of Eleanor's body atwitch, as though the looming Houses of Parliament above looked down on her with a condemning eye. She found herself turning to stare at every flicker of the lamplight, conscious that her near-panic might be infectious, but unable to control herself. Something was quite simply *wrong* here.

Could years of rulership and authority somehow poison the foundations of a building? That hadn't happened in France. She'd never perceived anything like this there – even in the Temple prison with its trapped inmates. And even Bedlam hadn't felt like *this*.

But her frequent glances to left and right made her the first to see a body.

She caught at Chauvelin's sleeve, unwilling to speak a word – none of them were certain how far sound might carry down here – and pointed at the protruding, somehow pathetic buckled shoe which stuck out from behind a pile of crates. He followed her gesture, nodded, and then touched Lady Marguerite's shoulder, beckoning her over to look.

The man wore a plain servant's livery. He was simply unconscious, thank the heavens, and from the trails of dust, he had been dragged behind the crates after he'd been knocked out. That must have been the League, Eleanor decided. Lady Sophie's agents might also have knocked people out with blithe abandon, but they'd have had no need to hide his body.

Eleanor saw a brief wave of relief touch Lady Marguerite's face as she inspected the man, possibly looking for a face she might recognize, and grateful not to see one yet. In silence they resumed their journey.

The cellars seemed to go on and on – larger than the ones below Bedlam, or the ones beneath any noble house Eleanor had ever seen. The rooms, tomblike in their stillness, opened onto one another. They were filled with mysterious crates and barrels, piles of staves and racks of bottles, wardrobes which smelt of decaying lavender and fleabane, leather-bound boxes with heavy metal locks, and even the odd tombstone set into the walls. Fear began to ebb a little. Even the most ardent terror could only twist the stomach and dry the mouth for so long before one began to disregard it. Lady Marguerite turned right and left, and right again, as though she knew the map by heart, following some invisible route. But Eleanor could feel the dead air stretching out to either side, wider than she could measure. If there were vampire forces down here searching for the League, then she could only pray they were following false tracks, wandering into dead ends and wasting their time . . .

Then a pistol shot rang out from ahead, echoing in the shadows so that it was hard to tell how close or far away it was. But there was nothing else it could have been, nothing for which it could be mistaken. Lady Marguerite stiffened, then closed the shutter on the lantern till only a thin line of light emanated from it. She gestured for silence – even more silence – and drifted forward like a ghost.

Garbled words drifted from ahead. '. . . surrender! You're surrounded!'

Eleanor twisted her fingers, hooking a breeze around them, and sent it running ahead to carry back the conversation more clearly.

'Sink me, I do believe you've overplayed your hand.' Sir Percy's tones were unmistakable. 'Hasn't anyone told you that murder's still a crime in England, old fellow? What are you going to do, tear us to pieces and then claim to the Bow Street Runners that you mistook us for Easter bouquets and were horrified by how out of season we were?'

'And who will come looking for you, here beneath the Houses of Parliament?' Whoever the man was, he was making a valiant attempt to sound threatening. Eleanor had been threatened by truly dangerous people, however, and by comparison he merely sounded like a pouting brat stamping his foot.

Sir Percy laughed – his genuine laugh, the intelligent, amused one, rather than his braying Society snigger which all but confirmed his idiocy. 'Zounds! Haven't you ever heard of the practice of leaving a letter behind before you go on a dangerous mission? I may be the greatest fribble at Court, but even I've read those novels!' He paused. There was whispering. 'No, wait, I do believe you're right, Tony – the whole point of those novels is that the heroines *don't* leave any letters behind them. Deuced inconsiderate to their rescuers, I call it.'

'Stop trying to waste my time!' the other man snarled. 'My shot will have been heard. Soon my brothers and sisters will gather to bring you down—'

'You could try it on your own,' Sir Percy suggested. 'Far less crowded that way. I say . . .' More whispering. 'You aren't Georges de la Fontaine, are you? I could have sworn we met at someone's ball, but I didn't recognize you under all that dust. This place is dreadfully taxing on a gentleman's clothing. And while we're at it . . .'

'Yes?'

'Catch.'

Glass shattered. A smell – no, a *stench* – of garlic powerful enough to rise up and walk on its own washed towards them. There was a scream. Abruptly running feet came pounding in their direction, and before Lady Marguerite could step back, the stranger was among them. He paused, looking around the group, clearly having expected someone else, and his teeth flashed white and sharp in his mouth.

Chauvelin stepped to one side, then closed in behind the vampire, one hand on his shoulder. In the dim light from the part-closed lantern, Eleanor saw the flash of a pistol in his other hand. He cocked it, pressing it against the vampire's back, and pulled the trigger.

The vampire coughed, shuddered, and blood poured from his mouth. He crumpled. Chauvelin stepped back fastidiously, letting him collapse to the floor.

'A common reaction,' he said to Eleanor, possibly mistaking her frozen horror for interest, 'when they have not been vampires for long. Only the older ones crumble to dust, as de Courcis did at Bedlam.'

'Yes,' Eleanor choked. Out of the corner of her eye she could see Lady Marguerite putting an arm around the trembling Fleurette's shoulders, turning her face away from the body on the floor.

'Squeamishness will do you little good now. We should hurry. Two shots? Every other sanguinocrat in these cellars will be on us in a few minutes. Madame, with me, if you please.' He gestured for Lady Marguerite to continue forwards.

'You trust me to go first?' she said, raising an eyebrow.

'I trust your husband and his men not to shoot you on sight.'

Lady Marguerite actually giggled, though it was difficult to tell whether it was genuine humour or nervousness. She passed Fleurette gently to Eleanor, then led the way, opening her lantern to its full extent.

It wasn't hard to tell where to go. One merely had to follow the abominable reek of garlic, and when closer, the light. Eleanor had no objection to garlic in the proper quantities – unlike vampires, who abominated the stuff – but this was ridiculous. Even worse, the smell from the sewers was *still* with them – so oppressive that Eleanor could hardly breathe.

The League were lurking in a cellar two rooms along. Some of them Eleanor only knew vaguely – Philip, Jeremiah,

George, Armand Saint-Just. But Tony and Andrew were there too – Andrew having his arm bound up *again*? – and Sir Percy himself.

But Charles? Where was he?

They were crowded around a part of the wall, behind a semi-stockade of crates which had been pulled out of place, their marks clear in the dust on the floor. A lantern nearby was fully open, shedding its jumping light on the wall, where Tony and Jeremiah were fumbling with something Eleanor couldn't make out.

Sir Percy had raised his pistol, but on seeing who it was he deliberately, almost ostentatiously, lowered it and crossed to take his wife in his arms. 'Faith, Marguerite, I'd rather have seen you half the world away from here. What of that promise you made me?'

'I may owe you obedience twice over, as a member of the League and as your wife, but there's no promise I'd ever keep if it meant losing you.' There was an edge to her voice, as though they'd had this discussion before.

In the end it was Sir Percy who looked away. 'It seems you've brought us reinforcements. Well, ladies, gentlemen, we've been played a deuced unfortunate trick by luck. There's a hidden passage in the wall here, but de la Fontaine interrupted us before we could all slip through, else he'd never have caught us.'

'Where is Charles?' Eleanor demanded, stepping forward.

'Nowhere else but here.' Tony touched a point on the wall, and a panel swung open. A dusty Charles stepped out, brushing cobwebs from his hair.

He saw Eleanor, and his eyes widened in shock. 'You were supposed to be away from here and safe!' he exclaimed.

'Nowhere is safe,' Chauvelin cut in. 'Blakeney, before this descends into further sentimental recriminations, allow me to explain.'

His brief summary was muted by Eleanor being in Charles's arms, distracted for a moment from fear, vampires and stench.

Sadly it didn't last long. Charles released her. 'What, pray tell, is the point of my hazarding my life to keep you safe if you endanger it like this?'

'I might ask you much the same question,' Eleanor returned through gritted teeth.

'Believe it or not,' Chauvelin said aside to Sir Percy, 'we did actually come on more urgent business than simply allowing Citizen Dalton to vent her feelings. There was some minor talk of a trap, and assisting you in escaping from it.'

'Do you not understand that I want you to *live*? I have no interest in being saved by your noble self-sacrifice!' Eleanor grabbed Charles by the shoulders and found the strength to shake him. He was astonished enough by the gesture that he actually swayed.

'I fear the two of you must continue this discussion later,' Lady Marguerite said, her mouth twitching as she tried not to smile, 'or I shall have to rap you both over the head with my fan. Do not ask me where I would find a fan: it is a woman's business to know these things. Percy, what shall we do?'

Sir Percy shook himself as though coming out of water, and his presence was suddenly brighter and more vital than the lamplight. 'Well, heaven may grant us another minute or two, but it won't be long till other vampires come to investigate those pistol shots. And they have forces closing in around us, if all you say about a trap is true. If some of us enter the passage, with luck the others may be able to ward off any attack and slip away in the confusion—'

'You put too much faith in Providence, Blakeney,' Chauvelin snapped. 'Believe me, I have no wish to remain in your company, but by now there will be no escape. And the longer we stand here talking, the more chance of being caught.' His eyes were on Fleurette, and Eleanor knew his daughter must be his primary concern. Guilt pricked her. Fleurette was the *last* person who should be trapped down here with them.

'Oh, I wasn't suggesting that *you* leave us,' Sir Percy said amiably. 'I've a great deal to discuss with you. But it must wait. Very well, then. Tony, get that thing open again. Andrew – was it quite necessary to stop that pistol ball?'

'It was the same arm, too, dash it!' Andrew declared angrily. 'I'd near as dammit got it mended properly, and now that fellow's perforated it once more. Any more of this and my demned doctor's going to refuse to treat me!'

'A few more guineas and he'll bandage it up, even if you shoot holes in it half a dozen times a year,' Sir Percy retorted. 'Armand, give me a hand with these crates. Charles, Eleanor, if you've quite finished looking into each other's eyes—'

'Of course, Chief,' Charles said dutifully, one hand still on Eleanor's.

Eleanor dragged her attention from Charles's face. She had to be strong. They'd come so close to uncovering what the vampires had kept hidden down here for centuries; they were at its very doorstep. She couldn't let herself be distracted at the last. At least she'd make sure that Charles and the others got out of here alive. That would make it all worthwhile.

Wouldn't it?

Then she heard the distant echo of a voice carried on the breeze, perceptible even through the encompassing stench. She couldn't tell who it was, but if it was close enough to hear . . . 'Someone's near!' she whispered.

'Charles, get through that hole and guard the other side,' Sir Percy ordered, lowering his own voice. 'The women follow, then the rest of us. Stay back behind these crates – they'll give us cover from pistol shots. Now!'

The panel in the wall reopened, and Charles stepped through. It was concealed in the timberwork, an opening barely a couple of feet wide and only four feet high. The air that came from beyond smelled just as foul as the rest of the sewers. Was this entire place contaminated with the reek of ages past?

Fleurette had been watching the whole encounter with an air of cheerful friendly interest, but Eleanor knew her well enough to recognize the nervousness beneath her bright surface. She quickly gathered her skirts and followed Charles, ducking her head as she squeezed through. Eleanor and Lady Marguerite were bundled behind the crates by the other men of the League, obedient as ever to Sir Percy, to wait their turn.

A voice carried through the deathly still rooms, turning Eleanor's blood cold in her veins as it reached them. It was a sweet voice, a persuasive voice – one that she knew very well indeed. And it was barely a room away.

It was Lady Sophie.

'Percy? My dear Percy? I'd like to propose a parley. Don't go, I beg you – there's still a way that all this can be resolved.'

CHAPTER TWENTY

Silence filled the room for a moment, then Lady Sophie began again. 'My dear Percy—'

'The name is Blakeney, madam,' Sir Percy said. 'Will you be joining us?'

The League had crowded behind the stack of crates – inadequate shelter though it might be – like cats trying to press themselves into the smallest possible space. Sir Percy had turned his lantern so that its beam fell across the doorway, but Lady Sophie was invisible in the room beyond, without even revealing her silhouette or a fold of her dress.

'I was rather hoping you might come out to me. The odour of garlic . . .' She gave a slightly theatrical sigh. 'Not *insuperable*, you understand, though it is rather unpleasant. I would not want you to think it is some manner of absolute barrier against our presence, whatever popular superstition may say.'

'I assume, madam, that you do not speak in the royal we. No doubt you have friends with you?'

'I have other people with me,' Lady Sophie confirmed. 'The degree of their friendliness is open to debate. Which would be why I suggest we talk, now, before either of us is forced to take irreparable measures.'

'It strikes me, madam, that the measures so far have all been on your side rather than ours.' Sir Percy gestured for Eleanor to take her turn and enter the passage.

But she hesitated. What if – God forbid – there was some sort of mass attack by Lady Sophie and what were surely her vampire companions? In that case, Eleanor would be needed to hold them off while the others retreated.

She looked for strength inside herself, but found merely bravado and weakness. Only two days ago she'd been in Bedlam, being bled and drugged and purged. But she'd come this far, made a devil's bargain with Chauvelin . . . She had to be strong enough. She *had* to.

'You have no idea what you're toying with. That little witch has poisoned your minds against me. She has exerted her powers to bemuse and confound you.'

Sir Percy raised an eyebrow, and it was actually *perceptible* in his speech, even if Eleanor hadn't been able to see him. 'I do beg your pardon, madam, but are we referring to the young woman whom *you* pressed upon *us*? The one whom we recently rescued from unjust confinement in Bedlam? 'Pon my soul, madam, you have a strange definition of power. One might almost think she was the woman of wealth, rank and property who could snap her fingers and command servants, while you were the maidservant in her house, dependent on her generosity and goodwill, who could be condemned without trial at a moment's notice. It staggers my comprehension. I implore you, madam, reconsider your words lest I perish from shock.'

'My dear Percy, pray discard your facade. We are past the time for such things. Why are you down here in the first place?'

'Why?' Sir Percy laughed. 'For the same reason as always, and all my friends with me. For the love of the game, madam. For the love of sport. For excitement. For the thrill of it. We are Englishmen, madam, and we enjoy such things. I might ask rather why *you* are here. What has threatened you so greatly that you're dabbling your dainty feet in the filth, mud and dust with the rest of us?'

'Consider your position,' Lady Sophie said, ignoring his question, her voice as soft and flowing as honey. 'How likely is it that you'd have abandoned your mission in France to delve here beneath the Houses of Parliament, were it not for some toxic influence upon your mind? I don't blame you. I had no idea of the girl's devilish powers when I offered her to your household. I'll admit my own errors, but I ask you to consider the fact that you may have been deceived.'

Her words hung in the air like poisonous fumes. Eleanor bit her lip. Surely nobody would believe this sort of accusation just because she spoke it out loud.

'What sort of power could lure you into collaborating with Citizen Chauvelin of France?' Lady Sophie went on. 'What deception would convince you to try to save the National Convention from their well-deserved fate? You of all people know the misery they have inflicted on the persecuted people of France. How can you have so utterly changed your ways, forsaken your loyalties? Think, Percy, I beg you! It's true, we vampires do preserve the old stories – and some of those stories are about witches. Little Nellie is a sneaking, conniving, desperate woman who seeks her own advantage and has been playing you and your men as pawns in her game. I rue the day I ever set you in her path; I think I must have been bewitched myself to do so. She plays the innocent dove, but beneath it all she's the serpent. What she does is *unnatural*. And as they say, false in one thing, false in all.'

'Not to put too fine a point on it,' Andrew cut in, 'but you're a vampire who drinks blood, madam. It's a strange thing to hear you call someone else unnatural.'

'Excuse me? My dear Andrew, we have been here throughout the history of this country. We were here under the Lionheart, under the Confessor . . . I dare say that my name is older in this land than yours is. I simply have a different diet.' She paused. 'And better manners.'

'My temper may not be at its best at the moment, madam, due to having been shot in the arm just now by one of your minions.'

'Really? And who killed de la Fontaine?'

A faint smile touched Chauvelin's lips as he quietly reloaded his pistol.

'Let us save the minor recriminations till later, Andrew,' Sir Percy advised, 'and busy ourselves with the major ones. Madam, you make all manner of claims about Eleanor Dalton, but offer very little evidence. Given everything else you have done, why should we believe you?'

'Everything else *I* have done? Why am I the target of your accusations?'

'You had my wife accused of treason,' Sir Percy said, paying out the words like a hangman's rope. 'What do you expect me to make of that? Do you think I will take that lightly, madam?'

Lady Sophie sighed. 'It is possible that some of my allies took unwise action. I'm not such a fool to do something which would make you my absolute enemy. Really, have you nothing better than that to throw in my face?'

'Leaving us locked in cages beneath Paris so we might drink your blood and be turned into your slaves?'

This time the pause was more significant. 'I have no idea why—' she began.

'Madam,' Sir Percy said wearily, 'we *recognized* you. Perhaps you have grown used to operating in the shadows without let or hindrance, but matters have changed. The world has changed. I do not condone the Revolution in

France, God forbid, but England does not suffer despots – even invisible ones. The steps which you have taken only prove our point. The English people – egad, the French ones too – have the right to be more than mere cattle.'

'I've fed my people!' Lady Sophie snarled back at him. 'No peasant or farmer on my estates has ever hungered, no matter how feckless their whims! I rule my people, yes, but I protect them too! Did little Nellie ever complain of hunger or mistreatment? Was I ever cruel to her?'

'Before or after you sent her to Bedlam?' Sir Percy asked blandly.

'That is different. I have no mercy on traitors. But I do protect my own, Percy, and that includes those who share my blood. Do you not see that if word should get out about certain powers that a few of us have, a very few, then all hands would be turned against us? Can you not imagine the possible consequences? Lies in every journal, slander on every street corner – it would be worse than France! I will *not* be blamed for acting to protect my own!'

'Faith, and I might have given that argument some credence, had you not used those *rare* powers to enslave my brother-in-law,' Sir Percy returned. His humour had entirely slipped away, and nobody could have mistaken him for a fashionable man about town. 'By your own argument, I've every right to protect *my* own.'

'But I have far more to protect than you do,' Lady Sophie said softly. 'Sometimes hard choices must be made, I fear. Citizen Chauvelin understands that, while you . . . you play at being a hero, you and your wife. I supported you. I am one of your own kind! Why must you turn against me now?'

Sir Percy brought down a hand in one abrupt chopping motion. 'Madam, because you are a most damnable liar and tyrant. That is why.'

'And you are a fool!'

'But an honest one,' Sir Percy said. 'So, madam, what terms can you possibly offer which will satisfy us both?'

'I take it you speak for all your men?'

Andrew, Tony, the others – they all nodded. Sir Percy's gaze moved to Eleanor, just as if she were the equal of the men around her. She knew then, for certain, that he didn't believe – had never even considered believing – Lady Sophie's words about her. There was no hesitation in his questioning look, no thought of caution. She nodded in return, her heart brimming with thanks.

Lady Marguerite simply smiled at her husband.

Chauvelin stood silent, thin-lipped, brows drawn together, a figure in black in the dim light, bitterness in his eyes. Eleanor wondered what he was thinking. At least there was no way in which selling out the League to Lady Sophie could make matters any better for *him*, or else he'd have been considering the possibility. He must have hoped she'd leave London with him rather than come down here, under the Houses of Parliament. The string of events which had brought them to this place had collapsed on him like some disastrous building, and caught his daughter in potential ruin as well.

'I believe I do,' Sir Percy answered.

'Then let me make you an offer. If you truly disagree with our – my – guardianship of the country, and my alliances with other vampires, then take a position among us and change our direction. My dear Percy, perhaps we are in need of better leaders. And if that's so, then I ask you to help provide that leadership. Abandon your pretensions towards fashion and frivolity. Do something useful with your life and wealth. Do you truly want to help? Do you want to preserve England from the revolutions abroad? From the war in France? We have power which we will share with our allies.'

Sir Percy's face was expressionless as the other men exchanged glances. Eleanor wanted to scream out that it was all a lie, but . . . what if it wasn't? Perhaps if better people were vampires, then the country would move in a better direction. How simple it would be, to sidestep all the complications of elections and Parliament and political parties, to see to it that the *right* decisions were made. She could think of a few things herself which she'd like to see changed. Could it be this easy, this obvious a choice, to accept the lesser evil in exchange for a greater good?

How easy it would be to do what the vampires did, what the Committee for Public Safety did, and perhaps, what the mages of old had done. To be the ones who made the decisions and held the power of final judgement. To stamp one's own seal on the world and change it . . . for the better, of course. Sir Percy was a good man, and Lady Marguerite a good woman. The League were good men. If *they* held the balance of power . . .

A faint memory of Anima's words once more whispered in her mind, like a half-forgotten Bible verse or sampler motto. *I think the problem which lies at the heart of all this is that no vampire can remain virtuous. They may begin with the best of intentions, but nothing lasts . . . It isn't the sinners I should have been blaming, it's the sin . . .*

'And your enemies?' Sir Percy said.

'We cannot afford to have mercy on our enemies. If you tell me no, Percy – if your friends tell me no – then I will be forced to take brutal measures. I will not be happy to do so, yet I have my own people to protect, as I said. Even the ones who know nothing about this, the ones who think they can live happy, peaceful lives without meddling in politics, the ones who sleep away the centuries ignorant of the world around them. I have a remit to guard them – do you understand that? It is my task to help them *survive*.

And for that, there is nothing I will not do. Forget this folly of an English gentleman's code of honour. Think instead of life or death.'

Sir Percy took a deep breath. 'You might as well make the threat formal, madam, though I suspect I can already guess what form it may take. Better to have such things out in the open, don't you think? At least then we know the face of our enemy.'

'As you wish.' Lady Sophie was closer now. From where she crouched, Eleanor could see the edge of the other woman's dress through the doorway, a fragment of pale silk that caught the light. 'I did not wish to take this course of action, but since you drive me to it . . . All of you have loved ones. Wives, parents, friends. Suzanne Ffoulkes, who was Suzanne de Tourney, Yvonne Dewhurst, to name only a couple. Do I really need to make myself explicit?'

Eleanor saw the anger in the faces of the men beside her. Andrew and Tony were the first to react at the mention of their wives, but the others weren't far behind. Anger – and then fear.

And if she knew I was here, Lady Sophie would probably have mentioned my mother too. She could only pray she was still alive, and that Lady Sophie considered her relatively unimportant. Just one more farmer's wife . . .

'You'd have them accused of treason, as you did Lady Blakeney?' Andrew snarled. He wasn't often roused to fury, but the threat to his wife had brought out every ounce of temper in him.

'No,' Lady Sophie said calmly. 'Even I would have trouble exercising quite that much influence on our judiciary. I am merely saying that they might suffer some unpleasant accident. The world is harsh, my dear Andrew. As a man of noble blood, you have been spared a great deal of it, but misfortune can reach even to high places. Let us suppose you manage to escape these cellars. Do you truly wish to spend the rest of your lives watching every shadow?'

'You're not omnipotent!' Tony said coldly, his usual good humour washed away. 'Perhaps you can call on a few servants to assist you, but—'

'But you cannot be *certain*,' Lady Sophie cut in. She sounded so old, now – her voice was laden with the weight of centuries upon centuries, and while it might come from a human throat, it was utterly inhuman in its lack of understanding or compassion. She knew, she understood, yet she simply did not *care*. 'I have more friends than you might think. Where I do not have friends, I have allies, and where I do not have allies, I have the money to ensure faithful service. Your choice is quite simple. Join me or have your loved ones die. I am not bluffing. Necessity drives me, and if a few innocents must die to ensure my safety, well . . . it is nothing I have not done before.'

'Madam,' Sir Percy said wearily, 'even the jackals of the Revolution have a more sympathetic manner of putting things than you do.' As he spoke, he leaned across to reach into a satchel that Tony carried, pulling out a corked flask of liquid.

'Do you think that I'll do any the less to you because I haven't mentioned your wife, Percy? Perhaps I should have made this approach to her instead of to you. She has always struck me as cool-headed and practical – and deeply in love with you, too.'

Eleanor saw Lady Marguerite bite her lip so as not to reply, but her eyes blazed with fury.

'I request your indulgence while we discuss this matter for a moment,' Sir Percy said. 'And if manners won't oblige you to withdraw, then—'

He lobbed the flask into the empty doorway, and it shattered on the flagstones with a spray of liquid. Abruptly the stink of garlic, which had reached the level of being barely tolerable, once again rose to a miasma which would sicken even those who liked a clove or two in their soup.

Sir Percy drew a pistol from his pocket, cocked it and fired in the direction that the flask of garlic distillate had flown. A quick scuffle of movement indicated that someone had dodged it, but it was unclear who or how many might be out there alongside Lady Sophie.

'Listen,' he said, his voice very low, the cellars still ringing with the echoes of the pistol shot. 'Marguerite, Eleanor, Chauvelin – she doesn't know *you're* here. We must find whatever it is she's so desperate to protect that she'll risk herself to keep it secret. You go on through that panel and finish the job while we provide a distraction. I have faith in you.'

Chauvelin took it all in in barely a moment, while Eleanor's mind was still spinning. He jerked a quick nod and moved to ease the panel open again.

'Distraction, Chief?' Tony said softly.

'Time for some open rebellion.' Sir Percy's teeth glinted as he grinned. 'I'm about to tell you we utterly refuse, at which point you'll do your best to bring me down and take Sophie's deal. If they rush us, they'll be able to force the entry, so we'll delay them by letting them think we're doing their job for them. Knock the crates to cover the panel while we're at it. Let's see how long we can spin it out. Now move!'

Eleanor stumbled through the panel and into Charles's arms, followed by Lady Marguerite and Chauvelin. As the panel closed silently behind them, she heard Sir Percy declare, his voice pitched to carry, 'This isn't the time for mutiny, Andrew. We need to stand together on this. The woman's bluffing.'

'I don't think she is,' Andrew said. Then there was the

sound of a blow, and the noise of a scuffle beginning, as the five of them hastened away down the corridor.

The corridor was narrow, with barely room for two to walk abreast, and even then only if they were prepared to walk shoulder to shoulder. Charles took the lead, Lady Marguerite beside him. The light of the lantern he carried swayed from side to side, picking out joins in the stone-work. They would have gone faster, but there was only one lantern between the five of them, and none of them knew the way.

'I'm sorry,' Eleanor said softly to Fleurette beside her. 'I didn't want you to be dragged into any of this.'

'Sorry? Why should you be sorry?' Fleurette looked as though she'd been sipping from some forbidden flask of strong waters. 'This is my chance to help against a villain so infamous that even the English and the League revolt against her!'

'Excuse me? *Even* the English and the League?'

'My daughter's understanding is excellent,' Chauvelin said from behind, a note of pride in his voice, 'though I too would rather she were not here.'

'Ah, but you have never flinched, Bibi,' Fleurette said gaily, 'and your daughter can do no less.'

'Hsh!' Lady Marguerite hissed from ahead. 'Voices!'

They all fell silent and stole forward, and after a moment Eleanor too heard fragments of phrases coming from ahead. It didn't sound like normal speech, though; it was oddly cadenced, the tones seeming to advance and retreat like waves on a beach.

Abruptly they became clear, as the corridor opened into a small chamber. The words seemed to drift down from above. 'Should I call upon the Honourable Member to explain the possible dangers associated with this choice?

No, gentlemen, I think not! Because we already have proof that he will not answer!'

Charles raised his lantern. The room they were in was actually furnished, rather than serving as storage. The lantern light fell on a large oak chair, which looked as old as the ones Eleanor had seen in Anima's memories, as well as a desk and a set of shelves crowded with scrolls. All of them were thick with dust, as was the floor, with only their footprints to disturb it.

Chauvelin looked up at the ceiling. 'A listening post for the House of Commons, I believe,' he commented. 'Perhaps there are other such nooks scattered through the building.'

'No doubt we'll find Lady Sophie's fingerprints on the original plans for the architecture of this building,' Charles said.

The voices followed them down the corridor as they hurried on. 'While I agree with my honourable friend that there are indeed certain hindrances, nay, even moral ambiguities associated with the suggested course of action,' another voice droned, 'I believe that it is in the best interests of England – that motherland whom we so well love, or as Shakespeare would have it, this royal throne of kings, this scepter'd isle . . . Now is the time to take advantage of the disorder in France, gentlemen! If it is true that, as they say, the National Convention has moved against Robespierre and his followers, then what better moment for our forces to press the assault? And what better weapon with which to do it! No other nations would dare to take this step, but we . . .'

'Could something have happened in France, Bibi?' Fleurette asked softly.

Chauvelin frowned. 'I am a day or two behind the news, but it seems unlikely. No doubt this is wild rumour.'

His words were firm enough, but it seemed to Eleanor

that his voice was just a fraction uncertain. Wanting to hear the rest of the speech, she twisted her fingers in an attempt to call a breeze which would bring the words to their ears.

The omnipresent stench filled her throat. She choked, doubling over, falling to her knees, coughing as though she had been afflicted with consumption. Although she covered her mouth with her hands in an attempt to stifle the noise, it set the echoes trembling.

Charles was beside her in a moment, forcing the lantern into the hand of an unimpressed-looking Chauvelin, an arm around her waist. 'Eleanor? What is it?'

Eleanor managed to spit on the floor, and it cleared a little of the corruption which seemed to paint the inside of her nose and throat. 'I'm sorry,' she husked. 'I was trying to call a breeze. It's this smell. It's so foul. Do you suppose there's another entrance to the sewers along here?'

The others exchanged glances, frowning. It was Fleurette who spoke. 'But, Eleanor, there is very little smell here, except for the odours from where our shoes and clothing touched the sewer mud earlier. If anything, it is strange because there is *no* smell; it is old and dry and empty.'

Eleanor blinked at her in confusion. 'But it's disgusting! I thought it might get better as we left the sewers behind, but the further we go the worse it gets . . .'

She fell silent as realization struck her. If she was the *only* person who could smell this stench, then it must be because it was a thing of magic – or vampires.

Chauvelin seemed to have come to the same conclusion, albeit through his own perspective on what she was, and he gave a satisfied nod. 'Proof – if we needed it. What we seek lies ahead. It has poisoned this whole area, and she can sense it, even if we cannot. We must hurry. Even Blakeney at his most annoying cannot delay them forever. Assist her,' he directed Charles, taking the lead.

Charles helped Eleanor to her feet. 'I'd offer you a hand-kerchief to hold to your nose, or perfume to distract you, but I fear there are no convenient supplies available. The most I can give you is oil of garlic.'

'I feel a little better now that I have some idea of what it is,' Eleanor said with a weak smile. It was a relief to be able to lean on Charles, even if it wasn't strictly necessary. The comfort of his presence made her feel a thousand times better. She tried not to think about how temporary it must be.

'A similar problem arose in Oxford, as I remember it,' Charles said. 'Yet that worked to our advantage.'

Eleanor nodded. They were both keeping their voices quiet, so as not to trouble Chauvelin with talk of magic which he'd no doubt feel obliged to contradict. 'Though that was the ghost of a mage,' she felt obliged to mention. 'Do you think a sufficiently ancient vampire would have the same effect on me?'

'Who knows?' He shrugged. 'Perhaps one of the old mages of yore could have told you.'

'Assuming they knew, or even whether they were correct,' Eleanor muttered. Some of the details which Anima had told her – such as the fact that no magic could survive past death – had proven to be true only in the vaguest or most metaphorical ways. Anima herself had been long dead, as had Matthew in Oxford, yet they had bound their spirits to places or objects before they died, and their magic had survived as long as their ghosts did – or vice versa. And Bernard, under Mont-Saint-Michel, had cast himself into a sleep which had endured for over five hundred years – even though he'd then survived less than an hour after waking. Mages might die like humans, but there seemed a great deal of room for shuffling, lingering and general equivocation on the border between life and death.

She decided to change the subject. But what was there they could safely discuss? Especially with Chauvelin before and Lady Marguerite and Fleurette behind? She couldn't tell him about the promise she'd made to Chauvelin; he would no doubt be furious and complain that she had sacrificed herself – after running off with the League to get *himself* killed while keeping her safe, the hypocrite. And as to what was happening with Sir Percy and the others whom they'd left behind . . . well, they could only hope, and pray, and hurry faster, wishing that this wretched winding corridor would come to an end and lead *somewhere* other than eternally onwards.

'Have you noticed the architecture?' he asked.

Eleanor bit her lip so as not to say, *No, Charles, I have been too busy hurrying down this corridor and nearly fainting. And besides, it is so dark one can barely see the walls on either side even with the lantern.* Instead she peered at the walls and floor. 'It looks old,' she said, without much hope of accuracy. 'Older than Mont-Saint-Michel?'

'Far older,' Charles said with unwarranted enthusiasm. 'I believe the stonework is *Roman.*'

'So yes, older than Mont-Saint-Michel,' she agreed.

'Don't you remember? Bernard told us that vampires were first heard of during the Roman wars in Britain, while Nero was emperor in Rome?'

Eleanor's grasp of Roman history didn't extend much further than Bible readings concerning decrees being sent out under Caesar Augustus, that all the world should be taxed, resulting in Joseph and Mary travelling to Bethlehem. However, she took Charles's point. 'Then perhaps—'

The entire group came to a stop. There was a door ahead of them – a wooden door, which surely could not be Roman, but which was most assuredly locked. Chauvelin thrust the lantern into Lady Marguerite's hands and went down on one knee, removing some wire implements from an inner pocket. 'Hold it steady,' he ordered her.

'I *have* done this before,' Lady Marguerite replied, focusing the lantern's beam on the lock.

'Do you think this dark cellar may hold some ancient vampire, the source of all their race?' Fleurette asked Eleanor.

'Perhaps,' Eleanor said hopefully. 'Or maybe some precious source of vampire blood from which their longevity and strength springs. Whatever it is, Lady Sophie is desperate to defend it – and we must hope it can be used against them.'

'Yes, let us hope so,' Charles said. His arm tightened around Eleanor. 'The current situation is hastening on to catastrophe. If that bill they're debating should be passed—'

'A bill?' Eleanor was vaguely aware that Parliament passed bills, but was not sure of the differences between bills, laws, decrees, or other types of political governance.

'We overheard Parliament's deliberations a few minutes ago through those spyholes.' Charles glanced towards Chauvelin, who was manipulating the tumblers within the lock, then back to Eleanor and Fleurette. 'They are considering increasing the numbers of vampires, so that these may join our soldiers in France. When we – the Chief and I – reached London, it was in all the papers that Parliament was sitting late tonight to debate the subject.' His expression was grim; clearly he was not suffering from any kindly illusions on the subject of what hungry vampires might do in enemy territory. And further down the line, how might Lady Sophie use such a vampire army to her grasping ends? How far would vampires go to defend themselves? Frightened of the future and of the world changing, terrified of the revolution in France spreading from nation to nation . . .

'But that would be pure cruelty!' Fleurette protested.

'True, my dear, but it might also secure a victory without further drains on the army or the public purse,' Lady Marguerite commented without looking away from the lock. 'There's also reason for concern about the reaction of other countries – Austria, Italy, and so on. Will they condemn England's actions? Or might they do the same?'

Eleanor could imagine it as though it were a satirist's print in one of the newspapers. France portrayed as a helpless victim, Liberty in her red, white and blue, being savaged by a pack of slavering vampires dressed in the uniforms of the various nations' armies. Would that force the National Convention to come to terms? Or would it rather rekindle Revolutionary fervour, leading to further executions? Her head swam with horrible possibilities.

'I have it,' Chauvelin said. He straightened, putting away his lockpicks and reclaiming the lantern, as the door swung open.

Light shone from the room beyond.

CHAPTER TWENTY-ONE

While there was light beyond, there was also the stench of power which was so utterly repulsive to Eleanor's own senses. She felt as though she was reaching into the heart of a dung-heap, afraid that something within it would suddenly *move* and squirm against her fingers.

For a moment they all hesitated – and then crowded through the door. Chauvelin took the trouble to close it behind them, and Eleanor heard the lock click shut once more.

The room was empty, with neither furniture nor decorations, but its sole feature drew all eyes: a waist-high cavity inset in the far wall. A body – a man's body – lay within it, sidelong to the room. A huge, heavy pane of glass sealed the cavity off from the rest of the space. It was like the tomb of some saint or bishop in a cathedral.

'How is this place lit?' Lady Marguerite asked. There were no lanterns or candles, no obvious means of illumination, yet somehow thin rays of light fell from the ceiling to bathe the sleeper in a numinous glow. Strangely, it reminded Eleanor of a child sleeping with a candle next to his bed, lest he should wake from nightmares and find himself in the dark.

Charles looked up at the ceiling, and for a moment his eye-glasses reflected the light. 'I believe there must be shafts with mirrors set in them, leading to the rooms above,' he said thoughtfully. 'When they are lit, the illumination is conducted down to this room.'

'This is not the time for a discussion of architecture,' Chauvelin said. His face was drawn thin and sharp, and his eyes burned with hatred. He had clearly found something he loathed even worse than the detested Scarlet Pimpernel. 'Let us break this glass and make an end of things.'

Charles touched the glass hesitantly, turning his head to eye it sidelong and judge its depth. 'I fear it is more than an inch thick. How could such a thing have been installed down here? Faith, it's as though the fellow were in an aquarium.'

Eleanor pressed against the glass, the other two women beside her, trying to get a better view of the figure within. While undeniably male from his features and beard, he was dressed in a robe of some sort, which Eleanor thought was white beneath the dust. He lay there with his hands folded on his chest, preserved like a fly in amber.

'The glass is marred here,' Lady Marguerite said, touching an area by the man's face. 'Look, it's been worn away – it is scuffed compared with the rest of the surface. Eleanor, can you burn through it or break it somehow? I fear it will resist a pistol ball.'

'I can try,' Eleanor said, her stomach queasy with nerves as much as with sickness. She hardly dared believe that they'd found what they were seeking, what Lady Sophie had fought so hard to protect. She set her jaw and tried to focus her will – to regain the certainty and the power which she'd possessed before Bedlam, and before descending into the bowels of this place.

'Yet why haven't they buried him?' Charles said uncertainly.

'If I were trying to conceal some ancient vampire of great power, I'd bury him rather than leave him on display. 'Tis not as if they need to breathe, or have any necessity for light. Is this our true target? Or is it some manner of fake, left here to divert us?'

'No,' Eleanor said before he could hypothesize further. 'This is . . . it. Him. I'm not certain of how to phrase it – I'm no trained scholar – but this is the source of the power which I've been feeling for this past hour. I'm certain of it.' She didn't have the words to explain how she could feel it. Perhaps this was something Anima could have explained to her – but Anima was gone, and there were no other mages left to help Eleanor understand the nature of this power.

A sudden crash from the door startled them all. They turned to see the timbers shudder in the frame. Had it not been so solidly built, so firm on its hinges, then Eleanor thought it might have given way at that first assault.

There was no time left.

Eleanor laid her hands against the glass. Anima had once been able to bring down a manor house by running lightning through its stones, shattering it so that those who came to investigate afterwards had thought it must have been brought down with gunpowder. Surely, *surely* Eleanor could break a simple pane of glass? Even though her body was still weak from the travails of Bedlam, even though the stink of this ancient vampire's power made it hard for her to breathe, let alone draw on her own power, and even though she was an untrained novice with no idea what could be done or how to do it . . . If she didn't manage to do something now, then they were all dead or worse.

She heard the others speaking, heard the repeated crashing against the door. She ignored it. She called on all her anger.

Lady Sophie had handed her off to the Blakeneys as a pawn (and oh, didn't Lady Sophie bitterly regret that now?), as though she was lending them a piece of *furniture*. The Blakeneys had led her on with promises of future money and appeals to her sense of duty and honour, dragging her to France, putting her in constant danger as though it was a *game*. Chauvelin and all the other enforcers of the Republic – the high, virtuous, ethical Republic – had threatened to send her to the guillotine if she didn't turn her coat and spy for them, for all they called her *citizen*. The royalist vampires lurking beneath Paris had chased her through the sewers, threatened her to force the rest of the League to comply with their wishes and promised to turn them all into obedient slaves. Castleton had supervised her detention in Bedlam, had seen to it that she was bled and dosed daily, had said he'd lock her away there for the rest of her life among the screaming lunatics. And Lady Sophie – her yet again, the source of all this, the *fons et origo*, to borrow Charles's phrase – was going to see them all dead or damned before she'd allow the truth to become known about how the vampires were manipulating England, and France, and probably all the other countries where vampires could use chains of blood, money and power to bend politicians and rulers to their will.

And she, Eleanor, was just a maid, a commoner, a woman, and England was never going to have a revolution as France had done. And even if perhaps, in her heart of hearts, she dreamed of noblemen being thrown down and forced to work for a living, aristocrats having to chop wood and draw water, common men and women sitting in Parliament and giving orders to the King, making just laws and celebrating liberty, as France had tried to do (and maybe still could if people like Fleurette were in power rather than ones like Robespierre) . . . England *would not change*. Because it was not to the benefit of those in power for anything to change, and ninety-nine times out of a hundred, the grip of an aristocrat's hand was as cold and vicious as that of a vampire on the throats of those below them.

And behind it all, she'd lost Charles. She'd made that promise to Chauvelin and she'd have to keep it, and she was going to lose the League as well, and England, and everything. Perhaps it was the honourable thing to do to keep her word, and maybe that sense of honour would sustain her at some distant point in the future when she was alone in France, because even Fleurette's friendship might no longer be enough . . .

Lightning crackled and spat where her hands touched the glass, but it wouldn't go *into* the thick transparent pane. The blue-white flare outlined her fingers and even seemed to glow through them, showing the shadows of bones beneath her skin. She threw herself into it – all her will, all her determination, all her anger . . .

. . . yet it wasn't enough.

She was on her knees, tears running down her face, leaning forward with her hands on the floor to keep herself upright, and it hadn't been enough.

The room was full of shouting people. Eleanor stared at the floor in front of her, almost too weary to lift her head, but when the skirts of a familiar dress came into her field of vision, she found the strength to manage it. She looked up at Lady Sophie.

'Well,' the older woman said. How old? Eleanor had no way of knowing. 'I suppose I should thank you for testing my precautions, but between you and I, little Nellie, you came closer to inconveniencing me than I find truly comfortable. How you found your way here . . .' She twitched a shoulder. 'Still, that is of little importance now. I will ask more questions later. Now are you going to threaten me with your flames again?'

'If I could, I'd already have done it,' Eleanor said numbly.

Her bones ached with utter exhaustion. Every breath was an effort. She looked around the room. The others were all restrained, held in place – by men or vampires? It didn't matter. They were all servants of Lady Sophie. 'Please, milady. Let them go.'

Lady Sophie sighed. 'Now why could you not have been so reasonable earlier? Castleton, I question my judgement in placing this child in your custody. Apparently she merely needed a firm correction, rather than the sort of brutal mistreatment you were inflicting on her.'

Castleton was standing behind Lady Sophie, his white hair and his clothing sodden and foul with Thames water. The satchel was clenched under his arm, but it was so soaked and leaking that Eleanor doubted any of the documents within could have survived. His right eye had developed a tic. 'Yes, milady,' he said in colourless tones, visibly holding on to the reins of his temper by a single finger.

'But I cannot bring myself to blame you for it, considering what a foolish little minx she is.' Lady Sophie boxed Eleanor's ears, hard.

If Eleanor hadn't already been on her knees, the blows would have left her there. She bent over, her head spinning, trying to retain her consciousness. She could hear Charles and Fleurette calling out amid the buzz which filled her head, and the thought that they were here, trapped with her, about to die like her, brought new tears to her eyes.

'Milady,' Castleton said, 'I beg of you, explain. This place, this woman's powers, this . . .' He gestured at the man behind the glass. As Eleanor looked up at him, she saw the burning, thwarted curiosity in his eyes, the desperate urge to *understand*. 'Is he some progenitor of ours? The first of vampires?'

Lady Sophie touched her lips for a moment as though to hide an expression, and looked to the point that was scuffed on the glass, by the sleeping man's cheek. 'No. He is no vampire. He is . . .' She trailed off, as though considering the most appropriate words.

'He's the man you love,' Lady Marguerite said.

Lady Sophie pivoted to look at her, moving as quickly as a snake. 'Be very careful, Marguerite. Your husband is useful to me alive; your death, on the other hand, would solve any number of my problems and tie up the loose ends of this situation rather prettily. Nobody will look too deeply into the disappearance of an accused spy.'

Lady Marguerite tossed back her hair and stood proud and defiant, as though the men holding her by either arm were merely stage properties or supporting actors, rather than minions of her enemy. 'Why, madam, 'tis nothing but the truth. What woman comes to visit a man in such a place as this, to sit beside his sleeping form and press her lips against the glass that covers his face, save for one who loves him? I can tell it merely from the way you gaze upon him.'

'You may perhaps understand a little of my feelings,' Lady Sophie said begrudgingly.

'How could I not, when you hold my Percy in the palm of your hand?' Somehow Lady Marguerite slipped from the grip of the two men who had her arms, and went down on one knee in front of Lady Sophie in a billow of skirts. 'Must I beg? If I must, I must. I'll take whatever blame you may wish. I'll confess myself to be a spy for the Republic and endure whatever penalty the law may exact, without a single attempt to clear myself.' Her eyes held Lady Sophie's as though she was hypnotizing the vampire; she drew attention to herself as if she was a lodestone and they were all needles, helplessly spinning to point at her. 'Do you not believe I love Percy enough to do this? What must I do to convince you?'

Yet Lady Sophie's words were echoing in Eleanor's head.

He is no vampire. But if so, who or what was the man who lay here, unmoving, unchanging, uncorrupted? What power had flooded the cellars beneath the Houses of Parliament so thickly that Eleanor could scarcely breathe? What sort of man could cast himself into a sleep which would last for centuries?

Oh, Eleanor knew the answer to that one.

Was this why Chauvelin had detected traces of guilt in Matthew's suspicions of what lay hidden down here? Had some mage, centuries – no, more than fifteen hundred years – ago, cast a spell which had lingered all the way down the years until now, preserved by his slumber? Because a mage's spell could last until he died, and he quite simply had not died?

And who was he to Lady Sophie, or she to him?

'Convince me?' Lady Sophie wound a ringlet around one finger thoughtfully. 'Why, yes, I suppose there is one thing you could do. Castleton, give me that knife you carry.'

Castleton's eyes widened, but he obeyed without hesitation, passing it to Lady Sophie. The narrow piece of steel gleamed in the thin light which filtered down from above, drawing all eyes.

'Slit little Nellie's throat for me and I'll believe you,' Lady Sophie said, smiling sweetly.

'No!' Fleurette was the first to cry out in protest, with Charles a moment later. 'No, madame, how can you demand such a thing? Would you make her a murderer in order to save her husband? Have you no care for her immortal soul?'

'Don't do it, milady!' Charles demanded, struggling in the hands of the men who held him, who had his arms wrenched up behind his back. His eye-glasses fell to the ground. Someone stepped on them, grinding the glass to fragments. 'You can't trust them to keep their word.'

'She can,' Lady Sophie said, smiling. Her mood seemed

sweeter now that she held the whip hand. 'I can manage
you others, but little Nellie? No. I fear she is too much of a
risk. I should have disposed of her far earlier. I blame myself.
She will die in any case, Marguerite, so why not dispose of
her for me and convince me that you are telling the truth?'

Chauvelin said nothing, but Eleanor could see an
unpleasant knowledge in his eyes. She remembered the story
which he'd told her, and others had confirmed, about how
Lady Marguerite had reported the Saint Cyr family to the
forces of the Revolution after they'd beaten her brother
nearly to death. A cold uneasiness squirmed in her own
stomach as she watched Lady Marguerite's hand move
slowly towards the knife.

Slowly. That was the most important thing. Lady
Marguerite wasn't a woman to hesitate and be uncertain;
quite the contrary. But she *was* an actress. If she was playing
for time, or to get her hands on a weapon, then it was
Eleanor's part to seize the moment and take advantage of
the lack of attention on *her*.

Because there was something she could do, now she knew
the truth. A mage's spells lasted as long as they lived, and
a mage could stay sleeping for centuries, far past the natural
time of his death. But once he woke up – ah, then matters
changed completely. She'd seen it under Mont-Saint-Michel.
Bernard had slept beneath it for over five hundred years,
but once he'd awoken time had descended upon him like
an avalanche, and he hadn't lived out the hour.

If she could only reach through to him with her power,
and wake him from his sleep . . .

'But, milady,' Castleton protested, 'there is so much we
still have to learn! The woman has secrets she has yet to
reveal. What if she has allies ready to attack us?'

'Us?' Lady Sophie's tone of voice made it clear, for a
blazing moment, just what she thought of Castleton grouping

himself together with her. Then she smiled. 'Ah, my dear boy, I have so much to tell you, though not in front of careless ears. You have proven yourself worthy of my trust. Once I explain, you will understand why so much of this is necessary.'

Eleanor breathed out. The last tattered shreds of her power mingled with her breath, flickering through the miasma which filled the room like a footman darting through a busy crowd. She looked up and met Fleurette's eyes as that power touched the other woman, and she saw Fleurette suddenly smile in bright clear understanding, and felt the other woman's acceptance and offering of strength.

'Do you really believe her, Castleton?' Charles demanded. 'You've sold yourself for continued life – I understand that, man! – but I beg of you, don't be a damned *fool*! You'll be nothing but her cat's paw for the rest of eternity, begging for a fraction of her secrets. You already know too much for her liking. I'd lay good money on the fact she won't let you live out the night. We studied together at Oxford. We were friends. Do you not see what you have done to yourself?'

Chauvelin's eyes flicked to Fleurette, then to Eleanor, and narrowed in sudden suspicion of what he couldn't see. 'And what of France!' he snarled, forcing his way into the conversation, drawing Lady Sophie's attention. 'Do you truly think you can reclaim power there, after all that the Republic has achieved? I may be lost, but my fellow citizens will root you out, woman. There is no place for sanguinocrats in the world any longer.'

'I have the right to live!' Castleton snapped at Charles, ignoring the rest of the room. 'If the world has nothing to offer me except rotting lungs and an early death, then be damned to the world! How can *you* judge me?'

Eleanor needed more. She breathed out a second time, and her power reached to Charles. His face was alarmed for a moment as he sensed her touch, her wish, and then softened, accepting, his dark eyes gentle. 'I fear you've run up a debt beyond your ability to pay,' he said to Castleton. 'But whether it be this world or the next, we must all answer for it in the end.'

Eleanor closed her eyes. She shaped her power, and the power of her two friends – freely offered, freely given, freely agreed – into a single thread, with her will a needle at the end, probing for a way in. The sleeping mage might lie behind a mighty pane of glass, set in ancient stonework heavy enough that it would take a dozen men to break it down, with all the Houses of Parliament above pressing down to keep him sealed away and surrounded by a morass of his own power over a thousand years old . . . but there was no chink so fine that air could not pass through it, no crack so small that a tiny draught could not slip in and past. She probed here and there, up and down, from ceiling to floor, seeking an entrance.

'You will be useful,' Lady Sophie said to Chauvelin, still smiling. 'What better agent than one in the heart of the Committee of Public Safety? Once you are convinced to assist us . . . And I can even promise that your daughter will be safe here. Far safer than in France.'

Finally, Eleanor found an imperfection in the mortar. The breeze carrying the thread of her power slid through it, moving in the tiny spaces and cracks between stones and mortar, from side to side, as though she were stitching a new pattern into the wall. She could sense the other mage's power more thickly around her with every inch she gained, like congealed mud stiffening into solidity, as foul as though she were inhaling decay directly into her nostrils.

'Now take the knife,' Lady Sophie coaxed Lady Marguerite. 'Do you want to save your husband? This is the only way. What's one life, in comparison to his life? What would a thousand other lives be, when it comes to *his*? We understand each other very well, my dear, we are very alike. Yes . . .'

Eleanor distantly felt someone's hand knot into her short hair, tilting her head back. *Please, no*, she prayed with half of her mind, *no*, but still she forced her will forwards, keeping her eyes closed, her focus on the sleeping mage.

Finish my task, Anima had said.

For a moment she felt cold steel against her throat . . . and then there was shrieking, and a thrashing of bodies, and she was free of Lady Marguerite's grasp.

'You devil!' Lady Sophie screamed. 'You dare – you *dare* – to raise your hand against me? You think you had a chance to touch me? What of your husband?'

'I did more than touch you,' Lady Marguerite returned, somewhat breathlessly, 'and if you think my Percy would forgive me if I came to him with the blood of an innocent on my hands, madam, then I believe *that* is the difference between us.'

Eleanor's power touched the sleeping mage.

And he awoke.

CHAPTER TWENTY-TWO

It would have been vastly preferable if the ancient mage's awakening had been a subtle thing, barely noticeable, signalled perhaps only by the flickering of an eyelash or the slight twitch of a chest once more inhaling.

Instead, power cascaded back through the narrow thread which linked him and Eleanor. It was a reaction as violent as though she had jabbed him with a pin to wake him and he had thrown the entire bed at her, covers and all. The air around her caught fire in a blue-white haze which she could see even through her closed eyelids. People jumped away from her, screaming. The thick miasma of old magic in the air trembled and churned, congealing like spoiled milk, and Eleanor shuddered to think what might respond to it.

The flare of power vanished, leaving Eleanor blinking, her vision full of black spots. Her links to Charles and Fleurette had broken in that outward gush of power, frayed and burned like silk. Her head was spinning, her body humming with unwanted, unhealthy reaction, but she had just enough sense left to throw herself to one side as a pistol ball struck the floor where she'd been kneeling.

'What have you *done*?' Lady Sophie's voice cut through the room like a knife, silencing her servants and even

Castleton. If before she had been deadly, now she was out-and-out murderous. She tossed the empty pistol aside, her fingers crooked into claws.

Eleanor caught hold of the wall and groped her way upright, swaying. The floor seemed to be shivering beneath her feet – or was this merely a perception unique to her, like the smell of power? 'Look and see,' she said, her voice shaking. 'I woke him.'

The man in the alcove moved. His hand jerked, spasming, then slowly rose to brush dust from his face.

Lady Sophie turned to look, and all the love Eleanor had ever seen between two people – between the Blakeneys, in Charles's eyes when he looked at her – was in her face. For a moment she almost seemed alive, dazzled by something she had never dared hope to see again. The remaining light in the room seemed to flicker around her as she raised her own hand towards the glass, as if she could reach through it and touch him.

A line of grey ran through the man's hair, then another. His eyes opened.

At the same moment, out of the corner of her eye, Eleanor saw one of the two vampires holding Fleurette shudder, releasing her arm as he staggered to one side. He had been a handsome man, but now he was visibly dwindling, as though afflicted by a tertiary fever, the skin dragged so tight on his face that he seemed all skull. He looked down at his hands, mumbling in shock as they grew thin, dwindling to skin and bones.

Lady Sophie was across the room before Eleanor even realized that she was moving. She caught Eleanor by the throat, nails piercing her skin, and forced her back against the wall. Her breath smelled of violet pastilles and blood. 'You've killed him,' she hissed.

'He should have died centuries ago,' Eleanor gasped. Her

heartbeat was drumming in her ears. She could barely hear Lady Sophie's voice, let alone the others.

The room seemed full of a dreadful suction. Eleanor felt as though she was dangling above a whirlpool which vented and drained itself into the man behind the glass. He slowly raised himself on one elbow, looking at her and Lady Sophie, and reached out towards them.

Charles crashed into Lady Sophie and Eleanor from one side, sending the three of them sprawling. Lady Sophie's fingers left long scrapes on Eleanor's throat as she twisted herself free, rolling across a paved floor which seemed horribly unstable, a bare film of stone stretched across deep flowing currents. Lady Sophie kicked back in a flurry of silk skirts, tossing Charles halfway across the room and sending him crashing into the wall.

There were bones everywhere. Bones and clothing and dust. Where had the vampires gone?

The entire world seemed to be dissolving into a series of disconnected moments, like beads on a string. Lady Marguerite, the knife still in her hand, threw herself at Lady Sophie, but Castleton caught her hand, dragging her back. Chauvelin fired at Lady Sophie, the crack of his pistol echoing in the enclosed space. She slipped deftly out of the way of the ball, and it tore a hole through her glove and arm but missed her heart. Her face was a painted mask, her eyes like poisonous black stones. Now she was as Eleanor had once seen Marie Antoinette – a dead thing masquerading as a living one.

And behind this dance between the living and the dead, through it all, power was draining into the ageing mage and going – where? Eleanor didn't know. Thoughts fell into place in Eleanor's dizzy head like cards in a game of Patience. *It's a spell. Lady Sophie may have been the first vampire, but every vampire since then has been a part of it, willing to share their lives to support it. Now the mage has woken up, he's drawing on that power to try to sustain himself, taking it back from the vampires. But it isn't working.*

With every shuddering breath, the mage behind the glass aged further towards death. His hair had fallen away. His fingers were swollen at the knuckles, cramped into claws, and his skin sagged on his bones. His gaze met Eleanor's through the glass, and she saw not one trace of regret or sympathy or acceptance, only a dreadful anger and bitterness.

Fleurette tried to support Eleanor to her feet, but the ground seemed to be trembling beneath her and she couldn't manage to stand. 'Tell me what to do!' she demanded of Eleanor.

'Do? You can stand away and let me dispose of the slut!' Lady Sophie snarled. Charles had managed to get between her and the women, but she backhanded him, knocking him to his knees. 'Lucius saved me when Boudicca and her armies sacked London. He promised he'd do anything to preserve my life – and he did! But he said the spell would only last while he lived, and with all his power spent . . . he slept. So I kept him safe. I guarded him!' Her voice was drawn as fine and furious as the catgut of a violin. 'I did everything, and now because of the mischief and malice of a group of fools, a nitwit and a harlot, their idiot followers, peasants who rose up against their rightful owners, and this little *slut* who should have been willing to give her life to serve her mistress . . .'

Eleanor drew on what she had left, what Fleurette could offer her, but the flame which glowed this time was no more than a pearly shadow, barely visible in the lit room. She had nothing but prayer. And deep within, she wept that an act of love had resonated down through the centuries to such monstrous effect, and so steeped in blood.

'For seventeen hundred years I have kept him safe.' Lady Sophie advanced on Eleanor, inexorable, slowed by the flame but not stopped. 'I have guarded and governed those whom I created, and their own vampire children. Even through the most difficult times, when the mages turned against us. I have guided this country, this world, towards the best possible future—'

'Sanguinocrat,' Chauvelin said, cutting through her tirade. 'You have done nothing except for your own safety and preservation.'

'I have a right to live!' she screamed.

The light finally went out behind the ancient mage's eyes. His lips moved in a silent word – and then he was gone. His cataracted eyes closed, and he slumped forward, his body crumbling to bones and dust, as though Death had swept his robe over him and reclaimed the too-long-delayed soul.

The thick miasma poured into the room faster and faster, flowing towards the skeletal remains.

Lady Sophie looked at the remains in the niche and turned away from Eleanor to press her hands against the glass. 'Lucius?' she whispered. 'Lucius, my love . . .'

Death – true death – swept over her, swift and perhaps merciful, catching her as her words echoed through the room. Her eyes, her hair, her lovely skin, her hands that Eleanor had once manicured, her red lips, all went to dust in a moment. Her dress cascaded to the floor in sighing folds of silk.

In the sudden silence, the thought filled Eleanor's mind: *What have I just done?* She'd been deliberately trying to break the spell which preserved Lady Sophie by waking the now-dead mage, and she'd realized this might propagate to other vampires, but dear God in heaven . . . She'd just killed the ones here, and what about other ones elsewhere? All the other vampires out there in England, in other countries, the evil and the good alike, the ones who murdered and the ones who merely wanted to survive. What had she done?

The stench of the dead mage's power still swirled around her, moving through the room and out into the tunnels in a great outpouring of released tension. It was seeping into the stones, flooding downwards and outwards towards the river, uncontrolled and loose.

Strangely, Castleton was the one vampire still standing. He shuddered, leaning against the wall to support himself, and his breath – yes, he *breathed* now – came in great racking gasps that turned into a painful cough. When he removed his hand from his mouth, it came away red with blood.

The pistol in his hand rose to point at Eleanor.

'Tell me one thing,' Castleton said, his voice raw. 'I have given my life, my soul, for the knowledge to truly *understand* the fundamentals of this world, and the time to do it in. I have no regrets. I'd do it again. But if so, then why should this knowledge, this power, these *secrets*, have come to an ignorant girl who'd rather spend her life sewing and serving? To someone like you?' He cocked the pistol, and Eleanor felt her heart jump at the click of metal against metal. 'Why you and *not me*?'

Eleanor had no answer. Everything seemed a blind gamble, dice thrown on the table by Sir Percy's favourite goddess, Luck. Her resemblance to Marie Antoinette, her presence in Lady Sophie's household, the encounter which had caused her to be possessed by Anima's ghost, her own potential to become a mage, all of it . . . what *was* the reason? Why should so great a possibility have been placed in her hands – and what had she ultimately done with it?

What indeed.

She looked up at Castleton, at the muzzle of his pistol, and had no response.

Charles stepped between her and Castleton. 'Don't,' he said. 'My friend, don't.'

'She's killed me!'

'You're still alive.'

'And I'll be dead within a few years. You know that.'

Charles . . . laughed. The sound was raw, uneven, but genuine. 'Castleton, hasn't this all shown us how little we *do* know? You're alive again. Put down that gun. If we're all to perish down here, then don't let the last act of your life be one of murder.'

Castleton hesitated, and Charles caught his wrist, dragging the pistol to point upwards. Castleton's finger spasmed on the trigger, but the ball went wild, embedding itself somewhere in the ceiling. With a moan of despair he let the pistol drop, covering his face with his free hand.

Fleurette helped Eleanor to her feet, and she was grateful for the other woman's support, but there was something vitally important she had to communicate. It took her a moment before she could remember what it was.

'We have to get out of here,' she said.

'I am certainly in no mood to stay.' Chauvelin cast a glance around the room and the piles of clothing and dust. 'I believe we have accomplished more than we hoped for.'

'Are there more enemies hidden deeper in?' Fleurette enquired, with a cheerful enthusiasm which Eleanor could not share. 'We should force their surrender now, while we have the advantage.'

Eleanor shook her head, trying to find the proper words. The miasma of old power was rising like water coming to a boil. It wasn't just her imagination; the ground deep beneath was trembling. 'I fear that the dead mage – Lucius – the echoes of his power, the water and earth are rising against us . . .' There was no visible sign of any peril, but her skin prickled with the oppressive nearness of danger, as though they were beneath a thunderstorm and the lightning was seeking targets. 'We need to get out! Now!'

'Then let's not stand around,' Lady Marguerite said briskly. 'Charles, help Fleurette support Eleanor. I'll take the lead. Chauvelin, bring up the rear and assist Castleton here.'

Her tone was entirely neutral, and Eleanor couldn't help wondering just what sort of 'assistance' she might have in mind. But she was distracted by Charles slipping an arm around her waist and lending her his shoulder; she wanted nothing more than to rest next to him.

A piece of mortar fell from the wall.

Charles paused, still supporting Eleanor, to touch the place where it had been, probing the crack between stones with the tip of his finger. 'Subsidence, perhaps?' he hazarded, ignoring Lady Marguerite's gesture towards the doorway. 'Or . . . I believe it feels wet. The Thames . . .'

A moment of horrified realization struck them, and then there was no further need for Lady Marguerite to urge them onwards; they were all hurrying, even Castleton. Lady Marguerite snatched up the lantern by the remains of the broken door, still lit and burning – had it really been that short a space of time since they had entered the room? – and they stumbled back through the corridors, coming to the listening room . . .

For some reason there were no pompous speeches or hypocritical references to *honourable members* and *learned friends* echoing down. Instead there was shouting, loud and incoherent, each interrupter drowning out the previous speaker, with yells for *Silence!* achieving nothing but more noise.

The walls were trembling. It wasn't just the swinging beam from the lantern causing them to appear to shake: the stones were truly shuddering in place, fragments of mortar falling away.

A light ahead – another lantern. Sir Percy's voice called, 'Marguerite?'

'Percy!' Lady Marguerite took a deep near-sobbing breath of relief, but her voice was steady when she spoke again. 'We must flee! Sophie is dead, but the water is coming in – we must escape or we'll all be drowned!'

Sir Percy didn't waste time asking for details. 'Hurry!' he ordered. 'You're almost out!'

He and the others were waiting in the cellar with the secret door. Piles of clothing and dust indicated what had happened to the vampires left to guard them. 'No time for explanations now,' Sir Percy greeted them as they stumbled one by one through the panel doorway, 'and no way out through the sewers. We'll have to go up into the main House and make our exit that way.'

The panicked escape became a rout. Fresh gusts of sewer air and Thames stink followed them as Sir Percy hurried them all to a staircase. These smells were foul, but still preferable to the odour of ancient power which eddied beneath them in what felt, to Eleanor's dizzied mind, like a growing whirlpool, dragging downward at them with every step they took. *Perhaps power comes in through mages and goes out through mages,* she thought foolishly, *and when there isn't a mage any more, the power has to go somewhere, into the earth and water . . .*

It took all her concentration to put one foot in front of the other, and to try not to be more of a burden to Charles and Fleurette than she already was. She could see the traces of fighting on the other men of the League. They'd paid for every minute they'd gained for Eleanor and her group.

But they were all alive. That thought kept her moving forward, stumbling up the stairs, her body aching with every step. They were alive. She was alive. *Charles* was alive.

And in that moment, she understood why Lucius had done what he did. She could understand it, even if she didn't condone it.

The stairwell gave out onto a ground-floor passage – visibly a servants' passage, seeing how plain and discreet it was – but Sir Percy didn't gesture for them to halt. Instead he urged them on, moving to the rear to support the coughing Castleton and letting Andrew take the lead.

'Can we not pause?' Fleurette asked. 'Eleanor is exhausted—'

'We cannot afford to be caught. Even the Pimpernel might have difficulty explaining his illegal presence here in the Houses of Parliament,' Chauvelin snapped. 'And as for mine, as a member of the Committee for Public Safety . . .'

'Lud, I believe I have the reputation to carry off any drunken frolic to which I care to put my name,' Sir Percy said cheerfully, not slowing his pace. 'And as for random assorted Frenchmen—'

The building shook. Stones and timber creaked and shivered. Crashes and screams came from all quarters.

Sir Percy frowned. 'Deuce take it, I'd have thought they'd have the sense to evacuate by now!'

'Well, they are politicians,' Lady Marguerite murmured.

'Gentlemen – no, not you, Charles, but everyone else – scatter and see what you can do to get this place cleared of anyone who'd need orders to leave,' Sir Percy commanded. 'But don't take too long: I fear we have only minutes. The rest of you, with me, and that includes Castleton here. I have some questions for you.'

'If I survive,' Castleton muttered.

'You're not going to cough your lungs out between here and the nearest door.' Sir Percy threw open another door, hurrying them through. The decor abruptly became rich and classical, spared only from being lush by its evident age. It might have been expensive – it probably still was expensive – but it was also visibly decades if not centuries old.

A bustling troop of serious-looking men rounded the corner, and one came to a stop on seeing Sir Percy, raising his quizzing-glass. 'Blakeney? Good heavens, man! What are you doing here? And what's going on? Why—'

'Not when the building's falling down,' Sir Percy ordered, somehow taking control of the group despite his workman's clothing and the general disorder. He took the fellow's arm and marched him towards what Eleanor hoped was a way out, the other men following like hypnotized chicks. 'Can't allow a fellow of your importance to risk himself,' he said persuasively. 'I mean, what would your people back in Huddersfield do without you – or was it Hoxleigh? Or Horton? Geography was never my strong point, you know . . .'

'Don't be ridiculous, old fellow. Nothing but a mere earthquake.'

'Thought we didn't have earthquakes in England,' another muttered.

'Ah, but when I was in Brazil, we had them all the time—' the first began.

'I am reassured as to France's safety,' Chauvelin muttered, his eyes on the expostulating Member of Parliament.

He was interrupted by a hideous noise from the ceiling, as though the very timbers and joists were screaming in pain. Plaster rained down, an elegantly sculpted boss landing with a thud barely inches from his foot.

More of the ceiling shattered. Fleurette stifled a scream, her knuckles against her mouth. 'Hurry!' Lady Marguerite ordered. 'Forget decorum and run!'

The walls seemed to lean inwards, flexing out of true. Paintings toppled to the ground, ornamental vases fell, glass windows broke, and *finally* other people in the building seemed to accept that something was wrong. Within half a minute their group was joined by others, until they were lost in a stream of men complaining loudly to each other, but – thank heavens – wanting to do so outside. Eleanor would have been lost in the crush if not for Charles and Fleurette supporting her, helping her keep her feet. She could still smell the stink of power from below, but now the whirlpool seemed to be paused on the edge of some giant breath – no, a giant suction, ready to pull down anything and everyone within its sphere.

'It's coming,' she gasped. 'It's nearly here . . .'

They stumbled out into the night air, into an ornamental courtyard filled with a mass of men, both gentlemen and servants, who apparently thought that once outside they had no need to move further away. 'See,' Eleanor heard one man say to another, 'I told you this was merely the over-excited folly of some new fellow only just elected. Why, any old building creaks and groans a little from time to time . . .'

Then the world seemed to exhale.

Eleanor looked back, like Lot's wife, and saw it: the first slow crumpling of the roof, the shuddering of the whole Palace of Westminster as foundations gave way, its cellars filled with the Thames and collapsed, and windows shattered like thin panes of ice. The rows of spires and the elegant battlements, dark against the clear night sky like chess pieces, rocked and tumbled, crumbling inwards.

One could not hear the screams of the onlookers over the dreadful noise of the building's destruction.

Even when Eleanor closed her eyes, she could still see the utter collapse and wreckage – and over it all, like some destroying angel, the face of Lady Sophie as she cried out to her lover before falling to dust.

CHAPTER TWENTY-THREE

Outside, it was raining – a thin grey mist of rain which leached the heat from the summer day. It wasn't enough to restore the grass or bushes, but it was more than enough to dampen muslin dresses and wilt stiff proud cravats. Eleanor lay in her bed and stared at the ceiling, pondering how best to pack in order to travel to France.

Of course, she hardly had a great deal to pack. She'd accumulated a couple of new dresses and a number of keepsakes since coming to the Blakeneys, but it would probably still all fit into her original portmanteau.

She'd been thinking about what had happened under the Houses of Parliament, and . . . well, common sense told her that surely what she'd done must have had *limits*. Perhaps Lady Sophie had perished, and all the vampires close to her, but what of France? Or the world beyond that? She couldn't truly bring herself to believe that her single action in breaking the ancient mage's spell might have extended so far. She wasn't sure she wanted to even consider it. Because if that was true, then she'd truly killed them . . .

No. It was folly to think that way. Better to focus her mind on her own immediate problems. She would be allowed out of bed in a day or two, and then she would have no further excuses left; she would have to go to France with Chauvelin. She'd given her word. She might not be an English gentleman, but . . .

Irritably she wriggled up into a sitting position, tugging the pillows into place to support her. Lady Marguerite had placed her in one of the guest bedrooms at Blakeney Manor rather than leaving her in the servants' attics, but even while it was nicer, it was . . . boring. People were too busy to see her. The window overlooked a significantly dull part of the gardens, too. She'd been assured that everyone was alive and healthy, so she couldn't fret about that – at least, not too much – but all she'd had in the way of company was a couple of quick visits from Lady Marguerite and Fleurette.

The thing that really gnawed at her, though, was that she was no longer part of the household. The other maids didn't look at her the same way any longer. They didn't share gossip. They didn't share jokes. They'd been aware that *something* was odd about her earlier – Alice wasn't the only one to have suspicions – but now they were certain it was true. Eleanor might not be a genuine lady of quality, but she wasn't one of *them* any longer either.

She stared at the rain-smeared window glass and imagined turning back the hands on a clock, returning to where she'd been a year ago. At Basing Manor, in the summer heat, chopping vegetables and scrubbing dishes . . .

There was a brisk knock on the bedroom door. Eleanor hastily scrubbed a hand across her eyes, tweaked her bed-jacket (far too expensive for her, a gift from Lady Marguerite) into better order and called, 'Come in!' There was very little point in considering modesty and the propriety of enter-taining men alone in her bedroom by now, after all.

She was rather disappointed when it was Chauvelin who entered. The man was positively jaunty, with a spring in his step and a sparkle to his eye. No doubt, she reflected sourly, he was looking forward to bringing her back to France as a feather in his cap. Or should that be a rosette on his hat, to be sufficiently modern and Revolutionary?

'It's good to see you awake,' Chauvelin said, taking a seat by her bed without waiting to be asked. 'A little more colour in your cheeks, I think? It would seem that having blood constantly drawn is not healthy for the individual in question, and that you are much better when that regimen is stopped. No doubt this will come as a surprise to many doctors.'

'I feel much better, sir,' Eleanor admitted. 'Is Fleurette well?'

'She is also fully recovered, and will be spending a little while with you after I have finished.'

Eleanor knew all too well what he must be here to say. Her time had run out. 'I should be ready to travel in a few days, sir,' she muttered. Perhaps . . . no, it would only hurt even more if she wished to be able to see Charles once again, before she lost him for ever. At least she could be glad that he was well and safe.

'That will be unnecessary.' He paused, extracted his snuffbox and took a pinch of snuff. 'You are no longer required – by me, or by France on the larger scale.'

Something between relief, joy and an unhelpful feeling of resentment at being unnecessary flooded through Eleanor. So the vampires *had* all been eliminated? And – a less welcome thought – their blood was on her hands? 'They're *all* dead?' she whispered.

A thin smile curled Chauvelin's lips. 'You have not been permitted the newspapers or journals, have you? So you will be out of touch with the latest developments. I believe they did not want to . . . disturb you.'

Eleanor was by now quite thoroughly disturbed. 'Please

explain,' she said, hoping that his malicious enjoyment of her shock would outweigh any urge he might have to hoard information to himself.

'Your action a few days ago had benefits quite beyond anything we could ever have conceived possible, or what we expected before going into that chamber.' He considered his snuffbox again, drawing out the moment, then put it away with a faint air of regret. 'As far as can be discovered by the most ardent of searches, there are no more vampires. Anywhere.'

Eleanor had seen Lady Sophie and the other vampires in the cellar fall to dust, and Castleton's transformation back to a normal humanity. She'd *known* what this implied. Yet she had quite deliberately not wanted to think too closely about how this might have played out around the world. 'No more vampires . . .' she said, trying to conceive the idea. It was too huge, too shocking, to encompass. England, France, beyond; Austria, Italy, Hungary, Russia, other places of which she'd never heard.

Dear God, what had she done?

'Control your tendency to mope,' Chauvelin advised her briskly. 'You have done the world a service. You have done *France* a service. However, in doing so, you have caused a certain amount of confusion. Vampires have fallen to dust in all nations, or returned to their prior lives, and a great many people now claim they were influenced against their will to act in certain ways. And – possibly not very interesting to you but highly significant to other people – the disposition of money and estates has been thrown up into the air, as vampires were notably prone not to leave wills behind. I understand that the lawyers are making merry, even if nobody else is. And, of course, there is the minor issue of the physical collapse of the Houses of Parliament. A wide variety of conspiracies are being blamed, though nobody has yet come forward to take responsibility. The Lords and Commons are highly discommoded, and are trying to agree on where to meet in order to direct the nation's policies. I believe a committee has been put forward to discuss the matter. In short, England is in chaos, and so are many other nations. Few places in this world were without vampires.'

Eleanor tried and failed to imagine what was happening everywhere outside this room. 'No wonder nobody has been coming to talk to me,' she said, still dazed.

'Well, you can hardly blame Sir Percy Blakeney for taking advantage of a confused situation,' Chauvelin said, malice salting his words. 'I believe that in the confusion the charges of spying against Marguerite Saint-Just have been dropped, which should please you.'

Eleanor sighed in relief. 'It does, very much. Thank you for telling me that, citizen.'

'A mere nothing.' He brushed a fleck of dust from his sleeve. 'However, there have been troublesome developments in France which require my attention. No doubt your friends in the League will be glad to pass on the details.' His tone was now positively sour; whatever had happened must not be to his liking. 'I will be able to act with more liberty on my own. You are not only unnecessary, you have become an encumbrance rather than an asset. With no more vampires, we no longer need a weapon against them. As a result, I will not be holding you to your word. Your life is your own. I trust you will not waste it.'

Further relief broke over Eleanor like a wave, drowning her fathoms deep in gratitude. She would have kissed Charles if he'd been there. She very nearly kissed Chauvelin, but she managed to restrain herself. '*Thank* you, citizen,' she said with deep gratitude.

'I would like to hope you will do something useful with your . . . talents.' *But I doubt it* hung in the air behind his words. He rose to his feet, closing his snuffbox, the interview clearly at an end.

'But what about Fleurette?' Eleanor asked.

'She will be temporarily remaining in England,' Chauvelin said reluctantly. 'Until the situation in France is more settled, I prefer her to stay here. I have faith in her common sense, and I trust that your League will treat her as an honoured guest and keep her safe.'

'I'm sure they will all be very kind to me, Bibi.' Fleurette had evidently been listening at the door. She stepped in, radiant even in the gloomy light of the rainy afternoon, enchanting in a pale blue gown which Eleanor's trained eye recognized as one of Lady Marguerite's favourites. 'I may even be able to persuade them to change their ways.'

'Now that would be a miracle.' Chauvelin inclined his head to Eleanor. 'I will leave you to my daughter. I expect to depart within a few hours. Adieu, Eleanor Dalton.'

'Goodbye, Citizen Chauvelin,' Eleanor said. She wasn't sure what to feel about him – hatred or regret, friendship or dislike. She was still too elated by the news that the bargain was void and he didn't want her any longer. She was *free*.

Fleurette took Chauvelin's place as the door closed behind him, seizing Eleanor's hands in hers. 'Oh, Eleanor, I'm so glad we're all still alive!'

'As am I,' Eleanor said with feeling, returning the clasp. 'Once more, I'm so sorry you were brought into all this, Fleurette. I shouldn't have endangered you—'

'Oh, fie!' Fleurette said with an airy shrug. 'Purely for being Bibi's daughter, I am in danger. Is it not morally better for me to be in danger because I have chosen to take action, rather than merely be an incidental target of opportunity?'

Eleanor felt a jab of unworthiness. She herself hadn't *chosen* to take action for the most part; she'd been dragged into it. Fleurette's virtue was a shining example to all those around her – and to be honest, rather hard to live up to. She decided to focus on more important matters. 'So you're staying in England?'

'For the moment.' Fleurette squeezed her hands again. 'Then, once things are more settled, Bibi will need my support in France.'

'I notice,' Eleanor said carefully, 'that you're not saying *when Bibi sends for me*.'

'You notice very accurately, Eleanor! But Bibi will be fretting about me. Truly, the best thing I can do is rejoin him as soon as possible, for his own peace of mind.'

'But the danger—' Eleanor started.

'Oh, I will be very careful, I assure you. And I'm learning so much here. Tony, Andrew and their wives, and all the others, are so willing to talk to me about how they do things! In the meantime, I have letters to send to France as well. The people whom I met in Mont-Saint-Michel – Madame Thiers and all the others – we promised to stay in contact. I want to find out what they are doing for the good of France and see whether I can help them. Besides, everything is so confused. I don't know how much Bibi told you before I started listening . . .'

'He only said *troublesome developments*.' Eleanor mimicked Chauvelin's tone, and both women giggled.

'Ah.' Fleurette grew more sober. 'Well, it seems that Citizen Robespierre – you know him?'

'Mostly by reputation, though I did see him once at a distance,' Eleanor admitted. In her position, it would have been near-impossible not to know of the leader of France, the head of the Committee of Public Safety.

'He has been accused of conspiracy, arrested and sent to the guillotine,' Fleurette said bluntly. 'Others of his close allies also. The National Convention is in turmoil, and Bibi will not talk to me about it, but I know he has received sealed letters which cause him grave concern.'

Eleanor couldn't help thinking that Marie Antoinette would be pleased. The once Queen of France, turned vampire – and now presumably turned human again, though it might do little to save her neck if she was caught by the Paris mob – had predicted that the increased weight of the laws in France would eventually turn upon the ruling party. Though for it to happen within a couple of months was perhaps faster than she had expected . . .

'What will your father do, with Robespierre gone?' Eleanor asked. If the Committee of Public Safety was shaken, then would one of its most favoured agents still have any influence? Chauvelin might be walking into just as much danger as . . . well, as Sir Percy did every time he went to France.

'I don't know exactly, but France *needs* men of integrity like him.' Fleurette spoke with absolute certainty.

Though it didn't need guillotines, Eleanor thought . . . yet wasn't it appropriate that Robespierre had gone to one himself?

'You are thinking too heavily, Eleanor,' Fleurette chided her. 'France is not your problem – unless you *choose* to come and help me, of course! You've already done your part. God blessed you with a great gift and you fulfilled his will, granting peace to the vampires.'

'Is that truly how it seems to you?' Eleanor asked quietly. She couldn't help thinking about it. Her mind returned to it again and again, like a tongue probing an aching tooth. Those people had been alive, as much as one could call vampires alive, and now they were quite definitely dead – save for those like Castleton, who'd still been within the span of their natural life. Even for those of them who had been actively malicious, there were now no possibilities of repentance, no second chances. It was as though she had sent thousands to the guillotine. And as for the vampires who had simply wanted to exist a little longer, who had paid for any blood they took, who were essentially as blameless as they could be, who had perhaps even been friends of the Blakeneys and Charles and the others . . .

'That is simply how it is.' Fleurette shifted her grip to Eleanor's shoulders and gave her a little shake. 'You are too hard on yourself. Vampires were the work of that ancient mage. Even if he was trying to save her life, I'm certain he hadn't intended what came of it seventeen hundred years later. Lady Sophie was not a good person! I'm not even certain that he was. You simply caused him to cease his spell, and saved all our lives in the process, as well as many others' too. But now you have other things to worry about, and so do I.'

Eleanor didn't think she was going to be able to shrug it off as lightly as Fleurette, but . . . the other woman wasn't necessarily wrong, either. And how would that mage have felt about the war between the vampires and the mages which saw the near extinction of his kind? This was not a good problem to brood on alone. She was fortunate to have friends who would help her carry her guilt.

She was, she decided, very fortunate.

'That's better,' Fleurette said as Eleanor smiled. 'Now, let us see about getting you up and dressed!'

'Why so enthusiastic?' Eleanor asked.

Fleurette dimpled. 'Oh, I believe there might be someone downstairs who would like to see you but doesn't wish to intrude on a lady's bedchamber. And you don't wish to sit and frowst in here all day, do you?'

'No,' Eleanor said, already thrusting back the counterpane. 'I certainly don't. Why didn't you tell me this in the first place?'

'What, and interrupt our pleasant conversation?' Fleurette's smile was a trifle melancholy. 'After all, it may be a while before we can sit together as intimates again.'

Eleanor paused. 'Fleurette, surely you don't think I'm going to simply forget about you? Besides, you're going to be in England for a while yet to come. Whatever may happen . . . we can write to each other, we can meet in the future. Your father may have said *adieu* to me, but I'm not saying that to you. Even when you go back to France, surely it will be no more than *au revoir* between us.'

'I would have liked to have you as a sister so much,' Fleurette said.

'We *are* sisters,' Eleanor vowed, 'in every way which counts.'

Charles was waiting downstairs in one of the drawing rooms, sitting in the bay window seat with a newspaper sagging across his lap. He seemed to have fallen asleep there, his head bowed on his chest, but as Eleanor entered the room he looked up, blinking. The pages of the newspaper drifted in all directions as he jumped up to wrap her in his arms.

It was so . . . *good* to know she was there with him and he was safe. It would have been easy to close her eyes and dissolve against him, to laugh, to cry, even to kiss him, but any of that would have taken away from the glorious comprehension that he was *there*, and he was there for *her*.

It was perhaps another ten minutes before they had finally disentangled themselves from each other and were sitting together in the window seat. Charles had apologized a dozen times for not coming to see her more often, for not being there when she awoke, and she had forgiven him as many times and apologized for not waking up sooner. They were generally in a pleasant haze of amiability with each other and with the world.

It was Charles who broke this spell. 'Eleanor,' he said, 'I must speak seriously with you about our future, my love.'

Reality came trampling back in, as welcome as unwanted visitors proposing to make themselves at home for the fortnight and bringing their families with them. 'I know what you once suggested,' Eleanor said reluctantly, 'but as much as I care for you, I fear it wouldn't work. I couldn't sustain the pretence of being a French heiress for more than a few days. Your father is not a stupid man . . .'

He laid his finger against her lips. 'M'dear, I'm flattered you have even remembered the idea and considered it. No, I have something else in mind. But before I propose it, I wanted to ask you first: could you content yourself with living somewhere other than England? For a while, at least? And in some position that hardly suits what I would like to give you?'

Eleanor was torn between affectionate tears and gentle annoyance. 'Charles, I beg you to tell me that you have not accepted any offers from Chauvelin to become an appendage of his in France!'

'What? Oh, no, devil take it, certainly not! To even consider the idea – I'll assume he was the one who suggested it? Well, I assure you that the very vestige of such a thought never even crossed my mind. Unless it were the only way to be with you,' he added.

'I'm somewhat reassured,' Eleanor said drily. She indulged herself by looking at him once more. The rain had stopped but the clouds still hung above, and the afternoon sunlight was pale and uncertain. It gleamed on his eye-glasses – new ones – and on the buttons of his coat, the buckles of his boots, the familiar fond lines of his face. He was no fashion-plate like Sir Percy, but with the eyes of love (she could admit it now) she found him all the more handsome. His thin features, his keen eyes, his long hands – even his occasional careless lapses, the ink stains on his cuffs, the way that he would peer at her and ask her opinion on questions about which she knew nothing, because he expected cleverness of her . . .

'My question, Eleanor,' he prompted her.

'Oh.' She blushed. 'Charles, while I love England, I'm more concerned that the two of us might have some hope of a future together. If you have found some path which will allow us to take it – without giving up your own birthright and family – then I beg you to share it with me! And I have no concerns as to my position, only yours. Have you forgotten that I've spent the greater part of my life behind a broom and scrubbing the dishes?'

'But have you no wishes of your own?' he pressed.

Eleanor hesitated. 'I do have one desire,' she confessed. She might no longer be a maidservant, she would never be one of the nobility, but she knew one thing that she wanted. 'I find it difficult to believe that the vampires destroyed all mages and all records of their existence as thoroughly as they claimed. I need to know more about what I am, what I can do, and I would welcome the chance to learn from other mages who know more, if they exist. Perhaps I can do something to help revive their way of life, as Anima would have wanted – to teach men and women who might have the potential but live and die while never knowing it, as might have happened with me. But I am not sure where or how to look for such things . . .'

Charles reached across and tipped her chin up so that she looked him in the eyes. 'My sweet, I thought this might be the case. And don't you think that such things would intrigue me as well? If there is a hidden history to the world, by God I'd like to know it! Your interests are mine as well as your own.'

'Then you have an answer to that?'

'To that and more. But first . . .' He lowered his voice to murmur in her ear, 'Do you think the Chief or milady are listening to us?'

Eleanor giggled, again. It felt strange to be able to laugh with such unconcern, with no threat hanging over her or those for whom she cared. 'If they are,' she whispered back, 'then I hope they allow us a little more time before they interrupt.'

Ten minutes later, the Blakeneys came strolling in, and Eleanor and Charles broke apart, jumping to their feet.

'Sit down, sit down, my dears!' Lady Marguerite said with a laugh. She disposed herself in a chair facing them, spreading out her skirts with fingers that delighted in the fine muslin. She was in pale green this morning, and her unpowdered hair outshone the clouded sun. 'I'm so glad to see you up and well again, Eleanor – and so lively!'

Eleanor could feel the blush which climbed from her shoulders to her cheeks. 'Thank you, milady,' she mumbled.

'I'd make a similar joke at Charles's expense, but he's already sharing your blushes,' Sir Percy said, leaning on the back of Lady Marguerite's chair. He was once again dressed as a full exquisite, with a neckcloth like Alpine mountains and lace at his cuffs, as well as boots that glowed as if they'd been polished with champagne. Which they probably had. 'A great relief to see you up and around once more.'

'Will the League continue, Chief?' Eleanor asked. Was the League even still needed, if Robespierre had fallen and France was in turmoil? Or would it be twice as bad now that the regime had changed?

'That's a matter for the future,' Sir Percy said blithely. 'If we're needed, then be assured we'll still be playing the game. But if not – well, England requires some attention, and my beloved Marguerite is also encouraging me to turn my eyes homeward. The country is changing, and I believe that perhaps it's the duty of an English gentleman like myself to take some responsibility for what it'll become. The others are all occupied with their own pursuits, too. Andrew's teaching his Suzanne to shoot a pistol, while Tony's buying himself a balloon and swears he'll master the science of aeronautics. We're all vim and vigour, my dear.'

'Indeed,' Lady Marguerite agreed. 'My brother Armand will be returning to France, to serve his country in her need – though not on the same ship as Citizen Chauvelin, I assure you.'

Sir Percy leaned forward. 'But since we haven't been listening at any doors, I'm afraid it falls to me to ask Charles if he's broached the matter under consideration.'

Charles coughed. 'Well, to be frank, Chief, I was working my way round to it. Didn't care to be too hasty, and we might have been a little distracted. Fact of the matter is, Eleanor, I've a suggestion which I'm hoping may please you.'

Eleanor looked between the three of them – the Blakeneys and Charles, all smiling, all confident in their knowledge of the secret. It reminded her of days very long ago, crowded around the fire at Christmas with her mother hiding presents beneath her apron. She couldn't spoil this happy air of cherished secrets and expected joy. 'I'm all ears,' she said.

'Well . . .' Charles adjusted his eye-glasses and took a deep breath. 'What would you say to St Petersburg? It's in Russia,' he added hastily.

Eleanor knew very little about Russia, save that it was large and cold. 'Isn't that where your father was threatening to send you?' she asked, casting her mind back. It seemed months since she'd met the man, and it would hopefully be even longer until she saw him again. 'I thought you hated the idea.'

'Well, at the time I had other things that were more

important. But now . . . I might possibly have already written to him to say that I'd take up the task,' Charles admitted. He folded his hands together to stop their nervous twitching. 'Full of apologies, and all that, publicly remembering my duty to my family, admitting everything that I'd done wrong and hoping to win back his favour by a few years of labour out among the Cossacks. Very touching, I assure you. And not something he can easily recant or forbid me from doing, given that he's so often threatened me with a position as factor over there, watching out for his interests.'

'You've already written?' Eleanor said uncomfortably. Of course she wanted to be with Charles! But this all felt pre-arranged, one more event in her life which had been settled by other people to suit them.

'I'll take it back if I must.' Charles leaned forward, meeting her eyes. 'If you don't want it, then I'll find some other way, whatever it may take. But this would solve so many problems, and it would only be for a while. We can come back in a few years' time, with some sort of story about our meeting and marriage which will appease Society and cause them to ignore us in the future. And it's a fascinating city, I'm told. Lots of books. A great deal of art. Positively over-flowing with embroidery.'

'And besides,' Sir Percy broke in, 'we have to get you out of the country.'

'Me?' Eleanor exclaimed, surprised.

Lady Marguerite nodded. 'Unfortunately for us all, my dear, Castleton got away during the confusion, while the Houses of Parliament were tumbling down, and he's been making an ass of himself.'

'My beloved wife uses language suitable for polite company,' Sir Percy added. 'I have stronger terms for the fellow.'

'Well, heaven forbid that I should be exposed to improper

language, given how spotless and innocent my life is,' Eleanor muttered. She was wishing Castleton at the bottom of the Thames. 'When you say he's been making an ass of himself, milady . . .'

'It's been easy enough to contradict the *ridiculous and lying* accounts which he's been spreading about what took place beneath the Houses of Parliament,' Lady Marguerite said airily. 'What's more inconvenient is that he's been making contact with other men – and women, too – who were vampires. They were young enough to have returned to life rather than perish as did the older ones. A few are pleased by the turn of events, but more of them are, I fear, decidedly displeased. Fortunately my dear husband's reputation is notorious enough that Castleton's having great difficulty in convincing them that he's a master manipulator and their arch-nemesis.'

Sir Percy flicked his fingers casually. 'Few people will ever appreciate the lengths I go to for my art,' he murmured.

'Unfortunately, a number of them are looking for a scape-goat – and they know who you are and what you look like. They may not believe everything Castleton says about magic and mages, but they're keen to find someone to blame for their own sudden change in circumstances. There's also the matter of the Houses of Parliament collapsing. Such hysteria you never did see! Faith, and they call *us* the excitable sex. Talk of traitors, of gunpowder, of spies, of whatever. You can scarcely meet a friend at the moment without them asking for an opinion on the matter. We think it best to hide any possible loose threads – especially those who most unfairly don't have rank or birth to protect them. So you see, my dear Eleanor, it behoves you to rusticate for a little while and stay out of sight.'

Eleanor's stomach was crawling with a new dread. 'They're looking for me personally?' she asked, controlling her voice with an effort. Members of the nobility – wealthy people, powerful people – with a grudge against her . . .

'My dear, we've frightened you.' Lady Marguerite's eyes were kind. 'We had no intention of doing such a thing, merely of impressing on you how important it was.'

Eleanor was about to retort that whatever they'd intended, they'd *succeeded* in terrifying her, but then she remembered Lady Marguerite herself had been charged with treason and spying less than a month ago. When one weighed the whole of Bow Street and the majesty of the British law against a few offended once-vampires, was there really a comparison?

She held her tongue and forced herself to consider the matter seriously. The most important thing was that she'd be with Charles, and that he'd found a way to escape from his father's shadow, at least for a few years. This was enough to build a new foundation. It was a chance to be . . . someone else, neither maid nor League. A chance for her and Charles to create – or discover – themselves as they wished to be.

'Charles,' she finally said, 'I think that's very clever of you. I'll go with you, wherever you want – even to Russia. Is Russian a hard language to learn?'

'We'll study it together,' Charles vowed, and brought her hands to his mouth, kissing them. 'But I'm told many of them also speak French there. You need have no fear of being silenced.'

Lady Marguerite tactfully glanced aside. 'And of course, there's no reason why you should go *directly* to Russia,' she said. 'Why, there's the whole of Europe between you and that country! Or there certainly *can* be, depending on how you plot your travels on the map. You might want to avoid France – for the moment, at least – but Percy and I can give you the names of friends in a dozen other countries on the way who'll be glad to have you as guests. The state of war across Europe has fallen into confusion with the general vanishing of vampires, which should make travel a great deal easier. Most to the point, if the two of you wish to research local legends in Europe about mages and the like, I can think of no more convenient time to do it.'

Her words seemed to offer everything Eleanor could ask for. It was like a fairy tale told to a child. Yet – perhaps – it might be true. It wasn't the dream she'd once had, of being a modiste and sewing for an exclusive clientele. But conceivably it might even be something better than that.

Yet practicality insisted on having a final word, as though it wished to bring all her castles in the air tumbling down. The part of her that was used to living on a servant's wages could barely conceive what it might cost to waft elegantly through Europe. 'But – will it be manageable . . . financially?'

'You must allow me to use my magical powers of wealth and influence, m'dear,' Sir Percy scolded her. 'I may not be able to snap my fingers and summon lightning, deuce take it, but I can do as much for bankers and men of business!'

'I once promised you that we'd place you at the best modiste in London,' Lady Marguerite said quietly. 'We may not be able to do that, as matters stand, but you've more than earned all that we can give you. Both you and Charles.'

Eleanor's cheeks were burning, and she couldn't look anyone in the face. She'd wanted to earn her independence, to find a life where she wouldn't be constantly dancing attendance on a master or mistress, or liable to be thrown out on the street for a moment's 'insolence'. Having riches poured into her lap like this felt . . . wrong. It didn't happen to people like her.

Yet what sort of person was she now, anyway? She was sitting here among the Quality, wearing a dress that was nearly as good as Lady Marguerite's own. She could speak French like a queen, and English like a commoner. She had some friends who were noblemen and others who were revolutionaries. She was a mage, and she needed to discover more about what that actually meant – and where her powers came from. Were they part of the natural world, as Charles believed, or something God-given, as Fleurette would tell her? What sort of new world might they help build?

And she was in love with Charles. These people, her *friends*, were offering her a way to be with him. How could she object to their kindness?

Pride was the death of revolutions. She simply nodded. 'Thank you,' she said, tears pricking at her eyes. 'Thank you, Chief, milady, Charles . . .'

'We'll be expecting regular letters, my dear,' Lady Marguerite said. 'And we'll be seeing you on the first step of your way. We sail in the *Daydream* with you in two days, as you begin your slow bridal tour towards Russia.'

'But I haven't even proposed to Eleanor!' Charles protested.

'From the way you were staring into each other's eyes when we came in, I fancy the whole thing's settled,' Sir Percy said.

'But it'll take weeks for the banns to be read in church!' Eleanor objected. She knew she couldn't possibly travel alone with Charles without the formal ceremony of marriage.

Sir Percy drew out an envelope from an inner pocket of his coat – a masterly feat, since the garment was cut so elegantly tight that it seemed there was no room between it and his body for even a single sheet of paper. 'Allow me, m'dear, to introduce you to this special licence which I obtained for you this morning.'

'But . . .' Now that this last, final escape was in front of them, Eleanor hesitated on the brink. Was this really the right choice? Would Charles actually be happy, separated by thousands of leagues from his family home, and . . . with her? Was this new path what she truly wanted?

Sir Percy offered Lady Marguerite his arm to help her rise. 'Faith, my dear pair, this isn't a leisurely stroll. This is a rescue, and as such, I'm snatching you out of danger by any means possible. One last mission for the League of the Scarlet Pimpernel. And I trust you remember the rules for such rescues?'

Eleanor and Charles looked at each other.

'No time for objections,' Charles said, a slow smile coming to his lips.

'No complaints,' Eleanor chimed in.

'Excellent. In that case . . .' He smiled, and there was all the amusement and challenge in his smile that there had always been. 'A carriage to the church is at the door, and it's deuced bad form to keep everyone waiting.'

Outside, the rain had stopped and the clouds were parting. The August sun shone bright and brilliant, like a design embroidered with gold thread on blue velvet. Eleanor clutched Charles's hand as she rose, and she knew that even if they were leaving England for now, they would return in time.

After all, she had so much to do. Anima had passed the burden of duty to her, as well as the gift of power. The Blakeneys and all the League had helped her on her way. Chauvelin had given her back her freedom. Fleurette believed that Eleanor had been given her magic to make the world a better place. England might need her in a few years' time – and she should answer that need.

Most of all, Charles would be beside her, and they would help each other on their way.

ACKNOWLEDGEMENTS

I would like to thank everyone who's been involved in the writing of this trilogy. My editors (story, line, copy and otherwise); my publishers; my agent; my beta-readers; and my friends and family who supported and encouraged me; and everyone who's read and enjoyed the books. Lucienne Diver, Rebecca Needes, Charlotte Tennant, Grace Barber, Olivia-Savannah Roach, Claire Baldwin, Sophie Robinson, Holly Domney, Charles Stross, Elizabeth McCoy, Rachel McMillan, MJJ, Sarah McDonagh, Naheeda Aslam, Hazel Brear, Maureen Atkinson: to all of you and to everyone else whom I have not been able to mention, I am most heartily thankful.

I would also like to thank the authors of various books which I have used for research. *Citizens* by Simon Schama; *Revolution* by Peter Ackroyd; *Enlightenment, English Society in the Eighteenth Century* and *Bodies Politic* by Roy Porter; *Passengers* by James Hobson; *A People's History of the French Revolution* by Éric Hazan; *Behind Closed Doors* by Amanda Vickery; *Bedlam: London's Hospital for the Mad* by Paul Chambers; *Living the French Revolution, 1789–99* by Peter McPhee; and numerous others. Any errors in the fiction of this book are entirely my own insertion.

And then there's Georgette Heyer. I'm a lifelong fan of her historical fiction (not quite as keen on her detective fiction, but to each her own) and I can't deny that even though most of her novels are set a little later than the events in this trilogy, they absolutely were an influence on my writing. (At least I didn't have Sir Percy belong to the Four Horse Club – and believe me, I was tempted.)

Writing a protagonist from a completely different time and with a very different mindset to my own presented multiple challenges, but the one I found most difficult was in terms of her internal simile and metaphor. When we think of something as being 'as fast as X' or 'as strong as Y' or 'as elegant as Z', we do it in terms of our own knowledge of the world around us. In 1793–4, a character's knowledge of the world would have been entirely different. Does one mentally compare things to a tidal wave or an earthquake when one has never seen such things and barely knows they exist? What cultural touchstones would such a character have from their reading, the stories they're told and the world they know? It's been an interesting exercise.

We live in a world which contains other people, all of whom have as little – or as much – right to exist and thrive as we do. I think that pretty much everyone in this story, at some point or other, declares that they have 'the right to protect their own' or 'the right to live', and feels that they're entirely justified and ethical in doing so. And thus we get both despots and revolutions. If anyone has a good answer to this, then I hope that the world finds it at some point. On the whole, looking at history, cooperation seems the most viable strategy . . .

I first read the Scarlet Pimpernel books as a teenager, and while I loved parts of them while disliking other parts, they've stayed with me for more than forty years. All due respect to Baroness Orczy, who gave us these entertaining characters, and I hope that I have in turn entertained my readers. And if in a hundred years someone's writing their own stories about Eleanor and Charles and Fleurette . . . I wish them the very best of luck. What better monument could any writer have?

ABOUT THE AUTHOR

Genevieve Cogman started on Tolkien and Sherlock Holmes at an early age, and has never looked back. On a perhaps more prosaic note, she has an MSc in Statistics with Medical Applications and has wielded this in an assortment of jobs: clinical coder, data analyst and classifications specialist. Although *The Invisible Library* was her debut novel, she previously worked as a freelance roleplaying-game writer. She is the author of the Invisible Library series and the bestselling Scarlet Revolution trilogy. Genevieve's hobbies include patchwork, beading, knitting and gaming, and she lives in the north of England.